"You are a rake."

Quinn grinned down at her. "Thank you."

"*Stop* saying that! That is not flattery." Belle swatted at his hand until he pulled it away from her bosom and she could quickly fasten up the bow and cover herself. But even then he didn't move away and continued to stare down at her, like a starving man before a feast he wasn't allowed to enjoy. "You have a certain reputation, you know."

His grin faded abruptly. He stared at her curiously, as if reassessing her and finding her not at all what he'd expected.

Then he shrugged, his eyes gleaming mischievously. "Yes, I do. And one that is well-earned, I assure you." He leaned in closer, his voice dropping to a deep rumble as he added, "If you're interested in learning more about men than you can discover from your books, I'd be happy to teach you."

Teach her? The offer was indecent, yet her stomach somersaulted at the unexpected temptation. To be in Quinn's arms, to experience what she was certain would be expert instruction on making love, with no one knowing but them...

Sweet heavens, she'd gone utterly mad to even consider such a thing!

and gloriously complicated...the author balances the dark with a light, witty humor and a sexual tension that adds sizzle to every scene...*How I Married a Marquess* is intense, satisfying, and cleverly unpredictable. Consider me a freshly minted fan of Harrington's style of happy ever after."

—*USA Today*'s *Happy Ever After* blog

"The Secret Life of Scoundrels comes to a rousing conclusion as Harrington delights the readers with the charming characters, fast pace and unique story. This talented writer crafts romances that captivate, touching readers' hearts while bringing smiles to their lips."

—*RT Book Reviews*

"Extremely entertaining...I enjoyed this well-written tale."

—RomRevToday.com

ALONG CAME A ROGUE

"Harrington creates fast-paced, lively romances with unconventional characters and plot. For her second novel, she adds heated sensuality and a gothic twist. There is little doubt that she is fast becoming a fan favorite."

—*RT Book Reviews*

"In this thoroughly entertaining story, seduction and adventure take center stage. Nathaniel is far more honorable than he will admit, and Emily far braver than she ever imagined. Together, they form a formidable pair that readers are certain to love."

—*BookPage*

WHEN THE SCOUNDREL SINS

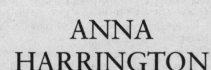

ANNA HARRINGTON

FOREVER

NEW YORK BOSTON

Copyright © 2017 by Anna Harrington
Excerpt from *As the Devil Dares* © 2017 by Anna Harrington
Cover design by Elizabeth Turner
Cover illustration by Chris Cocozza
Cover copyright © 2017 by Hachette Book Group, Inc.

Forever
Hachette Book Group
1290 Avenue of the Americas, New York, NY 10104
forever-romance.com
twitter.com/foreverromance

First Edition: August 2017

Forever is an imprint of Grand Central Publishing. The Forever name and logo are trademarks of Hachette Book Group, Inc.

The publisher is not responsible for websites (or their content) that are not owned by the publisher.

The Hachette Speakers Bureau provides a wide range of authors for speaking events. To find out more, go to www.hachettespeakersbureau.com or call (866) 376-6591.

ISBN: 978-1-4555-9728-4 (mass market), 978-1-4555-9727-7 (ebook)

Printed in the United States of America

OPM

10 9 8 7 6 5 4 3 2 1

Dedicated to
Sarah Younger,
who convinced me to write about the
Carlisle brothers,
and
Brittney Papadopoulos,
the little sister I always wanted

Special thanks to
Michele Bidelspach, for being such a
fabulous editor,
to Jessie Pierce, for putting up with my
e-mail requests,
and to Maria Rose, for naming the butler

PROLOGUE

Mayfair, London
April 1816

Eyes widening, eighteen-year-old Annabelle Green stepped back from Quinton Carlisle, against whose hard front she'd just so scandalously pressed herself. She brought her hand against her lips. Swollen, hot, wet…Oh heavens, he'd been *kissing* her.

Dear God, she'd let him!

She bit back a groan of self-recrimination. *Let?* She'd practically jumped into the scoundrel's arms to be kissed.

"Annabelle?" he asked softly with concern. The noise from the Countess of St James's crowded ball barely reached them beneath the thick rose bower at the rear of the garden, where dark shadows cocooned them together.

She stared at him, for the life of her not knowing what to say. A few minutes ago, she'd slid out the library terrace door to escape the crush of the party, to take a short turn around the garden. To give herself a few minutes of peace when she wasn't the object of whispers and laughter from the other ladies at the ball who thought she was overreaching. She was only a lady's companion, after all, with no real right to wear silk and jewels or to dance with eligible gentlemen.

But she'd come across Quinton Carlisle in the shadows. And then she'd found herself in his arms, being given the most incredible kiss imaginable.

"Are you all right?" he pressed. From the expression on his shadow-darkened face, he was just as bewildered as she was.

"You—you kissed me," she whispered around her fingers, still pressed to her mouth.

"I certainly did." A devilish grin quirked at this lips. "And you kissed me back."

"I did not!"

He arched an amused brow at that wholly obvious lie.

Annabelle groaned. It hadn't been only a kiss, either. It had been a full-out embrace, eager and hungry, with nibbles and sucks and wandering hands—

"I'd like to do it again." He stepped forward to close the distance between them. His hot gaze dropped to her mouth. "Very much."

Her hand fell away from her lips, not to encourage him but because she was utterly confused. What on earth had come over them? "But we don't even like each other!" she squeaked out.

Well, he didn't like *her*, at any rate.

He was Quinton Carlisle, for heaven's sake. She'd known him since she was ten. He had a quick smile that always set butterflies swirling in her belly and a golden handsomeness she was certain would have made Adonis jealous. One of London's most charming scoundrels, he turned the heads of bored society widows and wives everywhere he went, even at just twenty-one. Belle would have had to be dead or eighty not to be attracted to him.

But he was also the bane of her existence. He never seemed to tire of teasing her, just as he had since they were children. They were friends, certainly, but this season he seemed to take great delight in angering her until flames could have shot out of her head. While she might have fantasized about him, he certainly never gave a second thought about her.

Until tonight. When his arms had been around her. His hard body had pressed against her soft one, and his lips had played over hers, teasing kiss after kiss from her until she thought she might explode from the throbbing ache he spun through her.

Oh, what a delicious mouth he had! No wonder all those women in the *ton* practically threw themselves at him. When he knew how to kiss like that, why would they care about his reputation as one of the wild Carlisle brothers?

But *Belle* cared. Her reputation already hung by a thread, simply because of who she was. Nothing but the homeless daughter of one of Lord Ainsley's former housekeepers whom he and Lady Ainsley had pitied enough to take in, a penniless companion whose mother was dead and whose convict father was serving in prison. Despite Lord and Lady Ainsley's attempts to bring her into society's graces, not one person inside that ball tonight was willing to accept her. And all of them let her know it, too. Repeatedly.

Now she'd put even that tenuous position into jeopardy. Heavens, how could she have gotten herself into this situation? With Quinton Carlisle, no less! Her head swam with it.

"But I do like you, Belle," he corrected in a deep and husky voice.

Then her head practically whirled itself right off her neck. He...*liked* her?

His mouth hovered just above hers, close enough that she felt the heat of his breath shiver across her lips. "I can show you how much if you don't believe me."

She pressed her hand flat against his chest to keep him away, although her traitorous fingertips curled into the brocade of his waistcoat to keep him right there. "Why did you kiss me like that?"

He lowered his head, to briefly bring his lips to hers. Yet that kiss was so much more than a peck. It held promises of all kinds of wicked things he'd do to her if she let him...all kinds of deliciously tempting things. "Because I wanted to."

He grinned at her in the shadows, then leaned in to kiss her again, this time with clearly more in mind than a mere touch of lips—

Her hand flew up to his shoulder, stopping him. "*Why* did you kiss me, Quinton?"

He shifted back at that, perplexed. Then he answered softly, "Honestly? I don't know."

Oh, that was *exactly* the last thing a young lady wanted to hear after giving away her first kiss! He couldn't even come up with a good lie to explain himself, or some affectionate compliment that he was so expert at giving to other ladies.

Apparently she didn't even merit empty flattery.

His eyes gleamed. "Annabelle, you're definitely not the sort of woman I normally end up with in the shadows."

The raw honesty of that burned into her chest. But he chuckled, as if he found their predicament humorous.

She blinked but couldn't clear the gathering tears from her eyes. "Was this only a joke to you?" Just another way for him to tease and torment her? She knew he was a rascal, but she never thought he'd stoop so low as this!

His expression grew serious beneath the shadows. "At first, yes," he admitted. "But it didn't end that way."

Anger and shame pulsed through her. With a soft cry, she shoved him back. She turned to hurry out from beneath the bower—

And tripped.

Her toe caught on a root, and she fell forward. Off-balance and unable to stop herself, she hit her shoulder on the post framing the entrance. The loud rip of tearing fabric sounded in her ears only heartbeats before her knees hit the dirt. For one moment, she could do nothing in her stunned shock but rest there on her hands and knees, her head hanging with mortification and her bodice sagging loose.

"Belle!" Quinton knelt beside her and reached for her arm. "Are you hurt?"

Squeezing her eyes shut against the hot tears, she shook her head. A lie. Because her heart had shattered.

He helped her to her feet. With her arms clamped tightly over her bodice to keep it in place, as if she could also physically fight back the embarrassment pouring through her, she wrestled her arm free from his grip. Her vision was too blurred with tears and shadows to see his face clearly—oh, she was glad of it! She couldn't have borne to see his pity. The humiliation would have killed her.

"Are you all right?" he quietly demanded, taking her shoulders in both hands so she couldn't pull away again.

A sob choked from her. "My dress…" She'd ruined the expensive ivory and pearl silk gown that Lady Ainsley insisted she wear for her first ball. Her ripped bodice gaped open over her breasts, the skirt stained with dirt.

"Let me help." He reached for her.

"Go away!" She twisted away from him. "Haven't you done enough to me tonight?"

He stared at her incredulously, his lips parting at her angry rebuke. Then his eyes narrowed. "I've done *nothing*—"

"Carlisle!" A man's voice rang out through the quiet of the garden, followed by a jarring laugh. "There you are!"

"*Christ*," he snapped out, then tried to remove his jacket for her. But it was too late.

Two men came upon them in the dark garden, with lit cheroots and glasses of whiskey in their hands. They froze when they saw Belle in her torn dress and Quinton half out of his jacket. Then lecherous grins spread across their faces, their teeth gleaming in the moonlight.

"And he's busy," the first man drawled.

The second one looped his arm over his friend's shoulders and tapped his glass against the man's chest. "Deliciously so."

Fresh humiliation cascaded through Belle, and she cringed at the lascivious looks the two men gave her, slowly raking their gazes over her from her dirtied hem to her torn bodice. She turned away, but it was too late. They'd surely recognized her, even in the shadows. And what they must have thought she and Quinn had been up to—

"Go away," he growled, stepping between her and the men. His hands drew into fists at his sides.

The first man tsked his tongue. "And let you have all the fun?"

Belle recognized him—Burton Williams, Viscount Houghton's youngest son. Her stomach sickened. *Oh God, not that scapegrace and male gossip!*

"I never would have figured you for a piece like this, though," Williams muttered disdainfully.

Belle's chest tightened so hard that she couldn't breathe, that she was certain her heart would stop beneath the pressure of it. She lowered her head to hide her face as the first tear slid down her cheek.

"Go away," Quinton repeated in a snarl through gritted teeth. "This isn't your concern."

Ignoring that, Williams laughed. He was having far too much fun chiding Quinn and humiliating her to leave. "Tore your dress, did you, pet?"

The other man slapped Williams on the shoulder and gestured toward her skirt. "Before or after she was on her knees, do you think?"

Quinton's broad body stiffened with anger so intense that it pulsed palpably on the midnight air. "Leave," he ordered. "And don't say a word about this to anyone."

"Or what?" Williams taunted, throwing his glass away into the bushes to empty his hands to fight.

Amusement fled from the two men. Their faces turned hard, and they pulled themselves up straight. Tension sizzled like electricity in the air.

"Quinn, don't." She rested her hand on his right arm to stop the fisticuffs that were about to occur. Because if a fight broke out in the garden, then everyone in the ballroom would surely come pouring outside to see. All of London would find her looking like this and make the same assumption about her and Quinton that Williams and his friend had. "Just walk away. Please."

His eyes flashed like brimstone. "And let them get away with insulting you?"

"Yes!" she choked out, afraid she would burst into sobs. "It doesn't mean any—"

"Tupping a bluestocking?" The friend laughed. "That's desperate."

"Unless bluestockings taste like blueberries. Do they, Carlisle?" Williams took a step toward Quinn. "Is she a ripe juicy blueberry, ready to pop on a man's tongue?"

Quinn's arm muscles tensed beneath her fingertips as she felt his simmering anger flame into rage.

"Quinton, don't do this," she begged. "*Please.*"

But he shrugged her hand away and stepped forward, fists clenched and heading straight into the fight. In an instant, punches hurled between all three men, followed by the sickeningly dull thuds of landed fists.

Panic surged inside her. She couldn't be caught out here, not looking like this! Not with one of Mayfair's favorite rakes bare-knuckle brawling over her.

Without thinking, only knowing she had to get away before she was seen, she ran toward the house. She was desperate to find the retiring room, to hide there until Lady Ainsley could rescue her and put an end to this nightmare.

"Belle, wait!" Quinn called out. She glanced over her shoulder only long enough to see him land a punch that sent Williams reeling. "Stop!"

But the *last* thing she would do was face him in her disgrace, or watch him get himself beaten up over her. When she heard him running toward her, the fight abandoned to chase after her, she hurried faster through the dark shadows toward the terrace door. Her shaking hand grabbed for the door handle—

"Annabelle, no!"

She flung open the door and rushed inside. Then halted in mid-step to suck in a soft scream of surprise when she saw four of the *ton*'s biggest busybodies sitting in the library. They stared at her, as if she belonged in the mews rather than in the grand town house with them. Then their gazes roamed slowly over her, taking in the torn and sagging bodice, the dirt stains on her skirt... *Oh God.*

Quinton arrived at her side a heartbeat later, looking disheveled and mussed from the fight. Knowing smiles spread across the women's faces, and their eyes gleamed like hyenas relishing a feast. A scoundrel and a woman they considered too ill-bred to ever be one of them—

He shed his jacket and placed it over her shoulders to cover her, but it was too late. The damage had been done. Her ripped and dirty dress provided all the proof—and ammunition—they needed to ruin her.

CHAPTER ONE

Cumbria, England, Near the Scottish Border
September 1822

Annabelle paused as she walked with Lady Ainsley through the gardens at Castle Glenarvon, glancing up at the late afternoon sun as it slowly lowered toward the horizon. Another day gone.

Her chest tightened painfully as she whispered, "Only one month left."

The dowager viscountess wrapped her arm around Belle's and gave a resolute nod as she patted her arm. "There's still plenty of time."

Belle wasn't so certain. Hadn't the last four years passed in the blink of an eye, only for her to still be unmarried one month before her birthday and the deadline for her inheritance?

Drawing in a deep breath, she looked across the gardens to the sweeping views of the Cumbria estate she loved, with its river and glen, and farther out across the fields of heather leading away to the blue mountains in the distance. Given as a gift to a favorite of the crown during the English civil war, the estate had been created to hold the border against Scottish invasion. It had passed down through the late Lord Ainsley's family as a treasured, if financially meager, property located so far north that a strong wind could have toppled it over into Scotland.

Yet Annabelle loved every rock-strewn, heather-tufted inch of it. After a childhood spent moving from place to place, sometimes in the middle of the night to flee her father's creditors and often not knowing when the next meal would be, the peace and permanence of Glenarvon still seemed like a dream to her. And in one short month, when she turned twenty-five, the property would be hers.

If she married.

Or she would lose it forever if she didn't. The estate would go to the Church, and Belle would lose everything...the mountains and the wilderness, the darling sheep and their pastures, even the little pond where she swam on summer evenings. The only true home she'd ever known.

That was the unbearable situation she found herself in. Just as she knew that it was all the fault of love.

Sensing her distress, the dowager added quietly, "We only wanted the best for you, my dear."

"I know." Belle squeezed her arm affectionately and turned away before Lady Ainsley could see the hint of tears in her eyes.

Lady Ainsley and her late husband were fond of Belle and always had been, ever since she came to live with them when she was ten. Her mother had died of fever, and her father, who had never been a part of her life except to cause misery, had been sentenced to prison two years earlier. She'd had no relatives to take her in.

Because her mother had once worked for the viscount, Lady Ainsley wanted to help by raising her to be her companion, since the viscountess had no children of her own. So they welcomed her into their lives and treated her as well as they would have their own daughter. Truly, as well as Lord Ainsley's three daughters from his first marriage, with a wonderful education, all the dresses and accessories she wanted, and a safe and stable home. They also wanted her to be well-protected for the rest of her life. So Lord Ainsley had willed Castle Glenarvon to her, held in trust by the new viscount—but only if she married by the time she turned twenty-five. Then, the property would have been overseen by her husband and untouchable by her thief of a father.

But the road to hell was paved with good intentions, and by trying to protect her, they'd inadvertently harmed her. Because her twenty-fifth birthday was now only a month away, with no husband in sight.

"We have a plan, and it will work," Lady Ainsley reminded her, referring to the series of teas and parties they'd planned on hosting. All of the area's most eligible gentlemen would be invited, to give Belle a chance to meet them and decide if any might do for a husband. A rushed season in miniature.

Of course, the time had finally come to also reveal that Castle Glenarvon formed her dowry. With the viscountess's permission, Belle had always kept that secret, except from a few trusted persons who held a vested interest in the property...the estate foreman, the family solicitor, and Sir Harold Bletchley, who owned the neighboring estate. She'd feared being inundated by fortune hunters who wanted the land more than they wanted her and terrified that she'd end up in a marriage like her mother's. One in which her husband's lack of love for her would turn the union into a nightmare.

But now, with a looming deadline and a dearth of suitors, she had no choice but to reveal her dowry. And no choice but to consider a marriage of convenience.

"There is always Sir Harold," Lady Ainsley tossed out offhandedly. "He would make a fine husband."

Belle stiffened, certain Sir Harold *would* make a fine husband. Just not for her. Not if she wanted to enjoy any conversations with her husband other than those about hunting and hounds.

Oh, Sir Harold wasn't a villain by any stretch. But neither was he the kind of man she suspected would make her happy. One who saw his wife as a true partner in marriage, one equal to the task of running the estate and deserving of his respect.

Lady Ainsley ticked off his qualifications as if she were reading an entry in *Debrett's*. "He has his own property and a goodly amount of wealth, the respect of the aristocracy, a fine family history.... By all accounts, he would be quite an advantageous match for you. You should reconsider his offer."

Belle fought back the urge to cry. Lady Ainsley was being helpful, in her own way. And she wasn't wrong. A young lady with Belle's pedigree—or rather, *lack* of one—would never have been able to marry a gentleman any other way except by bringing an estate as her dowry. But Belle had never cared about social rank or her place in society, except to please Lord and Lady Ainsley. Whether society spurned her for the rest of her life or welcomed her with open arms, she couldn't have cared less. She'd turned her back on them six years ago when they'd all turned their backs on her. The *only* thing that mattered to her now was that she be allowed to keep living right here in the home she loved, surrounded by the people she cared about.

She just hadn't planned on being forced into a marriage she didn't want in order to do it.

"I do not believe that he and I are well-suited," she countered before Lady Ainsley considered her silence to be an acquiescence. "I believe I should look elsewhere."

"As long as you keep looking," Lady Ainsley warned with all the worry and affection of a true mother. "I fear you've grown opposed to marriage."

"I'm not against marriage," Belle defended herself. "It's a perfectly fine institution." But neither had she ever been one of those young ladies who eagerly sought it out, who spent all their waking hours preening and plotting to snare the best husband, one of high rank and large fortune. "But I want a marriage based upon respect, friendship, shared interests . . . love." Then she added softly, certain the dowager could hear the admiration in her voice for the two people who had become a second set of parents to her, "The kind of marriage you and Lord Ainsley shared."

Marrying for love was a quaint notion, to be sure, one that certainly flew in the face of modern convention, when affection was the last consideration for a marriage match among ladies of the *ton*. Yet Belle had seen firsthand with her own mother what could happen to a wife who had trapped herself with a man who cared nothing for the true partnership a marriage should be.

Belle wasn't brilliant at math, but she could certainly count to nine months and knew that her untimely arrival had forced her parents into marriage. There was no love between them, and Marcus Greene thought he had the right to control his wife, if not by direct orders and insults than by his fists. He'd never provided a sound roof over their heads or adequate coin with which to buy bread and cloth—often none at all—preferring instead to spend his nights drinking and his days drifting from job to job, unable to keep one for longer than a few weeks. His wife and child had been dragged along in his wake, without means of escape. The drunkenness became worse, the beatings fierce and frequent, the debts higher...until he was arrested for theft and sent to prison. His gaol sentence had been his family's path to freedom.

But while her mother's situation exemplified the misery that a marriage could be, Belle had also witnessed the true partnership that Lord and Lady Ainsley had shared. Oh, they certainly fought. Angry words had been exchanged, once with the viscountess refusing to leave her boudoir for a week until Lord Ainsley apologized. But the viscount would never have cursed her or raised his fists in anger. They both dearly loved the other, and that love made all the difference.

It all came down to love, Belle was certain.

Or to the lack of it.

Given all she'd witnessed, if faced with the choice of marrying a man who did not love her or remaining unmarried, Belle would have gladly become a spinster.

But she could never utter that last aloud for fear it would break the dowager's heart. And in her current situation, with her home hanging in the balance, it seemed she no longer had a choice.

"I want a good marriage for you, too," Lady Ainsley agreed. "Which is why I sent for Quinton Carlisle."

Belle tripped.

Stumbling to regain her balance, she turned to stare at the

viscountess, her eyes wide as saucers and her mouth open. She struggled to find her voice in her shock, finally squeaking out, "*Why?*"

Lady Ainsley kept her gaze straight ahead. "To assist in your search for a husband, of course."

Belle gaped at her, stunned. *That* rascal, to help her find a suitable husband? What did he know about husband hunting, except for how to avoid the marriage shackles for himself? *Good Lord.* It was a measure of how desperate they'd become that Lady Ainsley felt compelled to invite that devil here.

Oblivious to Belle's deep breaths to regain her composure, the viscountess led her forward through the garden. "I tucked in a note to him when I wrote to his mother last month, to congratulate Elizabeth on finally marrying off one of her sons without scandal. Rather," Lady Ainsley corrected, "with *little* scandal. Trent married the niece of one of his tenant farmers, after all. I am certain tongues were wagging all the way to Cornwall over that."

Belle hadn't seen that note, or she certainly would have burned it. Which was most likely why the viscountess hadn't told her about it until now.

Dread pinched her stomach at the thought of seeing him again. "But why Quinton?"

"Because we need his help." The dowager turned to gaze across the glen in the distance. "If anyone can sort suitable husbands from the undesirables, it will be my great-nephew."

Ha! The only *help* Quinton would give would be to cause problems. Just as he'd always done for her.

In the past, whenever they'd met on those rare occasions when Annabelle accompanied Lord and Lady Ainsley to London, that scoundrel had taunted her mercilessly. Like one of those boys in the schoolyard who enjoyed pulling a girl's braid just to capture the attention of her ire. Over the years, the torment only grew, and it seemed that the more aggravated she became, the more he enjoyed it.

Until her London season, when he'd finally gone too far.

"You know what happened between us, my lady," she whispered, struck by how painful that memory was, even now. The *very* last person Belle needed interfering in her life was the man who was responsible for driving the final nail into her reputation's coffin.

"Yes." Lady Ainsley's lips pressed into a tight line. "Which is another reason I asked him here. This is his last opportunity to apologize to you."

Not likely. The Carlisle brothers never apologized for the havoc they wrought, and she doubted Quinton had changed so much in the past six years that he'd become remorseful.

Besides, she didn't want an apology. Forced contrition on Quinn's part wouldn't begin to make up for the trouble he'd unleashed upon her life. Thanks to that ill-fated night in St James's garden, she had no proper suitors. She'd been clinging to the edge of society by her fingernails as it was, and every soiree she'd attended that season only reinforced how different she was from the ladies who were born into the upper class. Although the viscount and viscountess adored her, there was no changing who she and her father were—the companion and the convict.

Before that night, gentlemen had paid her little attention. But after, she might as well have been invisible.

Which had been fine with her then. But now time was running out, and she'd have to choose from among a gaggle of men who wanted her only for her inheritance. Worse was her lingering fear over Glenarvon. To be forced into a marriage without love was bad enough...what would she do if she accidentally picked a man who refused to let her run the estate? Glenarvon would become joint property, with her husband having ultimate say over it. A good husband would let her run it as she saw fit, but there was no guarantee that the man she married wouldn't turn out to be exactly like her father—a liar, gambler, thief, abuser...with no way to be certain of his true character until it was too late.

Lady Ainsley continued, "And with the potential for fortune hunters to come crawling out of the woodwork as soon as they learn of your dowry, we will need a man's strong presence to keep them all in line."

"Did you tell him the real reason for the invitation?" A niggling guilt that they were ambushing Quinton pricked at her. Or rather, that Lady Ainsley had ambushed *her* with her outrageous plan to bring that rogue here.

The viscountess feigned insult at the gentle accusation. "He is leaving for America, and I desire to see my great-nephew one last time before he goes. I am an old woman, and I might not live to see his return visit."

Belle arched a brow. She'd grown to know and love Lady Ainsley as much as her own mother, and *that* was clearly a skilled dodge if ever she'd heard one.

So no, Quinn hadn't been told the truth.

But the dowager wasn't wrong; she was along in years, and Belle couldn't bear to think of losing Lady Ainsley as she'd lost her mother and the viscount. She guiltily bit her bottom lip. "If it makes you feel better to have Lord Quinton here, then I suppose—"

"It does."

That came rather quickly. Belle eyed her suspiciously.

Quinton Carlisle wasn't the only one being manipulated by Lady Ainsley's scheme to find Belle a husband. There was no way out of the marriage stipulation for her inheritance, and Lady Ainsley was doing everything she could to make certain Belle didn't lose her home. Belle couldn't fault her for the sentiment.

But the execution—especially Quinton's involvement—was certain to prove disastrous.

"I am a practical woman, Annabelle," Lady Ainsley explained. "Sentiment only takes one so far. At some point, practicality must enter the room."

Belle supposed so. She only hoped she could find a way to make it leave again.

"Perhaps Ainsley and I were wrong not to force Quinton to marry you six years ago," the viscountess said thoughtfully. "If we had, you would not be in this situation now."

No, her situation would have been *worse*. Which was why she'd begged Lord Ainsley not to push for marriage with Quinton as a way to salvage her reputation after the ball. Being forced to wed would have done nothing to help her standing and everything to ruin both their lives by creating a marriage of animosity and regret. She'd never seen the viscount so angry, but he'd finally relented and let her return quietly to Glenarvon, to put London and that horrible night behind her.

As for Quinton, she suspected that the rascal knew how close he'd come to being leg-shackled then and now would never set foot on Glenarvon land, summoned by his great aunt or not. Belle took comfort in that. After all, there was already enough trouble in her life as it was.

No matter. Quinton Carlisle was the last person she wanted to think about. Not when the sunset was this beautiful and the evening most likely one of the last warm ones of the year.

"If you don't mind, my lady." Belle slipped her arm from the viscountess's. "I'd like to take a walk down by the pond, for some fresh air before dinner."

"Very well. I shall see you at dinner then." She tilted her cheek toward Belle so she could kiss it.

Belle obliged with a smile.

Lady Ainsley walked on toward the house, and Belle sighed out a grateful breath as she hurried away in the opposite direction, toward the end of the garden and the little path lying just beyond. One way led uphill to the tumbled ruins of the old castle, the other down toward the glen and the secluded pond. She turned downhill, her feet moving quickly over the familiar path she'd walked at least once a day for the past fifteen years.

For the first time all day, she felt at peace, and she hummed a soft tune to herself as she reached the edge of the pond and began to undress. Her worries slipped away as easily as the layers of her clothing. For a little while at least, she could forget about her troubles and simply enjoy the summer evening.

With a small shiver as she entered the cold water, she took a deep breath and plunged forward, to swim out into the center of the pond as she did on most summer evenings. As always, she had the glen to herself. The men were all up at the stables, where they kept their quarters, or had returned to their families and homes in the village. There was no one to see her through the thick bushes lining the pond's edge or to invade her peaceful solitude.

She closed her eyes and let the cold water refresh her, cooling away the frustrations that had engulfed her life.

But it couldn't stop the sorrow that swept over her whenever she thought about the possibility of losing Glenarvon if she didn't find a husband. The estate had been a refuge for her, free from the horrors of her childhood, where she'd always had a warm bed to sleep in and food free from the mealy worms she remembered picking from the flour with her mother. What would she do if she no longer had the security of this place and these special moments? How would she ever be happy again, forced away from all she held dear?

"Well, well." A man's deep voice pierced the quiet evening. "What have we here?"

Spinning around, Annabelle gasped with surprise. Her arms flew up to cover her bare breasts, and she dropped down until the cold water came up to her chin, hiding all of her beneath the pond's surface.

Unable to see his face as he stood silhouetted against the setting sun behind him, she stared at the tall stranger standing at the edge of the pond, right beside her pile of clothes. She swallowed back both her startled fear and her mortification, and anger flared inside her. To sneak up on her like this when she was alone, naked, and vulnerable—how dare he!

"Who are you?" she demanded in her sternest possible voice, which dripped with irony given the weakness of her current position. Heavens, she couldn't even run away! "What do you want?"

An impish grin blossomed through the shadows darkening his face. "Belle," he called out, a laughing lilt to his rich voice, "is that you?"

Her shoulders sagged beneath the water. God help her, she would know that grin anywhere. That handsomely smooth smile that could charm the king out of his crown...

"Quinton Carlisle," she called out tersely, peeved that he'd picked here and now of all times to arrive.

Typical Quinn. Always showing up at the most inconvenient moments. And incidentally—as if he had some sort of a rogue's sixth sense for it—where currently stood a naked woman.

The last time she'd seen him, he was just twenty-one, fresh out of Oxford, and well on his way to becoming a rake even then. He and his two older brothers had cut a swathe through London's most notorious venues that season, as if competing to outdo each other with drunken debauchery. The three had been the foremost topic of retiring room gossip, with the quality unable to believe that the Carlisle brothers belonged to their hallowed ranks. But while the ladies scorned them in public, privately they swarmed to them. Especially to Quinton, whose charming smile had them eagerly surrendering their hearts. And other body parts.

No wonder he hadn't paid her much notice that spring, except to torment her. Why would he give any mind to a shy country girl who felt more at home in bookstores than in ballrooms when he had the sophisticated ladies of the *ton* vying for his attention? She should have known when he charmed her into surrendering her first kiss that she meant nothing to him. Such a goose she'd been!

"So it *is* you." With an amused glimmer in his blue eyes, obviously thrilled that he'd caught her in such an embarrassing situation, he lowered himself onto his heels and closer to her level. "Up to your neck in it as ever, I see."

"And you, as ever a bother," she muttered, goaded into the same bickering they'd engaged in when they were children. Old habits were hard to break.

He gave a short laugh. A lock of blond hair fell across

his forehead as he removed his beaver hat and ran his fingers through the thick waves, which were just as golden as she remembered. His crooked grin grew impossibly brighter.

Oh, she knew that look! And knew well the effect it had on women. Even now, having experienced the devilishness that lurked behind that angelic face, she felt that charming grin swirl through her, so intensely that it curled her toes into the muck at the bottom of the pond.

He pulled off his leather riding gloves and slapped them against his hard thigh as if finding her in such an embarrassing—and increasingly colder—position was a grand joke. "I wasn't certain if it was you," he taunted, "or if mermaids had come to Scotland."

"We're in England," she shot back. The pest aggravated the daylights out of her—always had, blast him. "But if you'd like to travel on, Scotland is just ten miles that way." She gave a jerk of her head toward the mountains in the distance. "Safe travels!"

Instead of being offended, he laughed, his eyes sparkling brightly. That, too, was typical of Quinn—boundless energy and a magnetic personality. "Your loyalty to crown and country is admirable, Belle, but I don't think 'Rule, Britannia!' applies to duck ponds."

Oh, the devil take the man! Pressing her lips together tightly, she glared murderously at him, not trusting herself to respond without saying something she might regret.

He was just as aggravating as she remembered, despite being six years older, more mature, and definitely broader and more muscular. A sinking dread fell through her that Lady Ainsley had made a terrible mistake by inviting him here. How on earth was he, of all men, supposed to help her find a husband—something she didn't want in the first place?

But her primary concern at the moment wasn't his aunt and how the two of them were going to resolve the mess that the late viscount had created in her life—it was getting out of the pond and over to her clothes without Quinn seeing her naked. And judging from the relaxed way he rested back on his boot heels, his forearm lying casually across his thigh, he didn't plan on being a gentleman and leaving.

"Lady Ainsley is up at the house," she informed him, goose bumps forming on her skin. Good Lord, the water was cold! A few minutes more, and her teeth would chatter.

"I know. My brother Robert is with her," he explained. "But the groom said *you* were here, and I thought I'd say hello before settling into the house. So... hello." Even in the dim light of the fading sunset, his eyes sparkled like the devil's own. "This feels like old times."

Old times she very much wanted to forget.

When her eyes darted longingly to her clothes at his feet, he followed her glance. "Are you really...?" He gasped in feigned shock as he reached down to hook a finger in her dress and lift it from the ground. "Goodness, Belle! You all truly do live wild here in the borderlands, don't you?"

Despite the chill of the water, her face flushed hot. Leave it to Quinn to so cavalierly point out that she was naked.

She sighed in aggravation. And shivered with cold. Her teeth began to chatter, and as she shook, she prayed he couldn't see it. Or anything else he shouldn't see. "Would you please—"

"My, my, how careless!" With a shake of his head, he clucked his tongue. "Some wild animal could stumble upon your clothes and carry them off, or the wind might simply blow them—"

"Quinton James Carlisle, don't you dare!" But her threat lacked all force, since she could do nothing to stop him. And drat him, he knew it, too.

Which only caused his grin to widen. She could see on his face how tempted he was to do just as she feared and walk away with her clothes, leaving her as naked as Eve in the garden. The deceitful snake!

"Same Belle I remember." He laughed good-naturedly, as if he truly were happy to see her. "Tell me, do you still prefer books to people?"

"Certain people, yes," she bit out. *And especially you.*

As if he could read her mind, he nearly doubled over hooting with laughter. The rotten scoundrel actually laughed! When he should have had the decency to be remorseful about what he'd done to her all those years ago.

In frustration, her hands fisted beneath the pond's surface. "*Why* must you always insist on tormenting me? We're no longer children."

"No, we're not." His gaze darkened heatedly as his eyes fixed on her, a look that proved he was pure man. "But teasing you puts a fire in your eyes, Belle," he drawled in a silky voice, "and I've always liked seeing the fire in you."

She shivered. This time not from the cold.

But his smooth words couldn't be trusted. That much about him hadn't changed, although the rest of him was most definitely different...taller, broader, more solid. And impossibly more masculine. The tight fit of his buckskin breeches accentuated the hard muscles of his thighs and his narrow waist as much as the redingote stretching tight across his back exemplified the wide breadth of his shoulders. Since she'd last seen him, he'd transformed into a golden mountain of man, just like his older brothers, yet retained the same charismatic grin he'd possessed since he was a boy.

If he were anyone else, she would have said he was attractive. Perhaps even handsome. Unfortunately, she knew the Carlisle brothers and was well aware of what lurked beneath their captivating exteriors. Sebastian was the serious one, Robert was the risk-taker, and Quinton...well, Quinn made his way through the world by his charm.

But his charisma no longer worked on her. She'd gained immunity. The hard way.

For a fleeting moment, she was tempted to show him exactly how much fire flamed inside her and simply walk out of the pond and collect her clothes, as bare bottomed as a newborn babe. Wouldn't she just love to see the startled look on his face! Because she was certain he thought her incapable of doing anything so daring.

She trembled at the enticing idea. Despite the cold, an odd yearning of excitement fluttered up from low in her belly. Certainly the girl he knew before would never have considered it, but the woman Annabelle had become might just do something that unexpected. Something so bold that he—

She sneezed.

"God bless you," he offered, then trailed his hand through the water at the pond's edge. "Brrr! That is rather cold, isn't it?"

Her eyes narrowed to slits. She distrusted herself to speak, knowing this time she really would say something indelicate.

"Better come out now, Belle. You're turning blue." His eyes gleamed with enjoyment at toying with her. "Like a blueberry."

Her breath strangled in her throat. *Blueberry.* Her eyes stung at his thoughtless words, and her chest panged painfully. To be that unkind to her even now after all these years as to bring up that horrible night—but he only continued to smile at her, oblivious to the cruelty of his offhanded comment. Of course, Quinn wouldn't think anything of it. His reputation hadn't been ruined because of a fight. His heart hadn't been shattered. But *hers* had.

Although she could hide her body beneath the water, she couldn't conceal the dark humiliation gathering on her face like storm clouds.

From his puzzled expression, he'd noted the sudden change in her but didn't realize the full implication of what he'd said, and she didn't dare speak past the knot in her throat to explain for fear she might cry. Because she would never allow herself to cry in front of him, *never* show him how much he'd hurt her.

"Belle, are you— Oh Christ." His grin faded, and his eyes softened apologetically. "I'm sorry. It was so long ago that I'd forgotten all about it."

But she hadn't, and never would.

He rose to his full height, then turned his back to her and walked off a few paces to give her privacy. All his teasing vanished. "Come out whenever you're ready."

* * *

With his back turned and his eyes focused on the darkening shadows cast across the countryside by the sunset, Quinn heard the soft splash of water as Belle moved quickly toward the bank.

He smiled. Annabelle Greene. Quick-tempered, defensive,

serious...exactly as he remembered. When they were children, she'd been a bluestocking whose nose was forever pressed into one book or another. So he'd nicknamed her Bluebell, a combination of her name and bluestocking, just to antagonize her. The name stuck.

So did his enjoyment of irritating her.

He hadn't lied to her—he liked seeing the fire in her eyes, always had. Perhaps it was because all the society ladies he knew kept their true emotions carefully hidden. Not so with Annabelle, whose pretty face had never been able to hide what she was thinking, whose bright smiles had always lit up a room.

Maybe it was even simpler than that. As he'd ripened into manhood, he'd come to realize how close anger lay to passion. Fires stirred by teasing were nearly as sweet as those flamed by desire.

"Are you all right?" he called out over his shoulder. Then he added, just to taunt her, "Bluebell."

"I-I'm fine!"

He heard her teeth chatter. Guilt stabbed him for keeping her in the cold water longer than he should have. Or perhaps her answer was forced out between teeth clenched in anger. *That* would certainly be the Annabelle he knew.

Good Lord, had it really been six years since he'd seen her?

The last time had been in London when she was starting her first season. As a late bloomer not yet grown into womanhood, she'd been at that age when her curves were just beginning to blossom and soften. The stick-with-ears she'd been all her life had grown into her long legs and big honey-hazel eyes, her gawkiness turning graceful and her shyness mellowing into a natural demureness. The Bluebell had suddenly turned interesting, even to the jaded buck he'd already become.

Then he'd kissed her.

He remembered the sweet tang of honey on her lips, the wild scent of heather that clung to her skin, the pliant softness of her curves...the utter confusion that gripped him afterward. She was the Bluebell, for God's sake. Aunt Agatha's companion. Innocent and inexperienced. And wholly intriguing for all of it.

Six years had passed, and he hadn't seen her since. Based upon the barbs they'd just exchanged, though, she hadn't changed. And oddly enough, he was more relieved than he wanted to admit that she hadn't.

He offered affably, unable to stop himself, "Need any help with your stockings?"

"Just stay right where you are!"

"But I'm very good with ladies' stockings," he drawled.

"Oh," she muttered beneath her breath, "I'm sure you are."

He chuckled. Same old Annabelle, all right.

Good to know that some things hadn't changed, especially when everything else in his life was turning on end. Including the unexpected invitation to visit Glenarvon, which had nearly knocked him flat. Aunt Agatha had implied in her letter that she had financial matters to settle, which only boded well for him.

"Lady Ainsley said you'd planned to travel to America," Belle called out from behind him. "Is it true? Are you really going?"

He smiled at her stilted attempt at casual conversation. Or rather, at her not-so-subtle attempt to suss out when he planned to leave. "Yes."

But first, he needed to pay his respects to his aunt and

collect whatever funds she had for him. Beggars couldn't be choosers, and he needed every penny he could get his hands on for what he had planned. To say his prospects as a third son were limited was a grand understatement. Oh, certainly he'd proven himself successful in managing the family's estate, assisting Sebastian after he'd inherited. More successful, in fact, than anyone who knew of his wild reputation would ever have imagined. In just two years, he'd increased estate profits by over fifteen percent.

But it was Sebastian's estate, not his, and he'd always chafed under the title's shadow. Proving himself on his merits meant that he had to find another path for himself, where his own capabilities decided his success and where his connections to the Duke of Trent meant nothing.

"To New England or Virginia?" she persisted, as if this conversation was nothing more unusual than discussing weather over tea. As if she wasn't naked.

"South Carolina, actually."

"Why?"

He grinned at her interrogation. "I promised my father."

"No," she corrected. "I mean, why South Carolina?"

"An old friend of my father's lives there." Asa Jeffers had served in his father's regiment during the first war with the Americans, then stayed on in the former colonies after the war, where he'd bought a significant amount of property outside Charleston along the Ashley River and settled down to raise a family. But he and his wife had only daughters. "He's getting up in age now and has no one to continue working the land for him. So he's putting it up for sale."

"And you're going to buy it?"

"I am." Just as his father had arranged. Richard Carlisle had understood Quinn's need to make his own way and hadn't dissuaded him when he'd set his sights on America. He'd encouraged them, in fact. Quinn couldn't afford the property by himself, even at the generous price Jeffers offered, so his father agreed to loan him the money. There was only one condition: that Quinn would allow Jeffers and his wife to live out their remaining days on the property, that he would care for them there.

And Quinton had every intention of keeping this last promise to his father. The *very last* promise, in fact. Because the letter from Jeffers, agreeing to the terms of sale, had arrived just three days before the accident that took his father's life. Quinn's plans had been put on hold after that, but he'd used that promise to find his way out of his grief and to be strong for his mother when she'd needed him.

Jeffers graciously understood Quinn's need to remain in England, to help his family through their mourning period and to assist Sebastian in running the estate until a proper land agent could be hired. But their mourning was now over, and a good agent had been hired. And Quinn was needed in Charleston. He couldn't be there at his father's side to take care of him the night he'd had the accident that took his life, but he could take care of Asa Jeffers.

"Then shouldn't you already be on a ship sailing for the west?" Belle asked.

Good question. Time was running out. He had to make his way to Charleston before the new year, when Jeffers would no longer be able to hold the land for him, having to sell before taxes were levied. Given the need to be on a ship bound for America in just four weeks in order to meet that deadline, this trip to the borderlands wasn't convenient. But he wasn't too proud to pass up any additional funds Aunt Agatha might be willing to provide that would help his new venture to found not only his own American estate but a trade business, as well.

"I will be soon enough," he answered resolutely.

Of course, he also knew that the visit to Glenarvon meant seeing Annabelle. They hadn't last parted under the best of circumstances, but he'd assumed that they could tolerate each other for a few days before he rode on to the coast. Then his future would begin. And not a moment too soon.

"Quinton! You got dirt in my stockings!"

He grinned. Yep. The same Bluebell he remembered.

Unless...

How much *exactly* had Belle changed during the past six years?

The temptation to satisfy his curiosity was too great to ignore. And who could really fault him for taking a quick glance? After all, any man would be curious about a woman he hadn't seen since she was eighteen, since the night she'd kissed him breathless.

"And look! There's grass all over my dress."

Would she be the same gangly girl he remembered? Would she still be nothing but skin and bones, sharp angles, and big feet? Fate would undoubtedly make him pay for this, but he couldn't help himself—

He glanced over his shoulder.

His breath hitched in his throat when he caught sight of her in the fading golden-purple sunset, all curvy naked and dripping wet, her body half turned toward him as she hurried into her clothes. *Sweet Lucifer.* Full breasts with dusky-pink nipples drawn taut from the cold water, round hips, and long legs that stretched all the way from her toes to her... *Well.* She'd certainly grown into her feet, all right, along with the rest of her.

He swallowed. Hard. The Bluebell had become a woman.

And God help him, he wasn't prepared for that, or for the visceral reaction in his tightening gut. Good Lord, for the *Bluebell*. And when she turned to drop her shift over her head and shimmied it down over her breasts and hips, unknowingly teasing him with another angle of her ripe body, the new view ripped his breath away.

He turned around before she caught him staring at her. Fisted at his sides, his hands trembled, and he inhaled deep, slow breaths to steady himself.

Well. Some things had certainly changed in the past six years. In all kinds of new and interesting ways.

"Just one moment more," she called out. "I can't quite reach..."

More fabric rustled behind him. Quinn imagined her lissome body twisting to reach behind her to fasten her dress, her breasts straining tantalizingly against her low-cut bodice as her back arched. One long leg would be half exposed by a raised skirt revealing the lacy edge of her stocking, which he could slowly roll down her thigh and follow along in its wake with his mouth.

"I'm almost through!"

Squeezing his eyes closed, he tried not to think of how round and full her derriere was as she bent over to slip on her half boots. He blew out a harsh breath of aggravation. That she of all women could elicit such a response from him that even now his cock tingled—

"Hurry up, will you?" he prodded irritably. Because he wasn't certain how much longer he could stand there, not looking.

"There," she announced. "I'm dressed."

Thank God. He turned.

And froze beneath the full force of her presence.

Sweet and genuinely enchanting—and far more beguiling than he remembered—Belle gazed up at him through long, lowered lashes. In her sprigged muslin dress, with her damp, caramel-brown hair now pinned into place, she looked perfectly proper, as if she hadn't just been caught swimming naked. She barely came up to his shoulder yet packed the punch of an Amazon with her quiet allure and natural grace. Gone was her insecurity, replaced by a shining confidence he remembered seeing in her only once before, right as she'd wrapped her arms around his neck to kiss him.

She held her hand out to him, and he caught the scent of heather wafting on the air. The same wild, floral perfume he remembered. Her cheeks pinked delicately, and the tingle in his cock turned into a longing ache that twined up his spine.

She said softly, "Welcome to Castle Glenarvon." She added with a touch of begrudging politeness and a flash of her eyes that reminded him of smoldering coals right before they flamed into a fire, "I hope you enjoy your stay."

CHAPTER TWO

There you two are," Lady Ainsley called out as Belle and Quinn entered the drawing room.

Belle sent her an apologetic smile for taking so long to return, then gave one to Robert, Quinton's older brother, in welcome as he rose to his feet at her arrival. He seemed happy to see her again.

More importantly, he hadn't fled. Which meant that Lady Ainsley had yet to acknowledge the real reason behind his brother's summons to the borderlands, most likely waiting until Belle was in the room.

She bit back a groan of embarrassment. She'd hoped that the viscountess had changed her mind about this mad scheme of hers—

"I imagine that you and Quinton had a great deal to discuss," Lady Ainsley added hopefully.

No such luck. Her stomach sank as her last tendril of hope for reprieve fled.

"Not really," Belle dodged, refusing to acknowledge her predicament to the two men until she absolutely had to. The entire situation was embarrassing enough. The last thing she wanted to do was admit in front of that scoundrel Quinton that she'd been unable to find a husband. No, not *unable*. More like purposeful evasion. And truly, with the way the men in her life had behaved, could anyone blame her for not being eager to shackle herself to one of their kind?

But now, she no longer had a choice.

Lady Ainsley's lips tightened knowingly at Belle's answer, clearly not the one she wanted. "Regardless, I am glad you've returned."

The viscountess's eyes narrowed curiously on Quinton, as if sizing him up.

Belle frowned. Did Lady Ainsley regret her decision to bring him here, now that he stood before her in flesh and blood?

Apparently not, because his aunt's gaze softened with an optimistic gleam. Belle's stomach sank further, this time all the way to her knees.

"Now that we're all present," the viscountess announced, "Quinton, Robert—welcome to Castle Glenarvon."

"Thank you, Aunt Agatha." When Quinton placed a kiss on Lady Ainsley's cheek, the dowager flushed a happy pink even though she waved him away with a feigned scowl. She fooled no one. His aunt held great affection in her heart for Quinton, always had. Even when the rascal didn't deserve it. "I'd never pass up the chance to see you." Ignoring her unconvincing *humph* of disbelief, he jerked a thumb toward his brother. "Robert, though, tagged along in order to flee from a woman."

"I wasn't fleeing," Robert interrupted with a touch of aggravation.

"As much as escaping," Quinn clarified quickly.

Robert nodded. "The lifelong shackles of domestication—"

"And matrimony—"

"But any escape from matrimony—"

"—is a good escape."

"Indeed!" they finished together.

The two men turned to look at Lady Ainsley, as if expecting some kind of reaction to their rapid-fire exchange. But the dowager only stared at them as if they were both bedlamites.

And truly, even Belle didn't know what to say to that, her mouth falling open, speechless. The Carlisle brothers had always possessed an uncanny ability to finish each other's sentences, but this was . . . astonishing.

Having long ago grown used to the brothers' antics, Lady Ainsley claimed back the flow of conversation. "So good to have you both here." She darted a sideways look at Belle. "However, I did not invite you here to avoid weddings. Quite the opposite, in fact."

Sobering quickly at her pronouncement, the two men exchanged a bewildered glance.

Then Quinton ventured with a grin, "You invited me here because you wanted to see me one last time before I left for America." When his aunt hesitated to answer, his grin faded. "Didn't you?"

Lady Ainsley's ramrod-straight spine softened at that, as if she fully realized that this visit could very likely be the last time her old eyes laid sight on Quinton. "Of course I wanted to see you. I am very fond of all of Elizabeth's children." Her lips twisted into a judgmental grimace. "Although surely you boys take after your father's side of the family and not mine."

The two men grinned, and Belle was struck by how similar

they looked. Like two life-size bookends, right down to the same broad shoulders, golden hair, and midnight-blue eyes.

"You are always welcome to visit." Lady Ainsley admitted after a fleeting pause, "But that was not my prime motivation."

Belle couldn't breathe as the room tilted sickeningly beneath her. She held her breath, dreading this moment...

"Then why were we invited?" Quinn asked.

The question seemed to hover in the air like a trail of smoke. Knowing what was coming, Belle dropped her gaze to the carpet as embarrassment heated her cheeks.

"Because Annabelle needs a husband," Lady Ainsley announced without preamble.

Oh God. Belle's stomach plummeted right through the floor.

"Pardon?" both brothers rasped out simultaneously, their deep voices thick with bewilderment. And panic.

Mortification surged through her. Oh, she simply wanted to crawl under the settee and die!

With her cheeks heating, she glanced up to find Quinton staring at her. His puzzled gaze raked deliberately over her, as if he'd never seen her before. As if it had never occurred to him that she might become some man's wife.

Belle rolled her eyes. The rascal was probably terrified that his aunt meant marriage to *him*. Which only made Belle's face heat even more with embarrassment. And irritation. After all, there was nothing wrong with her, for heaven's sake! She'd make him a fine wife. If anything, he was the one who wouldn't do for a husband for her if she proposed to the scoundrel and—

Oh.

Her heart skipped as an idea began to take shape at

the back of her mind. A thoroughly desperate, utterly mad idea.

A *proposal*...

Lady Ainsley explained quietly, "My late Ainsley insisted that Annabelle be taken care of after we'd both gone, to ensure a living and home for her. So we established an inheritance which would do exactly that." Her shoulders lifted as she drew a deep breath. "We wanted to protect her from anyone who might try to do her harm, just as we wanted her to share her future with a loving husband, who would help her oversee her finances and provide the love and support she deserves. The same kind of marriage I shared with my Ainsley."

"That was very kind of you and Uncle Charles," Quinton murmured, drawing a concurring nod from Robert.

"We thought so," Lady Ainsley agreed solemnly, her concerned gaze drifting to Annabelle, who looked away, unable to bear the viscountess's helpless concern. "That was also why we attached a stipulation to the inheritance."

Robert frowned. "Which is?"

"That I marry by the time I reach my twenty-fifth birthday," Annabelle interjected grimly, to save Lady Ainsley from having to speak it. To ease at least a portion of the guilt Belle knew swirled inside the kind woman over this. She and Lord Ainsley had only wanted the best for Belle, and Belle had let them down by not finding a husband.

By not wanting one at all, if truth be told. Not unless she married for love.

"If I marry by then," Belle continued quietly, not daring to meet Lady Ainsley's gaze for fear one of the two women might break into sobs, "I will inherit Castle Glenarvon. If not, it goes to the Church."

As the days grew closer and closer to her birthday, it seemed as if exactly that would happen. Unless... Belle took another glance at Quinton. While entering a love match no longer seemed an option, at the very least she wanted a husband who would allow her to keep the estate and run it exactly as she pleased. Someone who wouldn't interfere.

Or who *couldn't* interfere.

Hope fluttered inside her. The scoundrel might just prove helpful after all.

"So you understand that we must find her a husband." The viscountess shifted her gaze between her two nephews. "And I expect both of you to help."

"Help *how*, exactly?" Robert asked suspiciously.

"In two days, after Sunday service at church, we will casually announce that Belle has been given a generous dowry. The estate of Castle Glenarvon." The dowager's lips twisted distastefully at all that implied. "I expect word to flood through the countryside and for suitors of all kinds to inundate our front hall in order to declare their intentions to marry her. We will have to choose the best man from among them."

"But that's..." Quinn began thoughtfully, his voice trailing off as he closely watched Belle.

Like auctioning me off to the highest bidder? But Belle didn't dare speak that aloud, knowing how much it would wound Lady Ainsley.

"Exactly like any other young society lady who debuts in London and makes her intentions to marry known," the dowager finished. "The only difference is that those ladies have several seasons to choose a husband, whereas we have only four weeks."

Belle cringed. Lady Ainsley made it sound like a battle plan for capturing the enemy.

"Which is why we need you two here," the dowager continued. "Annabelle lacks male relatives to help her with the formalities of being courted and to sort the viable suitors from the undesirables, so I have called upon you to assist us. You will fill the role of guardian. Suitors will approach you, and you will put them through their paces. If you decide they are good enough to court Annabelle, you will give your permission. If not, you will ensure that they leave and do not bother her again."

Belle kept her gaze glued to the carpet, unwilling to raise her eyes to see how Lady Ainsley's plan was settling on the two men. Nor did she want to face the recrimination—or worse, the laughter—she knew she'd see on Quinton's face.

"That is our plan," the viscountess finished. "And it will work. We have not yet given up hope."

But Belle had. *Almost.*

She stole a surreptitious glance at Quinn as the desperate idea at the back of her mind now blossomed into a real possibility. *A proposal.* It was ludicrous and reckless, absolutely mad—

And quite possibly the only good solution she had left.

Quinn arched a skeptical brow. "It takes a scoundrel—"

"—to know a scoundrel?" Robert finished just as warily.

"Exactly." Lady Ainsley nodded imperially. It was a credit to the two men that they hadn't either burst into laughter at her scheme or fled.

Quinn shook his head, the lunacy of this plan visible on his face. "Aunt Agatha, you know we'd do anything for you and Annabelle." He flicked an apologetic glance at Belle. "But Robert and I don't know any of the local gentlemen here."

Robert agreed cautiously, "We wouldn't know who to recommend or chase away."

"You will do fine for what I have in mind." Lady Ainsley inhaled a deep breath and squared her shoulders. "Desperate times call for desperate measures, do they not, Annabelle?"

"Yes," she murmured thoughtfully. Oh, what she was considering was certainly desperate!

"And you have no suitors now?" Quinn turned toward Belle. "No one who holds an affection for you?"

That stung. Because of him, she hadn't had any serious suitors since the night of the St James ball, but then, neither had she encouraged any. All the men in her life had proven to be disappointments, either brutally controlling her or actively working to harm her. Even Lord Ainsley, whom she loved like a father, was now directing her life. Why would she be eager, then, to chain herself to one for the rest of her life?

"There is no one," she admitted, trying unsuccessfully to ignore the aching humiliation darkening her chest. Society regarded an unmarried woman of twenty-five as being "on the shelf." A pleasant way of saying *unwanted spinster*. They viewed her lack of marital status as an indication that something was inherently wrong with her, something lacking in her as a woman that made men shun her. Belle was doubly damned. Not only had her reputation been ruined six years ago, but she also lived between worlds as a lady's companion, where she wasn't good enough to marry into society and too good to marry an ordinary man from the village.

She might as well have been invisible. And sexless.

Until recently, none of that had bothered her. She'd viewed unmarried life as her path for independence. No man to control her or tell her what to do, no husband to yell or raise his fists in anger. She could dress however she preferred and spend her time on whatever activities she wished, and never would she be uprooted from her home again due to the actions of a man.

That was the bitter irony of her situation. A man once again had control over her life, albeit this time from beyond the grave, while only another man could save her.

"The gentleman who owns the neighboring estate has offered marriage," Lady Ainsley commented, sensing Belle's distress. "Sir Harold Bletchley. He is Annabelle's leading suitor at the moment."

Quick dread swept through her, and Belle glanced frantically at Quinn. "He is not my suitor," she corrected the dowager as gently as possible. She didn't want there to be any confusion in Quinn's mind about her relationship—rather, her lack of one—with Sir Harold. "We are not courting, and I have not accepted any offers, from Sir Harold or anyone."

Now that Quinn was here, she might never have to. For the first time, a glimmer of hope about her situation tingled inside her.

"Although he has offered in the past and would gladly court her," the viscountess interjected. "He is quite fond of Annabelle."

Perhaps. But he seemed even fonder of her inheritance. "I was hoping someone else might come along," she explained. "Someone better suited for me."

Her gaze drifted to Quinton. By the luck of fate, she might have just found that man. And right in the nick of time.

"It takes three weeks to read the bans," Robert reminded them. His concerned gaze softened on Belle. "You're not giving yourself much time."

"I've procured a special license," Lady Ainsley informed them. When they all looked at her in surprise, she explained, "The archbishop is a family friend."

"Of course," Belle mumbled, her shoulders sagging. Apparently, even God wanted her married.

"We're planning the wedding festivities to coincide with her birthday," the viscountess continued. "Both tied up perfectly together."

"I see," Quinn said slowly, although Belle knew from the quizzical expression on his face that he barely understood any of it. Or exactly how he and Robert had gotten snared in her mess.

"Considering Belle's situation, and *all* the events that brought her here," his aunt pressed, not so subtly reminding him of his role in her predicament, "you will be happy to assist us, won't you, Quinton?" It was not a question.

He held her gaze for a long moment, the pause before he answered so thick with tension that they could have swum in it. "Of course."

The dowager nodded, pleased at his answer. "Just as Annabelle will be happy to let you help her find a husband."

Annabelle smiled at the unwitting irony in the viscountess's words. "Absolutely thrilled."

Quinn's sapphire-blue eyes narrowed suspiciously. He recognized her comment for the lie it was, even if he had no idea of the true motive behind it.

"Ah." Lady Ainsley sighed gratefully when the butler appeared in the doorway. "There's Ferguson now."

The butler bowed to the viscountess, then to the room at large. "Dinner is ready, my lady."

"Very good." Lady Ainsley put an end to the conversation by offering her arm to Robert to escort her into the dining room, leaving Belle with...

Quinton.

She sucked in a deep breath to steady herself and to keep

from saying anything she might regret. It wouldn't do to chase him away now that he was her last best hope. Having no other choice, she took his arm.

As they followed slowly behind Robert and the viscountess, he leaned down to bring his mouth close to her ear. "What the devil is going on here?"

"Lady Ainsley explained everything," she whispered, her cheeks heating. "She wants your help in finding me a husband so I can meet the conditions of my inheritance. That's all."

His gaze narrowed suspiciously. "You're lying."

"I am not."

He flicked a pointed glance at her blush. "Like a rug."

She rolled her eyes. Darn that blush, and double darn that responding grin of his! The rascal infuriated her to no end. Yet her silly heart also skittered traitorously at the warm tickle of his breath against her earlobe.

She grimaced at herself. Such a hopeless goose! Even caught red-handed in a lie, with her world ready to crumble around her—even knowing what a scoundrel he was—she couldn't help the familiar pull of him. The same one from six years ago which had gotten her into this mess in the first place. And if she wasn't careful, her goose would be good and cooked before it was all over.

As they entered the old banqueting hall turned dining room that soared two stories high from its stone floors to the wooden beams above, he gave a friendly tap of his shoulder against hers. "Tell me the truth," he cajoled. "Do you really want my help in finding a husband?"

"More than you realize," she murmured honestly.

He asked bluntly, "Why?"

She certainly couldn't tell him *that*! If he discovered her new plan before she was ready to share it, he might very well leave right now. And then where would she be? So she purposefully misunderstood his question and answered, "Can't I call on an old friend when I need him?"

With his lips twitching at that blatant evasion, he led her around the table that could accommodate over fifty people to the four settings laid out for them at the far end near the fireplace, where Robert had already seated the viscountess.

"We were a lot of things, Belle," Quinn admitted sotto voce, the deep sound falling through her like warm summer rain. "But we were never *friends*."

Her mind filled with the memory of their kiss beneath the rose bower, the solidity of his body pressing against hers, the surprising softness of his warm lips...Fresh heat flashed through her. To think that her future now lay in this rascal's hands— She hated that she'd sunk so low that she had to ask for help from *him*.

Yet there was something sweetly fitting that the man who broke her heart and made her swear off men and their insincere charms should now be the only one who could save her.

"I'll explain everything later," she murmured. "I promise."

He slid her a disbelieving look, yet acquiesced. "All right. I'll leave it alone."

Relief poured through her. "Thank—"

"For now."

He pulled out her chair for her. She shot him an aggravated grimace before slipping into her seat.

He leaned over her shoulder and warned, "But one way or another, I will get the truth from you. Even if I have to tie you up and torture you."

Her breath caught in a silent gasp. Before her befuddled

mind could come up with a proper response to *that*, he'd already moved away to take his own seat. She stared after him, but the infuriating pest didn't so much as glance in her direction so she could give him the cutting glare he deserved.

Belle chewed her bottom lip and stared at him across the table as the footman carried in the first course. Oh, he was certainly not happy at finding himself coerced into helping her acquire a husband. From the trapped expression on his face as he turned to speak to Lady Ainsley, Belle suspected that he might not be any more receptive of the scheme she now turned over in her mind. But there was no other way to keep her home, not without the possibility of bringing down upon her head the same sort of miserable marriage her mother had.

Lady Ainsley was right. Desperate times called for desperate measures, and she could think of nothing more desperate than what she had in mind. Because she now knew what had to be done.

She needed to marry Quinton Carlisle.

* * *

Quinn's eyes narrowed on Belle across the drawing room, where they'd gathered after dinner. *What was really going on with the Bluebell?*

Dinner had been pleasant enough, he supposed, except that he'd spent half of it wondering about Belle's situation and the other half contemplating how much fun it might be to actually tie her up, given the glimpse of her he'd had at the pond.

His aunt's announcement that Annabelle had to get married had stunned the daylights out of him. He'd heard of similar stipulations by members of the quality to force their children into doing their bidding, especially to second- or third-born children, who didn't have the restraints of entailments and the pressures of continuing peerages that the heirs had. One way to ensure that sons and daughters married suitably and settled down into respectable adulthood was to control their purse strings.

But for Belle, it made no sense. That a proper gentleman from a respectable family would ever attach himself to her was highly unlikely, regardless of how sizable her dowry. Surely his uncle had realized that. What the late Lord Ainsley should have done was give her the property outright, to establish a home and living for her in case she remained unmarried.

What Uncle Charles had actually done, however, was force her into the very real possibility of falling prey to a fortune hunter. Which gave veracity to Aunt Agatha's explanation for why she wanted him here.

But it didn't begin to clarify everything.

Whatever Annabelle was hiding, he would discover it eventually. And she knew that, too, based on the way she'd kept her distance ever since they'd gone through after dinner. As if she couldn't trust herself near him. Even now, she played at the pianoforte on the far side of the room, pretending to ignore him and missing half the notes in her lack of concentration.

The butler slid open the double doors, and a footman carried a coffee tray inside. He set it on the sideboard and retreated from the room.

"Ah, the coffee's arrived," Aunt Agatha commented as she picked up a discarded ace in the card game she'd taken up with Robert. "All of you help yourselves. We don't stand on formalities in the evenings here at Glenarvon."

Ferguson's heavy sigh said otherwise, but the butler dutifully arranged the coffee for service, then stood to the side and waited to pour cups.

Belle rose from the pianoforte and crossed the room to request a coffee.

And so did Quinn. As Ferguson reached for the coffeepot, he stepped up beside her. "Belle."

Her pink lips parted in a peculiar mix of nervousness and awareness that reminded him for a moment of a hare who knew it had stumbled into a snare but couldn't flee for falling deeper into the trap. She stared straight ahead, unwilling to look at him. Which made him only more determined to discover the truth.

Ferguson finished pouring and held out her cup.

As she turned to walk away, Quinn took her elbow and stopped her, forcing her to remain at his side unless she wanted to cause a scene. She tensed with a shallow gasp, and he felt that soft breath shiver through her beneath his fingertips.

"A coffee for me, too, Ferguson," he requested, although he didn't have a taste for it tonight. But it gave him a good excuse to remain at her side.

The butler nodded and reached to pour a second cup.

"The truth now, Belle," he pressed. "Why do you really want my help?"

She hesitated, and for a moment, he suspected she might tell him. But her eyes flicked with uncertainty at the butler. "I cannot say right now," she answered quietly. "There are too many ears in the room who might overhear."

Ferguson bristled at the comment, caught in his eavesdropping. Quinn thought he heard a soft *humph* sound beneath the butler's breath.

"You can't avoid me for long," he warned. "I deserve answers."

"I told you—"

"You've told me practically nothing." He took the proffered coffee from Ferguson, who turned away with a sniff of pique and politely put several feet between them. "Except enough to raise my suspicions."

She scowled. "Now you're just being dogged."

He let that insult slide, knowing she wanted to make him angry enough that he'd leave her alone. Not a chance. He hadn't believed one word of that sentimental cock and bull story she gave earlier about wanting the help of an old friend.

"I plan on hounding you until you give in and tell me the truth," he warned. With a self-assured grin playing at his lips, he added as rakishly as possible just to goad her, "And I always get my way with women."

"*Not* with this one," she replied haughtily and pulled her elbow away, but not before her cheeks pinked. Shaking her head, she muttered beneath her breath, "I had absolutely nothing to do with bringing you here. That was all your aunt's doing." Then she paused, her lips parting in soft hesitation, as if considering what to say, how much to divulge… "But I do have an idea for how to get us out of this mess."

Interesting. He leaned in closer—

"Come join us, you two," Agatha called out, interrupting them. "We need more hands to play at whist."

"Of course." Belle smiled at his aunt as if she and Quinn were discussing nothing more important than the evening's weather. But as she turned to join the game, she paused to briefly rest her hand on his arm and lowered her voice. "Meet me in the library at midnight."

A midnight meeting in a room only a bluestocking would pick. Not the kind of midnight assignation with a woman he usually found intriguing, but the Bluebell had pricked his interest. In more ways than one.

And he couldn't resist teasing her about it. "A midnight tryst?" He faked astonishment. "Why, Belle, I'm shocked at you."

For a heartbeat, she froze, astounded at his insinuation. "It isn't like that at all!"

When he grinned at her, her shoulders slumped in irritation. She blew out an aggravated breath, knowing she'd risen to the bait exactly as he'd wanted.

"Someday, Quinton Carlisle," she seethed, "you're going to regret all the childish torment you've done to me over the years."

Not as long as he could glimpse the fire he raised inside her. Like now. It was simply too delicious to avoid. "Perhaps," he agreed, then walked away to join the card game, chuckling low as her blazing eyes followed after him. He murmured to himself, "But today is not that day."

"Annabelle," Aunt Agatha called out to her, "we need you."

He had to give her credit as she plastered a carefree smile on her face and slid onto the chair at his elbow, partnering with Aunt Agatha against the two brothers and appearing for all the world as if nothing untoward had passed between them. Still, he placed his coffee safely out of her reach just in case she decided to fling it at him.

Ah, the Bluebell! Always so unpredictable and challenging, always so much fun to fluster and tease. And so much more interesting than those society ladies he associated with in London.

Robert dealt the cards, and as the tricks played out and trumps were taken, they fell into easy conversation. Aunt Agatha asked for details about Sebastian and Miranda's wedding, right down to what kinds of cakes were served at the breakfast. She guffawed loudly when Quinn described how Edward and Kate Westover's daughter Faith, who had been the flower girl, hit little Stephen Crenshaw, the ring bearer, over the head with her petal basket.

"The boy was born a marquess." Aunt Agatha laughed. "Best he get used to abuse while he's young. Especially that which involves irate females and flowers— Don't trump my ace again, dear."

"Apologies." Belle bit her lip and frowned at her cards, as if she wasn't certain which ones she still held in her hand. Her mind clearly wasn't in the game.

"I'm a great fan of flowers and women myself," Quinton murmured lazily as he counted the point in his and Robert's favor on the marker.

Belle's gaze slid sideways at the private innuendo, narrowing murderously on him. But his comment went right over the heads of Aunt Agatha and Robert, who paid it no mind.

Agatha shuffled the cards and dealt out the next hand. "And how is Elizabeth?"

Quinn frowned and answered quietly, "Mother's much better now."

But for the past two years, she'd been through hell. Richard Carlisle's unexpected death had nearly taken her, too, in her grief.

No, it was more than mere grief. It was an inconsolable anguish that devoured her from the inside out, such pain and desolation that she'd barely survived it. In those first black weeks after his father died, Quinn had sat at her bedside and held her hand for days at a stretch, begging her to drink some water or broth, to eat anything in order to keep up her strength. Instead, she'd wasted away, until Dr. Brandon called him and his siblings together to tell them that he now worried that she might also perish.

So Quinn returned to her bedside and begged her again, this time not to die. Not to leave him and the family alone without her.

She'd heard him through her grief, and slowly, she'd recovered. Eventually, she'd moved out of her mourning and returned to society, going so far this past season as to sponsor Miranda Hodgkins and help with the wedding when his brother Sebastian fell in love with the girl. But even now she wasn't nearly the same vivacious and energetic woman she'd once been. A light had dulled in her with Father's death, one Quinn wasn't certain would ever shine as brightly again.

"I was worried about her," Aunt Agatha murmured. "I regret that I wasn't able to go to her during her mourning, but it was so close on the heels of my own dear Ainsley..." Her voice trailed off. She didn't look up from her cards, but Quinn could see the glistening of tears in her eyes, and his heart tugged for her. His aunt was another widow whose loss of a husband had nearly ended her, as well.

And *that* was why he planned on remaining a bachelor. What good could come of marriage? All the marriages he knew were either ones made as advantageous matches for acquiring property or position, in which both spouses grew to detest each other—if they'd ever liked each other in the first place—or love matches. But in the end those were just as bad, if not worse. Because love always ended. *Always.* And nothing was left but grief.

Marriage might be fine for other people, those like his sister and brother, who needed their spouses the way flowers needed water to bloom. But not for him. He'd never let himself need a woman that much, or ever let a woman need him so much that she'd come to grief over him.

Besides, there was no room in his life for marriage anyway, now that his future was settled in America, where he looked forward to years of long days and hard work to prove himself successful.

"Miranda helped a great deal with Mother's mourning," Quinn said thoughtfully. And thank God she had.

"Especially when she married Seb," Robert interjected. "Mother's in heaven now that she's got two of her children happily married off."

"And giving her grandchildren," Quinn added.

"Which takes the pressure away from us." Robert grinned.

"For a while anyway." He slid his brother an amused glance across the table. "Because she's hoping for another wedding by next summer."

"Oh?" Belle glanced up at Quinn, with a stricken look almost as panicked as the one Robert shot him. "You're not... are you, Quinton?"

"Not me, but Robert," he informed them, much to Agatha's delight and Robert's chagrin. And to Belle's visible relief as she slumped back against her chair. *Odd.* "He's been courting a general's daughter in London. A lovely girl named Diana Morgan, who has a penchant for growing roses." Because he wanted to see the fire spark inside Belle again, and divert this conversation from weddings, he added, "If I remember correctly, Annabelle, you also had a fondness for roses."

Belle's mouth fell open at that private tease. She darted a

panicked glance at Lady Ainsley, but the viscountess noticed nothing untoward. Then she jutted her chin into the air and gave a haughty little sniff. "I suppose I used to when I was younger... and *extremely* foolish."

Instead of being piqued as she wanted, he gave her a grin, which only caused her to simmer in her seat.

"You've trumped my ace again," Agatha sighed with exasperation.

"Apologies," Belle mumbled, this time unable stop a pretty little blush that pinked her skin all the way up from the back of her neck to her cheeks.

Sweet Lucifer, he was beginning to like that blush.

Unable to say what it was for certain about Annabelle that pricked his puckish nature, but only that he couldn't resist, he murmured, "In my experience, roses can be quite beguiling."

She shot him a quelling look. "Roses are a menace. They might seem all sweet and charming from a distance." Belle laid down the knave of hearts to take the trick and ignored the puzzled expressions on Agatha's and Robert's faces at the peculiar turn of conversation. And that she'd distractedly claimed a trick won by Robert's king. "But beneath their pretty exterior exists nothing but thorns."

Lady Ainsley looked at her peculiarly. "But you spent all last spring putting in a rose border along the south terrace."

A caught expression flashed across Belle's face. Quinn felt a sharp stab of guilt for teasing her.

She drew a calming breath. "Not all flowers are bad, though, I suppose," she acquiesced. "Lilies, poppies, daisies—"

"Bluebells?" he asked innocently, taking a sip of coffee to hide his grin. Apparently, that stab of guilt hadn't been so insurmountable after all.

She froze for a single beat. Then, more calmly than he expected, she slowly laid down her cards and rose to her feet. "I regret that I am tired and have a headache," she announced. "A very large, very *pestering* headache."

When Quinn opened his mouth to respond, she sliced her gaze sideways at him and narrowed her eyes to slits. He wisely closed it again.

"If you all will excuse me, I need to retire. Good evening." She nodded at Lady Ainsley and Robert, then glared at him. "*Quinton.*"

She walked stiffly out of the drawing room, holding her head up in an imperial posture, surely learned over the years from his aunt.

"What on earth…?" Agatha commented as she laid down her cards, the game over. Then she arched a brow at Quinn with an expression somewhere between amusement and accusation.

"Apparently, she was very tired," he murmured with a touch of remorse. Already, he missed her company. Without her presence, the room seemed inexplicably empty.

Except that as Belle had walked from the room, he'd seen the fire in her that he'd come to crave. He would never deny himself a chance to see that, along with that telltale blush that stained her cheeks. A blush whose deeper meaning he was very much beginning to understand.

And liked a great deal.

CHAPTER THREE

Blast it!

Pain shot through her foot as Annabelle stubbed her toe against one of the chairs in the dark hallway. Grabbing at the throbbing toe with her hand and hopping on one foot, she muttered a string of curses beneath her breath, all of them aimed at Quinton Carlisle. Only he could cause this much trouble when he wasn't even in the room.

She blew out a heavy sigh and hurried on.

The house was silent around her, except for the faint tolling of the long case clock on the first-floor landing as it struck midnight, and without so much as a slant of moonlight to guide her, it was also dark enough that she could barely see. But she knew her way blind through the house—well, she reconsidered as her toe throbbed, perhaps not *quite* blind. Yet she loved every inch of this two-hundred-year-old perpetually drafty house, with its worn carpets and faded draperies, its solid furniture, and most likely a family of mice inhabiting every wall.

This was the place where she felt most at peace in the world, where she felt safe and loved. The place that made her heart full. *Home.* She couldn't imagine ever living anywhere else.

Perhaps now she wouldn't have to.

Wrapped in a white shawl over her cotton nightdress, she made her way through the dark house, too afraid that someone might see if she lit a candle and wonder what she was doing prowling around like a thief in the night. But Lady Ainsley had been snoring as loud as a mill saw when Belle passed her room, and the rest of the house was just as dark, with all the servants gone to sleep.

So far, though, there was no sign of Quinton. She hoped that he'd be enough of a gentleman to meet her. Failing that, then enough of a mercenary to discover if Lady Ainsley had intended any funds for him at all. She'd welcome either reason as long as he heard her out.

He had absolutely infuriated her earlier. What on earth had he been thinking? All those sly innuendos...and right in front of Lady Ainsley, no less. Belle had no choice but to feign a headache and flee before she did something she would regret. Or before she had to admit to herself that Quinn could still tie her belly in knots. Which only made her angry at herself that he could still affect her, even after everything he'd put her through.

Heavens, how desperate she'd become to be willing to put up with that scoundrel! But there was no legal way out of the inheritance clause. She and Lady Ainsley had thoroughly exhausted that route with the family's solicitor after the viscount passed away. It was marriage or nothing, and if she wanted assurances that the man she married wouldn't steal Glenarvon away from her or treat her unkindly, then Quinton Carlisle was now her last hope.

She reached the library and slipped inside, only to find the room dark and empty. But she wasn't yet ready to give up. Two things she knew for certain about Quinn were that, one, he never missed a midnight meeting with a woman, and two, he was always late. To everything.

So she crossed to the reading table and lit a candle, prepared to wait. Taking the curled handle of the little brass holder, she was drawn to the tall shelves of books. She lifted the candle to read the titles embossed on the leather and cloth spines, and as she moved the light across the rows of books, she trailed her fingertips over each one, unable to keep herself from touching them.

She loved books. Oh, how could anyone not? The way they smelled of pulp and rainy afternoons, the soft scratch of the paper beneath her fingertip as she turned the pages, all the wonderful knowledge and adventures held within their covers just waiting to be discovered—she loved everything about them. But most of all, she loved the way they had always brought her comfort. Given the choice between sneaking off to read a book, where she could let her imagination run wild and believe anything was possible, and being forced to be polite even as people cut her directly to her face, well, she'd gladly choose a book any day.

Wondering if she should take one back to her room with her, knowing that trying for sleep tonight would be a lost cause, she paused with her fingertip on the spine of *Don Quixote*. One of her absolute favorites. After all, didn't she know firsthand the futility of tilting at windmills, yet still feeling compelled beyond reason to try anyway?

Her body tingled with sudden awareness, feeling him before she saw him as Quinn stepped up behind her from out of the shadows. She swallowed. Hard. Thank goodness he'd come. She would have felt a wave of relief if not for the nervous somersaulting of her stomach.

He lowered his head over her shoulder, his mouth close to her ear. "You know, Annabelle," he murmured. The warmth of his breath tickling across her cheek sent a cascading heat swirling through her. "With your hair down like this, in that white nightdress, you look…"

She held her breath, foolishly hoping for an affectionate compliment—

"…more like a ghost than a Bluebell."

She rolled her eyes in exasperation. The man was impossible!

But aggravatingly, she also knew exactly how much she needed him. And what a terrible wound to her pride *that* was. That the only person who could save her now was him—oh, fate must surely be having a good laugh at her expense!

She faced him and caught her breath. He stood close. Uncomfortably close. So close that if she simply leaned forward, she could bring the front of her body against his hard chest. Her heart—the traitorous, silly thing—began to race. He wore only boots, breeches, and a shirt scandalously untucked around his hips. For a moment, he reminded her of a rumpled highwayman who lived outside the proprieties of society, and not at all a gentleman.

Heavens, she'd been reading too many books to confuse Quinton Carlisle with a dashing villain! Yet despite herself, her eyes trailed lingeringly up his roguish state of undress, over the open collar of the shirt, which exposed the bare skin of his neck and just enough of his chest for her to note the outline of the hard muscles beneath.

Perhaps not a villain, she conceded. But certainly dashing, drat him. Oh, why couldn't he be hideously featured with the charm of an old boot? Marriage to him would be so much easier if he were repugnant.

As her gaze finally rose from his chest to meet his blue eyes, she remembered to breathe. "Quinton."

"Annabelle." He gave her that same lazy grin that always sent butterflies fluttering in her belly. Even knowing what a rascal he was, she couldn't help being attracted to him. Somewhere down deep she wanted to believe that he was more than just the devil who antagonized her to no end, that he would repent his past ways and treat her differently going forward.

Was she a fool to hope for that? Or would he be the same scoundrel he was before? *He* certainly hadn't been affected by that encounter in the St James garden, while she'd nearly melted into a puddle at his feet.

His lips tugged into a faint smile, as if recognizing the confusion warring inside her. He took the candle from her hand to place it on the shelf behind her. But instead of stepping back, he kept his hand resting on the shelf, effectively holding her trapped between his large body and the bookcase.

His shadow-darkened eyes flicked to the book she'd been touching when he found her. Even in the dim candlelight, she saw amusement dance in their depths.

"You like Cervantes," he commented, keeping his voice low to match the quiet of the sleeping house around them.

She caught his scent, a delicious masculine combination of tobacco and port. Nervousness pinched inside her. "I like windmills."

He laughed softly, his eyes shining.

Embarrassment washed through her. *I like windmills?* Oh, what an inane thing to say! None of his sophisticated London ladies would have ever uttered something so ridiculous. No, they would have known the exact right turn of phrase to capture his attention and prove their urbanity, to persuade him into doing their bidding—

"I like windmills, too," he confessed, his voice a deep purr that tickled down her spine and left her breasts feeling strangely heavy. "Well, I like Cervantes, at least."

She blinked, surprised. "You've read *Quixote*?"

His lips twitched, although she couldn't say whether with amusement or pique. "I studied at Oxford, you know. I'm not a complete dullard."

"I've heard about what you and your brothers did at Oxford," she challenged with a dubious quirk of her brow, "and I don't think any of it involved books."

He gave another soft laugh. Well, at least he found her amusing, although Belle wasn't certain that was a compliment.

"There are lots of ways to gain a life's education," he informed her, his sapphire eyes sparkling in the candlelight. "Not all of them are found in a lecture hall."

"You're probably correct," she admitted grudgingly, loath to admit that Quinton Carlisle might be right about anything. Overseeing Castle Glenarvon since the viscount's death had proven a wealth of hands-on knowledge for her that couldn't be learned from books, although she was certain that wasn't the kind of life lesson Quinn had in mind. Not this scoundrel.

The corners of his lips curled higher, surprised that she would agree with him. Then he shook his head. "I can't believe it's been six years. At first, I thought you hadn't changed, but now..." he murmured as he stared intently into her face, a touch of incredulity lacing through his voice, "I see it's more than I realized."

Her pulse quickened. Well, *he'd* certainly changed. Quinton had matured into a more solemn man than he'd been before, despite his perpetual teasing of her. The candlelight accentuated his strong cheekbones and the smooth panes of his face, even with the faint stubble of a midnight beard darkening his skin, and his hair appeared even thicker and silkier in the faint glow. So soft and inviting that her fingertips itched to touch it.

But Quixote and his windmills—and Quinn himself—had taught her that appearances were often deceiving. Especially charmingly rakish ones.

"You look much more like your father now," she commented, nervously licking her suddenly dry lips but only serving to draw his attention to her mouth. Which made her even more nervous, so nervous that she couldn't stop the trembling of her fingertips as they wrapped into the skirt of her night rail. "But you're still a troublemaker."

A faint smile played at his mouth. "And you're still a bluestocking," he countered. Unintentionally simmering a slow heat low in her belly, he reached up to tuck a stray curl behind her ear. "Still retreating to the sanctuary of your library."

"Because books are usually more pleasant than most people," she answered, swallowing hard when he trailed his fingers down the side of her neck. She forced out, not at all as firmly as she'd hoped beneath his soft touch, "And more trustworthy."

Ignoring that jab, he slid his hand lower to let his fingers play at the edge of her shawl. "Yet there are things that people can do that books can't." His fingers tugged gently at the shawl and pulled it down her shoulder to reveal the scooped neck of the nightdress beneath. His gaze flicked to the small patch of revealed skin at the base of her throat, then back to her eyes. "All kinds of interesting things."

She should stop him, swat his hand away, shove him back—but she couldn't bring herself to do it. Just as she couldn't hold back the hot shiver that swept through her or the gooseflesh that formed on her skin. His touch was proving to be as equally intoxicating now as that night six years ago.

"Then I have no interest in learning them," she countered, although from the way her blood hummed, her body was *very* interested.

Madness—that after what he'd done to her, she could ever want to be in his arms again. Yet she desired just that, although that could never happen. Kissing him once had ruined her reputation. Kissing him again might destroy her entire future.

She thrust her chin into the air. "I know of your reputation."

"Thank you," he half purred.

His finger hooked beneath the wide shoulder strap of her sleeveless nightgown and slid it slowly down her arm. But this time, with a stretch of bare shoulder revealed to his eyes, he didn't bother feigning propriety by looking away and instead flamed a prickling heat beneath her skin everywhere he gazed.

She pulled in a deep breath to steady herself. Oh, *why* did she always go light-headed when she was alone with him? "That was not meant as a compliment."

"Wasn't it?" His mouth crooked into a lazy grin. His fingertip traced smoothly over her shoulder, drawing aimless yet tantalizing designs on her skin. From the odd mix of soothing caresses and searing strokes he gave her, Belle was certain he was branding her body with each small touch. "Then how exactly did you mean it?"

He fogged her brain and made thinking difficult. At that moment, through the confusion his nearness churned inside her, all she knew was the feel of his fingers tugging once more at the shawl to reveal even more of her to his eyes. And she let him, enjoying the nearness of him. It was like eating too many sweets, knowing that it wasn't good for her but desiring the pleasure anyway.

She forced out in a hoarse whisper from suddenly thick lips, "That you're a rake."

He smiled down at her. "Thank you."

"*Stop* saying that. That is not flattery." She gave him her best affronted governess stare, when what she actually wanted to do was take a single step forward and place herself in his arms, to experience once more the delicious strength of him she remembered. She couldn't help herself. Despite knowing what a scoundrel he was, she was still drawn to him. Even against her better judgment.

He shrugged, his eyes gleaming mischievously.

She saw in that unguarded sparkle the same glint he wore whenever he teased her, and she *knew*— Oh, that devil! He knew exactly what he was doing by murmuring to her like this, playing with her shawl and night rail . . . flirting with her until she was ready to blush. Or scream in aggravation. The rascal was *enjoying* putting her off-balance!

Not knowing he'd been caught, he leaned in closer, his voice dropping to a deep rumble as he added, "If you're interested in learning more about men than you can discover from your books, I'd be happy to teach you."

Keeping her annoyance in check, she flashed him a saccharine smile. "Ah, I see...*fiction*." To throw an even larger bucket of cold water over him, she forced herself to drop her gaze down his front and linger at his groin, then remarked regretfully with a sympathetic shake of her head, "And a very *short* story at that."

At her cut, his lips tightened for only a heartbeat before returning to the same charming grin as before. "*Epic*, I assure you," he drawled.

Her patience snapped. She slapped at his shoulder with her open palm. "Quinton James Carlisle!" She scowled, no longer able to hide her aggravation. "*Why* do you always insist on goading me?"

With a deep chuckle, he gave her a crooked grin and leaned down, as if sharing a secret. "Because you always make it so much fun."

She gave a frustrated sound somewhere between a growl and a cry. "Be serious for once, will you?" How could he find such pleasure in tormenting her at a time like this? She heaved an exasperated breath and ground out in grudging admission, "I need your help."

He froze. The amused smile that had been on his face vanished. The teasing rogue she remembered from years before disappeared, replaced by the serious man he'd become.

"What's wrong, Annabelle?" Concern underpinned his masculine timbre. "What can I do?"

She exhaled a long sigh of relief at finally being able to broach her plan with him. But she needed more courage to get through the rest of this conversation. "There's a bottle of

Bowmore hidden behind the Bibles." She nodded toward the shelves on the other side of the room. "Fetch it, will you?"

"Behind the Bibles?" he repeated, dumbfounded.

"It's where Lady Ainsley keeps her best scotch," she explained, fighting back an affectionate smile for the viscountess. "She's a staunch believer that religion should always be followed by a stiff drink."

With a deep chuckle, knowing his aunt well, he turned away to do as she asked.

"Bring me a glass, too, please," she called out as she sank onto the settee. This was a conversation best conducted sitting down. In case one of them fainted.

He threw her a surprised glance over his shoulder. "The Bluebell drinks scotch?"

"Good single malt she does," she clarified, a bit peeved. Did he think her so dull and boring as all that? "Why are you surprised?"

"Because whisky—even good single malt scotch," he corrected as he reached behind the row of Bibles and found the bottle hidden there, "is not a drink usually taken by ladies."

"In the borderlands, most ladies prefer scotch." Including Lady Ainsley. The scotch distillers, who had known the viscountess for years, always made a point of stopping at the estate on their way south to let her sample their finest stock. And she wasn't alone in her penchant for good drink. Here in the northern wilds, scotch whisky was mother's milk. "You've spent too much time in London with those frilly petticoats of the *ton*."

"Perhaps I have," he mumbled thoughtfully as he picked up a glass from behind the nearby hymnals and carried it and the bottle back to her. He splashed the golden liquid into the tumbler and held it out to her.

"Thank you." She gratefully swallowed down the small amount of scotch as he sat on the settee next to her and kicked his long legs out in front of him. Whatever edge to her nervousness that the whisky had dulled was immediately sharpened again by his closeness. But she couldn't very well demand he move away, not with what she was about to ask of him.

"Now, tell me what's wrong." He slid her a sideways glance, one whose hard expression told her that he would brook no dissembling. "What kind of trouble are you in that Aunt Agatha brought me here under false pretenses?"

Annabelle winced inwardly at that reminder that Lady Ainsley had lied in order to help her. "She had to, because you wouldn't have come if you knew the truth."

His mouth pulled down. "What truth is that exactly?"

She held out the empty tumbler and gestured for him to refill it. And this time, no small splash, either. He complied and poured a generous two fingers' worth.

She was conscious of his sapphire eyes training on her as she drank a long sip. When she lowered the glass, he took it from her hand to drink after her.

"I'm in a terrible situation," she whispered, pressing her fingers to her whisky-wet lips. "And I need help getting out of it."

He arched a brow. "Doesn't seem so terrible to me. You're on the verge of gaining an estate."

And an unwanted husband. She inhaled deeply. "I'm very grateful to Lord and Lady Ainsley," she began, a bit haltingly as she tried to stumble her way through her explanation. "They raised me as if I were their own daughter."

"I know." He finished the remaining scotch in a single swallow. "Aunt Agatha adores you."

Belle nodded glumly, her shoulders sagging. "And I love her. Which is the problem."

He frowned. "How so?"

"She wants the best possible future for me. So did Lord Ainsley."

"Which was why they put you into the will."

Another nod, impossibly even glummer than the last. "When Lord Ainsley died and the inheritances were settled, the title and all its entailed properties went to his late brother's son. Lady Ainsley received her dower, and his three daughters from his first marriage received equal portions of what was left. Except for Glenarvon." She couldn't stop her voice from trembling with grief for the late viscount, and with the gratitude she still felt every time she realized that he cared for her enough to include her in his will. "Which was saved for me."

"Very generous of him," he commented sincerely. "I've never heard of another peer leaving an estate to someone who wasn't a blood relative."

Belle knew how special she must have been to the viscount, and certainly he meant the world to her. She blinked back the stinging in her eyes. "He loved me like a true father. Far more than my own father ever did."

He frowned. "Then why not give you the property outright, rather than risk you losing it?"

She looked down at her hands as she held them in her lap, idly twisting her fingers. "He wanted to protect me."

The glass lowered slowly from his lips, and he stared at her, his eyes dark with concern. "From what?"

"My father," she answered quietly. Feeling him tense beside her, she took back the glass of whisky. "If I inherited without that clause, then my male guardian would have the right to control my property, as if it were his." She stared down into the empty glass. "So if my father were ever to return, if he asserted himself back into my life..."

Her voice trailed off. *Speak of the devil.* She didn't dare put her thoughts into words, for fear that the devil would appear.

"Which is why the property is only granted to me upon marriage," she continued, "when my husband becomes the man legally responsible for me." She took a deep breath and exhaled slowly, but it emerged far shakier than she intended. "That way, my father could never get his hands on Glenarvon."

"That was clever of Uncle Charles," Quinn commented. He knowingly quirked a brow. "Except..."

"Except that now I'm about to turn twenty-five without a husband in sight?" A grim smile pulled at her lips. The irony was biting. "I suspect Lord Ainsley thought twenty-five would be a good age to end the trust. After all, both of his wives hadn't yet turned twenty when he married them, and all three of his daughters were wedded by the time they reached their majority. He thought I'd do the same when he originally wrote the stipulation into his will, although by the time I'd turned twenty-one and had no serious suitors, he'd begun to rethink it." A knot of grief choked her throat. "But he died before he could make the change."

Self-consciously, she darted her hand up to swipe at her eyes.

Quinn silently reached for the bottle to refill her glass, as if he knew how much distress remembering that dark time caused her. But of course he would. He'd recently lost his own father.

With a trembling hand that jiggled the golden liquid in

the glass, she raised it to her lips and took a small swallow, more to give herself time to recover than for the taste of the stuff.

"So now I have four weeks to marry, or I lose my home," she whispered. Four *very short* weeks. "And not a proper suitor in sight."

"A beautiful woman whose dowry is an entire estate?" he murmured, shaking his head. "I'm surprised you don't have men bivouacking in the rear garden for their chance at you."

She couldn't help but smile at that ludicrous image. "Actually, only a handful of people know that I'll inherit Glenarvon." She protectively drew her knees up to her chest and drew the shawl tighter around her shoulders. "But now, we have no choice but to reveal it."

He shook his head. "You're setting yourself up for capture by a fortune hunter."

"Which is why you're here." The relentless frustration of her desperate situation sank over her once more. "To make certain that doesn't happen."

He gave a short laugh at the absurdity of that. "By sorting out the rotten apples?"

"Among other things," she replied carefully, studying him from the corner of her eye.

He took back the glass. "And if you don't marry?"

"Then the Church gains the estate," she whispered, so softly she feared for a moment that he might not be able to hear her. But his continued expression of concern told her that he heard every word. "Lady Ainsley and I would move into the dower house in London until she passes away, then most likely I would be placed into a cottage somewhere on one of the Ainsley properties, if the current viscount feels charitable. If not…" When her words started to choke in her throat, she cut herself off with a wave of her hand, but the tears were dangerously close to falling.

His eyes softened with concern. "Have you tried speaking with the solicitor, to find a legal way out of this?"

"Yes, and the stipulation cannot be altered." She sucked in a painful breath at the grief that clawed at her chest at being forced into a marriage she didn't want to prevent being torn away from the home she loved. Quinton had become her only salvation. "I have to marry in order to inherit."

"This Sir Harold whom Aunt Agatha mentioned—he's offered for you?" A casual question, certainly one he had a right to ask. Yet Belle thought she heard a deeper edge to it. When she nodded, Quinn said, "Then he's solved your marriage problem."

Oh, Sir Harold was the farthest thing from a solution! Surely, Quinn thought he was helping, but being reminded of that marriage offer only squeezed her heart tighter with desperation. "I don't want to marry him."

He frowned into the glass. "Why not?"

"I don't love him," she admitted quietly, fearing that he would think her a sentimental ninny for saying so. "And he doesn't love me."

He stared at her for a long moment, as if she were some kind of new creature in the Tower menagerie that he simply couldn't fathom. "Most husbands and wives don't love each other."

Hearing the cold truth from him didn't ease the dread weighing heavy in her chest. Or the fear that she'd end up trapped like her mother. "I don't want to be one of those women."

He gave a faint shake of his head. "You might not have a choice."

How well she knew that! "At the very least I want a husband who will treat me like an equal partner." One who would never put her at the mercy of his whims, who would never shout at her or raise a hand to her. Who wouldn't attempt to take Glenarvon away from her or interfere with how she wanted to run it.

He frowned. "That doesn't sound like this Sir Harold of yours."

"He isn't *mine*." And God help her, if she were lucky, he never would be.

"Better set your sights on another husband, then," he advised, swirling the scotch in the glass. "And quickly."

"I have," she replied soberly.

"Oh?" He raised the glass to his lips. "Who?"

"You."

* * *

Quinn choked on the scotch.

Coughing to catch his breath, he stared at her incredulously. She seemed like a perfectly normal woman, sitting there calmly, her big honey-hazel eyes watching him guilelessly. And yet...

Wiping at his mouth with the back of his hand, he sputtered, "Are you *mad*?"

She sighed patiently. "If you would just hear me out—"

"We *cannot* marry!"

Her calm appearance only worked to send his galloping heart into a furious tattoo, and he resisted the urge to leap to his feet and run. Which was what he usually did whenever any woman discussed marriage in front of him. And *this* one had the spine to actually propose.

"Not only do we irritate the blazes out of each other, but I'm on my way to America—immediately." He raised his arm and gestured in what he hoped was a westerly direction, too stunned to be certain. "I have land waiting for me. If I don't leave, and soon, I'll lose it."

"I won't keep you here longer than absolutely necessary, I promise," she assured him. She leaned slightly toward him, a fresh intensity glowing in her. "But this can help both of us," she cajoled, a soft desperation coloring her voice, "giving me the estate under my own control and sending you off with more money at your disposal."

His mouth fell open. *Good God...* "You're serious."

She gave a sober nod. "Very."

Unable to sit still any longer, he shot to his feet and stood there awkwardly, running a shaking hand through his hair. Half of him wanted to flee and the other half was shamelessly curious about her scheme. After all, he'd come here in the first place for money. But marriage...*Sweet Lord.* Just pondering it made his blood run cold with panic and his palms turn clammy.

She uncurled her legs from beneath her and sat forward on the edge of the settee, then paused to bite her bottom lip, as if deciding whether to press on. "Besides," she ventured cautiously, "I'm only in this situation because of you."

He gaped at her. "How is this *my* fault?"

"Because of that fight with Burton Williams," she answered quietly.

His eyes narrowed sharply as they slid over her. She was skating on thin ice if she thought she could guilt him into marriage. More resourceful women had tried, and it had gotten them nowhere. Just as it would with her...despite the odd pang of unexpected remorse pinching his gut.

Damnation, he *had* caused problems for her that night. But not enough to wed her because of it. "It was ill-conceived, I'll admit—"

"Immature," she corrected.

That stung more than he wanted to admit. "Misguided," he clarified, crossing his arms over his chest. "But Williams was insulting you."

The truth was that the bastard had done a helluva lot more to her than that. In the weeks following that ball, Williams had branded her a poplolly. He'd made certain that all his cronies at Boodle's had a good laugh over finding Quinn with Lady Ainsley's companion, all ripped and rumpled— along with several other more salacious adjectives as the story passed through the *ton*.

"I'm an impoverished lady's companion whose father is a convict," she said quietly. "Do you think that was the first time I'd ever been insulted by someone like Burton Williams?"

He blew out a hard sigh as the pang of remorse blossomed into full-out guilt. She'd never have been accepted by society, no matter how much his aunt and uncle wanted that for her. But that night certainly hadn't helped.

"I need your help," she pressed delicately. "You owe me, Quinton."

She was wrong about that. He certainly didn't owe her *this*. "I am not marrying you, Annabelle. That night was nothing more than an accident, and you bloody well know it."

"And several kisses, don't forget," she whispered.

No, he hadn't forgotten. How could he? It had been a surprisingly passionate encounter that left him craving more, even as unpracticed and innocent as she'd been. All these years later, and after dozens of other women who did far more with him than simply kiss, that night with Annabelle was still embossed upon his mind. His senses tingled even now at simply remembering it.

But *marriage*...

"For God's sake, Belle," he ground out in exasperation. "What you're proposing—"

"Yes," she replied urgently, "exactly that! I am proposing." She gave him a bright smile, but he could easily see the nervousness behind it, so much nervousness that she trembled. "Marry me, Quinton, and in exchange, I'll pay you a portion of the annual estate profits. That way, we both win. I get to keep Glenarvon, and you get additional funds for your new life in America."

A proposal. Good heavens, she truly meant it. "Marriage," he stammered out. Even though he was certain she'd said it, he couldn't quite bring himself to believe— "To you?"

"A business arrangement," she clarified. "As you said, the quality marry for money and land all the time. Why should this be any different? Only on a much smaller scale."

"I'm not quality," he protested. When her lips curled in amusement at his self-deprecating slip, he rolled his eyes with a grimace. "You know what I mean."

"You are, Quinn," she assured him, although he was certain that bit of flattery was meant to sway him toward marriage. But it would take a helluva lot more than a compliment or two to get him to leg-shackle himself. Especially to someone like Annabelle. She was the kind of woman a man could fall in love with. And if he wasn't careful, he'd find himself permanently ensconced in some barren sheep pasture in the borderlands. "Why do you think all those women in London throw themselves at you?"

Despite pointedly arching a brow, he wisely kept his silence. This was not the time to explain to her the darker pleasures of society entertainment.

"Will you do it, then?" she pressed. "Will you marry me and help me out of this mess?"

"And right into another." He shook his head, flabbergasted that he was having this conversation. "You said yourself that you don't want to marry without love. You and I are most definitely *not* in love."

"I no longer have a choice. I *have* to marry. But if I cannot marry for love, then marriage to you is perfect," she rationalized, "because emotions will never get in the way, and you'll let me run Glenarvon as I want."

"Because I'll be on the far side of the ocean!" he nearly shouted in exasperation.

A slow smile pulled at her lips, reminding him of the cat that got into the cream. "As I said, perfect."

He blew out a harsh breath. "Belle, for God's sake—"

"At the very least I should be able to marry a man I know won't hurt me," she interrupted. Her smile faded beneath the brutal honesty of that comment, which sliced straight through his chest like a knife. "And I know you well enough to know that you'd never harm me on purpose."

His shoulders slumped beneath the weight of fresh guilt, and he sank back down onto the settee. "Good Lord, you *are* mad."

"Yet there is a method to it," she answered, her eyes gleaming as she paraphrased Shakespeare and proved again that she was the same bluestocking he'd always known.

He nearly laughed at the irony. While she loved attending the theatre, he loved getting ladies alone in private theatre boxes.

The two of them were oil and water.

And yet, a dependable allowance from Glenarvon would certainly make life easier for him, he couldn't deny that. Helping her secure the estate for herself would also more than repay her for that night six years ago.

But marriage...*Good God.*

"If you agree," she urged, doing her best to sway him, "we still have time to read the bans and won't need the special license."

He sent her a sideways glance. "We're less than ten miles from Scotland, Belle," he reminded her. "We don't even need that."

"There!" She gestured emphatically with her hands as if her lunacy made sense. "See how convenient this is? Almost like fate."

He rolled his eyes. "Or a phony invitation to a scheming plot."

"That, too." She reached for the bottle of scotch and refilled the empty glass he still held in his hand, although he'd lost his taste for the stuff. "Once we're married, we'll travel to Newcastle. I know a trustworthy banker there who can set up financial arrangements for you to receive an allowance in America." She put the bottle down and leaned back against the settee. "It won't be much at first, I'll admit, but I have plans for the estate which should increase our profits nicely within the next few years."

He grimaced, not knowing whether to be tempted at her offer or terrified to within an inch of his life. "You've got this all figured out, haven't you?"

"Desperate times," she answered solemnly, repeating his aunt's words to him, "desperate measures."

She slowly removed the glass of scotch from his hand. He

watched as she took a sip, noticing the soft undulation of her elegant throat and the glistening of her wet lips after, and he felt that swallow sink all the way through him.

He was in serious trouble.

Of all the woman he'd known in his life, none of them had ever been more dangerous than Annabelle Greene as she sat there in her white cotton night rail with its ribbon bow and dipped her finger into the scotch, then raised it to her lips and sucked off the droplets clinging to her fingertip. With an outward appearance so innocent-looking that he felt the urge even now to pull her into his arms to protect her, while beneath lurked a siren who had him wanting to pull her into his arms to satisfy a far darker urge, she was a trap just waiting to be sprung. Add to that the financial boon which could be his—

Dangerous? Good Lord, the woman was downright deadly.

Unable to resist touching her, he reached out to caress her hair, which cascaded in a riot of caramel-colored curls around her shoulders. "If I agree to this plan of yours—and I'm not saying that I will—" A silky lock curled around his finger. "Do I get to leave as soon as the honeymoon is over?"

A soft sigh escaped her, her shoulders sagging as visible relief surged through her that he was agreeing to help. Or at least not running away. "That's exactly what I want, too."

He fought back a smile of pleased surprise, not expecting her to be so bold—and wonderfully direct—about the marriage bed. Perhaps he'd wrongly underestimated the Bluebell. Perhaps a hellcat lurked behind those blue stockings of hers. "Is that part of your proposal, too, then?"

She nodded earnestly. "If you'd like it to be."

"I think I'd like that a great deal," he murmured, not

believing his good fortune. His eyes dropped to the top swells of her breasts, just showing above the scooped neckline, the bow nestled in the valley between. Lucky bow. But he'd never bedded an innocent before—how much did Belle know about the pleasures of wedding nights? "You're prepared for marriage, then?" He paused before adding, to make certain she understood, "For a proper marriage?"

"Of course I'm ready." She looked up from the scotch, and her lips tightened with ire. "I've been running the estate myself for years."

He chuckled softly. *Bluestocking.* "That's not what I meant."

She puzzled. "Then what did you—"

He grabbed her by the front of her shawl and tugged her to him, catching her off guard as his mouth found hers, to take the kiss he'd been craving for years.

Her mouth was warm, deliciously soft, and oh so inviting. She tasted intoxicatingly of the north…the spicy tang of scotch, the floral of heather, the boldness of the wilderness. The tip of his tongue traced along the seam between her lips in hopes of coaxing her into opening for him so he could taste all of her.

She trembled but didn't pull away. When he nibbled at the corner of her mouth, she acquiesced with a soft sigh and parted her lips. It was all the invitation he needed. He greedily swept his tongue inside and relished the sweetness he found there.

He'd kissed more women than he could remember, but none were as sweet as Annabelle. That was what he remembered from that night beneath the rose bower. More than the way she'd arched herself against him, more than how her hands had tangled in his lapels to draw herself closer, even more than the fumbling of hands reaching wherever they could touch...he remembered how delectably sweet she tasted. Like chocolate, wine, and woman. Even now that same rich, luscious flavor pulled straight through him and made him ache for more.

God help him, he wanted to devour her.

His lips slid away from hers to nibble along her jaw and down her neck. When he flicked the tip of his tongue against her racing pulse in the hollow at the base of her throat, she whimpered, and the soft sound shivered through him. Unable to stop himself, he traced his fingertip along the scooped neckline of her night rail to the bow and pulled the ribbon loose, letting the thin cotton billow open. His mouth followed after, to slide over that smooth stretch of flesh between her collarbone and the start of the valley between her breasts. He groaned. Sweet Lucifer, even her skin tasted sweet.

"Quinton," she breathed plaintively against his hair as he dipped his head to place a single kiss on the top swell of her left breast. Just inches below his lips, he could see the outline of her dusky nipple straining against the white cotton.

He captured her breast against his palm through the thin night rail and teased at the nipple with his thumb. Even as he felt the bud harden beneath the caress of his fingers and her resulting shudder, he contemplated pulling the night rail lower to reveal a single, luscious breast to his eyes, to his mouth—

Cold wetness poured over his head.

"What the hell!" He scrambled to his feet and wiped his hand through his scotch-soaked hair as rivulets trailed down his face.

"There will be *none* of that," she warned, putting up her

hand to half scold, half fend him away, her other hand still firmly gripped around the now empty glass. But her tremulous voice lacked conviction. She was as equally aroused by that kiss as he was. He could see it in the way she trembled and in the parting of her wet lips, but the frustrating bluestocking wouldn't let herself give over to it. "No wedding night, no marriage intimacies of any kind," she explained. "Our marriage would be purely a business arrangement, nothing else." She shot him a determined glance, and from the way she struggled to catch her panting breath, he wondered which one of them she was trying to convince. "*Nothing* else."

Gritting his teeth tightly in equal parts humiliation at her rejection and frustration from the brief taste he'd had of her, he wiped his hand over his face and flung away the drops of scotch. "Fine," he bit out. The liquid ran down his neck, and he grimaced as he added beneath his breath, "I doubt I'd survive anyway if this is how you'd welcome your husband."

"Be reasonable." Her chin jutted into the air with irritation. "With you on the other side of the world and me here, if we consummated, what would happen if we…if we…" She turned away to set the glass down. Her hand shook.

"Got with child?" he ground out irritably as he swiped at the cold trickle dripping beneath his collar. *Damnable woman.* "There are ways to avoid that."

She gave him an odd look. "I was going to say develop feelings for each other," she confessed softly, "although I'm certain there are ways of avoiding that, too."

An invisible fist squeezed his chest. That was exactly what he feared, as well. Because if a man latched himself to a woman like Annabelle, how would he keep the little hellcat from getting beneath his skin? Or into his heart? Would even an ocean's distance be far enough?

When his eyes solemnly found hers, she quickly covered any vulnerability by forcing a haughty sniff. "Regardless, the risk of complications doesn't seem worth a night of what Lady Ainsley assures me is not very enjoyable for the bride anyway."

He would have laughed at that, if he wasn't soaked through to the skin and reeking like a gin palace. "Aunt Agatha is wrong," he assured her, only to face her dubiousness when she silently raised an eyebrow in reply.

But he would get nowhere attempting to win an argument over how much she would enjoy being intimate with him, not with his reputation and her intellect to fight against. So Quinn wisely kept his silence.

He stared down at her, her lips reddened from his kisses and her night rail rumpled at her neckline, revealing more flesh than she realized. With her hands now folded primly in her lap, she looked every inch like a virginal seductress. One he very much still craved, despite the glass of scotch over his head, which was nearly as good in tamping down his arousal as a bucket of cold water.

But damnation, she was right, and he knew it. He maintained a healthy respect for the complications that could arise from sharing a bed, yet disappointment still panged hollowly in his gut. Over not possessing the Bluebell, of all women.

Sweet Lucifer, the *world* had gone mad.

"Will you do it, then?" Leaning forward on the settee, her fingers gripping the edge of the cushion, she looked up at him hopefully. "Will you marry me?"

His gut tightened at her modest proposal, the ramifications of which were anything but simple.

"I need to think about it," he deflected, unwilling to

answer while the heather scent of her still lingered on his body where he'd held her against him. While the thought of additional funds still tempted him.

"All right." Her slender shoulders eased down. "I'll give you time to decide."

"Thank you," he muttered, not nearly as relieved and hopeful as she was.

She rose to her feet and tied the ribbon bow securely at her neckline. His chest ached with disappointment. When he'd untied it, the sensation had been like unwrapping the most wonderful present he'd ever been given. Only to have it stolen away.

"But I'll need your answer soon." Her eyes darkened with a flicker of sadness. "If you say no, I'll have to find another solution. And quickly."

He swiped away the last of the scotch still clinging to the back of his neck and grimaced. "I would say that we should seal our agreement with a kiss," he joked grimly, "but you'd likely bash me over the head with the bottle for suggesting such a thing."

"I would never do that," she assured him as she slipped past him and glided from the room, pausing only to take the copy of *Don Quixote* from the shelf and tuck it beneath her arm. She added with an unrepentant smile, "It would be a waste of perfectly good scotch."

As she disappeared into the dark hallway, he caught a parting glimpse of her in the moonlight slanting in through the tall windows and illuminating the nightgown hanging loose around her. Her breasts and hips were silhouetted dark beneath the white cotton as if she wore nothing at all as her hair tumbled in silky waves down her back, nearly reaching her round bottom. His cock jumped eagerly at the rash thought of following her back to her bedroom, to convince her that marriage rights could be enjoyable for the bride, too. *Very* enjoyable.

And if he did that, the next thing to come crashing down over his head would be the *Quixote*. Along with all of his future plans for America and his promise to his father. Because he knew one thing for certain about the Bluebell. A man didn't give himself to a woman like her and then leave.

"Damned woman," he muttered and drank straight from the bottle.

CHAPTER FOUR

$\mathcal{Q}$uinn grimaced and rubbed at the pounding headache at his temples as he strode across the field, the pain a result of last night's unfortunate combination of too little sleep and too much scotch.

And not nearly enough Annabelle.

He flipped up the collar of his coat against his neck to ward off the drizzling rain that threatened to fall at any moment and the summer morning's unexpected cold. True to the north's unpredictable weather, clouds had moved in during the night and now hung low over the mountains and valleys, leaving the fields awash in a blue morning haze. The temperature had dropped a good twenty degrees. He would have said that the chill made it difficult to imagine Belle swimming in the pond, but he'd had a tempting glimpse of her there, and now that seemed to be the only thing he wanted to think about.

Good Lord, how the gel vexed him! He couldn't remember the last time he'd lost sleep over a woman, if ever, but that's exactly what she'd done to him. And not only because of that outrageous marriage proposal, although the prospect of wedding anyone certainly terrified him enough to ensure nightmares.

No. He was loath to admit even to himself that rest hadn't come because, in those few moments when he'd managed to fall asleep, his dreams were punctuated not by nightmares of marriage shackles but by erotic visions of Belle.

He groaned. *Not* erotic, not exactly. When he'd dreamed of Belle, he saw her in that white cotton night rail, the bow at her bosom untied and its ribbons streaming along behind her as she walked through the mists, her hair free and tumbling down her back. A smile on her face that made him ache, a laugh that lilted lightly on the soft air. Head turned to reveal her elegant neck. Slender legs revealed to the knees, and arms just as bare. Then she turned back and offered him her hand, to follow her down into the dew-covered heather . . . He'd glimpsed more of her at the pond than in his dream, yet he'd awakened hard as iron.

Oh yes. He had definitely lost his mind.

So at dawn he gave up all pretense of sleep and went down for an early breakfast, hoping to find Belle so he could answer her proposal and end his suffering. But Ferguson informed him that she was already up and outside, as was her habit most mornings. *Wonderful.* The aggravating woman was also an early riser.

Quinn rolled his eyes. He knew how to deal with ladies of the *ton*. Those women slept until noon, would never be caught dead in a library, and would certainly never drink scotch. Or pour it over a man's head.

But the contradiction that was Annabelle Greene

fascinated as much as it frustrated. The beautiful woman on the outside was a hellcat beneath, an intelligent and sharp woman who knew practically everything...except the effect she had on men. She infuriated him *and* intrigued him, and she had him still wanting to tease and torment her like a kid, just so the man he'd become could selfishly see the fire inside her. How was it possible that the same woman who had him wanting to yank her into his arms also had him wanting to put an ocean between them?

Madness. Madness that she should have ever considered him for her proposal. That Aunt Agatha thought he could be her protector.

Apparently lunacy was contagious.

He reached the crest of a small rise overlooking the south pasturelands and saw her. Dressed in men's trousers and work boots just like the workers around her, complete with a tweed cap covering her hair, she helped to heave a thick post out of an irrigation ditch and onto the creek bank.

Quinn let out a frustrated breath. Apparently, nothing about Belle was typical.

With all the grim resolve of a man going to his own execution, he started toward her and the group of workmen gathered at the small stone structure at the side of the creek.

One of the men bent down to give Belle a hand up from the ditch, where she stood up to her knees in water. From the way none of the men laughed at her appearance when she scrambled to her feet, not only were they used to seeing her in workman's clothes but they were also used to being directed by her. He'd admit that knowing she'd inherit Glenarvon stirred jealousy inside him, when he would be forced to start from nothing. But he also felt admiration for her, because she didn't consider herself either above hard work or too delicate for it.

She rested her hands on her round hips beneath the long, brown coat, which reached to the tops of her muddied boots. Her shoulders sagged as she answered a question from one of the workman, "...damaged on purpose."

The man behind her lifted his eyes to Quinn as he approached. He cleared his throat loudly enough to cut off Belle's reply, then nodded past her to gain her attention.

Belle glanced over her shoulder and saw Quinn. For a heartbeat, she froze as uneasiness darkened her face. Then it vanished just as quickly, replaced by a bright smile that he knew was forced for the benefit of the men around her. Certainly not for him. From the flash deep in her eyes, he knew the Bluebell was still peeved at him for their misunderstanding last night.

"Lord Quinton, good morning." But she couldn't hide the surprise in her voice at his arrival, or a soft bit of sarcasm as she teased, "I'm surprised to see you up so early, given your reputation as a Corinthian."

He laughed. *A Corinthian?* Well, he'd been called a lot of things by women before, but never that. "Not everyone in London sleeps until noon, Miss Greene," he countered good-naturedly as he stopped in front of her. He was suddenly very aware of the men's eyes on him, sizing him up and wondering who he was. And what he wanted with Glenarvon's mistress.

She asked wryly, "Just half past eleven, then?"

"Quarter 'til," he sent back with a crooked grin.

"Well," she commented, "then you're a good four hours early to start your day."

She smiled, but he sensed an anxious dread beneath her

calm façade, noting the tense way her shoulders stiffened, how she clenched and unclenched her gloved hands nervously at her sides. As a woman donning men's clothing, her unusual appearance served only to make her somehow even more appealing. More feminine. And heartbreakingly vulnerable.

Guilt gnawed at his gut, yet there was no help for it. She wanted an answer, and he had no reason to delay the inevitable. In fact, if he'd had his wits about him last night, instead of being preoccupied with the way she'd felt in his arms, he would have told her his answer then and saved them both from this awkward meeting.

Yet whatever trouble he was about to cause her would be better dealt with sooner rather than later. Telling her this morning would give her more time to find a better candidate for marriage. It had nothing at all to do with wanting to avoid the confusion he felt about her. Or the persistent attraction between them, which had reared its head again last night and apparently still lingered between them so palpably that even now the air crackled with it.

At least that was what he kept telling himself from the moment he'd left his room to find her. If he repeated it to himself often enough, maybe he would start to believe it.

This morning, her eyes gleamed more green than gold in the veiled sunlight of the overcast sky. But the nervous flicker in their honeyed depths signaled that she knew why he'd sought her out. And that she'd already guessed his answer.

He felt the weight of the men's curious stares on him, not bothering to pretend that they weren't eavesdropping on the conversation. But this was *not* a discussion he wanted to share. He inclined his head. "Would you care to take a walk with me, Miss Greene?"

Her strained smile faded, and she hesitated. Then, with a stiff nod, she wordlessly turned to stroll along the creek, away from the worksite.

He fell into step beside her. They walked on together in silence, which soon became acutely uncomfortable, the tension between them as thick as the clouds overhead. He grimaced as he took a sideways glance at her determined profile. She was going to make him talk first, clearly, but he wasn't yet ready to broach the reason he'd invited her for the walk. Despite knowing what had to be done, he was reluctant to add to her troubles.

He glanced over his shoulder and asked, "What are you doing back there?"

"Repairs," she answered curtly. Instead of placing her hand on his arm, as any London lady would have done, she removed her muddied gloves and shoved both hands deep into her coat pockets. Not touching him. Did the little hellcat realize the cut she was giving him?

But of course she did. Apparently he'd underestimated how much that night at the St James ball had hurt her.

"What kind of repairs?" he pressed, wanting to draw her out and knowing how much the estate meant to her.

She eyed him suspiciously. "You really want to know?"

"Yes." He did. Surprisingly enough.

She hesitated, then relented on her silence. "The spillway gate for the irrigation ditch broke, and the south pasture flooded," she explained. "Our shepherd, McDougal, found it two days ago when he rode out to check on the sheep, so the men spent all day yesterday moving the flock into a smaller pasture until we can fix the gate and the land dries out." She glanced up at the gray clouds overhead, heavy with their promise of rain, and he could almost hear the curse she inwardly yelled at Mother Nature. "*If* it ever dries out."

Something about the way she described the damage pricked at him. "You don't think it was due to age and wear, though, do you?"

She hesitated a moment, then shook her head. "No," she sighed as if resigned to getting it fixed and forgotten as soon as possible. "Burns thinks it was done intentionally."

"Burns?"

"Angus Burns, my foreman."

Ah, the guard dog who had watched him so closely when he'd arrived at the stonework.

She explained, "His family has lived legally on Glenarvon land for five generations."

"Legally?" he repeated, sliding her a curious glance as she walked beside him.

"*Illegally* for far longer than that." Her lips curled into a smile, the first genuine one he'd seen from her this morning. "He helps me oversee the property and manages the building repairs and maintenance. He makes certain the work crews have no problem taking orders from a woman."

"I doubt you need anyone's help with that." Not based on the way the men paid attention to her instructions at the ditch.

A faint smile of pride teased at her lips, before a wrinkle of worry creased her brow. "It's been...an odd year," she confided, lowering her voice as they made their way toward the hill. "We've had more than our fair share of accidents and problems recently."

Struck by that, he halted and reached for her arm to stop her. His eyes searched her face for answers. "Are you in danger, Belle?"

"No! Of course not." She waved away his concerns with a scoffing laugh. "You wouldn't have been invited here if anyone was in danger."

"Annabelle." Her name emerged as a low warning. "Don't dissemble. Not with this."

"No one's been hurt," she admitted, "and no lasting damage has been done. But it's bothersome enough to distract from the real work of the estate."

Her denial didn't reassure him. "Enough to make you regret running Glenarvon by yourself?"

"Never." Determination flashed in her eyes.

She pulled her arm away and walked on, leaving him to catch up. *Stubborn chit.* He scowled as he fell into step beside her.

"The creek feeds into the irrigation ditch, as you saw," she explained with a wave of her hand, as if she were explaining the workings of the estate to a new hire, and most likely grateful to change topics. "When everything works properly, we can control the amount of water to the pastures. The creek joins the Arvon River at the bottom of the glen." She pointed behind them toward the glen cutting its way across the property. "That's how the estate got its name."

"Glenarvon," he murmured. "And the castle?"

She beamed, her smile full and bright. And full of love for the place. "The ruins lie up ahead on the hill above the pond."

The pond where Belle liked to swim at sunset. Naked. Quinn suddenly gained a new appreciation for history.

"It was built in the fourteenth century to guard this stretch of the river. Now all that's left of it are a handful of walls and tumbled stones." With pride ringing in her voice, as if daring him to contradict her, she added, "But I think it's beautiful."

"So do I." He stopped to pluck a wild rose from a bush growing alongside the creek.

She shook her head, clearly exasperated with him. "But you haven't even seen the ruins yet."

He shrugged and handed her the flower. "I believe you."

She stared at the rose, momentarily wary, as if she didn't trust it not turn into a snake and bite her. Then she mumbled, "Thank you."

She took the pale pink flower from his hand and raised it to her nose, then turned away quickly and began walking again, but not before he saw a matching pale pink blush color her cheeks. He was finding a new appreciation for those rose-pink blushes, too.

"But we're not stuck in the Middle Ages," she continued as she turned onto a narrow path snaking through the trees to the top of the rise. He fell into step behind her. "We're a modern country. Things are changing rapidly, and I have big plans for the estate and the village."

He smiled. Why was he not surprised? "Like what?"

"Well, first, I want to improve the village school." The description of her plans came slowly in her hesitancy to trust him. "I started the school three years ago, but I want to employ a good teacher from London or York who can teach the children the basics they need to know. Their numbers and letters, how to manage property, how to avoid being taken advantage of by unscrupulous millers and merchants—" She quickly ticked off the list on her fingers, her reluctance to share her plans with him now gone. "And especially how to read. All those skills they won't get as apprentices or might never get at all as tenant farmers." She glanced back at him, as if to gauge his reaction, before continuing up the path. "And I want to find a real doctor for the village, too, not just an apothecary."

As she continued to list all her plans, Quinn stopped and watched her walk up the hill ahead of him, now seeing her in a completely different light.

She wasn't just the bluestocking and lady's companion he'd always known. Annabelle Greene had grown into a capable estate manager with a just understanding of the importance a manor house had on its village's future. In fact, some of her plans were exactly what he wanted to do in America...to have a piece of land of his own to shape and to help the local townspeople. While he would have to spend years creating that dream, she had the opportunity within her reach now, the right vision for the future, and the determination to see her dream through.

But he couldn't be the man to help her reach it.

His chums at the clubs would have thought him daft to pass up this opportunity, given the terms that Belle had proposed...a share of the profits and the freedom to go on with his new life in America exactly as planned, fulfilling the promises he'd made to his father and Asa Jeffers. Any less scrupulous man would have immediately flung her over his shoulder and marched straight to Gretna Green to get his hands on everything she'd offered. And to get his hands on *her*.

But Quinn would never use her like that. Nor would he ever abandon his wife.

His eyes wandered over Belle as she climbed up the hill in front of him, unwittingly giving him a delectable view of her round derriere, made even more visible by the men's trousers.

He bit back a groan. Being an honorable man was beginning to lose its appeal.

As he followed her up the hill, the trees and bushes gave way to a clearing, and in the center stood the old ruins of Castle Glenarvon rising in a jumble of fallen stones and half-tumbled walls. But he could easily see the outline of what had once been a sturdy keep, with some of the ramparts still capping the tops of the remaining walls, which stood over two stories high in the far corner where they met. The rise gave breathtaking views of the river and glen to the west and the cloud-covered mountains to the north, while the ruins gave a sense of history and romance. As his eyes swept over the horizon, he realized why Annabelle loved this place so much.

And why she would hate him when he refused to marry her.

She sat on one of the stones and patted her hand on the rock beside her in invitation for him to join her. Fresh guilt clawed at his gut.

"Isn't the castle marvelous?" She smiled at him as he sat beside her. "I laugh every time I think about those wealthy lords to the south who are paying small fortunes to create follies in their gardens when our ruins are better than anything Capability Brown could ever have envisioned."

An uncomfortable silence fell over them as they gazed together at the ruins. Then he leaned forward with his elbows resting on his thighs, his hands clasped between this knees.

He said quietly, "I can't marry you."

She stiffened but otherwise didn't move. Didn't deign to look at him, only kept her gaze straight ahead at the estate spreading out before them. But Quinn felt the change in her, as her petite body turned as hard as the cold rock beneath him. And surely so did whatever small feelings of friendship she might have still carried for him.

"I'm on my way to America," he explained when she said nothing. That cold silence was more accusatory than he'd thought possible. "I've been waiting for this opportunity for four years."

Longer, if he were honest. The thought of striking out to America had been with him since that summer after he was graduated from Oxford, when he realized that the life of an English peer's son was not for him. Richard Carlisle had been supportive of the idea from the start, and Quinn had been determined to do exactly that and make his father proud of him.

"I want property of my own, a chance to prove myself apart from the title and the Carlisle name," he explained, sharing with her what he'd never told anyone else. Not even Robert. "No matter what success I find here, people will claim it was only because of Trent, only because I'm a Carlisle, and not because of any hard work or smart decisions I make. There's no way to escape Trent's influence without leaving the country."

And no other way to fulfill his promise to his father.

"I'm not asking you to give up that dream," she said quietly, finally breaking her silence yet still not looking at him. "You can still go to America and—"

"I will not abandon my wife," he stated firmly. He might be a scoundrel who was well on his way to being a rake, but he had that much honor, at least.

She said nothing, her gaze fixed on the horizon.

"This is my chance to make my own future, Annabelle." Surely, she understood that. "I have no way to do that in England. Land is too expensive here."

"Not if you marry into it," she countered in a whisper.

"It wouldn't be my land," he said quietly. "It would be yours." And he would be nothing but a de facto estate agent, this time for his wife instead of his brother.

He didn't think it was possible, but her body tightened even more, like the tension of a coiling spring. He could feel the emotion pulsating from her as her fingers gripped into the rock beneath her, so hard that her fingertips turned white.

He ran a frustrated hand through his hair. "I'm leaving this morning. As soon as I say good-bye to Aunt Agatha." And roused Robert from bed, so they could ride on together to the coast. Saying good-bye to his brother would be difficult enough, given how close they were; he didn't want to do it any sooner than he had to. "If we leave this morning, we can be to Keswick by nightfall."

"You don't have to leave so soon," she countered, seizing on a new line of attack. The hope he heard in her voice nearly undid him. "America's big. There's lots of land there for sale. You can buy another property if you lose this one."

"No, I can't. It has to be this piece of land." He stared grimly at his hands, folded between his knees. "It belongs to a family friend. He's been holding it for me but needs to divest himself of it by the New Year. He made me a good offer if I bought it and let him and his wife remain on the property." And Quinn had made a promise to do just that. A promise he had every intention of keeping. "They have no one else."

In the silence that followed, she sat unnaturally still, not even breathing. Then, so softly that the words were barely above a breath on her lips, she whispered, "*I* have no one else."

Anger pulsed through him, chasing on the heels of a flood

of guilt. *Damnation.* It wasn't his responsibility to secure her future when he had his own to worry about. Didn't she realize that?

He jumped down from the rock, then wheeled on her. "This is not my problem to solve."

Her own anger flared to the surface. "Isn't it?"

"Because of that damned fight?" *Christ.* Not this again! With frustration simmering inside him that she refused to leave that night to the past where it belonged, he planted his hands on the stone on either side of her and leaned in, her face level with his. Close enough that he saw the gold flecks in her irises when her eyes flared at his boldness. *This* fight was a long time in coming, and they would finally have it all out. Here and now. "Was I supposed to just stand there and do nothing while Williams said those things about you?"

"Yes!" She straightened her spine. "Better to be insulted than to have my reputation ruined, don't you think?"

"*I* didn't ruin your reputation," he countered. "That was nothing more than an accident and poor timing."

She imperially raised a brow, in a gesture that eerily reminded him of Aunt Agatha. "And was slamming your fist into Williams's jaw accidental?"

"No." He grinned, just to irritate her. "That was pure pleasure."

"*That* was your arrogance getting in the way," she snapped.

He gritted his teeth. "I was defending your honor."

"I didn't need my honor defended." She jabbed her finger into his chest. "But you wouldn't listen to me and had to throw your fists at Williams—"

"I did not *throw* my fists at him!" *Good Lord.* She made it sound like a grammar school shoving match. But if she thought she could guilt him into marriage, she'd better think again. He deliberately bit out each word, "That night was not my fault."

She cast him a contemptuous look, one so cold it shivered through him. "So you keep saying."

She looked down at the wild rose blossom she still held in her hand, then threw it away. She shoved him back, giving herself just enough room to slip to the ground and hurry away.

Oh no. That little force of nature was going nowhere! Not after the bomb she'd just exploded.

He grabbed her arm as she tried to step past him. "Listen to me, damn it!"

With a fierce yank, she tried to wrench herself away, but he held tight. He took both of her arms and pulled her up against him to hold her still.

"What do you want from me, Annabelle?" he demanded, unable to keep the exasperation from his voice. "An apology?"

"You can keep your apologies!" she spat back. So much anger radiated from her that she shook with it, her breath coming quick and ragged, her chest rising and falling rapidly. "I don't want them."

"Good. Because I'm not giving any." Her eyes blazed indignantly at that and stirred the burning inside him. "I'm not sorry for fighting over you that night. I'll never be." He pulled her closer as he leaned back against the rock. "But it's not the fight that upsets you, is it?"

"Let me go!" she hissed.

The hell he would. He lowered his head until his mouth nearly touched hers. Each panting little breath of hers fanned across his lips, and beneath his hands he could feel her pulse racing. "It's what happened before the fight that bothers you. How we kissed."

When her face darkened, he knew he was right. An electric thrill spun through him.

"When you played another one of your childish pranks on me," she ground out accusingly. "What was the goal that time, Quinton? To put me into tears by making me think you wanted to kiss me, when it was only a joke to you?"

He stared down into her eyes, seeing a heated mix of anger and arousal that had her nearly breathless. "I kissed you because I couldn't help myself."

She inhaled sharply at his confession, and his gaze dropped to her mouth and fixed there. As if he could devour her simply by looking.

"Because you were beautiful in the moonlight, because I wanted to taste your lips and feel you pressed against me." Then he dared to admit all— "Because I couldn't believe that the awkward little girl I'd spent years tormenting had grown into a woman who was so unaware of her own allure that she'd venture into the shadows of the garden with a rogue like me."

"You're lying," she breathed, stunned by that raw admission.

"I'm not." He shifted her in his arms, until he wasn't keeping her from fleeing but holding her willingly against him. "Or about how much I enjoyed that kiss." He felt the catch of her breath against his lips. "And so did you."

She swallowed nervously, and he suppressed the urge to place his mouth right there at her throat to feel the soft undulation beneath his lips. "I didn't."

"Liar," he rasped. "But if you don't believe me, I'm happy to prove it."

She narrowed her eyes. "You wouldn't—"

He lowered his head and kissed her, unable to resist one heartbeat longer.

Sweet Lucifer... Quinn knew kisses, and knew them well. He'd kissed more women than he could remember, and a misspent youth had made him good enough at it to turn half of those encounters into full-out seductions. But this, *this* wasn't just a kiss. This was so much more.

Those other kisses didn't leave him trembling the way that he trembled now. They didn't intoxicate him with the wild scent of the highlands and heather. They didn't leave his gut twisting into knots and his head spinning, or make the world fall away until he was aware only of the warm sweetness of her breath tickling at his lips, her soft body leaning into his in innocent invitation. But Belle's kisses did just that. They were addictive, leaving him hungering for a deeper taste...one which he knew he shouldn't claim yet desperately wanted.

But if this morning was to be the last time he'd ever get to see her, why should he stop? He'd have this moment together to remember her by.

And just like six years ago, he couldn't help himself.

"I remember everything about that kiss," he murmured truthfully against her lips, although at that moment he would have said anything to keep her mouth against his and her body leaning into him, tasting the unbearable sweetness of her. "And how beautiful you were that night. How alluring."

"Quinton," she whispered in a soft plea.

Another kiss, but this time, he took her bottom lip between his and sucked, eliciting a shiver from her as he drew her lip deep into his mouth.

She inhaled a jerking breath. Then the last of her stubborn resistance melted away, and she slumped bonelessly against him. His arms around her kept her pressed close, to prevent her from slipping down his body to the ground. Instead of pushing him away, her hand at his shoulder now fisted the collar of his wool coat in her fingers to keep him close.

Joy soared inside him at her capitulation, and he welcomed her response as her mouth softened against his and her body relaxed within his arms. Sweet and delicate, the kiss possessed none of the flaring passion nor the eager fumbling he remembered from six years ago—but it was just as magnetic, just as arousing. Even more so. Because her body was now softer and more yielding with her maturity, which only made him crave more.

"I remember this, too." He slid his thumb to her chin and gently tugged down, opening her mouth as he slipped his tongue between her lips.

A shameless lie. He hadn't kissed her so intimately that night beneath the rose bower. If he had dared to sweep across her inner lip like this, to delve his tongue inside the dark, moist recesses of her kiss and taste the sweetness hidden there like ambrosia—*God help him*, because even now her kiss heated him down to his core and left him shaking.

She whimpered softly. He responded to her growing arousal by cupping the back of her head against his palm, to keep her mouth captured against his as he began to thrust his tongue in rhythmic strokes between her lips. He knocked away her tweed cap and dug his fingers into her soft hair until it tumbled loose down her back, all the while not stopping in his relentless desire to kiss her the way no man had ever kissed her before. If he had to leave with only this memory to remember her by, then damnation, he wanted to make certain she never forgot *him*, either.

But when her lips closed tentatively around his tongue and took a gentle suck, he felt the unpracticed pull of her mouth straight down to his tightening gut. He was a fool to think he could control this encounter, now as swept up in the embrace as much as she.

"Annabelle," he rasped hoarsely, tearing his mouth away from hers to nip his teeth down the side of her neck and drawing a breathless moan of need from her.

Dear God, how he thrilled at those little sounds that came from her! Even now his cock tingled at her guileless response. She dug her fingers into his hair, and he gladly let her, because every electrifying scratch of her fingertips against his scalp sent shivers spiraling through him.

When she moved her mouth against his to kiss him back and nibbled tentatively at his bottom lip the way he'd done to hers, he groaned.

She pulled back, a worried frown marring her pretty face. "Is something wrong?"

He cupped her face between his hands and pursued her for another kiss. "Nothing."

Just everything. For God's sake, at that moment, he should have been packing his bags and readying his horse to leave, but he couldn't tear himself away. He tugged back the collar of her coat to gain access to the side of her neck where it sloped beneath her shirt, then licked at the patch of revealed skin.

She bit back another moan rising at her lips, and he smiled at her innocence as he sat back on the stone. To fight away the very thing that would bring such pleasure... Yet he understood her nervousness, because his own hands shook as he reached beneath her coat and encircled her waist to draw her onto his lap.

Trembling hands? He nearly laughed. The woman had *all* of him shaking! So much for his reputation as a rake if such an unschooled gel like Annabelle had him as nervous as a green pup, so nervous that his fingers could barely unfasten the buttons of her waistcoat.

"Quinn?" His name was an uncertain whisper.

"You're so pretty, Belle," he whispered, his hands gently pushing her waistcoat open to reveal the thin white shirt and the shadow of her breasts beneath in the blue morning light. He groaned—she wasn't wearing stays. "I had forgotten how much."

He trailed a hand slowly down her front and pulled at the shirt to draw the fabric taut across her breasts. Her nipples, already pebbled in arousal, showed dusky rose through the white material. His breath hitched at the sight of her. Sweet Lucifer, she was beautiful.

"Quinn." This time, his name was an aching sigh of permission as she arched herself toward him.

Unable to resist, he lowered his head and captured her right nipple through the thin fabric, finally taking the taste of her he craved.

A gasp of surprise tore from her at the intimate contact, but she leaned harder into him, her fingertips digging into his shoulders as she fought to regain the breath he'd so easily stolen from her. His pulse spiked. He couldn't remember ever kissing another woman who was so responsive to each little touch and caress. Even now as he suckled at her nipple, she trembled beneath his mouth, her eyes closed and her lips parted, as if having his mouth on her like this gave her the most intense pleasure she'd ever known.

When he lifted his head, he saw the wet circle his mouth had left through her shirt, the now translucent material tantalizingly encircling her nipple. He couldn't resist tracing his thumb over the hard bud and making her shudder before he leaned up to capture her mouth again. This time, she welcomed him eagerly with a hot, openmouthed kiss. One that left him hard between his thighs and throbbing for her.

He wanted to make her ache just as much as he did. With his left arm around her to keep her close, he shifted her on his lap, until she straddled him as he perched at the edge of the stone.

Her eyes flew open, and all of her tensed. She stared uncertainly up at him but didn't pull back. Instead, her arms tightened boldly around his neck, her breath coming in small pants of arousal. She bit her bottom lip.

He understood her hesitation—she didn't know if she could trust him with this embrace when he'd so foolishly wounded her after the last one. "I would never do anything to hurt you," he reassured her, despite the husky rasp of his voice, now thick with desire. "I only want to bring you pleasure."

Which was the God's honest truth. He'd never cared about pleasing another woman in his life the way he did with Annabelle. He found his own satisfaction in giving pleasure to her, and even now that sweet reward pulsed through him and left him insatiably wanting more. He wanted to bring her to bliss.

Not breaking eye contact with her, unable to tear his gaze away from her beautifully flushed face even if he'd wanted to, he lifted his right hand to his mouth and removed his glove with his teeth. He dropped it to the ground.

Her eyes widened nervously. "What are you doing?"

"I want to touch you, Annabelle," he purred and felt her sharp intake of air. He hadn't meant to sound so wolfish, yet he couldn't keep the arousal from his voice. "I've wanted to touch you for six years. Will you let me?"

His heart pounded so fiercely as he breathlessly waited for her answer that he suspected she could feel it—

"Yes," she whispered, the word shivering from her lips.

His body flashed hot at her soft permission. He leaned forward to place a tender kiss on her throat, making her eyes close again. A soft, shuddering sigh seeped from her. He placed his hand on her leg and slowly, so not to frighten her, slid it upward along her inner thigh.

She dug her fingers into his shoulders as his hand reached the juncture where her legs met. Her name fell from his lips in a low groan as he lightly stroked his thumb against her, down between her legs along the seam of her trousers. She trembled.

"All right?" he asked.

"Good," she whispered, simultaneously nodding and holding her breath.

With a smile at her contradiction of alluring innocence, he stroked against her again, this time harder and tantalizingly slower than before. She gasped, only for the soft sound to turn into a low moan of pleasure.

"Oh, that's—" She licked her lips as he continued to caress her through her trousers. "That's *very* good."

Her mouth found his again, and she kissed him ardently as her fingers ran through his hair in silent encouragement. She widened her thighs in shameless invitation, one he very much wanted to accept—

A shout went up from the fields below.

With a startled gasp, Belle slipped off his lap and staggered away from him, brought back to her senses by the intruding world around them. Her hand flew up to her mouth as she stared at him, moon-eyed and stunned, as if she couldn't believe what they'd done.

Instantly, he missed the warmth of her and the light weight of her small body pressing into his. He reached for her. "Belle—"

"*No.*"

The single word cut him to the quick. Dropping his hands to his sides, he tightened his jaw as he watched her fumble to fasten up her waistcoat.

"Damnation, Belle," he growled, unable to tamp down his anger over her rejection, or hide the frustration evident in his stiff cock. "You don't get to kiss me like that and run off the—"

Another shout went up. This time closer.

Her eyes locked with his for one pained heartbeat. In that moment's connection he saw both her desire for him and her regret. "Good-bye, Quinton."

As she turned away and ran down the hill, he saw that familiar fire blazing inside her, the one he loved so much to rouse. Always had, even when they were children. But they certainly weren't children anymore.

With a pained jolt, he realized, finally, why he so enjoyed tormenting her.

It wasn't because he enjoyed seeing the fire inside her, but because he enjoyed being the man who put it there. The *only* man who could stir the anger and passion inside her until it flamed through her like the shimmering of shaken foil.

And he'd never get to experience it again.

* * *

Belle hurried down the path and across the field toward the irrigation ditch. With each step she prayed that her lips weren't as obviously swollen and red as they felt beneath her fingertips and that no one who saw her would realize what she and Quinn had been doing. Yet thoughts of that wholly unexpected embrace swirled through her mind, confusing her and leaving her in a fogged daze.

Quinton had kissed her. Again. And oh, what a kiss, too. As delicious as she remembered.

No—better. Everything about this last kiss was right. More than right. She groaned—it was perfect. So perfect, in fact, that he had her wanting so much more than just a kiss and a fleeting touch. Which was not only delicious, but downright dangerous.

She'd gotten caught up in him, in the anger he always brought out in her, and then in the wonderful wickedness of his breath-stealing kisses and forbidden touches. But when she'd heard Angus Burns calling out for her, the aching arousal that had been surging through her vanished, replaced instantly by self-recrimination to find herself once more in that scoundrel's arms. And so shamelessly enjoying it.

To fall for his charms again— *Of course* he'd wanted that wanton encounter, because he was leaving and so could scamper off scot-free from any problems he might leave behind. She was such a goose! And especially since he'd refused to help her, putting her closer to losing Glenarvon.

When she approached the workmen at the ditch gate, she noted the progress they'd made in her absence, which only added more remorse to the mountain of guilt she already carried over Quinn.

"Looks to be done 'fore noon," Angus Burns announced as he climbed out of the ditch to stand by her side. Together, they watched as two men finished applying the mortar around the stones that held the gate in place. "'Tweren't much damage done. More o' a bother than anythin'.'"

"Boys from the village causing trouble," she muttered with a long sigh, her hands on her hips in frustration. If Quinton didn't send her to Bedlam, this string of recent troubles would.

"'Tweren't no boys," Angus countered in a low voice. He gestured toward the stones. "See them scrape marks there?"

She nodded faintly.

"Used a metal bar t' pry the gate loose, an' the force from the water took it the rest o' the way off. Whoever did this had strength i' his arms, lassie, an' meant to cause problems fer ye."

Her shoulders slumped. The self-recrimination and anger she felt over Quinn completely disappeared beneath Angus's grim words. What were a few kisses and touches compared to the reality of protecting the estate and the slew of problems that had befallen it lately?

Deliberate destruction meant to do harm...But *why*?

"Let's put a padlock on it," she instructed with a defeated air, not knowing what else to do to prevent it from being vandalized again.

"We'll build up th' side tracks, too, wi' more stone an' mortar. When we're through wi' it, lass," Angus assured her, nodding confidently at his men, "the only way to open this gate wi'out permission will be to hack through it wi' an axe."

She stared glumly at the new gate as it lay on the grass beside the ditch. "Let's hope it doesn't come to that."

"Aye." Then he slid her a curious, sideways look. "Ye came back from yer walk alone. Has the Englishman returned t' the house, then?"

She didn't dare raise her eyes to look at him for fear of what her old friend might see in their depths. "I would assume so."

They watched in silence as the men finished placing the last stone, then Angus pressed, "Is that Englishman visitin' fer a reason?" He lowered his voice so none of the men could overhear, "Perhaps 'cause o' yer birthday an' what it signifies?"

She grimaced. What it signified was a loss of any hope for a happy future, no matter the outcome. The exact opposite of what Lord Ainsley had wanted by including that entailment in his will.

But knowing Angus was fishing for information about Quinn, she dodged, "Lord Quinton is headed for America. Glenarvon is only a stop on his way to the coast."

"A demmed shame, then," Angus muttered. "'Cause he could be the solution t'yer problems."

"No," she assured him, turning to help the men with the last of the mortar. "Quinton Carlisle is a problem all his own."

CHAPTER FIVE

*D*amn damn damn damn *damn*!

Quinn stomped into the house and nearly growled at a footman when the man offered to take his coat and hat. "Where's the nearest whisky?"

The young man pointed toward the drawing room, not blinking an eye that the long case clock on the stairway landing hadn't yet struck ten. "Behind the potted palm, sir. Shall I fetch you a glass?"

"No." He blew out a frustrated breath and ran his hand through his hair. "I'll get it myself."

The footman nodded and wisely retreated. And Quinn charged toward the drawing room and the promised whisky.

What on earth had he been thinking to kiss Annabelle like that? Along with so much more he had no business doing with her at all. Something to remember her by? He laughed bitterly. Well, he certainly had *that*. Although remembering her wasn't what he wanted to do to her now.

The infuriating bluestocking had gotten into his head and under his skin, and what he wanted to do was dribble scotch over her ripe body and lick away every tempting drop, teach her all kinds of pleasures not found in her blasted books—

He threw open the drawing room doors and froze.

Lady Ainsley looked up from the settee, a cup of tea lifted halfway to her lips, while in the chair across from her lounged a man dressed in a tweed hunting costume. The man's eyes flicked disinterestedly in his direction, and he climbed slowly to his feet only when Aunt Agatha rose to hers.

"Quinton." A smile brightened her face. "Come join us for tea."

He fought to keep from rolling his eyes. Tea. *Wonderful.* When all he wanted to do was put as many miles between himself and Glenarvon as possible, before he did something he would regret. With the Bluebell. *Good Lord.*

But Aunt Agatha's request couldn't be ignored. With a welcoming smile he certainly didn't feel—and casting a longing glance toward the potted palm in the corner—he sauntered forward.

Agatha proffered her cheek to him, and Quinn nearly blinked at the unexpected display of affection. What had gotten into her?

But he did as expected and kissed her cheek. "Aunt Agatha, you look well-rested this morning."

Her sharp eyes swept over him. "And you look absolutely fierce."

"It's the weather," he deflected. "Too damp and cold for a good walk." But apparently not for other things.

The flicker in her eyes made him wonder whether she believed that bit of dissembling. But if she didn't, at least she didn't press. Instead, she waved a hand at the man with her. "Quinton, I want to introduce to you Sir Harold Bletchley, our good neighbor to the east."

And the man who wanted to marry Belle.

Quinn tensed, his eyes narrowing. Bletchley looked perfectly harmless enough, he supposed, although the man was at least fifteen years Belle's senior, with thinning hair and the start of a paunch around his middle. And an arrogance that reeked.

For the life of him, he couldn't imagine Belle being happily married to this man. Or kissing him as passionately as she'd just kissed him.

"Sir Harold." Quinn gave a stiff nod.

His aunt continued the introductions. "Sir Harold, this is Lord Quinton Carlisle, my great-nephew, come to Glenarvon to visit with us on his way to America."

"Carlisle." Bletchley didn't bother to nod, nor erase the bored expression on his face.

From the tea service and the way Bletchley and Aunt Agatha had been in polite conversation when he entered, Quinn suspected that Bletchley was here to pay a social call, although from his appearance, he'd given it little forethought. The mud on his boots showed that he'd been outside in the damp and found it acceptable to muck about the countryside before calling, as did the smirk on his face that Quinn had let the northern weather get the best of him.

Quinn disliked the man, instantly put off by his egotism. And by his early arrival. Dear God, did everyone in the north country wake with the bloody chickens?

"Were you wanting to speak with me?" Agatha inquired of Quinn, straight back to her no-nonsense self, now that pleasantries were over.

Clearly, this wasn't the best time to admit that he'd been looking for a bottle of scotch to dull his frustrations over scandalously touching the companion who was like a daughter to her. So he offered instead, "I've decided to leave today for the coast and wanted to say my good-byes."

An unexpected panic flashed over her wrinkled face. "But—but you're staying to help Belle. I insist!"

Quinn grimly shook his head, unwilling to divulge anything more about his sudden decision to leave. "I need to get on to America, if that's all right with you, my lady."

She stared at him silently for a long moment, as if she simply couldn't fathom him. Then she smiled tightly. "Of course," she assured him, the lie obvious. "Then your timing is impeccable, that you should be here to meet Belle's suitor."

Bletchley's thin lips curled with mock humility. "Now, viscountess, you know she hasn't yet formally accepted my suit."

Agatha waved her hand dismissingly. "Of course she will. And may I say how thrilled we are that you've declared your intentions? Aren't we, Quinton?"

He quirked a brow and drawled, "Ecstatic."

If Agatha heard the sarcasm in his answer, she made no reaction, her smile only widening on Bletchley. "Of course, Sir Harold first offered for her two years ago. But I didn't think she was ready for marriage then, especially given what she'd gone through in her only London season."

Quinn rolled his eyes. Would none of the women here let him forget that night? He bit back the offer to fetch Robert from bed so they could have his brother's help in roasting him on a spit in revenge. "How fortunate you persisted," he mumbled, drawing a surprised glance from his aunt.

Bletchley smiled lazily, as if marrying Belle were his

birthright. "As I've learned, hunting requires patience. All good things take time."

"Indeed, they do!" Agatha interjected before Quinn could say something entirely ungentlemanly about his so-called hunting of Belle. "And speaking of time, Sir Harold's family has been in the area for over five generations."

Quinn couldn't help himself. "Legally?"

"Pardon?" Bletchley frowned.

"Sir Harold inherited Kinnybroch nearly twenty years ago," his aunt hurried on, ignoring that small exchange, "which his family has owned since his great-grandfather received the estate for his bravery at Culloden." She slid Quinn a deliberate glance. "Isn't it wonderful that Annabelle might have the chance to marry into a family with such a distinguished history?"

"Wonderful," he repeated stiffly. He didn't give a damn about family histories when what mattered was Belle's happiness.

"Lord Quinton is the third son of the late Duke of Trent," she continued, turning to Bletchley. Then sadly shook her head. "You know the lot of younger sons. So he is leaving for America to start a life for himself there."

Quinn stared at her, dumbfounded. Did Aunt Agatha realize the unintended insult she'd just leveled against him?

But of course she did. The question now was why she'd done it.

"Yes," Quinn forced out, his smile never wavering as he pretended her comment didn't sting, "in the Carolinas. I plan on buying land there."

"Tobacco?" Sir Harold asked, amusement touching his lips that Quinn hoped to be what most English gentlemen considered nothing more than a glorified farmer.

"Rice and indigo, actually." He'd been working the numbers for the past four years and knew the best use of his money was to invest in those two crops. And not just in the profit from growing them but also in their storage, shipment, and trade, which was why he was fortunate that the land was so close to Charleston. With the help of Asa Jeffers, he could be both landowner and businessman. His father would be proud of the man he planned to become.

"You'll have slaves, then." Bletchley's words emerged as an arrogant sneer.

Hell no. Yet Quinn only shrugged. "No more so than any English landowner whose indebted tenants can never be free of the manor."

A strangled sound escaped from Aunt Agatha's throat.

But Bletchley only laughed. "Then you'll do well in America, with the rest of the colonists who detest us Englishmen. I only hope you don't find yourself being detested as well."

Oh, he was certain of that. Yet he grinned broadly, just to irritate Bletchley. "I'll take my chances."

A soft knock sounded at the door. "Excuse me, my lady." Ferguson stepped into the room. "But Cook would like a word with you. She says it is an urgent matter with the ovens, ma'am."

She hesitated with a glance between the two men, as if wary to leave them alone together, then sighed, realizing she had no choice unless she wanted to risk burning the house down. "If you gentlemen will excuse me."

She scurried out with Ferguson on her heels. An awkward silence fell over the room.

Quinn's eyes narrowed as he sized up Bletchley. So this was Belle's leading prospect for marriage.

No wonder she preferred to remain unmarried.

But Aunt Agatha had said she wanted Quinn's help to keep Belle safe from unsatisfactory suitors. Well, then, no time like the present to start.

He leveled his gaze hard on Bletchley. "You expect to marry Annabelle."

"Yes."

"What are you plans, then?" He folded his arms over his chest.

Bletchley smiled at that. "So you're her guard dog now?"

Knowing not to rise to the bait, Quinn said nothing as Bletchley went to the tea tray on the table and poured himself a fresh cup.

"Oh, you can be confident that I have lots of plans," Bletchley assured him. "The first thing we do is knock down the existing fences to enlarge the pastures and merge the flocks. Then, with the extra money on Glenarvon's books, we'll buy a herd of Highland cattle to graze on the slopes to the north." Bletchley gestured with this teacup between sips. "Close up the shearing and dairy barns on Glenarvon and double the size of the ones at Kinnybroch, renegotiate all the tenant leases and grazing rights." He glanced disdainfully around the room. "And let out this tired place, if I can find anyone daft enough to take it."

Quinn noticed that he never mentioned Belle. Not once. His intentions were purely mercenary. Just as Belle feared. "And the villagers?"

Bletchley blinked, surprised at that question. "What about them?"

"What plans do you have to help them?"

"*Help* the villagers?" Bletchley laughed as if it were the most absurd thing he'd ever heard, nearly spilling his tea.

Good God, this man was a completely wrong match for Belle. In every way.

"My concern is the estate." Bletchley reached for a biscuit from the tray. "Especially once it's folded into Kinnybroch. I'll have twice as much land then and considerable funds. Managing all that will keep me too busy to worry about the villagers. They can tend to themselves."

Dread prickled at the back of his neck. "Glenarvon will belong to Annabelle. She wants to run it herself."

Popping the biscuit into his mouth, Bletchley waved away his concern. "Once we marry," he explained between munches, "she'll come to see how much better it is to let her husband worry about such things. You know how women are. She'll be thrilled to spend her time enjoying trips to the dressmaker and planning parties, rather than fretting over the account books and getting her hands dirty in the fields. Besides," he continued with a smug grin, "we'll need an heir. She'll be increasing soon enough, and then all her attention will be on our child, where it belongs."

A quick stab of emotion pierced low in Quinn's belly at the thought of Belle with child. Of the hot fire in her tempered by the soft glow of motherhood. The sensation hit him so swiftly, so fiercely, that he nearly shuddered with it before he found his control.

Desperately needing that drink now, he crossed the room to the potted palm and from its fronds retrieved the hidden whisky he'd originally come into the room to find. With no glass at the ready, he poured himself a teacup.

"Annabelle's a smart woman," he commented. *Downright brilliant, in fact.* He corked the bottle and slid it into his rear waistband beneath his coat, then leaned back against the wall and studied Bletchley over the rim of his cup. *Far too brilliant for you.* "She's already running this place well, and she'll be able to handle both motherhood and the estate's management."

"Well, I'm certain she'll be too busy to manage once she has another child." Bletchley chuckled. "Or six."

Quinn glared at him. *Over my dead body.*

Bletchley smiled blithely. "We'll be certain to send you news in America when each of our children is born."

Quinn's hand tightened around the teacup until he thought he might shatter it in his palm as he fought back the urge to punch him. Bletchley cared only about the property and talked of marrying her as if he were acquiring a brood mare. Arrogant, pompous, misogynistic—

A movement at the corner of his eye captured his attention.

Through the tall window, he caught a glimpse of Belle returning from the fields, the collar of her coat turned up against the drizzle of the cold morning and her hair once more tucked beneath her tweed cap. Silhouetted against the gray clouds hanging low across the sky and the blue mountains in the distance, she looked for all the world as if she'd materialized right there from the mists. A fairy born of glens and mountains. A creature as wild and independent as the land around her.

Quinton knew then that he wouldn't allow anyone to take Glenarvon away from her.

Aunt Agatha swept into the room, nearly breathless in her hurry to return. Her eyes darted between the two men as if checking for wounds. "Disaster averted," she panted out. "The house won't…burn down…before dinner."

Bletchley smiled dutifully at her labored quip. But Quinn

only continued to glare coldly at the man over the rim of his teacup as he took a calming swallow of whisky.

Fanning herself as she regained her breath, Aunt Agatha sank gratefully onto the settee. "I'm so glad you two had the chance to talk." She poured more tea into her cup and added a dollop of honey. "It would have been a shame if Quinton had left before you had the opportunity to meet him, Sir Harold. Now knowing that Annabelle and Castle Glenarvon will be in your safe hands, Quinton can happily sail for America."

Like hell I will. Belle would be safer with Lucifer himself.

"Actually," Quinn announced as he pushed himself away from the wall and stepped forward as casually as if commenting upon the weather, "there's been a change of plans."

"Oh?" His aunt froze, the honey dipper poised in her hand accidentally filling her cup.

"I've decided to stay on as you asked, Aunt Agatha." He looked squarely at Bletchley, whose face hardened as he slowly realized what Quinn intended. "To help you with Belle's suitors."

"Wonderful!" Agatha distractedly stirred her tea with the dipper as a beaming smile spread across her face. "I mean, it would be *wonderful* if Belle agrees."

"Oh, I think she will." Quinn watched her raise the cup to her lips. When she made a face at the overly sweet tea, he sent her his most charming smile, although he planned on ruining her scheme to marry off Belle as thoroughly as he'd just ruined her tea. Then he turned toward Bletchley with feigned innocence. "Can't be too careful, you understand." He flashed a crocodile grin. "Seems there's a new fortune hunter dropping by every day."

"Of course," Agatha interjected quickly, as if fearing the two men might yet come to blows, "this is all about doing what's best for Belle."

Bletchley clenched his jaw and dutifully agreed, "Of course."

An awkward tension settled over the room. Bletchley glared at Quinn like a lion defending his territory.

Quinn grinned back confidently.

And Aunt Agatha had no idea where to look. Setting her tea aside, she cleared her throat and made a desperate attempt to change the direction of conversation. "I hope you two had a good chat about hunting and fishing while I was gone."

Bletchley scoffed. "I wish we'd discussed something as entertaining as hunting, but focused on business instead, I'm afraid."

"And Belle, don't forget," Quinn reminded him, just for spite. "Or is she nothing more than business to you?"

Bletchley narrowed his eyes. "Perhaps, Carlisle, you should rethink your plans—"

"Sir Harold is a keen marksman and avid hunter," Agatha cut in with forced enthusiasm. "Aren't you, Sir Harold?" When her question failed to draw his attention—and his ire—away from Quinn, she added skillfully, "He keeps one of the best hunting packs in the north."

That arrow hit its target, and Bletchley turned toward her, a pompous smile softening his face. "One of my proudest achievements, I'll admit. Just a few years ago, I had the pleasure of arranging a hunt for Wellington. Said it was one of the best he'd ever experienced." He flicked his fingers at a piece of imaginary lint on his sleeve. "In fact, I just purchased a new bitch from the Duke of Devonshire. Fine blood lines, that one. She'll whelp a good pup or two to improve the pack."

Quinn couldn't help himself— "Or six."

The glare Bletchley shot him was murderous.

"And you, Quinton?" Agatha interposed smoothly. "Do you enjoy the sport of hunting?"

He set down his empty cup on the tea table. "It doesn't seem like much of a sport to me unless the animals are also armed."

Agatha pursed her lips tightly, although whether to suppress laughter or a scolding he couldn't have said.

"Hunting takes skill," Bletchley defended peevishly. "Perhaps your lack of ability prevents you from appreciating it."

Quinn shrugged away the insult. "How much skill can it take to shoot a slow bird flushed out of a bush by a beater while a gamesman stands next to you to reload your gun?"

Bletchley turned red. He sputtered, "Now see here, Carlisle—"

A lilting laugh drifted from the doorway, musical in its softness. Quinn caught his breath at the sound that fell through him as gently as a warm summer rain.

Annabelle. He turned toward her, and his gut pinched at the sight of her. Even all wet and dirty from working in the fields, her hair coming loose from beneath her tweed cap, and a streak of dirt marring her cheek, she looked beautiful.

As she stepped into the room, she smiled a greeting to Aunt Agatha, then sent Quinn a puzzled glance at finding him here instead of upstairs packing.

"Sir Harold." She nodded to Bletchley. But her greeting was reserved, and instead of extending her hand to him, she immediately scooped up a cup and saucer from the tea tray so that her hands were full and she wouldn't have to touch him by presenting her hand.

Brilliant woman, Quinn noted with admiration. Too brilliant to be unhappily shackled to a fortune-hunting boor like Bletchley for the rest of her life.

"My apologies for interrupting," she commented. But a wholly unapologetic smile played at her lips. "So you were having a discussion about the merits of arming prey?"

Instead of going to Bletchley, Belle retreated a step away from the tea table to position herself beside Quinn, as if seeking protection at his side. The small movement sent an unexpected possessiveness sweeping through him.

"In my opinion," she teased as she raised her cup, "it would surely make fox hunting more challenging, although I'm not certain how it would work with larger game. However would deer pull the triggers without their hooves getting in the way?"

Bletchley stared at her as if insulted by her musings, and Aunt Agatha as if she'd lost her mind. Quinn grinned broadly.

She tilted her head, feigning deep thought. "Although I suppose we could arm them with bows and arrows." Then she added brightly, as if the solution were suddenly obvious, "They could draw the bowstring through the cleft in their hooves!"

Agatha choked on her tea. "Annabelle!"

She laughed at herself, drawing another smile from Quinn and something else . . . something deeper and more intense than he'd experienced even when he'd been kissing her. He couldn't put a name to it. But whatever it was, he liked it. A great deal.

"My apologies," she offered. "I was only joking. I didn't mean to offend."

But Quinn saw the unrepentant gleam in her eyes. Oh, she'd meant to do *exactly* that.

Mollified by her pretense of an apology, Bletchley nodded at Quinn. "You have excellent timing, Miss Greene. Carlisle and I were just finishing a discussion about future plans for Glenarvon." His eyes swept over her, and he frowned with displeasure. "I see you've been working in the fields again."

"Yes." She smiled, ignoring his silent criticism of her appearance. "After all, the cheapest worker on any estate is always the owner, because he's—"

"Already taken his share," Quinn finished.

She glanced at him in surprise that he could finish her thoughts, her pink lips parting softly. He held her gaze for a heartbeat in silent connection, and an inexplicable warmth blossomed inside his chest.

He thought he saw Agatha's lips twitch, but his aunt had raised her teacup to take a sip too quickly for him to be certain. "What were you doing, exactly?" she asked.

Belle shrugged dismissingly. "There was a problem with the floodgate."

A worried frown creased Aunt Agatha's brow, and she lowered her cup from her mouth. "More vandalism?"

"Nothing to worry about," she dissembled with a forced smile. "Mr. Burns and the men had it all fixed this morning. The sheep will be back in their proper pastures by the end of the week."

Belle's explanation mollified Aunt Agatha, but Quinn saw a glint in Bletchley's eyes. The man scoffed, "More proof that a woman has no business running an estate."

Belle stiffened at that. But Bletchley didn't notice. Or if he did, the obtuse man foolishly decided to ignore it.

Quinn said nothing, gladly letting the arrogant fop dig his own grave.

Bletchley continued, "I expect that mischief will stop soon, once you accept my suit and whoever is doing it realizes that a man is properly looking after the property."

"Oh." Her face fell. The amusement that had been there only moments before vanished, and she looked away.

"Have you decided on your answer, Miss Greene?" Bletchley pressed, with all the romantic finesse of a dead donkey. "I daresay, time is running out. Will I be allowed to formally court you?"

"Well, I…that is…" Belle stammered. Her gaze darted nervously to Quinton. In her eyes, he saw a warring desperation and sadness that tied his gut into a knot.

Agatha rose from the settee. "Sir Harold, perhaps you should discuss this privately with Lord Quinton. In lieu of a male relative, my nephew will be serving as Belle's—"

"We've been neighbors for years, with no secrets between us." Bletchley waved away the viscountess's concerns. "I know the predicament you're facing, Miss Greene, and there's no need to stand on formality with me." He smiled confidently at Belle. "Except that I would like to hear your acknowledgment that I have your favor."

When Belle hesitated, Aunt Agatha murmured, "Quinton?"

"Annabelle knows what's best for her," he answered quietly. "She doesn't need me to make up her mind." And, knowing how stubborn she was, to most likely do exactly what he told her not to.

Quinn's eyes fixed on Belle, even as hers were pinned to

her cup of tea, not daring to glance in his direction. Holding his breath, he waited for her to refuse Bletchley's suit. In the silence, his heartbeat thundered in his ears—

"Yes," she breathed, so softly that no sound crossed her lips.

But Quinn heard, and her answer reverberated through his chest with the force of cannon fire.

Lady Ainsley blinked, as if she hadn't heard properly. As if just as surprised as Quinn that Belle hadn't refused. "Pardon?"

"I said yes." Belle raised her chin and stared across the room at Bletchley as she grudgingly accepted his offer with all the emotion of buying flour from the miller. "I will allow you to court me, Sir Harold."

"Good," Bletchley commented so gleefully that Quinn expected him to rub his hands together. "Then tomorrow after church I'd be pleased to take you on a drive through the countryside."

Belle nodded, saying nothing, but she couldn't hide the grim sadness on her face. Or the sense of defeat that radiated from her.

Aunt Agatha smiled tightly at Bletchley. "Come, Sir Harold." She took his arm and led him toward the door. "I'll show you out."

As the dowager led Bletchley from the room, she glanced back at Quinn, giving him a look he couldn't comprehend in his stunned bewilderment over Belle's answer. Although what he sensed from his aunt was disappointment. In him.

Quinn crossed his arms and stared at Belle, who hadn't moved an inch. To agree to go through with this nonsense— with Bletchley! He was furious at her, and the little hellcat knew it, too. Which was why she refused to look at him.

But it wasn't just anger, it was also betrayal. Not for himself, of course. It would be ludicrous to say so, as much as to say he was jealous of Bletchley. He had no rights to her, no feelings for her besides friendship.

No—she'd betrayed herself. Surrendering so easily to a life with a man like Sir Harold was a betrayal to the strong woman he thought she'd become.

"Oh no, you don't," he ground out as he stalked toward her. "You are *not* going through with this."

* * *

"Quinn, please understand," Belle protested, retreating across the room from him. He was furious, with more anger than she'd ever seen in him. So much that it shook her to her core. Even the hand she futilely held up to keep him at bay trembled.

But he was relentless in his pursuit, stepping her backward until he'd trapped her in the corner.

"Why, Annabelle?" he demanded. "Are you that desperate that you'd consider shackling yourself to that pompous arse?" His jaw tightened so hard that the muscles in his neck jumped. He held his hands against the wall at her shoulders to prevent her from running away. "Do you *want* to marry him?"

She shuddered at the thought. "Of course I don't!"

"Then why—"

"Because I don't have a choice! I have to marry." She shoved at his shoulder, but the aggravating mountain of a man refused to budge. "And you said no to my proposal, remember?"

"Do *not* blame me for this," he countered, his sapphire

eyes flashing like lightning at midnight. "You didn't have to agree to his suit."

"What other option do I have?" Frustration trembled in her voice.

"To not marry," he shot back. "And certainly not to consider marrying Bletchley."

He didn't understand what Glenarvon meant to her, or he'd never ask this of her. "He might be my only solution."

He shook his head with bewilderment, as if he simply couldn't fathom her. "You can make your home anywhere. You shouldn't have to marry a man like Bletchley simply because you're too damned stubborn to live anywhere else!"

At the unwitting callousness of his words, something snapped deep inside her, and she felt it shudder through her soul. Her hands drew into fists as anguish and frustration overwhelmed her.

"What do you know about *home*?" she forced out the cutting question, her resentment of his interference surging to the surface and barely controlled. "You—who grew up in the same house, sleeping in the same bed every night, surrounded by family who loved you. Where the worst that happened to you was being denied pudding at dinner because you'd played a prank on one of the footmen or didn't finish your studies." His handsome face blurred beneath the furious tears stinging in her eyes, but she couldn't relent. "Did your father ever lay a hand on you or your brothers and sister? Or your mother?"

Shocked understanding began to darken his face. He whispered hoarsely, "Belle, what you—"

"While you were in your nursery, watched over by your nanny, I was being woken in the middle of the night to flee in the darkness because my father had gambled and drunk away the rent money. *Again.* I remember nights sleeping in doorways and in abandoned buildings, going without food for days, clothes worn to rags...hearing rats gnawing in the walls, picking out maggots from the flour so we could make bread, feeling the lice—"

She choked as the memories came rushing back so intensely that they strangled the words in her throat, so fiercely that she could once more feel the lice crawling on her skin and itching in her hair. She shuddered and squeezed her eyes closed, as much to shut out the look of shock on his face as the horrible memories of that dark time.

"We never stayed anyplace more than a few months—fleeing creditors and people my father had cheated. When he had a job and was sober, we were fine. And then something would happen to make him drink again, to gamble, to steal. To hit my mother." She inhaled sharply. "And me."

She felt fury rise in him, his large body stiffening with it. "Why didn't your mother leave him?" he whispered. "Take you and go?"

She shook her head, not daring to open her eyes and see his pity. "Go where?" She stifled back a bitter laugh. "We had no relatives or friends who could help us, and what constable would ever arrest a husband for beating his wife?"

With her eyes closed, she couldn't see him, but she felt him. He stood perfectly still, close but not touching.

"It was always like that," she whispered. Now that the words were pouring out, she couldn't stop them. "Always moving, never enough to eat...Except once, when I turned eight. That year for my birthday there was cake. Mama gave me a new coat and shoes, and there was a doll in a frilly pink dress." She couldn't help smiling through the tears at the memory. "She was so clean and bright, with ribbons and lace, and real blond hair. I'd never seen anything as pretty as that doll. I sat on the floor of the dirty shed where we were living and did nothing all day but brush her hair, for hours and hours..." She sucked in a jerking breath. "When my father came home, he took all my presents and sold them. Including that doll."

"Belle." He cupped her face in his hands. She felt his long fingers trembling against her cheeks.

She opened her eyes and stared up at him. "But that was also the birthday when I met Lord Ainsley for the first time. He'd heard that Mama was living in the area, and since she used to work for him, he stopped by to visit. I had no idea then that meeting him would be my real gift, because two years later, when my father was in prison for theft and my mother died of fever, Lord Ainsley came for me and brought me here, where finally I was safe and warm, where there was always enough food and beds and—" She choked back a sob. Pained pierced her with each secret she revealed, but she couldn't stop. Not until he understood. "I thought I'd arrived in heaven."

A tear slid down her cheek. She clenched her teeth, furious at herself for being unable to stop it.

"So *don't* talk to me of home and what that means when you've always had one. Or how I should simply walk away from mine." Her hand swiped angrily at her cheek to wipe the tear away. "Because you don't know what you're talking about."

He stared at her silently, his eyes dark and his body tense. After that outburst and brutal chastisement, she expected him to simply turn around and walk away, to leave her to her own mess.

But he didn't retreat, remaining close enough that she

could feel the heat of him down her front, could smell that delicious scent of port and tobacco she'd already come to associate with him. And oh, the strength of him! It seeped from every inch of him, this man who had never backed down from a fight in his life.

She tried to push him away again, but frustratingly, he still wouldn't move. Instead, the aggravating devil had the spine to step even closer, to wrap his arms around her and pull her against him.

Her chest burned with desolation, and she gave a wretched cry. As she tried to wrench herself away, he held tight, and worse—the more she struggled, the tighter he held her, until she had no choice but to wrap her arms around his waist, no choice but to bury her face against his hard chest as the sobs tore from her.

"Shh, Belle," he whispered soothingly, his lips brushing against her temple. "You won't have to leave here, and you won't have to marry if you don't want to. We'll find another way for you to keep Glenarvon. I promise you. I'm not leaving here until we do."

"How?" she mumbled against his chest, foolishly clinging to the faint pulse of hope he stirred inside her.

"I don't know, but we will," he declared resolutely, shifting back only far enough to tilt her face up until she had to look at him. The steely determination in his eyes took her breath away. "I *will* find a way."

She nodded, unable to find her voice. She wanted to believe him, wanted to trust that the answer was that simple... Quinton Carlisle wished it, and fate made it happen.

But she knew better. She'd never been friends with fate.

CHAPTER SIX

One Week Later
(Three Weeks Until Belle's Birthday)

$\mathcal{B}$elle glanced out the drawing room window as another gentleman departed quickly from Glenarvon's front door. Her stomach knotted. "I have a bad feeling about this."

"Another gentleman arriving?" Lady Ainsley looked up from the desk where she was scratching out notes for the upcoming party.

"No." She frowned, suspicion niggling at her. "Another one leaving."

Something was definitely not right here. Lady Ainsley's insistence that Quinton and Robert be put in charge of greeting potential suitors was surely leading to nothing but trouble. They were supposed to have been interviewing the callers to suss out the men's intentions, sorting the blatant fortune hunters from the true gentlemen. But from Belle's count as she watched the men come and go, the two Carlisles were sending away nearly all the men who'd arrived. Today, she'd estimated that a dozen gentlemen had ridden up the drive to call on her. Although it couldn't be possible, she was certain she'd counted thirteen who'd left.

None of the departing men appeared to be happy. Including the last one, who turned to cast a dark scowl at the manor house before mounting his horse and riding away.

"A good sign, is it not?" The viscountess pushed her reading glasses up the bridge of her nose. "It means Quinton and Robert are doing their jobs."

"Perhaps." Or perhaps they were only adding to her headache.

And what a headache this past week had given her! With no other choice now but to marry, Belle had allowed Lady Ainsley to surreptitiously spread the information that her dowry was the estate and that she was looking for a husband. There was no mention of the birthday deadline, now only three weeks away, but there didn't need to be if the number of men who began to call on her was any indication of the scheme's success. Dressed in their finest, with hats in hands, they'd descended upon the estate like a swarm of locusts, where the two Carlisle brothers were waiting for them. Apparently, in ambush.

It was clear after only a few days that putting those two rascals in charge of approving suitors was like letting foxes guard the henhouse.

No—like a couple of foxes who refused to let the henhouse be built in the first place.

"It will all be fine." Lady Ainsley turned her attention back to the to-do list for the house staff in preparation for the party. "I trust Quinton to do the right thing."

Belle silently arched a dubious brow at that.

"After he has exhausted every other possible avenue," the dowager added beneath her breath.

Disheartened, Belle turned away from the window and began to pace the length of the drawing room. Oh, why couldn't Quinn have simply done what she wanted for once and accepted her proposal? Short of being given Glenarvon outright, it would have been the answer to her prayers.

Two weeks ago, she would have laughed at that notion. Married to Quinton Carlisle, of all men! She never would have countenanced such a thing. But now, not only would it be the solution to her dilemma, it might actually be pleasant to have Quinn for a husband.

And *that* realization nearly tripped her in mid-pace.

It was true. Although she was loath to admit it, at times the pest could be...enjoyable. During the past sennight, the most aggravating man in the world had become her friend and confidante, and her best ally in this inheritance mess.

She'd enjoyed spending time with him, playing chess in the evenings and talking long into the night, hearing stories about his wild youth with his brothers and all the pranks he'd pulled at university which nearly got him expelled. She enjoyed the habit she and Quinn had started of taking afternoon walks around the property and the village, when she confided her problems with running the estate and he offered sensible solutions. She'd even found herself looking forward to their debates over the news in the *London Times* during breakfast and respecting him for his mind.

Quinton Carlisle had a *mind*...Whoever would have thought it?

"If you keep pacing like that, my dear," Lady Ainsley called out, "we shall have to replace the rug."

Belle stopped where she was, halfway across the room,

and with a heavy sigh, she turned to face the viscountess. But her uneasy fidgeting couldn't be suppressed. Not today. Not with Quinton and Robert doing God only knew what downstairs. And certainly not since she was stuck spending the day inside with Lady Ainsley, planning out the last details of the party, which should have been a happy occasion but now filled her with dread.

What had originally been planned to celebrate Belle's birthday had now turned into a de facto engagement party, when Belle would have to announce the name of the man she'd chosen to marry. With only one week to spare, it was the latest moment when she could make her decision and still have time to hold a proper wedding in the parish church. Anything past that... well, it was the anvil or nothing, and if she waited that long, she feared she'd end up with nothing.

Unable to pace, she nervously bit at her thumbnail.

"And then we shall have to replace your thumb, as well."

She scowled and dropped her hand to her side.

"I think we can find enough oranges to have sugared orange peels for the refreshments table," Lady Ainsley mused almost to herself as she scratched out a note in her planning book. "Six dozen oranges, then?"

"Whatever you think best." Belle paused at the window to look down at the front drive, just in time to see yet another gentleman arriving.

"I think three cakes for the party, don't you?" Lady Ainsley commented and added another note to her list. "Lemon, cinnamon, and chocolate."

"Whatever you think best." She couldn't help craning her neck to take one last glance outside the window, hoping against hope that the Carlisle brothers had found a good husband for her. One who would let her run Glenarvon without interference.

"What *I* think best," Lady Ainsley repeated with a trace of pique, "is that I would like your input on these decisions. This is your party, Annabelle. It should be exactly as you want it."

"It will be." A lie. *None* of this was how she wanted it.

She began to pace again, not giving a fig about the rug.

She'd resigned herself to having to marry. She'd given up on a love match; now she simply hoped for an innocuous marriage that did no harm. Such a life wasn't at all what she wanted, but Glenarvon would be hers, which was more than her mother ever had. In that, at least, she should have been happy.

So why did she feel like crying?

"The musicians have already been hired." The viscountess ticked off another item on her list. "I've requested that they play several waltzes."

Belle wrung her hands as her heart began to race and her breathing grew shallow. With the passing of each day, it seemed more and more likely that she would end up with Sir Harold. Would that be so awful, all things considered? He wasn't someone dashing and strong like Quinton, but was it fair to compare them? After all, not every man had Quinn's knack for land management, his skill for dealing with tenants and villagers, his foresight with accounts and repair lists...his extraordinary ability to turn a kiss into heavenly bliss.

"Also the extra footmen to serve the trays of champagne when the announcement is made."

And then there was Glenarvon to worry about. A woman running an estate was far from the norm, but this place was her life and all she wanted. She couldn't imagine what her existence would become if she couldn't do that.

"Of course, there will scotch for the men and punch for the ladies."

Her heart thumped harder and faster with each quick step she paced across the room, as if the floor would open up and devour her if she stood still. What would she do if she could no longer run the estate? Other things would fill the void, certainly. Overseeing the household staff. Being hostess for parties and soirees. Having babies that weren't created in love or passion—

"What do you think, Annabelle?"

"I don't want to marry!" Blurting it out before she could stop herself, she gasped, and her hands flew up to cover her mouth as she stared at Lady Ainsley with mortification.

The viscountess froze, her quill in mid-scratch. Then she slowly looked up at Belle, and the look on her face— was that happiness? Or was the woman simply stunned into disbelief?

"You don't want to marry Sir Harold?" Lady Ainsley repeated in a whisper.

"No," Belle breathed out between her fingers.

The dowager rose slowly, a look of hopefulness lighting her face. Or perhaps it was alarm. "Then... whom do you wish to marry?"

"I don't," she admitted. Guilt overwhelmed her because she didn't want to wound the viscountess or have the woman think Belle was ungrateful for all she and Lord Ainsley had done for her.

And *that* was an undeniable look of disappointment as her wrinkled face fell. "Not anyone?" She paused, as if waiting to be contradicted. "Not *ever*?"

"I don't want to lose Glenarvon," Belle amended in a breathy whisper. "But I don't want to be forced into marriage, either."

She knew the prison a marriage could be. The moment a woman married, everything she possessed—including her body—became the property of her husband, for him to mete out affection or punishment as he saw fit. Including taking away her property. Including beating her, if she failed to do as he wanted. There was nothing the law or the Church would do to stop him.

It was silly, she supposed, how much she wanted in a marriage. Like something from a fairy tale, she wanted to love and be loved. She wanted to share Glenarvon with her husband and create a loving and happy home for their children, all of whom would be created and raised with love. She wanted a husband she respected, one who respected and cared for her in return.

Now all those dreams were slipping through her fingers.

"Your situation is far from ideal, I admit," Lady Ainsley said gently, setting her quill and glasses aside. "But many women marry because they seek property or position, or because they need the help of their husbands."

She shook her head. "I'm capable of running Castle Glenarvon myself."

Lady Ainsley crossed the room to her and took Belle's hands in hers, the affection and concern the viscountess held for her visible in her eyes. "You are very much capable of running this estate. No one could ever love this place more than you, my dear, and no one knows its heart and soul better than you." She paused, her expression softening. "But with whom will you share your success?"

Belle couldn't answer around the knot of emotion

choking her throat, because in her heart she knew the truth, that the only man she wanted to share it with was Quinn. He was the only one who understood how much work she put into running the estate, how much sweat and tears.

But he wouldn't be here. He was bound for America. Already her heart grieved at the impending loss of him.

Lady Ainsley cupped Belle's face. "A husband provides support in so many intangible ways. Without a husband, who will be there to laugh with you and cry with you, to share all your frustrations and all your joys?"

Who, indeed? Belle didn't doubt the veracity of Lady Ainsley's words. Just having Quinton here for the past sennight had eased her burden, giving her someone to talk with and to lean on for help. It made obvious a gaping hole in her life she didn't know existed until he was there, filling it.

She swiped at her eyes. Oh, the devil take him! Quinn always managed to cause problems for her, even when he wasn't in the room.

"You do not have to marry Sir Harold. You do not have to marry at all, if that is what you wish." With an empathetic but faint smile, the dowager placed a motherly kiss to Belle's forehead. "I will always love you and do the best for you that I can." Belle's heart leapt at Lady Ainsley's quiet concession... until the viscountess sadly shook her head. "But I cannot save Glenarvon for you if you do not."

Numbly, Belle nodded and blinked back her tears. She should be grateful for all that Lady Ainsley was offering, that she would be able to stay with her in the dower house in London and continue on as they had... lady and companion, the daughter and mother neither possessed. It was more than Belle should ever have had, given her past. But knowing how fortunate she was didn't lessen the sorrow over all she'd lose if she didn't marry.

So she was back to where she'd begun. Having to marry a man who didn't love her so she could stay in her home.

Lady Ainsley kissed Belle's cheek. "Do not lose hope yet, my dear. If I have my way, everything will work out well in the end. Time will bear it out."

But time was the one thing Belle didn't have.

"You will find a good man to marry, I know it." Lady Ainsley gave her a conspiratorial smile.

Belle returned her smile, even as her hopeless heart sank to the floor, not at all certain of that herself.

Shouts rang out from downstairs—male voices raised in anger, followed by the sounds of stomping boots and slamming doors. She exchanged a worried glance with Lady Ainsley.

Oh no.

The viscountess bit back an unladylike curse. "What have those two done now?"

They hurried downstairs toward the commotion, arriving in the entry hall just in time to see one of the gentlemen callers turn to shake a fist at Robert and Quinton as they followed the man toward the front door. The same man Belle had seen ride up less than fifteen minutes earlier. His face was nearly as scarlet as his fancy silk waistcoat.

He saw Lady Ainsley and straightened his spine with an expression of pure righteous indignation. "You—" He snatched his hat, gloves, and walking stick from Ferguson as the butler stoically held them out. Then he gestured angrily with his stick to indicate the two Carlisle men. "You would condone this—this *outrageous* behavior, my lady?"

Quinton and Robert stiffened in response. The amusement Belle thought she'd glimpsed on their faces when they'd entered the entry hall had vanished, replaced by hard-set jaws and narrowed gazes. Two nearly identical mountains of men as they stood shoulder to shoulder, their feet wide and their muscular arms folded across their chests.

Belle bit her bottom lip, worried that one wrong word from the visitor would get him pummeled before she could stop them.

Lady Ainsley imperiously lifted her brow, as if offended. "Sir, my nephews have *never* behaved outrageously in their lives!"

Belle nearly choked at that whopper of a lie. But Robert and Quinton simply exchanged silent glances, then returned their stares to the man.

"They are acting at my behest." The viscountess leveled that comment with all the authority of her position. Belle could almost feel the iciness in her voice, as well as the unspoken dare for the man to contradict her.

"Then you need to speak with them. The things they had the nerve to ask me!" He jabbed his stick at them, and Belle caught her breath, wondering which of the two Carlisle men would first let fly his fists. "About my intentions, my net worth...if I'd ever seek a divorce— Surely you didn't authorize *that*!"

The dowager's eyes flicked curiously to Quinton, then narrowed on their visitor. "Did you think I'd so easily hand over my companion to the first dandy who arrived at my doorstep with posies in hand?"

At her subtle accusation, the blood drained from his face. His lips parted, as if to fling back some cutting reply. Then he clamped his mouth shut, wisely thinking better of leveling an insult at the viscountess beneath the Carlisle brothers' watchful eyes. Except to trade glances, the two hadn't moved an inch during the exchange. Like life-size copies of the Colossus of Rhodes.

He stalked toward the door. "I came here to pay my respects to Miss Greene. I did *not* come here to be insulted." He flung open the door without waiting for Ferguson to come forward and stomped outside. "Good day!"

Quinton closed the door after him. "And good riddance."

Momentary silence fell over the entry hall, then Lady Ainsley blew out a hard sigh and shook her head. "What on *earth* did you two do to that man?"

Quinton shrugged. "Exactly as you asked of us."

"Keeping the wrong men away from Annabelle," Robert clarified.

Then both men folded their arms over their chests again and leaned back against the wall. Belle blinked. It was like seeing double.

"But that man wasn't here long enough for you to find out anything about him," the viscountess scolded.

Quinton shook his head. "He was here long enough to answer our questions about his intentions toward Belle."

"And about the state of his finances," Robert added stepping forward. "I know businessmen, Aunt Agatha. I'm one of them. So I know when a man is pretending to know more about financial matters than he actually does."

Lady Ainsley tossed up her hands. "You cannot fault a man for wanting to improve his lot in life through marriage!"

"No," Quinn replied. "But we *can* fault the man for not knowing what to do with the financial gain once he possesses it. And for exaggerating his current business interests and fortune."

"Lying," Robert corrected bluntly.

Quinn summarized quietly, "He wasn't worthy of Annabelle."

Belle's startled gaze darted to him, and their eyes met. He held her gaze for several long heartbeats, long enough for butterflies to flutter inside her. And not just at the dark flicker in his eyes as he stared at her hungrily, as if he wanted to do nothing more at that moment than pull her into the library and kiss her senseless.

No—it was the protection he was offering, however misguided, that filled her with warmth and happiness. She hadn't expected that. And she liked it. Far more than she should have.

"You asked the man about divorce." Utter bewilderment darkened the viscountess's face. "What does *that* have to do with whether he's a fortune hunter?"

"We asked if he could ever foresee a situation in which he would seek a separation or divorce from Belle," Robert clarified.

Their aunt stared at the two as if they'd just sprouted a third head between them. "Why in heaven's name would you ask him that?"

"Not just him. We've asked all the gentlemen that," Robert said. "A determinate test to judge their character."

"But divorce is nearly impossible to obtain," Lady Ainsley reminded them. "Especially if the wife protests, which I am certain Belle would do."

Belle wasn't so certain of that herself.

"But separation isn't." Quinton said quietly, his gaze returning to Belle, "Under the law, the estate would become his, and he's no longer shackled to a wife he never wanted in the first place."

"*Not* if it's contracted in the dower," Lady Ainsley reminded them. "And it will be. I'll make certain of it."

"Which was going to be the next question put to him," Robert informed them.

"'Would you sign a marriage settlement in which all of Miss Greene's property remains hers to oversee and the profits held in trust for her alone?'" Quinton's gaze never moved from her, and the warmth that his possessiveness had flared inside her was now downright blazing.

"But he didn't make it that far." Robert had the good sense to look sheepish beneath his aunt's imposing stare.

"Obviously," Lady Ainsley muttered.

"He did the same as all the other gentlemen when we put the question to him." Quinton tore his gaze away from Belle to answer his aunt, and Belle palpably felt the loss of its heat. "Adamantly swore he'd never petition to divorce her, no matter what happened between them—"

"Became righteously indignant that we'd dare ask such a thing—"

Instead of finishing his brother's sentence, Quinn hesitated. He looked at Robert before saying thoughtfully, "Except one."

"One?" Belle asked, unable to keep the dejection from her voice. They'd spent the entire week interviewing potential husbands, and they'd only found *one* man they'd deemed suitable for her? The warmth inside her chest vanished, replaced by a cold misery. With no other solution in sight to save Glenarvon except marriage, Belle didn't have much time left to find a good husband, and they'd wasted an entire week. "Who?"

"George Smalley."

"George..." She choked on the name. A freehold farmer

to the north of Braeburn, Mr. Smalley was a widower thrice over and over two decades Belle's senior. Her hands drew into helpless fists at her sides as she demanded, "Why him?"

"He's the only one so far who answered the question correctly. When we asked him if he would ever divorce you, he shrugged."

"He shrugged?" Lady Ainsley's shrill voice echoed through the entry hall in astonishment. "*That* was the correct answer—a *shrug*?"

Robert explained, "Or at least not to protest so vehemently what they would do in the unseen future. Any man who protests that much has certainly considered doing just that."

Lady Ainsley stared hard at Quinton. "And is that the *only* reason you've been chasing away the men who have come to call on Annabelle?"

The question hung in the air for several silent heartbeats before Quinn answered, "Yes."

The viscountess's eyes narrowed, as if she suspected he'd just lied to her.

But Belle could have told her he hadn't. He was doing exactly what his aunt had asked of him—to sort out the men who weren't fit for her. Unfortunately, Quinn's opinion of who would make her a proper husband set standards so impossibly high that few would ever be able to meet them.

"Stop asking those foolish questions, and stop chasing the gentlemen away," Lady Ainsley scolded. "We have two weeks until Belle has to announce her intended, one week after that to have her married." Despite her anger, her eyes glistened with tears at the prospect, and Belle's heart broke to see it. "I am doing everything I can to help her. Can you two say the same?"

Quinn clenched his jaw, remaining silent. There was no good answer to that question, and all of them knew it.

Lady Ainsley turned on her heel and began to climb the stairs. "Annabelle, come. We have an engagement party to plan." She shot an icy glare over her shoulder at her two nephews. "*If* we have anyone left to betroth you to."

Instead of following, Annabelle remained. So did Quinn, although Robert wisely excused himself to return to the library.

"Divorce?" Belle bit out, adding frustration to the riot of emotions swirling inside her. "You thought asking about *divorce* was a good way to find suitors for me?"

"I'm protecting you, Belle." His blue eyes were steely hard with resolve. "It's a valid question."

"It's a terrible thing to ask, and you know it. A question no man could answer properly." She gestured her hand at him. "And what about you, Quinton? If someone put that absurd question to you, what would *you*—"

She froze in mid-sentence as an impossible idea struck her.

He frowned with sudden concern, reaching out to take her elbow to steady her. "Are you all right?"

"That's it, that's the answer," she whispered, almost afraid to speak it aloud.

"What is?" he asked warily.

"Divorce." Her heart had been so beaten and bruised in the past few weeks over the idea of marriage that she'd never thought to consider the exact opposite solution. "You'll marry me and then divorce me. You said you wouldn't leave a wife behind. This takes care of that." For the first time in four years, the weight of the world lifted from her shoulders, and she felt as if she could breathe again. "The will stipulated that I had to marry in order to receive Glenarvon. It never said I couldn't divorce and keep it."

He shook his head. "We cannot."

Desperation colored her voice, but she simply didn't care. This was the answer she'd been hunting for weeks to find—years, in fact. "I know it's not ideal. But it could be done if—"

"*No.*"

The force of that single word silenced her cold. She stared at him, her heart stopping as all the hope she'd felt only moments before ripped from her.

"Divorce takes an act of Parliament," he bit out. "You know that. And it's only granted on grounds of adultery."

She stepped back from him as the familiar hopelessness returned, this time so fiercely that she pressed her fist against her chest to keep from shuddering.

"I don't care," she whispered. She was now despairing enough to consider going through hell in order to remain here in heaven.

"I do." Heaving out a breath, he shook his head. "Damnation, Belle! What you're asking of me . . ."

His broad shoulders slumped in frustration. For the first time, she realized with a piercing clarity that he was just as aggrieved by all this as she was. Especially if he meant what he'd said about wanting to protect her.

But that didn't solve her problem.

"It would put you into an impossible situation," she finished quietly, dropping her gaze to the floor. She didn't have the strength to look at him.

"Both of us," he acknowledged firmly.

"But if we—"

"I won't *ever* get a divorce, Annabelle," he ground out,

silencing her. "I won't have either of us publicly labeled as an adulterer, no matter that we both know the truth. Six years ago, your reputation was ruined partly because of me. I won't allow that to happen again. Certainly not like this."

Her heart beat so hard that she winced with each jarring thud. Leave it to Quinton to be noble. She would have found it endearing if it didn't leave her once more without a solution. "But it's the only way left," she whispered.

"Not the only way." He stepped into the hall and bellowed toward the library, "Robert! I'm leaving for a few hours. Take over the interviewing, will you?"

Robert's muffled reply was inaudible, but Belle was certain that whatever he'd said was not charitable.

"You're a businessman, for God's sake!" Quinn shouted back. "Sniffing out fortune hunters is surely the domain of a businessman."

Belle's eyes widened. She clearly heard Robert's reply to *that*.

But Quinn only laughed and snatched up his gloves, hat, and a satchel sitting on the floor beside the side table, where he kept them since his arrival, to make escaping on afternoon rides across the countryside more convenient. Then he headed toward the door.

"I won't marry you, Belle, just to leave you behind. No man in his right mind would do that." As if to prove his point, he paused to rake his gaze over her, and heat seared her everywhere he looked. "But if this divorce loophole exists, then there must be other solutions, ones we haven't thought of yet."

Through the open door, Belle could see Sir Harold's curricle pull to a stop in the drive. He threw the ribbons to one of the grooms who came bounding up at his arrival, then jumped to the ground. When he saw Belle, he smiled, only for it to fade when he realized that Quinn stood next to her.

Quinton threw a resolute glance back at her before leaving. "Solutions which do *not* involve you marrying and losing control of Glenarvon."

Oblivious to Sir Harold's irritated scowl, Quinn slapped him good-naturedly on the back as they passed on the front steps.

* * *

Quinn glanced around at the local solicitor's office in Braeburn, the same village where Belle wanted to improve the school and hire a doctor. He wondered if she shouldn't first start with hiring a new solicitor.

The tiny, first-floor room was filled nearly from floor to rafters and overrun with piles of papers, stack of books, and ledgers in all states of mid-use, with a quill and inkwell located near each, although most likely half of those dozen or so inkwells hadn't seen a drop of fresh ink in years. All of them possessed a light tracing of dust to prove it. Maps covered what stretches of walls weren't blocked by pieces of heavy furniture too large for the room. A globe perched precariously free of its stand on the corner of the desk. Quinn couldn't be certain from his vantage point, but he thought he saw a Scottish claymore leaning behind the tall cabinet in the corner.

Which proved he'd been right in leaving Belle behind at Glenarvon. The damnable woman most likely would have used the bloody thing on *him*, if given half a chance.

He didn't blame her. He must have seemed like Lucifer himself to refuse her after she'd seized upon the loophole of divorce. But for God's sake, what other choice did he have? He'd nearly laughed aloud at that ludicrous notion, until he'd seen how serious she was about it.

But he was just as serious in refusing.

He hadn't lied to her. He would protect her. He would do anything he could in order to keep her safe and in control of Glenarvon, but he wouldn't marry her only to leave her. Intelligent, beautiful, and strong, with a kind heart the size of Scotland and a laugh that danced on the air like music—how could a man give that up once he possessed it?

In the past sennight, since the night Belle proposed, he'd let himself wonder what marriage to her would be like. Not those ridiculous propositions she'd made, but a *real* marriage. The kind his parents had. To spend days working the estate by her side, evenings talking quietly before the fire, and nights in each other's arms...It would be just as wonderful as he imagined.

Which was the problem. Because anything that wonderful was bound to lead to love. And love led to grief. *Always.*

The door opened.

Quinn rose to his feet as a paunchy, balding man in a brown wool jacket and matching waistcoat, knee breeches, and buckled shoes thirty years out of fashion shuffled into the messy office. Spectacles perched on his nose beneath a tricornered hat. Taken as a whole, he looked like an ideal banker for the late King George.

"No need, no need!" He gestured at Quinn to remain seated and walked the only clear path across the floor to circle behind his desk. "We don't stand on formalities here in Braeburn. Of course, we're too small a village to stand on anything!" He laughed at his own joke and introduced himself. "John Bartleby."

Quinn held out his hand in greeting. "Quinton Carlisle."

"Ah, the infamous Lord Quinton! All the village is abuzz about you and your brother. My apologies for not calling at Castle Glenarvon to welcome you to our little stretch of the borderlands." He leaned forward to shake Quinn's hand, then settled back into his chair, drawing a groan of protest from the wood frame beneath him. "It isn't often we get visitors of any kind in Braeburn, let alone a duke's brother—one set on voyaging to America, no less! And what be your plans, then?"

With a grin, Quinn reached into the satchel he'd brought with him and withdrew the bottle of Bowmore he'd liberated from Aunt Agatha's hidden stash in the music room, this one tucked within the pianoforte. The house was turning into a veritable treasure hunt of the best kind.

"Right now, I plan to raise a glass with one of Braeburn's most-respected residents." He set the bottle onto the only clear spot on the cluttered desk. "Unless you think it's too early in the day for a glass of fine scotch whisky."

"As I said," Bartleby commented as he examined the name on the bottle, then reached into a nearby cabinet to find two clean glasses hidden within, "we don't stand on formalities here."

Quinn grinned and splashed two fingers' worth into each glass. Braeburn was quickly growing on him.

"Your plans, then?" Bartleby pressed as he raised the glass to take a large swallow. "Forgive my curiosity, but it isn't often we get such interesting visitors to our High Street. Gives us the chance for vicarious living."

He nearly told the man not to bother, especially given the current confused state of his life. Instead, he settled back in his chair, prepared to spend all afternoon racing the man to the bottom of the bottle, if necessary, to find out what he needed in order to save Belle.

"I'm sailing to Charleston in a few weeks." He smiled, watching as Bartleby took another sip while he had yet to touch his own drink. "I've an offer in for a patch of land there, to grow rice and indigo."

"Ah, good! Very good." The solicitor smiled appreciatively at the quality of the scotch. "Good land, then?"

"Rich bottomland along the Ashley River."

Quinn took a small swallow of whisky, seeking comfort in the golden liquid. Bartleby's innocent curiosity served only to remind him that he needed to leave soon, or Asa Jeffers would have to sell the land to someone else. And he would break his promise to his father. He should have left two weeks ago, in fact.

Bartleby shook his head. "'Fraid I can't help you with anything in the colonies regarding your property."

"I'm here for local matters, actually."

"That's a different matter entirely, then." The man smiled, pleased to be of help. "What services can I provide to you, Lord Quinton?"

Quinn refilled the man's glass. "I'm curious about Annabelle Greene's inheritance from my great uncle, the late Lord Ainsley."

"Ah, protecting her, are you?" Bartleby leaned back in his chair with a knowing smile. "We're all quite fond of her—a good and kind lass, even if her choice in dress is a bit... unconventional at times."

Good Lord. Was there no one who hadn't seen Belle dressed in men's clothing? He answered casually with a patient smile, "She is unconventional, I'll admit."

"Yet we all think highly of her. I, myself, think of her

with as much fondness as I do my sisters." He gestured his glass at Quinn. "You must carry the same affection for her yourself."

Quinn grimaced inwardly. The affection he carried for Annabelle was far from sisterly. "So you understand my concern. Are you familiar with the terms of the will?"

"Of course! I was the one who helped the late Lord Ainsley fifteen years ago when he wrote it."

There! There it was. The reason he'd come here this afternoon with Aunt Agatha's best scotch in hand. If anyone could find a way to help Belle, it was Bartleby.

"The stipulation was my idea. Even then I knew marriage was the right path for her." The solicitor smiled proudly, and Quinn resisted the urge to plow his fist into the man's face in retribution for what he'd inadvertently done to Belle. "Glenarvon isn't a demanding property to manage, but estate oversight isn't fit for a woman's gentler sensibilities."

Quinn remembered how Annabelle had gotten into the mud with the men at the irrigation ditch and fought back a smile. No gentler sensibilities there.

He toasted Bartleby's legal abilities, knowing the man wouldn't notice the angry contempt behind it. "A fine inheritance clause, from what I understand."

"Indeed!" His chest puffed with pride. "Quite a legal maneuver, I must say."

"But my family has an attorney who swears that all legal clauses have loopholes." He casually offered the dare to be proven wrong. "Surely, even your clause has one."

"Ah yes." He nodded, and Quinn's heart skipped with hope. "A very large one, indeed."

Quinn leaned forward. "Which is?"

"*Was.* The loophole died with the late viscount," Bartleby corrected with a wave of his finger, the unsteadiness of his hand showing the immediate effects of the scotch. He smiled, taking Quinn deeper into his confidence. "The late viscount *was* the loophole!"

"Because only he could change it," Quinn supplied glumly.

The solicitor hesitated, his eyes gleaming, as if he had some great secret poised on his lips. Then he said, "Exactly."

A suspicion nagged Quinn that Bartleby had been about to say something else. "So there's no method for voiding the inheritance requirement?"

"None. Rest assured, she will be married." Then he laughed as a new thought struck him. "Which I'm certain Sir Harold Bletchley thanks God for with every day that passes closer to her birthday!"

Quinn didn't find that amusing. "So you've heard that Sir Harold Bletchley is courting her?"

"It's a *very* small village." He chuckled in amusement, the movement straining at the buttons of his waistcoat.

Quinn refilled both glasses although he'd barely touched his, then eased back in his chair as if they were two old friends who imbibed together regularly.

"I've heard rumors," he ventured casually with the blatant lie. He hadn't heard one whisper, but he knew men like Bletchley and what motivated them. "Grumblings from workers who aren't being paid, merchants whose bills are refused...Kinnybroch is in debt."

"Not just in debt," Bartleby informed him with a conspiratorial air, brought on by too much whisky. Then he countered in his attempt to better Quinn, but only letting slip more information than he realized, "Mortgaged to the rafters!"

Quinn wasn't surprised. But if Bletchley was that far in debt, it was worse than he and Robert suspected. He forced a scoff of disbelief to lure more information from the solicitor. "On whose authority?"

Bartleby leaned forward across the desk to confide, "I'm not just the resident lawyer but also a district officer for the Bank of England, per recognized right of the crown." He raised his glass in toast. "To King George!"

"King George," Quinn toasted back, starkly reminded that he sat in the middle of the borderlands where allegiance to the English king was still questionable.

Bartleby held up a finger for dramatic effect, and Quinn fought to keep from rolling his eyes. Then he reached down to his desk drawer, riffled through it, and withdrew a sheet of paper. He placed it onto a pile of ledgers covering the desk.

"What's this?" Quinn frowned.

"An advertisement." Bartleby grinned at it as if sharing a secret prize. "For Kinnybroch!"

Quinn lowered his eyes to the small sketch of the house and description of the property, followed by details of how to make contact to ... Mr. John Bartleby, Esquire, Official Conveyancer for County Cumbria.

He crooked a brow. Apparently, Bartleby *was* Braeburn Village.

The solicitor leaned forward across the desk and tapped a finger on the paper. "The bank gave notice of foreclosure last year," Bartleby confided, "but as the accountant for Kinnybroch and the Crown's official conveyancer—"

"Also the bank agent," Quinn reminded. "And the solicitor."

Bartleby's eyes shined with pride at his arrangement. "As

all four, I agreed with myself to give Sir Harold a reprieve from the auction block, confident that he would marry Miss Greene and gain the money to repay his debt." He finished off his glass. "So there you are. The perfect match!"

Quinn blinked, having lost the thread of this churning, whisky-confused conversation. Yet he was just as certain that the man would talk in the same broad leaps of thought if he were sober. "Pardon?"

"The perfect match," he repeated, as if it were obvious. "Marry each other, and all is right. But if she doesn't marry Sir Harold, they both lose their estates!"

"Sounds more like the perfect irony," Quinn muttered, glancing down at the advertisement.

"But of course they will marry," the eccentric man hurried on, kicking his feet up onto the corner of his desk. He waved his hand in the air. "She'll marry him, he'll marry her... and we'll all have a grand time dancing at their wedding!"

"Yes," Quinn forced out. "A grand time."

"And if they don't... Well, make an offer to pay the mortgage, and you can have your own estate." He picked up the advertisement and tucked it safely back into the desk drawer, then shook his head. "Ah, but you're bound for America, aren't you? What would you want with a place like Kinnybroch?"

What, indeed? Except that Glenarvon's worth was similar to Kinnybroch's, and if Belle didn't marry, the Church might very well offer it up on the auction block next to Kinnybroch.

That stirred a desperate idea. "I'm curious. What amount do you expect the winning bid to fetch?"

"Twenty thousand pounds." He reached for the bottle and

refilled his own glass. "Of course, that's only if it goes to auction, you understand."

"Of course," Quinn repeated, trying to hide his stunned reaction at the sizable amount. Twenty thousand pounds... *Good Lord.* The momentary fantasy he had of buying back Glenarvon for Belle vanished like smoke.

Even if he wasn't set on America, buying Glenarvon would still take every penny he had—and ten thousand more. He knew only one person with that kind of money. And turning to Sebastian for help when he'd made such a point of leaving to become his own man, free from his brother's duke-shaped shadow, was almost as distasteful as letting Belle marry Bletchley.

Quinn tossed down the rest of his scotch in a gasping swallow to chase away the helpless frustration nipping at his heels.

"To Castle Glenarvon." Bartleby lifted his glass in a belated toast to follow Quinn's lead in finishing off his glass. But he stopped himself, his hand raised halfway to his lips. A melancholy expression flitted across his face. "Although only for a few short weeks more, I'm afraid."

"Miss Greene plans on keeping the estate." One way or another, he thought grimly. "If she marries"—and he was doing his damnedest to make certain *that* wouldn't happen—"under the law, her husband cannot mortgage nor sell any land held as part of the dower." He was certain that Aunt Agatha would have a marriage contract drawn up to keep it safely away from both her husband and any heir of his who might turn on her.

"You are correct, sir." Bartleby raised a finger for emphasis as he noted, "*Post hoc, ergo propter hoc* is fallacious, of course, yet *ergo hoc sequitur quod* does occur, indeed!"

Quinn blinked blankly as the man laughed half-drunkenly at his own play on words. For the only time in his life, he wished he would have paid more attention to Latin lessons at Oxford. "Thus then," he translated from the far dark corners of his brain, "after something...follows something..."

"Therefore, this follows that!" He lifted his glass in a happy toast to Latin, then caught Quinn's bewildered stare. "Under the law, as well as Church doctrine," he explained patiently, "the wife becomes the property of her husband. *Ergo hoc sequitur quod*...her property becomes his."

"Not if she doesn't give her permission." He knew Belle well enough to know that she would rather die than sign over her home.

"Inconsequential, in my experience." Bartleby waved away his argument. "Even the most independent-minded woman eventually sees the folly of her ways and succumbs to her husband's wishes."

Quinn thought of the women in his family. Bartleby had never been married to the likes of one of those independent-minded women if he thought succumbing was a natural evolution of marriage.

"You don't know Miss Greene very well," Quinn muttered.

Bartleby laughed. "Does any man ever truly know a woman?"

In the past sennight, Quinn had come to know Belle quite well. The woman she'd become was simply amazing.

And one in desperate need of his help.

He reached into his jacket breast pocket and withdrew several bank notes. "I want to hire you, Bartleby."

The sight of the blunt instantly sobered him. "As I said, sir, I cannot help with—"

"To find a legal loophole in that clause you helped Lord Ainsley write into his will."

His face paled, but his eyes stayed on the money. "'Fraid it cannot be undone. I wrote it to avoid all loopholes."

"Divorce," Quinn bit out.

The man blinked. "Pardon?"

"Divorce is a loophole, isn't it? If Belle marries a man who agrees to not protest a divorce and contracts the estate into her dower."

"Well…I…." For once, the solicitor was at a loss for words. "I cannot imagine anyone who would *willingly*… And—and then the Church, of course…"

"But it is possible," Quinton pressed. "And she would get to keep Glenarvon."

Bartleby paled. "Yes, I suppose she would."

"If that loophole exists, then there must be others." Quinn placed half the notes onto the middle of the cluttered desk. "Find one."

"I—I cannot guarantee anything," he stammered out. "In fact, I doubt I can find—"

"But I'm sure you'll try." He set another note on top the stack. "Hard."

"Of course, sir."

Quinn nodded toward the money. "Failing that," he added, putting down another note, "then I want you to find out how to go about buying the estate back from the Church. Who will be responsible for assuming responsibility for it." Another note. "And how to go about approaching the man to purchase it." One last note. "Understand?"

"Very well, sir."

Quinn had no doubt that he did. But as he settled back in his chair and began to return the remaining notes to his jacket pocket, a new concern struck him. "It's my understanding that Lord Ainsley put in that marriage stipulation in order to protect Annabelle from her father."

The man hesitated. "From Marcus Greene, yes."

"Find him." He placed one last note onto the stack. "I want to know where he is." The *very* last thing Belle needed right then was for her father to arrive on Glenarvon's doorstep and cause even more problems for her.

"Yes, sir." Bartleby reached for the stack of blunt.

Quinn raised his glass to his lips. He wasn't any more optimistic about finding a solution now than when he'd stalked out of Glenarvon. But at least now the cogs were in motion. And when it came to Annabelle, he would take his victories wherever he could get them.

CHAPTER SEVEN

One Short Week Later
(Only Two Weeks Until Belle's Birthday)

$\mathscr{B}$elle stepped out of the predawn shadows at the edge of the pond and breathed a long sigh, expelling all the pent-up tension she'd carried on her shoulders for the past two weeks.

Since Quinn and Robert arrived, she hadn't been able to sneak away for her usual evening swims, instead having to remain at the house to help Lady Ainsley with hostess duties before dinner. So after yet another restless night, when there was no point in lying in bed any longer and trying for sleep that wouldn't come, she'd decided to selfishly enjoy the peace and quiet of a dawn swim before her day began. Before she had to face Lady Ainsley's plans to marry her off. Before she had to deal with all the estate's ongoing problems.

And before she had to suffer the continuous exasperation that was Quinton Carlisle.

Despite Lady Ainsley's close watch, the audition process

for future husbands—and truly, wasn't that what it had turned into?—was off to a less than auspicious start. After the first week, the score was Gentlemen Callers 2, Carlisle Brothers 28. Quinton was resolved to protect her, yet as equally resolved to never marrying her himself. And they had yet to find a way for her to keep Glenarvon except through marriage.

Her only consolation was knowing that Glenarvon would be hers and that she would never have to leave her home. Instead of being relieved, though, she felt trapped.

She removed her half boots and stockings, then walked to the edge of the pond to dip a bare toe hesitantly into the water to test it. A weary sigh escaped her. If only she could test the temperature of men this way, how much easier her life would be!

She reached behind her back to unfasten her dress—

"So you ventured out of the library," a deep voice drawled behind her. "I didn't think that was possible."

Quinton. She rolled her eyes. Of all the people to interfere with her one moment of solitude... "Books don't sneak up on people uninvited," she threw back pointedly.

He gave her a half smile as he walked down the sloping bank toward her. "Then invite me to swim with you."

She shot him her best ice-cold glare, knowing the answer before she even asked. "Will you behave yourself?"

His smile blossomed into a full-out grin. "Have I ever?"

"No," she answered earnestly and reached again for the back of her dress. "So you'd better go back to the house." She'd come here for a swim, and she wasn't going to let him stop her from taking this bit of solace. "After all," she muttered dryly, "you have a herd of husbands to prepare for."

"I wouldn't have to if you gave up this notion of marriage."

"You're right," she agreed with a heavy sigh. Her fingers worked free the half dozen buttons down her back. "You're *not* behaving yourself."

"Then I'll keep misbehaving until you come to your senses."

"What other choice do I have?" she challenged. "You'd rather I remain unmarried and lose Glenarvon?"

"I'd rather you be happy." His voice was quiet on the morning air, curling around her in the blue-gray shadows with its sudden seriousness. "Wherever you live."

Her throat tightened with emotion. "Now you're playing dirty."

Widening his stance, he crossed his arms over his chest, in his best impersonation of an unmovable mountain. "Whatever it takes, Annabelle."

Her shoulders sagged as the suffocating frustration she'd been living under once more settled over her. The moment of peace she'd hoped to have vanished like the morning fog. "I don't want to argue about this anymore." Shaking her head, she freed the last button and let her bodice sag loose. "So unless you've found a way out of this for me, there's nothing more to talk about."

She pulled down her sleeves, the bodice dropping around her waist and leaving her modestly covered in her stays and shift from the waist up.

His eyes flared, and his voice grew uncharacteristically hoarse as he demanded, "What are you doing?"

She paused, and beneath the curious warmth of his attention, a knot of nervousness tied in her stomach. But something deep inside her thrilled to it, too, that she'd caught him by surprise and inverted whatever bluestocking—and false—notions he held about her. She might be forced into marriage, but she certainly wasn't a mouse. And she'd never wanted to prove that to anyone more than she did at that moment to Quinton.

She forced down her rising nervousness and casually shrugged a shoulder. As if she removed her clothes in front of men all the time. "Undressing." *And hoping to make you leave.*

But when he didn't move, she gathered her courage, resigned what little dignity she had left, and dropped her dress to the grass around her bare feet.

"Annabelle, stop." He ran a shaking hand through his blond hair and looked away.

He was…*nervous*? She gave a soft laugh of disbelief. "I'm surprised that you're offended by the sight of an undressed woman."

"I'm not offended," he assured her. Then, as if to prove it, he let his gaze travel languidly over her. Everywhere he looked, heat prickled over her skin. "Quite the opposite, in fact," he murmured, and she felt a ribbon of heat slowly thread itself through her, from her breasts down to between her legs. "I'm only concerned about your reputation."

She laughed at the absurdity of that. Her life as she'd known it was ending, and he was worried about her *reputation*? Not one of the gentlemen calling on her cared whether she behaved properly, not as long as Glenarvon remained in her dowry. It would take more than getting caught taking a morning swim—even a naked one—to run them off. "My reputation be damned!"

Not caring if she'd shocked him with her outburst—good if he was!—she untied the front lacings of her stays and let them fall away to join the dress at her feet. Lifting her chin in defiance, she reached her hand up to the shoulder of the shift, preparing to push it down and remove even that last bit of clothing if she had to in order to chase him away...although she sent up a silent prayer that she wouldn't have to. Not in front of those blue eyes which now stared at her as hungrily as a tiger contemplating the best way to devour a gazelle.

"I'm going swimming, just as I always do. So go away if it bothers you." Her fingers trembled as they slipped daringly beneath the neckline of her shift. "If not, then..."

He crooked a brow at that, and she could read on his face the question of whether she was about to issue an invitation to join her for her swim. Oh, she should do just that! It would serve him right to have all his preconceived ideas about her destroyed.

She would enjoy it, too. God help her, even now her heart raced beneath his intense gaze, staring at her with such obvious arousal that she shivered from the heat of him. To have the full attention of a man like him on her, to know that he wanted her as much as he'd wanted those London ladies with their Parisian silks and well-practiced flirtations—

And destroy what little dignity she had left.

No matter how tempting, she wasn't ready yet to go quite that far. She still had her pride, albeit a dwindling amount of it each unmarried day that drew nearer to her birthday, and she wasn't willing to cast it aside. Not even for Quinton Carlisle.

"Then turn around," she finished, her shoulders sagging.

Blowing out a frustrated breath, he turned his back to her and looked instead at the cover of thick bushes and trees surrounding the pond.

She slipped out of her shift and dived quickly into the pond, the cold water engulfing her heated body and quenching the fires he'd started beneath her skin. With her quiet strokes through the water rippling the mirror-like surface, she swam out several yards as she always did, to that place where she could just barely reach the bottom of the pond with her toes and the water cooled up to her neck.

He turned around then to watch her.

"You should leave now," she told him, her voice quiet on the soft morning air.

He shook his head. "I'm staying until your birthday."

That wasn't what she meant, but her belly tightened into a knot of gratitude just the same. Quinn was irritating and bothersome, but he was also her ally. Of a sort.

"My wedding, you mean," she corrected, hiding the bitterness in her voice by dipping beneath the surface, then rising to smooth back her wet hair.

"Your birthday," he countered firmly, "by which time we'll have discovered a way for you to keep Glenarvon without having to marry."

The conviction behind his words showed her in spades how much he'd matured since the last time she'd seen him. The brash man she remembered who thought he could prove his manliness by cutting a swathe through London by drinking, fighting, and bedding every merry widow who smiled at him was gone, and in his place stood a man of resolve and ambition.

She stared at him through droplets of water clinging to her lashes. It wasn't hope that now warmed her belly and tickled at the backs of her knees. But something just as good.

He bent down to yank off his boot and dropped it to the grass beside her discarded dress.

"What are you doing?" she demanded, a prickling unease rising inside her.

He reached for the second boot. "Going for a swim."

"But you can't!" she protested with a soft gasp. "It's scandalous!"

He sent her a lazy grin. "My reputation be damned," he repeated, throwing her words back at her as he unbuttoned his waistcoat.

Fuming to hide the rush of nervousness, she slapped her hand on the water's surface. "Don't you dare!"

Ignoring her, he shrugged away his waistcoat and let it fall to the ground.

"Fine," she bit out, forcing herself not to care that he was undressing. Not one whit! "When we're found together like this, you'll be forced to marry me after all, and all my problems will be solved."

He drawled in a deep voice that wound a ribbon of heat all around her, even in the cold water, "Have to be caught together first." He pulled off his neck cloth and let it trail away to the ground. His eyes locked with hers across the surface of the pond. "And I don't see anyone in sight to catch us, do you?"

Anger flared through her. "You scoundrel!"

His only reply was a slow, wolfish grin.

She slammed her mouth closed. Oh, this was all her fault! She should never have agreed to let him help her find a husband, should never have proposed to him—she was mad to have thought of it, madder still to think she could trust him.

Yet when he stripped his shirt off over his head, she watched shamelessly. Her eyes traced over the hard muscles of his shoulders and along the trail of golden hair that dusted his chest and down across the ripples of his stomach, to disappear at his—*oh my*.

Working on the estate, she'd seen many shirtless men before, but never one who looked as mesmerizing as Quinton. Not just muscles, not just the golden look of him in the fading shadows, but *all* of him drew her, exactly as he had six years ago for that kiss beneath the roses. Exactly as he had last week among the ruins for something far more than only a kiss. And just as he did now, despite her knowing better.

With a crook of his brow, he silently dared her to keep watching as he reached for the fall of his trousers. Her breath caught in her throat at his audacity, but a throbbing blend of tempting curiosity and tingling excitement jolted through her as she watched him loosen the first button—

Dear God, *what* was she doing? With a gasp, she spun around and squeezed her eyes shut.

His laughter rang out across the quiet dawn. Humiliated anger burned in her cheeks. Oh, blast him, blast him, *blast him*! God had *never* created a more antagonizing creature.

A loud splash echoed against the trees as he dove into the water. She didn't dare turn to look, no matter how much she wanted to. Her heart pounded furiously at the soft splashing as he swam up behind her.

All kinds of sensations swirled through her at knowing he was standing right behind her in the water, as naked as she was...nervousness tinged with excited anticipation, an electric giddiness that left her light-headed, a craving to be kissed and knowing that if he slipped his arms around her, she wouldn't refuse. But not one of those emotions was embarrassment. Having him here with her like this, surrounded by the stillness of the pond and the blue mountains rising in the distance as the shadows of night faded into the golden hues of sunrise, felt *right*.

"Lucifer's balls, it's cold!"

She bit her lip to keep from laughing.

"Good God!" he exclaimed. "How can you stand this?"

She looked at him over her shoulder, a sly smile playing at her lips. "Can't handle a little cool water?"

"*Cool* water?" He grumbled, "There's an ice flow near the bushes!"

"Southerner," she mocked, fighting back a laugh.

He chuckled, the deep sound rippling to her through the water and tickling at her bare back. "If you can stand it," he declared, although his voice lacked conviction, "then I can stand it."

And also standing awfully close for a naked man. But she didn't have the willpower to step away. Not with the way her heart raced at having him so close. It was wholly improper, downright scandalous... and too thrilling to stop.

"Don't worry," she teased, despite her nervousness. For once she'd turned the tables on him and was enjoying it immensely. "I'll let you know when your lips turn blue."

"Well then." He drawled playfully as he stepped forward and slipped his arms around her waist beneath the water, "How can any man resist such a welcoming invitation as that?"

She gasped at the unexpected contact, sucking in a deep breath. His mouth lowered against her bare shoulder.

"Mmm...mermaid," he mumbled against her skin. "My favorite kind of seafood."

She laughed. Quinn was always a charmer, even when wet up to his ears.

Then his mouth brushed back and forth across her

shoulder, sending her heart pounding as he took increasingly bolder kisses.

She tensed in his arms. The playful teasing between them had instantly changed. An electric throbbing blossomed between her legs when he brushed her wet hair aside to nibble at the back of her neck. When his hands spread out across her belly, heat flared through her and curled her toes into the mud at the bottom of the pond.

He took another step forward until his body pressed against hers. Her back rested against his bare chest, and her bottom nestled against his... *oh my*.

"Annabelle," he murmured as his hand slid over her hip.

Beneath his caresses, the world and all her problems disappeared, until she no longer cared about anything except the wicked sensation of his warm hands on her water-chilled skin.

Yet she felt compelled to protest, albeit extremely weakly. "Maybe we shouldn't..."

"Can't help it," he admitted in a husky murmur, keeping himself pressed against her. "You're too tempting."

She was *tempting*? Impossible. Yet he didn't back away, didn't stop his hand from trailing down her bare leg—

She jumped, startled at the boldness of his touch.

"Relax," he murmured reassuringly against the back of her neck.

Relax? Was he daft? How on earth was she supposed to relax?

Yet she exhaled a deep breath and willed herself to unwind the tension spiraling tightly inside her. But the churning nervousness was simply too strong to will away, the growing tingle at her core too insistent to ignore. Each breath she expelled emerged as a tremulous shiver.

"It's only a touch, nothing more," he promised, although the husky purr of his voice curling through her was far from convincing. "We're up to our necks in ice-cold water. The last thing I'll be able to do is ravish you. Although"—he swirled his tongue along the outer curl of her ear and drew a hot shudder from her—"I'd be happy to try."

Oh, *that* certainly wasn't putting her at ease! "Quinton, be serious."

"I am. When I kissed you all those years ago," he whispered, his hand on her stomach tracing tantalizing patterns of seduction across her bare skin, "I had no idea that you would grow into such a temptress."

Leaving her light-headed and tingling, all her senses alive, the world around her spun into a swirling mass of contradictions. The heat of his lips on her cold skin...the warmth of bodies pressing together beneath the cold water...the silence of the wild glen around them while her heartbeat roared deafeningly.

And most of all, there was the contradiction that was Quinn himself. The pest who had always sent her pulse racing with anger was now a man who sent it cartwheeling with desire.

"Have I truly become that woman?" she whispered, all of her on pins and needles in anticipation of his answer. "Am I at all what you expected?"

A small pause..."No," he admitted quietly.

A stinging pain pierced her—

"You're more beautiful than I ever imagined."

She closed her eyes, unable to keep back a smile of happiness. Oh, he was still a charmer, through and through; it was in his nature. But only Quinn could utter such a piece of sheer flattery and actually mean it.

"Why does that surprise you so?" he murmured.

"Because no one has ever told me that before." That the first man to do so was Quinton Carlisle—she could scarcely believe it.

"You deserve to be told how beautiful you are. How brilliant and special." His hand caressed in long, slow strokes along her outer thigh as he murmured, "Especially by the man you marry."

She trembled and struggled to keep her wits through the delicious fog of wanton sensations he swirled inside her. God help her. She was losing the war already, and the battle had barely begun! "That...doesn't signify."

His lips caressed at her temple. "Then what does?"

"Mutual respect," she whispered. During the past few weeks, she'd resigned herself to her situation. A loveless marriage was inevitable. Now she only hoped it would be painless. "Friendship, caring..."

"And desire," he rasped hotly. "Never forget about that."

He drove her to distraction as his fingertips poised at the edge of her feminine curls yet teasingly refused to slip lower, to that aching place that now craved his touch. Her heart pounded like a drum, half in longing for his hand to drift lower, half in fear that it wouldn't. "That's not important."

"You know you want desire in your marriage," he admonished softly. "That you want to be touched, like this."

His hands slid up to capture her breasts. She gasped, her argument dying on her lips.

She closed her eyes and gave over to his caresses. And oh heavens, how good his hands felt...how thrillingly wanton and warm, and oh so wicked. Beneath his massaging palms, she rose up in the water until her breasts floated on the surface. She bowed her head and watched shamelessly as his fingers teased at her nipples until they ached, already puckered hard from the coldness of the water and throbbing in time with the pulsing heat flaring up from between her thighs.

She gave a frustrated whimper. No good could come of this. He was still leaving to put half a world between them, and she would still be forced to marry another... Yet she couldn't quash it, that delicious craving swelling inside her that only Quinn could satisfy.

She panted softly as her body arched back against his and shamelessly invited his touch. She couldn't stop herself. To be bare to his seeking hands yet still hidden beneath the mirror-like surface of the dark pond—a delicious contradiction. And when his fingers pinched her nipples and shot a shiver of pleasure-pain straight down to that aching place between her legs, she didn't *want* to stop.

"You enjoy being touched and pleasured. Even now you're craving it." His lips curled into a knowing smile against her temple. "You should have that, Belle. You should be with a man who wants to give you every pleasure you desire, a man who desires you in return."

"Desire... will come... in time," she somehow found the breath to force out as his hands left her breasts. While his right hand rested against her outer thigh, his left arm encircled her waist and held her tight against the cradle of his hips, his manhood pressing into her bottom.

"No, it won't." He nuzzled the back of her neck. "Desire is immediate or never, an unstoppable need to bury yourselves in each other until the two of you become one."

When he placed a hot, openmouthed kiss to her nape, she bit back a whimper on her lips. "I don't need to feel desire to be a wife."

He nipped sharply at her shoulder in punishment for that untruth. But instead of a rebuke, his bite sent a wanton shiver curling through her, followed by an immediate longing to have him sink his teeth into her flesh again.

"Your husband should make you feel wanted as a woman, Annabelle. He should give you everything you desire. Especially himself."

His velvety voice swirled through her, like a ribbon unwinding from a spool, puddling in silky softness between her thighs. He meant to chastise, but the eroticism behind his words left her aching with an intensity she'd never experienced before.

He lowered his lips to her shoulder. She whimpered at the heat of his mouth against her water-cooled skin, at the light nibbles he took of her flesh when what she wanted was for him to devour her whole. A new contradiction that had her head spinning and her body tightening like a coiled spring.

"You should have passion," he murmured against her wet skin.

"Passion is," she panted out as he once again cupped her breast and strummed his thumb over her nipple, "overrated."

At that wholly blatant lie, he laughed against her shoulder. A wickedly knowing sound, as if he'd read her body and found the truth there. "You've got so much passion in you already, Annabelle, just waiting to be released." His lips smiled against her bare shoulder. "You probably fantasize about it when you're lying in bed at night, unable to sleep. About what it would be like to have a man's hands on you, caressing you until you tremble with need."

Despite the cold water, her face flushed hot. "I don't.

I don't think about any man doing that," she countered. Sweet heavens, the last person she'd admit to having fantasies about— "Certainly not *you*."

He purred in a dark voice that dripped like liquid flames through her, all the way down to her toes, and made them curl into the mud at the bottom of the pond, "Would you like to think about me when you lie in bed? Because I'd very much enjoy making you do just that."

Her fingers dug into his arm as it circled around her waist, holding herself tight against him as she panted out, "You wouldn't dare!"

"Dare to make you want me?" The amusing disbelief lacing his voice spun fresh wariness in her belly. Taking her words as a challenge, his slowly slid his hand over her front and down...until his fingertips teased at the edge of the curls between her legs. "A beautiful, naked mermaid with soft skin and inviting lips, who's practically begging to be taught a very important lesson about desire..." He delicately kissed her nape, then smiled against her bare skin when she shivered. "What rake could resist?"

Nervousness tinged with quick arousal sent her heart somersaulting. At that moment, she knew exactly how charming he was with his deep purring voice, his deliciously scandalous words, and his wandering hands. He was pure danger. "I don't need to learn any lessons from you."

"Then tell me to stop." With a flirtatious tease, he combed his fingertips through her wet curls. His fingernails scratched tantalizingly at the soft skin beneath. "Tell me you don't want this."

Oh, she *should*. It would serve him right, the arrogant devil! But she couldn't. Because a dark part of her knew the truth. That this was exactly how she'd wanted to be touched by him, ever since that night beneath the rose bower.

"Or this," he drawled huskily, and slipped his hand down between her legs to finally give the caress she craved.

She gasped at the intimate touch, her breath tearing from her. The inhalation on her lips died into a soft moan as he slowly stroked her. *Oh sweet Lord…* The sensation was overwhelming, both tender yet exciting at the same time. She closed her eyes against the way his fingers played wantonly against her folds, her body yearning for every wonderful caress he was willing to give.

"Admit it, Annabelle," he rasped hotly against her ear. "Admit that you like this, that you like being desired."

"I don't," she panted, her pulse speeding at the sweet torture of having his hand against her. Biting her bottom lip, she fought back the urge to writhe her hips against him and bring him harder against her.

"Liar," he drawled with a throaty little laugh.

She exhaled a deep breath and willed herself to unwind the tension gripping her like an invisible fist. But the heat swirling inside her was too delicious to give up. Too temptingly exquisite to deny herself. Quinn was being so gentle yet firm as his fingers stroked back and forth against her that the anxiousness slowly eased from her, and she gave over to the pleasure.

Heavens, how good it felt! His fingers were wanton and wicked, wholly scandalous…simply divine.

Helpless beneath her rising arousal, she stepped her legs wider apart. "Quinn," she whimpered and turned her head to nuzzle her cheek against his shoulder.

He smiled triumphantly against her wet hair. "So you like that?"

"It feels—" Her suddenly thick lips could barely form the words as she capitulated beneath the truth. "Oh, it feels so very good!"

His fingers moved harder against her now, stroking farther into the hollow at her core and flitting teasingly against her intimate lips. Each caress slipped deeper... And *that* felt so very wicked.

"This is what a man can do to a woman," he murmured against her nape. "You deserve a husband who can give you such pleasures. You won't be happy with less."

He was right, God help her. Her body had craved this since that morning at the ruins when he first stirred the ache sleeping inside her. Now she longed for him to make the relentless throbbing even more intense, even fiercer, until it engulfed her.

He whispered hotly into her ear, "You need this."

What she needed was *him*, but he wasn't hers to have.

"No," she whispered, even as his clever fingers did such things to her that she could barely keep her breath. "You're wrong. I don't—"

A low moan tore from her as he stroked again, this time so deep that two of his fingers slipped inside her.

She shuddered at the delicious contradiction of his water-cold fingers plunging inside her warmth, at the way her soft body clasped hard around him. And at the biggest contradiction of all, that it had to be Quinn who shared this first intimate touch. Somehow she'd known that all along.

She grasped onto his forearm as the sensation swelled through her that she was rising up and floating away, yet she was desperate to stay with him, right there in the circle of his strong arms. He drew such pleasures from her that she could barely keep from crying out at the intensity of them.

Then his touch changed. No more teasing, flitting caresses. Now his hand worked in a steady, relentless rhythm to push her toward the breathless edge. Her thighs quivered as he continued to plunge his fingers into her warmth, swirling inside her and growing the ball of unbearable heat at his fingertips.

"You deserve to be desired, Belle." He licked at her nape. The erotic caress shivered through her, connecting the ache of her puckered nipples to the relentless throbbing between her legs. He delved his thumb into her folds, to tease against the aching nub buried there. "You deserve to have passion and pleasure. In your heart, you know that as well as I."

His words cascaded through her in a waterfall of flames, and the mounting ache at his fingertips grew more ferocious until she could no longer remain still. With a whimper of need, she writhed her hips against his hand to demand release—

A gasp tore from her throat, and her hips bucked against his hand. All the tiny muscles inside her clenched down around his fingers, then released in a shuddering, electric jolt. With a soft cry, she shattered and went limp in his arms. Her body pulsed with waves of pure pleasure that radiated out from his hand at her core, and she sagged down into the water, to welcome its coldness against her heated flesh.

He wrapped both arms around her and held her against him, murmuring her name against her shoulder.

As she regained her breath, the lingering pulses of residual release gradually ebbed away. And in its place came self-recrimination. Good God, what had she done? With Quinton! The most impossible man for her.

She struggled free of his arms and shoved herself away, hot tears blurring her eyes as she turned toward him.

Concern darkened his face. When he reached for her, she held up her hand.

"Don't," she warned.

He lowered his arms. The concern on his face vanished, and his jaw set hard at her rebuke.

Embarrassment squeezed her chest. Not that he'd touched her, but because she'd so shamelessly encouraged it. And because she now wanted nothing more than to do it again. Worse, she wanted even more. She wanted his hard body moving inside hers, giving her the greater pleasures she knew he was capable of bringing to her at the same time he soothed away all her pain and sorrow. Even now her body shook with longing for exactly that.

"It was only a touch, Annabelle," he reminded her. "Nothing more."

Oh, he was so very wrong about that! "You shouldn't have done that," she chastised, wrapping her arms protectively over her breasts, even though he couldn't see anything through the water.

"We both wanted that," he countered gently.

"That doesn't—" She choked on the knot tightening in her throat. Then, letting the anger come, she sought refuge behind it from the swirling confusion he'd unleashed upon her. "Thank you for the object lesson about desire," she bit out scathingly, jutting her chin into the air. "But I don't need any more of your lessons, nor do I want them."

He closed the distance between them with a single step before she could dart away, cupping her face between his large hands and tilting her head back. She saw his angry eyes blaze like blue flames for one heartbeat before he seized her mouth beneath his, daring to plunder her lips in one last blazing kiss.

Lord help her, she let him, even as tears stung at her eyes. Losing herself beneath his strength and fierce determination, she kissed him back. How could she not, when his kiss was so torturously delicious? Sweet yet passionate, and so full of promise.

He tore his mouth away from hers. "You need my lessons." His breath panted hot against her cheek. "More than you realize."

His burning gaze dropped to her lips as he slowly backed away from her, as if he were afraid of what might happen if he stayed, of what their anger might drive them to this time.

As he turned and waded through the water to the bank, she stared after him, averting her eyes only at the last moment when his hips emerged from the water.

A new ache thumped brutally inside her. Although she couldn't put a name to it, this longing was completely different from the desire to have his hands on her and his body inside hers, to be physically exhausted and satiated in his arms.

It was a longing to have *him*. All of him. Now and for the rest of her life.

And it terrified her.

Chapter Eight

With a groan of exertion, Quinn lifted the heavy stone from the ground and set it into place on the pasture wall, then straightened and ran his forearm across his brow to wipe away the stinging sweat dripping into his eyes.

"That one nearly did ye in, eh?" Angus Burns teased beside him as he set his own rock into place.

Quinn answered with a strained grimace, panting to catch his breath.

Burns slapped him good-naturedly on his back with a grin. "Only twenty more t' go!"

He glanced at the break in the stone wall, the same gap he and Angus had already spent most of the day attempting to close, and cursed beneath his breath at the size of the breach left to fill.

Burns laughed and reached for a smaller stone to plug a tiny hole.

The cool morning had given way to a warm afternoon,

with bright sunshine flooding across the pasturelands and the blue mountains on the horizon. It was a beautiful day, and Quinn had barely noticed any of it. His mind was on the same place it'd been since the evening he arrived and found that the Bluebell had grown into a capable woman, with a kind heart, full curves, and quiet dedication. One he couldn't seem to stop worrying about. Or keep from kissing whenever they were alone.

Kissing? He rolled his eyes. He'd done a helluva lot more than that.

Which was why he was out here in the fields with Angus Burns this afternoon, breaking his back mending walls, instead of inside the house with Robert, interviewing potential suitors. The last thing he wanted to do was find Belle a husband. Which was also why he'd marched straight back to the house after leaving her at the pond to swallow his pride and scratch out a letter to Sebastian, asking his brother to loan him the money necessary to purchase Glenarvon from the Church, should Bartleby not discover another viable loophole.

And after that morning's encounter at the pond, he also needed to expel the frustration of being able to touch her and hear her throaty cry of pleasure, yet not be able to share in that release.

God's mercy, she'd made his blood boil. So hot, in fact, that he'd very nearly carried her from the pond in his arms, placed her on the grassy bank, and taken her right there. Cold water be damned.

He grabbed up another stone and slammed it into position. What had stopped him from doing exactly that—the *only* thing—was that he would be obligated to marry her if he took her innocence. That's what well-bred gentlemen did when they ruined ladies like Belle. Even a scoundrel like himself couldn't escape that. And the last thing he wanted was marriage, knowing the grief that would eventually accompany it.

Nor was he willing to turn his back on the promises he'd made to his father and Asa Jeffers, which was exactly what he would have to do then. Because there would be no marriage of convenience, as Belle had proposed. No separation. Certainly no divorce. He was a Carlisle. The Carlisle men never abandoned the women who needed them, and she would never leave the borderlands. His future wasn't here among rocky sheep pastures and patches of heather. It was waiting for him in America, where he could be free to make a name for himself. Where nothing would hold him back.

But for one breathtaking moment in the pond, when he'd been watching her beautiful face as the pleasure overtook her, he hadn't been thinking about America or his promise to his father. He'd wanted nothing more than to remain right here. With her.

Growling angrily, he shoved the rock onto the wall and ground it into place with his shoulder.

"Ye tryin' to mend that wall," Burns piped up, "or smash them rocks t' bits?"

Christ. His shoulders sagged as he realized what he was doing and stepped back from the wall. "Apologies." He took a moment to catch his breath and ran a frustrated hand through his hair. "I was distracted."

Distracted? A damned lie. He was a helluva lot more bothered than that.

Quinn tugged off his gloves and leaned back against the wall, more to gather his thoughts than to take a rest. Never before had an innocent captured his attention the way Annabelle had. Not only the way she looked, with that soft caramel-colored hair and those graceful movements, but also her sharp mind that kept him tantalizingly on his toes. He liked the way he felt when he was with her, a feeling no other woman had ever given him—not as the youngest son of a duke or a rake, but a man in his own right. Strong and competent. One deserving of her smiles. One capable of protecting her the way she deserved.

"We'll be done 'fore long," Burns assured him, popping the cork from a water jug and taking a long swig. "Only a few more of the big ones t' place, an' the others'll fill in fast."

Quinn glanced at the remaining gap and wasn't so certain. "I know about the incidents of vandalism on the estate." Quinn waved away Burns's offer of a drink and jerked a thumb at the wall. "Was this another?"

Burns shook his head, took one last swallow of water, and corked the jug. "This here wall's needed t' be repaired fer a while now." He laughed good-naturedly and slapped Quinn on the back. "Yer just the first Englishman we've had a-visitin' who wasn't smart 'nough t' stay inside when there was work t' be done!"

Quinn grimaced. Not smart enough, indeed. Apparently not about anything these days. Especially bluestockings.

"Tell me the truth about Glenarvon." He stripped off his sweat-soaked work shirt and tossed it across the stones to dry in the sun. "Man to man." He fixed the foreman with a look. "How's Miss Greene doing running the estate?"

"The lassie's doing fair, fer a woman."

Quinn bit back a grin at that. Belle would have flayed the man if she'd heard that qualifier.

"She's got the accounts in order, the repairs bein' made, all the flocks an' livestock tended to as they should be. It'll ne'er make her rich, but she makes good work o' it."

He breathed a silent sigh of relief. It would have been un-bearable to think she might choose marriage only to save a home she would end up losing anyway.

"She's even managed t' hold on through th' lot of them incidents lately." Burns wiped his forearm across his fore-head to swipe off the sweat gathered there beneath the brim of his tweed cap. "But I'm right glad yer here now. I know th' lass appreciates havin' ye here, all the help an' advice ye've given her. An' 'specially as Sir Harold's been pesterin' her to turn over the runnin' of Glenarvon to him even now, not wantin' to wait 'til she inherits—fer that matter, since the bad luck began last year."

Cold warning prickled at the back of Quinn's neck. "You think Bletchley's involved?"

Burns spat on the ground and shook his head. "At least attemptin' to take a'vantage. After e'ery incident that man hurries o'er here, offerin' to do just that—take it off her hands fer her, let him manage the property." A sour expres-sion darkened Burns's weathered face. "I don't trust him none, certainly not wi' Glenarvon, an' not 'round the lass."

Quinn's chest warmed with private vindication. If Angus Burns didn't like Bletchley, then his own dislike of the man was justified. "She might very well end up having to marry—"

Alarm bells peeled across the fields. Shouts split the quiet afternoon.

Quinn shoved himself away from the wall and shielded his eyes from the sun with his hand as he looked across the pasture at the small collection of buildings housing the shearing shed and the dairy, the barns, and other outbuild-ings where most of the estate's day-to-day work was carried out. Men scrambled from the buildings and ran toward the last barn, while footmen poured from the house—

"The hay barn's afire!" Burns shouted.

Christ! Quinn raced toward the barn, with Burns at his heels.

By the time they reached the barnyard, the men had organized themselves into a bucket brigade between the water troughs and the barn, with bucket after bucket passed hand to hand along the line and back. But the small amount of water they managed to pour onto the flames wasn't nearly enough.

"Shovels!" Quinn yelled at the last men to arrive from the fields and gestured toward the equipment shed. They did as he ordered and grabbed up shovels, hoes, pitchforks—anything they could use against the flames—then braved the heat to get close enough to toss dirt onto the flames and to smack at the fire to try to control it. But the barn was full to the roof with that summer's cuttings of hay, all of it dry and ready to catch flame from even the smallest spark.

Knowing the barn was lost, Quinn yelled for the men to turn the buckets on the surrounding buildings to keep the fire from spreading and for the men with the shovels to beat out any sparks which drifted from the hay barn. Grain sacks were dunked into the troughs and used to beat at the flames to keep the fire contained.

Quinn raced to the barn doors and threw them open wide, and he, Angus Burns, and two other men rushed inside to save whatever equipment could be salvaged before the flames completely engulfed the building. A small wagon sat in the middle of the barn, while above it the loft blazed with the heat of an inferno.

He ran forward and grabbed up the tongue, then began to push the wagon forward and out of the barn. Each step was agony, his lungs breathing in smoke and heat, burning as if they, too, were on fire, and all his muscles strained painfully to slowly roll the wagon from the barn. But he wouldn't give up. As he rolled the wagon forward, his forearm brushed against the metal ring on the tongue. It burned his skin like a branding iron. He growled out a curse at the sharp pain, but he didn't slow in his steps.

Finally, the wagon rolled out of the barn and into the fresh, cool air, which slammed into him like a wall. He gasped, filling his burning lungs with air and panting to catch his breath. Tossing the tongue down, he turned to head back to the barn, to rescue whatever else was still inside.

Someone grabbed his arm. He stopped—

Belle stood beside him, her fingers pressing hard onto his bicep and refusing to let him go. Tears left streaks down her soot-dirtied cheeks; the hem of her dress hung torn and singed. "You're not going back in there!"

"There's another wagon—"

"No!" She fiercely clung to him, putting herself directly between him and the barn. "I won't lose you, Quinton. I won't!"

He glanced at the barn and all the frantic movement around them as the others fought to keep the fire contained.

"It's gone!" she choked out through her tears. "There's nothing more you can do."

"The hell there's not!" he snarled. He hadn't yet been able to find a way to save her from marrying, but he refused to simply stand there while this new destruction rained down upon her.

He yanked his arm away from her and ran across the barnyard to grab up a stack of wet grain sacks. Fighting back his exhaustion and the aching strain of his already sore muscles, he beat furiously at the pieces of flaming hay that drifted from the barn, then covered his face from the shower of sparks that flew high into the air when the roof caved in.

He felt the heat of Belle's eyes on him, as hot as the flames themselves, but he refused to look at her, refused to let her think him incapable of protecting her. She needed him, damn it, and he wouldn't let her down.

After several minutes of fighting the fire with the other men, still giving orders even as he worked himself into exhaustion, he finally turned back—

His breath caught at the sight of Annabelle, dangerously standing in the middle of the chaos with the men, shoveling dirt onto whatever flames she could reach. Her face was filthy with soot, her hair hanging half-loose down her back, and every few minutes she had to stop to beat at the hem of her skirt to keep it from catching on fire from the smoldering ashes and charred wood at her feet. Every shovelful of dirt was a futile gesture, but he knew he wouldn't be able to stop her. He might as well have asked her to stop breathing as to give up this fight.

Together, all the men and household staff fought the fire until it was contained, although the hay and wooden barn beams would burn on for hours, most likely through the evening and night, no matter how much water and dirt they poured onto it. They were all exhausted and filthy, each man going through the motions in stunned shock and silence.

When his arms finally burned with a strain that grew too painful to slap the sack against the flames even one more time, Quinn tossed the wet burlap to the ground and bent over, hands on knees, to cough away the last of the smoke in his lungs and regain his breath. He was covered with sweat, hay, and black ash, and still scandalously bare-chested from when he'd pulled off his shirt in the field, which now seemed like a lifetime ago.

Angus Burns limped across the barnyard to him, the

weathered Scot just as exhausted and filthy as Quinn. The collar of his coat was singed.

Quinn jabbed a soot-blackened finger at the charred remains of the barn and the flames still biting into the last of the wooden beams. "I want to know how this happened." Blinding fear for Belle squeezed his chest like a vise. This wasn't petty vandalism by a couple of boys from the village. This was deliberate, with all intents to harm Belle and the estate.

Across the barnyard, he saw Belle giving orders to the men, assigning shifts to watch the fire until it completely burned out, and asking others to keep on with the buckets of water and shoveling of dirt to quench the coals.

She paused to draw a deep breath. In that moment, she looked up and met his gaze across the barnyard. He saw the fear in her, the surrender... the utter hopelessness. No one could have stopped that fire after it started; the dry hay and wooden barn served as kindling to the biting flames and spread the fire so fast that extinguishing it had been impossible. Yet Quinn ached with self-recrimination that he'd failed to protect her when she'd needed him. Just as he'd yet been unable to find a way to save her from marriage.

He wiped his forearm over his lips and spat onto the ground, in an attempt to wipe the taste of the fire from his mouth. He promised Angus Burns in a low growl, "I will find the son of a bitch who did this."

And when he did, the man would pay dearly.

* * *

"You had no business running into that burning barn," Belle scolded Quinn, trying to keep the trembling worry from her voice as she gently applied Cook's salve to the burn on his forearm. The basement was empty. All the servants had gone to help with the barn, which meant she was free to give him a piece of her mind without anyone eavesdropping. "You could have been seriously hurt." *Or worse.*

Sitting next to her at the long worktable in the kitchen, letting her both tend his arm and duly chastise him for his foolish heroism, Quinn said nothing. And oh, if he knew what was good for him, he'd keep his silence!

Even as she slowly rubbed the salve over the blistering wound with her fingertips, careful not to hurt him, Belle was just furious enough to throttle him for risking his life. His charming grin was missing, for once replaced by a grim expression born of exhaustion and the same emotional drain she felt herself at losing the barn.

"Worried about me, Bluebell?" he asked gently.

"Of course I was," she snapped angrily, refusing to let him see that she was more upset than she wanted to admit. She reached for the bandage on the table beside them, and her fingers shook as she silently rolled the long, white cloth snugly around his forearm. "You could have been killed. How would I have explained *that* to your mother?" She pulled on the two ends of the bandage, drawing it down tight around his arm. "And now, I've got to spend my time mending you because of your foolishness."

He glanced down at the bandage, which was drawn so tight that it pressed a deep indention into the muscle of his forearm, and mumbled dryly, "Or saving my death for your own hands?"

She narrowed her eyes. "Don't think I haven't been considering the best place to hide your body."

She grimaced inwardly with guilt at the overly tight bandage and reached to loosen it. He'd terrified the daylights out of her when she saw him go running into the flames, risking his life to help her. Her heart had stopped with terror, and it hadn't started beating again until he emerged from the flame-engulfed barn an eternity later. He would have run back inside again to his death if she hadn't stopped him. Even now her stomach sickened at the thought of it.

That wasn't at all the Quinton she'd known from before. That scapegrace was gone, replaced by a mature and responsible man whom she'd come to depend upon.

What would she have done if anything had happened to him? Dear God, how could she have borne it?

She blinked back the stinging in her eyes as she loosened the bandage, her fingers shaking so hard at the thought of losing him that she could barely retie the ends. He watched her closely, which only made her shake harder and the tears burn stronger.

He leaned forward and turned his arm so that his hand slid warmly into hers, his fingertips caressing across her palm and sending a shiver up her arm. His blue eyes stared solemnly at her.

"It's nothing, only a little burn." He cupped her cheek in his free hand and made her look at him. "I'm fine, Belle."

She couldn't find her voice to reply without sobbing. Or cursing.

"Besides, you know I wouldn't have died in that barn." He grinned at her. "I'd never let you get rid of me that easily."

With a scowl, she shoved his hand away from her face. Only Quinn would tease her at a time like this! "Knowing you, you'd come back as a ghost and haunt me," she grumbled, "and then I'd be stuck with you forever."

His grin widened. "Would I be able to walk through walls? Because it would make haunting so much more fun if—"

"Quinton James Carlisle!" The aggravation inside her boiled over. "I swear, if you don't—"

He grabbed the front of her dirty dress and yanked her toward him, his mouth capturing hers in an unexpected kiss that stunned her into silence. At first greedy, as if he craved her taste like a starving man, his mouth moved hungrily against hers until she responded just as eagerly.

Then the kiss softened, until his lips lingered against hers in a series of tender little kisses. Until she sighed against his mouth, all the anger and frustration draining from her.

Releasing her dress, he leaned back in the chair. She opened her eyes to find his heated gaze on her. As if contemplating grabbing her for a second kiss.

God help her, she wanted exactly that. Since he'd arrived at Glenarvon, he'd given her such heated kisses and wanton touches that he'd kept her awake at night imaging all kinds of wicked fantasies—*those* were a trouble all their own.

So was the arrogant confidence on his face at so thoroughly kissing her.

She rolled her eyes. "You can't keep kissing me every time you want to silence me," she warned, reaching across the table for his arm to finish what she was doing before he kissed her, although for one disconcerting moment she couldn't remember what that was.

"Seems like a damned fine way to me," he murmured rakishly.

Her insides melted as a blush heated her cheeks. It seemed like a damned fine way to her, too.

But it couldn't continue. "Quinn, I don't think—"

"The barn was deliberately set on fire," he said quietly, suddenly serious.

Her fingers froze on the bandage as her eyes snapped up

to his, not needing a kiss to surprise her into silence this time.

"Arson," he clarified, keeping his voice low in case someone entered the basement. "That's why it went up so fast, not just because of the hay. Like the flooding of the pasture and all the other troubles you've had for the past year, someone set that fire to cause problems for you."

Her stomach plummeted. He'd given voice to her worst fears, yet she argued, "You don't know that for certain."

"I do." He placed his hand reassuringly over hers, and her fingers trembled beneath his. "Whoever is doing this meant to cause serious harm this time. But I won't let them get away with it."

Her heart stuttered at the sudden sobriety of his words. "*Why* would someone do that?"

"Perhaps to frighten away the men who want to marry you." His eyes darkened but never left hers. "Who benefits if you lose Glenarvon?"

Irritation sparked inside her. Now he was just being ridiculous. "The Church." She arched a brow. "And I doubt Vicar Halsey is out committing arson when he rides his rounds."

He grimaced and shook his head. "How well do you know Bletchley?"

She bit back a laugh. That was almost as ludicrous as the vicar. "Impossible."

His jaw tightened. "He's keen on marrying you."

She didn't dare let herself hope that the edge she heard to his voice was jealousy. She knew better. "Exactly. So what could he possibly gain by damaging the estate?" Besides, petty vandalism and arson weren't Sir Harold's style. Too messy. And too much work. If an activity didn't involve hunting or gaming, he couldn't have cared less about it. "You give him too much credit."

"Because I'm concerned about you, Belle." He stared at her gravely. "Especially since you've come to the decision to marry."

"I have no other choice." Her shoulders sagged in defeat. "You might be able to cut yourself off from your home forever, to put half the world between you and the people you—" Her voice choked on the word, her throat tightening painfully around it. Finally, she forced out, "*Love.* But I could never do that."

She saw the anger flash coldly over him at her accusation, but she didn't care. If he could so easily leave England, his home at Chestnut Hill, his family . . . *her*, then he would never understand her need to remain here at Glenarvon and her willingness to do whatever she had to in order to save the estate. And she doubted she would ever understand *him*.

"So if you aren't willing to help me, Quinton," she warned fiercely, "then at least stop making things worse."

As she rose to her feet to leave, he threw his uninjured arm around her waist and drew her back to him. With a small squeak of surprise, she tumbled down onto his lap.

Maintaining a steely grip around her waist with his arm to keep her from slipping away, he cupped his palm against her cheek. His blue eyes shined into hers like a moonlit midnight.

"Damnation, Belle," he growled. "I *am* trying to help you."

"No, you're not! You—"

"I've found another way to save Glenarvon," he grudgingly admitted.

She stilled instantly. Her hands, which had been shoving at his shoulders to free herself, froze as she searched his face. But a grimness darkened his features. If he'd found a way to save her, he didn't seem at all happy about it. She held her breath as she whispered, "How?"

"You buy Glenarvon back from the Church," he answered quietly.

She flashed numb, all her hope evaporating. "But I can't buy it," she whispered, so softly her voice was barely audible to her own ears. Disappointment burned inside her chest, and so did humiliation when she had to admit, "I don't have any money."

And no way to get any. She had no property of any kind to post as collateral against a loan, and no male relative who could sign a loan for her in the first place. Women couldn't get loans on their own, certainly not mortgages, and every clerk she approached would laugh her right out of the bank if she tried.

She looked away, not wanting him to see her helpless tears. He'd dangled hope in front of her, then cruelly pulled it away. Owning Glenarvon without a husband was just as unreachable for her as before.

"There is a way." He took her chin in his fingers and turned her face back toward him. "If you let me help you."

She shook her head. The familiar frustration came rushing back, and she sucked in a jerking, pained breath. "But you're going to America…"

"I am," he confirmed somberly.

She winced as an arrow of disappointment pierced her heart, deeper than she thought possible. For one fleeting moment, she'd dared to hope that Quinton had changed his mind, that he was offering to stay right here in England. She should have known better. After all, didn't she know better than most the ramifications of a father's influence on his child's life?

As if reading her troubled thoughts, he added, "But I can also make certain that you're safe here before I go."

She didn't share his conviction. "How?"

"By convincing Sebastian to buy Glenarvon." He grinned at her, but his eyes were just as troubled as before. "What's the point in having a duke for a brother if I never get to use him to my advantage?"

Belle stared solemnly at him. She couldn't join in his optimism. "But Sebastian will own it then," she reminded him quietly.

"And he'll let you live here and run the estate as you please." When she didn't react with joy or throw her arms around his neck, as he'd undoubtedly expected, he frowned. "That's what you wanted. To keep Glenarvon without having to marry. We've found a way to make it happen."

"But I won't own it," she breathed out. Speaking any louder would have shattered her heart. "It'll be Trent's, not mine."

"You asked for my help, Annabelle." He rubbed his thumb over the streak of soot dirtying her cheek, but the tender touch scalded. "This will keep you from having to marry."

But that was only a legal technicality. Because it didn't stop her from once more being at the mercy of a man.

A sadness crept up inside her as she stared into his face, seeing an expression there of such concern for her, such relief that he'd finally found a solution to her troubles, that it made her ache. He was trying to help, but how could he ever understand what it was like to be helpless? To be left vulnerable to the volatility of a man, who was stronger and harder? Who had the power to evict her from her home whenever he pleased?

But at least it was a new way forward, which was more than she'd had an hour ago.

Despite the fearful dread sickening in her belly, she gave a jerky nod of capitulation.

"Good." He reached up tenderly to tuck a stray curl behind her ear. "I've already sent a message to Sebastian explaining your situation and outlining the terms that will most likely be part of the sale. It might take some time to hear from him."

More time...the one thing she didn't have. One week from today was her birthday party, when she was supposed to announce the name of her betrothed. "And if he says no?"

The way his face darkened told her everything—that Quinton didn't know himself if the Duke of Trent would agree to help her. "Then we find our legal loophole," he said quietly.

And if we don't? But she knew the answer to that. It was the same dark, anguished-filled answer she'd had all along. She would have to marry a man who did not love her, putting her life and her happiness into his hands.

She wrapped her arms around Quinn's neck to hug him to her. She rested her chin on his hard shoulder and squeezed closed her eyes, drinking in his strength and resolve.

"We'll find a way out of this together, Belle," he murmured, nuzzling his cheek against hers. "I promise."

She desperately prayed that he was a man who kept his promises.

CHAPTER NINE

One Week Until Belle's Birthday

$\mathscr{B}$elle's shoulders sagged wearily as the crush of bodies, noise, and heat of her birthday-turned-betrothal party suffocated her. Tonight should have been the happiest night of her life.

Instead, she'd stumbled into hell.

With only one week left until her birthday, there had so far been no salvation for her. The tension inside her coiled tighter with each tick of the clock that brought her closer to midnight and to the moment when she would have to make her announcement. Mr. Bartleby hadn't found another legal loophole, and there had been no word from the Duke of Trent. Time had run out. Tonight, she would have to announce the name of the man she intended to marry. The man who would save Glenarvon for her.

And that man wasn't Quinn.

Mrs. Lambert from the village mercantile squeezed her hand. "Annabelle! Happy birthday, my dear."

Belle cringed inwardly as she returned the well-wishes with a smile she certainly didn't feel. She wanted to scream! Instead, she kept her smile glued in place, graciously accepted the congratulations of everyone who approached her, and pretended that her heart wasn't breaking. Both over her impending announcement of who she'd chosen to marry and over Quinton.

She'd spent the past week avoiding being alone with him in order to keep him—and herself—under control. There could be no more stolen kisses or deliciously wanton swims at dawn, because she didn't dare let herself be tempted by more.

But tonight, Quinton was nowhere to be seen. Not having him at her side to support her through what lay ahead curled a bereft loneliness through her, even in the middle of the crush.

"Congratulations, Miss Greene!" Mr. Bartleby bowed his head to her deferentially, a pleased grin on his face. "My wife and I are so very happy for both you and Sir Harold."

Her smile faded as dread knotted her belly. Her gaze darted frantically around the room. Where *was* Quinn?

Instead of finding him, her eyes landed on Robert, who gave her a reassuring smile as she spotted him in the crowd. He wove his way through the room to her and bowed with all the polish of a London gentleman, his shining blue eyes so reminding her of Quinn's that her heart stuttered.

"Happy birthday," he offered for the benefit of anyone around them who might have been listening. Then lowered his voice, "Or should I say congratulations on acquiring Glenarvon? You'll make a wonderful landowner and a good patron for the village."

Her throat tightened with gratefulness, and she managed

to force out a whispered, "Thank you." It was her first sincere expression of gratitude all night.

Mindful of the crowd around them, he lowered his mouth to her ear. "And my deepest apologies for any problems Quinn and I might have caused you, both this past fortnight and six years ago. We were only trying to protect you," he explained apologetically as he straightened away from her. "Then and now."

"I know." Her insides warmed at his sincerity.

He winked mischievously. "But sometimes we Carlisles can be idiots."

She laughed. Oh, such grand idiots!

But the Carlisle brothers had surprised her by the men they'd become. Age and their father's death had sobered them from their outrageously wild ways, even though they still possessed a love for life and took more risks than they should have. Richard Carlisle had been so proud of both of them, giving his children the love and support that a good father should. Sadness crept over her to think that Robert and Quinton were now driven by the urge to prove themselves to their father's ghost, when Richard Carlisle had always loved them with all of his heart and only wanted the best for them.

"Forgive me?" He took her hand and raised it to his lips.

She smiled through the tears that threatened at her lashes. "Of course."

He grinned at her, one that looked for all the world like one of Quinton's...but somehow wasn't quite the same. Oh, it was charming and brilliant, certainly. But it lacked the earnestness and warmth she'd always found in Quinn's smiles. A genuine love for life and unabashed exuberance.

Robert's smile only made her ache more for Quinn.

She glanced nervously past his shoulder, feeling like a goose for once again checking... "Is Quinton with you?"

"I don't know where he is." Then he added, his voice tinged with sadness, "Most likely halfway to Liverpool."

His words jarred into her. A stark reminder that in one week—perhaps even after tonight's announcement— Quinton would be on his way to America. And away from her. Forever.

Sobering at the sight of her troubled expression that Belle was unable to hide, Robert explained quietly, "He needs a sense of worth in his life, one separate from the family."

Her chest tightened at that very succinct, dead-on description of his brother. That was exactly the person Quinton had revealed himself to be—a man who wouldn't settle for anything less than proving his full value to the world.

"He hasn't had much chance to do that," Robert added, "and it grates at him. He thinks he'll be able to succeed in South Carolina."

Belle was certain of it. Since his arrival, he'd helped greatly with the estate, more so than she'd thought possible given the devil-may-care attitude of his younger days. He'd demonstrated a natural talent for estate management, and his charming personality was perfect for interacting with the tenants and workers. He'd be a grand success.

But she wouldn't be there with him to see it.

She forced a smile for Robert, hoping to hide the sorrow gnawing at her chest. "What do you think of his plans?"

"I think he's better off staying right here," he said seriously.

She nodded, sighing out the truth, "He belongs in England. He'll miss his family too much." A faint smile touched her lips. "As well as London and all the trouble he gets into there."

A knowing gleam flickered in Robert's eyes. "That's not what I meant."

He moved away to let the next person approach to congratulate her, and Belle stared after him, bewildered.

Not what he'd meant? If not England, then...

"Oh," she whispered, the sudden realization dawning on her. Robert's subtle comment sent a quiet warmth twisting through her, a tiny tendril of hope—

No.

Taking a deep breath, she quashed whatever reckless optimism had just flamed inside her. No good would come of dreaming of what could never be, and she could never admit the truth aloud. That she wanted nothing more than to keep him right there at Glenarvon. With her.

As if fate had heard her thoughts, the crowd parted. Only for a fleeting moment, but long enough to catch a flash of golden blond beneath the blaze of the chandeliers on the far side of the room—

Quinton.

Dressed impeccably, he wore a superfine black jacket and blue brocade waistcoat that further accentuated the rich gold color of his hair and the wide breadth of his shoulders. Muscular thighs stretched beneath white trousers that matched the snow-white of his cravat that boldly contrasted the midnight-blue of his eyes. He held a glass of whisky in one hand as he listened to the group around him, with his other hand tucked into the small of his back and his feet wide. Quiet confidence exuded from him—the perfect stance of a gentleman who knew exactly who he was and what he wanted.

Her body reflexively tightened at the sight of him. *Sweet heavens*...so handsomely formal in attire, so comfortably casual in stance. Of course, he stood with a group of women, but truly, where else would Quinn be but surrounded by ladies, their attentions riveted to him? Just as hers was. He smiled that beaming grin of his and made them all feel the full effect of his charm, as if each of them were the most beautiful woman in the room.

The scoundrel she'd known had grown into so much more, and she no longer saw him as an impish rogue but as the capable man he'd become. As the true partner and friend with whom she could share her life.

Somehow, when she wasn't looking, Quinton had found his way into her heart. Now, when she closed her eyes at night and dreamed of a husband, it was his charming smile she saw. The quiet evenings before the fire she longed to have were with him. The children she imagined had his same grin and sparkling blue eyes, his same golden-blond hair. And it was Quinn she fantasized about welcoming into her bed, the only man she ever wanted to give herself to.

In mid-laugh, Quinn glanced up and caught her watching from across the room. An electric jolt swept over her as his eyes darkened on her, a predatory look pulsing with so much possessiveness and desire that she trembled. He held her captive beneath his gaze for a mere half dozen heartbeats, but in that moment, he set her heart somersaulting. It was as if a silken ribbon joined them, one that tangled through her and made her a part of him, and him a part of her. She couldn't remember what it was like not to have that connection to his strength and warmth. As she drew in a deep, shaking breath and felt the rush of emotion slice through her, she knew then, without a doubt...

She loved him.

Then the crowd closed back in, and he was gone.

*   *   *

Quinn stepped out onto the terrace and drew in a deep breath of the cool night air to steady himself. *Good God.* Even standing across the ballroom from Annabelle tonight had been too close for comfort.

Rubbing his hand at the knot of tension now permanently lodged at the back of his neck, he moved into the dark shadows near the balustrade and turned back toward the house. Keeping his distance, he could see her through the French doors, watching her as she smiled at the guests. Over the past week, it had become harder and harder to keep himself from her. And tonight was torture. Seeing how beautiful she looked in her soft satin and lace as she outshined even the flickering candles in the chandeliers, knowing how much she needed him and how much more with each minute that brought them closer to midnight, remembering how sweet her kisses and how soft her touch—

Christ. He blew out a frustrated breath. If he wasn't careful and somehow ended up alone with her tonight, he wasn't certain he could stop himself from kissing her again. Or touching her. And if he did that, he wasn't certain he could stop himself from doing everything he could to save her. Including offering marriage.

Robert joined him at the balustrade. He followed Quinn's gaze through the French doors and commented quietly to keep from being overheard, "The Bluebell's quite a beauty."

More than beautiful. Tonight, she simply glowed. "Yes, she is."

"And you're a damned fool."

Quinn's eyes narrowed, his hands tightening into fists. He hadn't expected to pummel his brother this evening, but he was just frustrated enough to do exactly that. And enjoy it immensely. "Leave this alone."

Robert slid him a sideways glance. "Have you left Belle alone?" When Quinn didn't answer, he added, "Didn't think so."

Quinn turned on him. "It doesn't concern you."

"You're my brother, and I like Belle. So of course it concerns me." He withdrew a cheroot from his jacket's inside breast pocket and bit off the tip, then spat it away. His shoulders dropped with concerned sympathy. "What are you still doing here, Quinton?" He lit the cigar on a nearby lamp. "You should have been on a ship to America three weeks ago."

Damnably good question, which only tightened the knot at his nape. "I was trying to find a way to help Annabelle."

Robert puffed at the cheroot, the tip glowing red in the shadows. "Do you have feelings for her?"

"Of course." He forced a casual tone into his voice to hide his confusion over what feelings, exactly, he did hold for her. Because they were growing more mystifying with each day he spent in her company, until he now didn't want to think about departing for America and leaving her behind. "She's an old friend."

"Well, then, you're not just a damned fool." Robert fixed him with a hard look as he clamped the cigar between his teeth. "You're also a damnably bad liar."

Now *that* was overstepping. "Robert, I'm warning you—"

"You two are a lot of things, but you're not friends."

Robert's gaze turned somber. "At least not anymore. Are you, Quinn?"

His shoulders sagged under the weight of his brother's concern and his own confusion about Belle. "No," he admitted quietly, "we're not."

"Are you going to offer for her tonight, then?"

Through the doors, he saw Belle laugh at something one of the guests said. But even from this far away, he could see that her laughter was forced, and his chest tightened for the unseen distress she surely suffered tonight. "A scoundrel like me? I'm not the domesticating type."

"Are you certain about that?" Robert leaned back against the stone railing and thoughtfully studied the glowing end of his cigar. "She's an heiress in want of a husband, and you're a man in want of an estate. Seems like a perfect match to me."

"I'm a man whose future lies in America," he corrected. But that declaration sounded thin, even to his own ears. The same niggling unease that had struck him recently whenever he thought of resettling in America came back tonight with full force.

Robert flicked a bit of ash from the end of his cheroot and gestured at the house and gardens around them. "Why not remain right here?"

"I can't stay in England, you know that." Here he would be seen first as the duke's brother, second as a Carlisle, and never as the man he wanted to be—someone who succeeded on his own merits. In England, he knew people would always suspect that his success came from his brother's connections or his family's wealth, rather than his own hard work and intellect.

Although he had to admit to himself that traveling to

America was now starting to feel more like an obligation and less like his dream.

"You're only ten miles from Scotland," Robert argued, "as far away from London as you can get and still be in England. Any further away, and you'd be wearing a kilt. Sebastian's influence is growing, but even Trent's shadow can't follow you all the way up here."

He grudgingly admitted, "Perhaps."

In the few weeks he'd been in the borderlands, he'd come to realize that a different breed of men lived here. Tough and hardworking ones like Angus Burns who had been weathered by the northern winters into understanding the hard truth—that a man's worth came from his abilities, not his given lot in life. If anyplace in England provided an opportunity to prove himself, it was here.

Yet he'd promised his father America. "But I've got land waiting for me there."

Robert said around the cigar as he clamped it between his teeth, "You've got land waiting right here."

He shook his head. "I want a place where I can make a difference, under my own work and management."

"You can manage this place yourself and put into motion all those plans Belle has for the village and improving the estate. And you fit in well here. You won't be able to say the same about America." He gestured with his cheroot, indicating the house and the estate, even the unseen mountains in the distance. "Look around you, Quinton. Everything you want is right here." He added, "And a beautiful woman to share it with."

"Not everything." The estate would always be Belle's, not his. No matter what the law said about matrimonial property, this place would always belong to her, its heart and soul belonging to her alone. True, he wanted to be like his father, a man who would never lord rights and privileges over his wife and home. But Quinn also knew it would grate to know that he'd come into marriage as an unequal partner.

As for Annabelle...a man didn't give himself to a woman like her and walk away with his heart intact.

He turned away from the French doors. "Asa Jeffers needs me. I promised Father I would take care of him and his wife." He wouldn't walk away from that, even if the thought of leaving Belle grew harder to accept with each new day. "America was the path Father wanted for me."

"Yes. Because he knew how much it chafed at you to be the third son. Because he knew you'd need a way to prove yourself, away from the family's influence and the title. Because he knew that life in the military or the church would never satisfy you, that you wanted to work for a living." Robert put his hand on Quinton's shoulder, adding quietly, "Because he wanted you to be happy."

Guilt once more gnawed at Quinn's gut. Around them, the din of the party hummed low, and the soft night air gave an appreciated respite from the stifling heat and too-sweet odor of beeswax candles wafting through the overcrowded ballroom. All the guests waited expectantly for Belle to make her announcement and end their suspense.

All except him.

"Father thought America would give you that chance at happiness, so he arranged it," Robert said soberly. "But Jeffers doesn't need you. He doesn't have any sons, but he has successful sons-in-law who could take over the farm, or who would welcome him and his wife into their homes if they didn't want to work the land. He doesn't need you. *You* need him. That's why Father wanted you to go to

Charleston. He understood that part of your nature better than you did."

Struck by the concern in Robert's voice, Quinn slowly raised his eyes and met his gaze.

"You need to be needed, Quinton," Robert continued quietly. "Always have. All the schemes we planned out as boys, all the trouble we got into...you always had to be at the center of it. Every contest and bet you carried out was because someone else needed you to do them—whether to win money or just to have a good time. Father knew that about you. He wanted you to have the chance to prove yourself on your own merits, but he also knew that you'd only be happy starting a new life if you had someone who depended upon you, who needed your help."

His brother fell silent for a moment to study the glowing tip of his cigar, the same way Father always did when they smoked cigars in the dining room after the ladies had gone through. Quinton's chest panged hollowly at the memory.

"That's why you excelled at overseeing the properties when you took over as estate agent when Sebastian inherited," Robert continued quietly. "Because you were needed there. No one else could have done it, and you thrived at it. That's also why you were the one who spent so much time caring for Mother after Father died, because she needed you."

Quinn looked away, his eyes stinging. He gritted his teeth against the pain he still carried for his mother's grief. Always would.

"And you're still here, in some godforsaken sheep pasture in the borderlands, because Belle needs you."

With a skipping beat of his heart, Quinn snapped his gaze up to his brother's. Could Robert be correct?

"You don't have to go to America now. You've got every-thing you need right here to make yourself happy. You just have to accept it." He leveled a sympathetic look at Quinn. "Father wanted you to be happy, no matter where you ended up." He paused. "Does Belle make you happy?"

Quinton drew in a jerking breath and admitted, "Yes." That was the God's truth. He'd not been happier than during the past three weeks with Belle. "Very much."

"Then stay right here, where you belong."

A lead weight settled on his chest. The temptation Robert was dangling in front of him was a bittersweet one.

But he couldn't take it.

"I'm going to America as planned," he repeated, although this time the declaration left him wanting a good stiff drink.

Robert remained silent for a long while, then he drawled quietly, "And I'm leaving for London." He flicked the ash from his cigar. "Tomorrow morning."

Quinn stiffened at the news. He was parting from his brother far earlier than expected. "I thought you'd be riding all the way to Liverpool to see me off."

And with that, the very real possibility that Quinn might not see his brother again for years. If ever. After all, most people who crossed the Atlantic made one-way voyages.

Truly, he had no idea when he would be able to return. His mother could very well have passed away before then, given her age, which was why he was privately glad that Sebastian married Miranda when he did, to soften the blow of Quinn's leaving by giving her a new daughter to fuss over. God only knew when he'd see Josie and his nephew and niece again, or how many more children she and Ches-ney would have while he was gone. Seb and Miranda would be plagued by children; he was certain of it from the way those two stared at each other. And Robert would make good on his business ventures and become a wealthy trade merchant—he was already well on his way, in fact.

When Quinn did come back to visit in five years or so, there would be so many Carlisles running around Blackwood Hall and Chestnut Hill that he'd never be able to keep track of them all. And missing each of them terribly when he had to leave again.

Robert looked down as he rubbed the ash into the stone terrace with the toe of his boot. "I thought I was going there, too. But a business matter has come up. I received a message this afternoon. Those trade investments I made in India have finally paid off. The ship docked at Greenwich three days ago, and I want to be in London when the goods are auctioned." He paused to inhale a deep, shaking breath. "This is it, Quinn. The opportunity I've been waiting for. One which might very well turn into a partnership with a large trading company."

Might...Concern nagged at him. "Does Sebastian know what you're planning?"

Robert froze for just a beat, but Quinn caught it. They were brothers; of course he noticed everything about him. Hadn't he wanted nothing more when he was a boy than to be just like Robert, looking up to his older brother the way boys now idolized Gentleman Jackson or Wellington?

"No, and I don't want him to. Not yet. If plans develop as I hope, then I'll be able to launch a successful life for myself, just like you. Only in a civilized country." Robert shot him one last warning look to mind his own business. "I'll tell him soon, but *I'll* tell him—not you."

Although Robert's assurances eased Quinn's suspicions, it didn't erase them. Still, he knew from experience—and several bloodied noses—not to meddle in his brothers' affairs. Besides, he had his own troubles to deal with...one particularly stubborn, inexplicably alluring, honey-eyed trouble, to be exact.

"Speaking of Sebastian," Robert commented as he reached into his breast pocket and retrieved a note. "This arrived for you a few minutes ago from Blackwood Hall."

His heart lurched into a booming beat as he accepted it. The answer to his proposal to buy Glenarvon. Just in the nick of time, too.

Quinn mumbled his thanks and somehow kept from ripping it open right then. Belle's last best hope lay inside that note.

"I'm leaving first thing in the morning," Robert told him. An amused grin spread across his face. "After tonight, our interviewing services won't be necessary anymore, which Aunt Agatha must surely thank God for." Then his smile faded, and he tapped his shoulder against Quinn's. "If you're going to America, you should leave with me."

"I want to stay a bit longer, to make certain everything is settled well for Belle." He'd made a promise to protect her, and he meant to see that through.

"She won't need your help with that."

Quinn shook his head. "Contacts and property deeds can be complicated. She'll need someone to—"

"*Quinton.*" His older brother fixed him with a steely look. "After tonight, she won't need you anymore."

Robert's words came like a punch to his gut.

Quinn turned his back to Robert, to lean over the balustrade and stare out into the dark garden, until he could regain his breath. He knew tonight was coming, knew she'd decided to take a husband...But down deep, he hadn't truly been prepared for riding away and leaving her behind.

But what other choice did he have?

Robert asked bluntly, "Do you love her?"

Quinn sucked in a deep, steadying breath to quell the riotous confusion of emotions that had swirled through him since the evening he arrived and saw Belle again, and admitted, "I don't know."

With a disappointed shake of his head, Robert stubbed out his cigar on the balustrade, then tossed it away into the dark garden beyond. "Well, you'd better figure it out soon. Because in less than two hours Belle's going to pledge her life to a man." He pushed himself away from the railing and walked toward the French doors, sliding a parting glance backward at his brother. "I'd hoped it would be you."

The doors closed after him, muffling the noise of the party beyond to a low drone.

Quinn squeezed his eyes shut. *Damnation.* What Robert wanted of him—didn't his brother realize the impossibility of what he was asking? He had an agreement with Asa Jeffers and his wife, to let them remain on the land where they'd made their home for decades. And he'd promised his father, the *very last* promise he'd made to him in the days leading up to the accident that claimed his life. How was he expected to break it? And for what reason—a woman? What would Father say to that?

He deserved an opportunity to prove himself, damn it! He'd worked hard and earned this chance for a new life, away from England and all the difficulties that came with being a duke's son. And a Carlisle. Life would be much easier in America, where no one cared about titles or would say that his success was only due to family connections. Staying here would be more difficult, where everyone doubted him, where failure was expected and success to be credited not to his merits but to his family.

He caught his breath as that realization hit him. Did he really want a life of *easy*? That's what America would be, compared to England.

A worse thought chilled him—was an easy future what his father had in mind when he encouraged Quinn to leave England? For Christ's sake, even finding the land to purchase had been done for him, neatly arranged by his father and handed to him like a gift.

If that was what a life in America meant, could Robert be right? Was he better off staying here?

Except that staying here meant having to marry Annabelle. Could he ever let Belle into his heart, or allow himself to enter hers? Because love ended. *Always.* That was the last lesson his parents' marriage had taught him, one he'd learned the hard way.

Love...the one thing he promised himself he'd never do.

But he could help her with Glenarvon.

He tore open the message and froze as he scanned Sebastian's scrawled writing. Then he crushed the note in his hand and threw it to the ground as he turned on his heel to stalk back inside.

* * *

"Ladies and gentlemen!" Ferguson called out, his head held high and his chest puffed out beneath the garish-colored waistcoat he wore as tonight's Master of Ceremonies.

Annabelle smiled. She adored him and all the other servants at Glenarvon, and a fresh stab of guilt jarred through her as she thought about what might happen to them in only one short week. Those who weren't old enough to be pensioned would be moved to other Ainsley properties, and several of them would be making the move to the dower house in London. And her right along with them if she didn't accept Sir Harold's offer.

The engagement was expected, of course. All the guests had assumed she would choose him, and Harold, himself, hovered nearby all night. As if the announcement had already been made and the marriage was now fated. All the guests were happy for her.

But she was utterly miserable. Despite all her resolve to avoid a marriage of convenience, one which held no love and might end up as awful as her parents' marriage, that was exactly where she'd found herself. The irony was bitter.

Ferguson tapped his staff against the marble floor and announced proudly, "The first waltz of the evening!"

The orchestra struck up the opening flourishes, and each note jarred into her. She'd been so busy greeting guests and thanking them for their kind felicitations that she hadn't realized the dancing had started.

A hand closed over her elbow from behind.

Her heart leapt into her throat. Quinton! With a bright smile, she turned—

"Sir Harold." Her breath caught in a painful inhalation at the sight of him, her chest hollow with disappointment. But her fake smile never wavered, not even as her heart plummeted to the floor.

"The waltz is beginning." With a smile, he gestured toward the dance floor with a sweep of his arm, as confident as everyone else in the room that she would choose him at midnight. Without a better suitor in sight, he had good reason to assume so. "Shall we?"

"Of course," she whispered.

He led her forward. They moved into position, and the sweeping first bars of the dance sounded through the room. Belle took a deep breath as he stepped her into the waltz, struck by the realization that she'd never danced with him before and didn't know what to expect.

What she found was boredom.

Oh, Harold was a good dancer, knowing his steps and turning through them with precision. But the waltz reminded her of sitting through the music recital of someone who didn't want to play—technically precise but utterly lacking in engagement. And passion. At least, thankfully, he didn't try to hold a conversation with her, so she didn't have to fake interest as well as a smile. She didn't think she could have endured it.

So they danced on, turning around the floor...stilted, uncomfortable, silent. A horrible, sinking feeling in her stomach told her that their marriage would be no different. Stilted. Uncomfortable. Horribly silent.

Harold came to a sudden halt in the middle of the dance floor.

She gasped in surprise, stopping quickly to keep from crashing into him. The other couples scattered around them as they continued on in their steps, yet all craning curious necks to see what was happening. Including Belle, who rose up on tiptoes to peer over his shoulder to see—

Quinton.

He grinned at her. "May I cut in?"

Her eyes widened. She'd never seen a couple interrupted like this before—oh, it simply wasn't done! Yet there he was, a shining contradiction of gold and black, with the audacity to interrupt. And her heart soared.

"Go away, Carlisle," Harold muttered threateningly, yet he smiled at Quinn as if they were old friends for the benefit of the curious eyes watching them. "I'm waltzing with my fiancée."

"I haven't agreed to that yet," Belle reminded him as she shrank away.

"But you will." He might have let Quinn stop them in their steps, with no other choice unless they wanted to trample over the top of him. But Harold wasn't giving her up, his left hand holding fast to hers, his right resting possessively at the small of her back. "It will be midnight soon, and you'll have to make an announcement if you want to keep your home." He added, smiling down at her, "I'm the best choice, and you know it."

He was right. She swallowed hard to keep down the nausea roiling in her stomach at the thought of being married to him. Oh, she was going to cast up her accounts right there in the ballroom!

"Then even more reason to let me dance with her." Quinn's charming grin only brightened as he slapped Harold good-naturedly on the shoulder, although Belle suspected that what he truly wanted to do was punch him. "If you'll have her for the rest of your life, then the least you can do is let me have her tonight. For one last dance with an old friend."

If. Belle's chest squeezed so hard that she winced. Even now Quinton still held out hope that she'd refuse Sir Harold. But he might as well have been whistling in the wind for all the difference it would make.

"You don't get her, Carlisle," Harold half hissed. To anyone watching, the two men were simply having a convivial conversation, but tension seethed palpably between them. "Not tonight, not ever."

Quinn's eyes flashed dark and territorial, and her breath caught in her throat. That was the same look he'd worn six years ago in the St James garden, right before he pummeled Burton Williams. Were the two of them bold enough to come to blows right here on the dance floor?

She felt Harold's hand draw into a clenched fist against her back. Good Lord—apparently, they were *exactly* that bold!

"Please don't cause trouble, both of you," she chastened, then turned to Harold. "Besides, you don't like to dance anyway. Quinn is doing you a favor by waltzing with me."

Quinn eyed her knowingly, the corner of his grin twisting up wryly at that.

"Fine. Finish the damned waltz, Carlisle." Quick anger pulsed visibly through Sir Harold, although Belle wondered which he was more furious about—losing the waltz or losing it to Quinton. He released her and bowed stiffly over her hand, a wicked smile touching his lips as he kissed her fingers. "After all, we'll have every night for the rest of our lives to dance together."

Appalled at his innuendo, Belle snatched her hand away. Harold turned on his heels and tried not to stomp away, the current loser in the strange rivalry that had sprung up between the two men.

"Shall we?" Quinton held open his arms.

Belle stared at him uncertainly. She should have refused to change partners, should even now walk away. Being cut direct in the middle of the dance floor was the least he deserved for nearly fighting over her again, for potentially ruining her life once more by driving away her last best hope for keeping Glenarvon.

But she couldn't bring herself to leave, and the siren song

of being held in his arms proved impossible to resist, even for half a waltz.

She stepped into position, and he twirled her lightly into the waltz. They danced together fluidly, as artlessly as if she were born to be in his arms and follow his lead. Smooth, graceful...magical.

She stared up into his eyes as he turned her effortlessly about the floor. He held her closer than he should have, brushing an almost imperceptible caress of his hand against her lower back, but she was helpless to make him stop.

Her awareness of his solid body only heightened with each turn and brush of her skirts around his legs. The familiar ache he'd always been able to stir inside her blossomed with an electric tingling that spilled through her, all the way out to the tips of her fingers as he held her hand in his. She breathed deep his rich, masculine scent of tobacco and port, and her head spun as they danced together, all of him engulfing her senses until she trembled.

Aware of the attention of the crowd on them, aching with the frustration of his nearness, and unable to bear the heat of his hungry stare another moment—"Quinton," she breathlessly whispered in a plea for mercy.

"I'll ask one last time, Belle." He squeezed her fingers as they rested lightly in his and sent a shiver racing up her arm, to land heavily in her breasts. "Don't get married. Aunt Agatha will take care of you. She'll always give you a safe home, if not here then in London."

Her shoulders sagged. She was so very weary of fighting this battle. "It's too late." Emotionally drained, she shook her head sadly. "We're standing in the middle of the engagement party."

"Your *birthday* party," he corrected firmly. "The announcement hasn't yet been made. You can still change your mind."

"I can't." With only one week until the will's deadline, there was no more time to delay. The announcement had to be made tonight in order to have time to negotiate the marriage contract and plan the wedding. Tonight was simply a foregone conclusion of what everyone already knew was inevitable. Everyone except Quinn, apparently. "There isn't time."

"Don't do this, Belle. Don't shackle yourself to a man who—"

"Quinton, stop!" She squeezed her eyes closed for only a moment, but even then, she saw his handsome face, the concern for her in his eyes. Which only made the sharp pain inside her chest flame more fiercely. Because his concern wasn't enough to save her from a marriage she didn't want and her home from being taken away, not enough to save her heart from *him*. The only man she wanted to marry. The man she loved. "Please . . . there's no help for it now."

"The hell there's not," he growled.

"Let it go, Quinton," she breathed, unable to find her voice for fear of sobbing. The burning desolation in her chest was scalding. "Let *me* go."

The orchestra sounded the last flourish and ended the waltz. Regretfully, she shifted out of his arms and mechanically sank into a curtsy. Then she turned and walked away, blinking back the blurring in her eyes but keeping the false smile firmly in place.

He took her elbow as he fell into step beside her to escort her from the floor. She trembled at his touch. Daring to take a surreptitious glance at him, she caught her breath at the hard determination in his expression, his jaw clamped tight and his eyes staring straight ahead as if he couldn't bear to look at her.

"I'm not giving up, Belle," he promised in a low, intense voice.

She forced her smile to widen even as her heart broke. It was almost midnight. "Perhaps you should."

He hesitated, then said quietly, "I've heard from Sebastian."

She tripped. His grip tightened on her arm and caught her, keeping her upright, even as she turned and stared at him, stunned. New hope blossomed in the barren desert that her heart had become tonight.

"That's why I was late for the waltz," he informed her stiffly. "His reply came right before the dance started."

She held her breath, waiting on pins and needles. "And?"

"He's willing to help purchase Glenarvon."

Relief cascaded through her, her knees going weak. She would have surely fallen to the floor if not for Quinn's strong hand on her arm, still supporting her.

"Oh, thank God," she breathed, unable to speak louder through the turbulent rush of emotions pouring through her. At the last possible moment, an answer to her prayers ... But why wasn't Quinn happy for her? Why did he look so angry? She stopped, dread rising inside her. "Quinton?"

"He's willing to put up half the money," he muttered, his jaw working so fiercely that the muscles danced in his neck. "Ten thousand pounds."

"Half?" she repeated, desperately praying she'd misheard. It might have been a single pound from the difference that much would make. Her heart shattered where she stood, and she pressed her fist to her chest to keep from screaming. "Then he hasn't saved me at all."

"He wants me to put up the rest," he added, once more taking her arm and leading her on as whispers began to rise around them.

She shook her head, her eyes blurring so much that she could barely see the floor in front of her. "You can't."

"I have enough money," he bit out.

"You need that money for America," she whispered. The weight sinking back onto her slender shoulders was crushing, and she had no idea how she kept from falling to the floor beneath it.

He repeated firmly, "I have enough money, Annabelle. You won't have to marry."

"No, I won't let you." If her heart hadn't already broken, his offer would have made it sing. Instead, grief blackened her insides. "Your dream is America, and I want that for you."

"Damnation, Belle—"

"No!" she choked out. "And please, *don't* mention it again." Dear God, she couldn't have borne it! To come so close, only to have all hope dashed once more... Any more would end her.

They arrived back to Lady Ainsley, and their argument fell silent. Yet she could tell from the glint in his eyes that this discussion was far from over.

But once midnight came and she made her announcement, it would no longer matter.

"Are you all right, dear?" Lady Ainsley frowned with concern and gave her hand a motherly squeeze.

Belle nodded, not trusting herself to speak.

"Quinton." Lady Ainsley narrowed her gaze on him.

Instead of recrimination, though, Belle thought she heard a touch of pleased admiration in the viscountess's voice as she scolded, "Do you often go about stealing waltzes?"

"It wasn't much of a theft," he joked, but Belle could tell that his heart wasn't in it. After all, she knew his teasing ways better than anyone. "After all, I brought her back."

When what Belle wanted was to run away together. What was left of her heart burned like brimstone in her hollow chest.

"Imp," Lady Ainsley chastised him for forcing his way into the waltz…or was it for bringing her back? Belle couldn't be certain of anything as the grief of losing him threatened to engulf her. Then the viscountess turned to Belle, and her features softened. "You'll need to make the announcement soon. Will you be able to do it?"

"Yes," she whispered, wishing she could have been more resolved. Instead, dread seeped through her. She felt cold and feverish in turns, and she would have cast up her accounts right there if she hadn't already been so upset that she hadn't been able to eat anything all evening. With each heartbeat, every inch of her seemed to be screaming out for her to say no, to flee…to save herself.

Hell. She'd been cast into hell. And there was no way out.

"Whom will you choose?" Lady Ainsley asked quietly, her eyes drifting to Quinn.

Now that the moment was finally arriving, Belle still couldn't bring herself to put voice to it, as if speaking it made it real. But what choice did she have? Lose the only real home she'd ever had, or…"I'll marry Sir Harold," she breathed out, "if I must."

Through the watery tears she no longer bothered to hide, Belle saw Quinn stiffen, then silently turn and walk away.

He left the ballroom, slipping out through the open terrace doors into the dark gardens.

Then the crowd swarmed in to offer more good wishes and congratulations, separating her from Lady Ainsley, smothering her. The noise rose and swirled through her head, somehow both numbing and sickening at the same time. She felt as if she were falling away, with no one to stop her fall...

No one but Quinn. Just as he'd been trying to do since he arrived.

The truth slammed into her like lightning, so fiercely that it ripped her breath away, and a soft cry fell from her lips—

She could never pledge her life to a man she didn't love. Not even to save Glenarvon.

She'd been wrong, so *very* wrong! How foolish had she been to think she could find happiness by marrying only for her inheritance? How would she not cringe whenever her husband touched her? Or stop the relentless tears if he never came to understand how much her home meant to her, even after she'd sacrificed her life, heart, and soul for it? How could the home she loved not become a prison in the face of all that?

Certainly, ladies married for fortune and property all the time, without a care toward love. But she wasn't one of those ladies. Not in men's work clothes, with her books and evening swims. Never had been, and *never* would be.

In that heartbeat of clarity, she realized what she wanted, what she *had* to do—

God help her. She chose Quinton.

With her frantic heart pounding so hard that the rush of blood in her ears was deafening, she pushed through the crowd and ran outside into the night after him.

* * *

Quinn bit out a savage curse as he stalked to the far end of the walled garden to lose himself in the shadows. But even all the way out here, he could still hear the party, muffled and distant, yet loud enough to plague him.

Damnation. He ran a shaking hand through his hair.

Belle was going to marry Bletchley. And there wasn't a damned thing he could do to stop it, unless he wanted to storm back inside and embarrass her in front of everyone. With that, he would ruin both her engagement and any chance she had of remaining in her home. Besides, the minute he opened his mouth, everyone in the room would think the same thing—that he wanted Belle for himself.

What he *wanted* was for Belle to be happy so he could travel on to America and not feel guilty that she'd entered into a loveless marriage. That was all. It wasn't as if he were in love with her himself.

In love with Belle? Laughable! She was the *Bluebell*, for Christ's sake! He didn't love her. He *wouldn't* let himself love her, just as he wouldn't let himself love any woman.

But that resolution was becoming harder to keep.

He heaved out a frustrated breath. A bluestocking with the heart of an angel, she had him wanting to protect her with a determination he'd never felt before.

Yet he'd failed to do just that, and in one hour, she'd be at Bletchley's side, announcing her wedding plans.

With a curse, he slammed his palm against the stone wall.

"Quinton."

The soft voice swirled through him, prickling the little hairs at his nape. He froze, except for the fierce pounding of his heart.

Appearing out of the darkness like a ghost, Belle came toward him through the shadows. Her hair shined dark, the sage-green dress she wore tonight showing white in the faint light of the sliver of the crescent moon lying low behind the distant mountains. Silent and ethereal... like a figure from a dream.

As she stepped slowly toward him, he held his breath, fearing she was nothing more than a wishful illusion.

"Belle," he whispered. He drew a deep, tremulous breath. The sweet scent of heather surrounded her. "What are you—"

She placed her fingers to his lips. "Hush."

Then she rose up on tiptoes and touched her lips to his in a featherlight kiss that left him speechless. He was too entranced by her magical spell to put into words the emotions and desires pulsating through him.

When she lowered herself away, he pursued, his mouth lowering to capture her lips and his eyes closing against the painful sweetness of her. Soft, delicate... enchanting. He whispered her name and lifted his hands to cup her face and hold her still as he deepened the kiss, as he sought to fill up his senses with her.

But with a soft laugh, she slipped away. Taking his hand as she broke the kiss and lacing her fingers through his, she led him into the darkness beyond the garden walls.

He followed, a willing captive. In the dim moonlight, surrounded by midnight shadows, she guided him across the lawn and down the path through the trees like a sprite from a fairy tale. Whenever he tried to take her into his arms, she danced ahead just out of reach and taunted him with the soft, seductive sound of her laughter.

The path emptied into the clearing surrounding the old

castle ruins. When they reached the outer wall with its tumbled stones, she stopped and leaned into him, letting his mouth possess hers and his arms encircle her. With a soft moan, she parted her lips, and he swept his tongue between them, to taste the sweetness inside.

Then she was gone from his arms again, the seductive sprite slipping away deeper into the ruins.

He chased after her. His arms ached to hold her, his body throbbed to enjoy hers. This time, he didn't want to stop with a kiss and a touch. He wanted to possess her. He wanted *all* of her, every aggravating, independent, brilliant, beautiful bit of her.

He found her at the heart of the ruins, standing in the castle's keep and softly panting, breathless with anticipation. Even in the shadows he could see her body trembling and her bright eyes shining with nervous excitement as he moved toward her.

"You can't leave your own party," he drawled, his voice hoarse with desire. He wanted her—*Sweet Lucifer*, he wanted her more than he'd wanted any woman in his life! But he wanted her coming freely to him because she wanted *him*. And no other reason. "You need to get back before you're missed."

"I don't care!" She laughed, and the lilting softness fell through him like a warm summer rain. She held out her hand to him, and he stepped forward to take it, letting her draw him to her. "I don't want to think about the will, or marriage, or the estate..." Her breath tickled warm and sweet against his cheek as she leaned against him and brushed her lips tantalizingly along his jaw. "And I don't want to be at the party a moment more."

Even as his heart raced with desire, he took her arms and

set her away. He had to make certain—"What *do* you want, Annabelle?"

"You."

His cock stiffened instantly at the breathless whisper, spoken so softly that he barely heard it. He stared down at her delicate face in the shadows, fearing that she truly was nothing more than a fantasy after all.

"When you took the waltz, you said you wanted one last dance." She stepped forward, bringing her body against his, her arms entwining around his neck. "But I want more than that." Her fingers played in his hair, and each innocent caress sent a jolt of aching need shivering through him. "I'm yours for the night...if you want me."

CHAPTER TEN

$\mathscr{B}$elle held her breath as her trembling fingertips combed nervously through his silky hair, waiting for him to say something...*anything*. But he didn't, and in his silence, each beat of her heart pounded like a drum, so loud she was certain he could hear it.

Yet she couldn't help herself. She knew she'd made the right decision not to marry, no matter how fearful the prospect of leaving her home. Just as she knew it was right and good to be here with Quinton. There would be no wedding night for her, no marriage bed—there would be only tonight, and she wanted to share it with Quinton. Every inch of her, full heart and soul, begged for exactly that.

Yet what she wanted was more than just the physical touches her body craved. She wanted the comfort she knew Quinn could bring her, his strength and reassurances, his resolve never to surrender even when she herself had given up. She wanted him. *All* of him, right down to that charming grin. If only for tonight.

When he didn't answer, her fingertips stilled. She stared up at him, confused. "I thought..."

"You thought what?" he pressed, puzzling her further. Instead of the desire she expected to see on his face, a mask carefully hid his thoughts.

Not at all what she'd expected. "Apologies." Her cheeks heated with humiliation. And confusion. But she'd seen his desire with her own eyes! How could she have been so wrong? "Apparently, I was mistaken."

When she moved to step away, his hands slid down her arms and pulled her against him, stopping her. "You thought what, Annabelle?" he murmured, each breath tickling hotly against her lips.

She shivered, drinking in the heat and strength of him. "That you wanted me," she breathed. "Do you?"

Sliding an arm around her waist to keep her hips pressed against his, he cupped her face against his palm and brushed his thumb over her bottom lip. Each little caress spun an electric tingle through her. "Very much."

She gasped as his fingers trailed down her neck to touch her racing pulse in the hollow at the base of her throat. His lips curled into a pleased smile. The *most* confusing man, and the most thrilling she'd ever met. More—he was protection and security. And when he touched her, he felt like...*home*.

His fingers paused in their downward caress at the neckline of her dress. So close but not yet touching the swells of her breasts now rising and falling rapidly as she fought to keep both her breath and her wits. He brushed his lips against her ear. "But do you want *me*?"

Heavens yes. She trailed her fingertips across his cheek, wanting tonight with him more than she'd wanted anything in her life. Perhaps as much as she wanted Glenarvon. He was leaving, she was staying…and tonight she simply didn't care about the future. All that mattered was being as close to him as possible, both body and soul. She would worry about the morning when it came.

His eyes shined brightly in the darkness. "Do you, Annabelle?"

If he only knew what she really felt for him! She gave a throaty laugh, only for the sound to catch in her throat when he captured her breast against his palm, cupping her fullness in a gesture so possessive that she shuddered from the intensity of it.

His fingers teased lightly at her nipple through the silk of her gown, and a wisp of pleasure drifted through her. Her breasts grew heavy and warm, and she leaned harder against him, begging him with her body to give her more.

"Well…to be honest," she panted out beneath the wonderful sensation of her nipple pebbling against his palm, "you were…my second choice."

His hand stilled. "Oh?"

That was definitely jealousy! And her heart soared with it. "But Angus Burns was busy, so—"

"Bluestocking," he growled as he captured her lips beneath his to give her a blistering kiss whose hunger stole her breath away.

She clung to him as he ravished her mouth and left her craving more. Even now, pressed against him with her arms wrapped around his neck and the heat of his body soaking into hers, she still wasn't close enough.

A soft moan of need rose from her lips. "I want you,

Quinton," she murmured as he drank in her words. *I love you*... Not a single doubt existed inside her about giving herself to him tonight.

Still kissing her, he carefully maneuvered her backward, and she went willingly. All of her prickled with pins and needles of nervous anticipation, but oh, how much she wanted this! When he lowered his head to kiss her again, her body arched against his with a whimper of willing capitulation.

He released her from his arms only long enough to strip out of his jacket. As she watched him, her stomach somersaulted with pure nervousness. He was undressing. If what she wanted to share with him tonight happened, then of course—but heavens, he was *undressing*! She trembled with trepidation...

Until he draped the jacket over the waist-high stones behind her.

She blinked, puzzled. "Why did you do that?"

He grinned. "So I can do this."

His hands encircled her waist and lifted her easily off the ground, to set her on top the low wall. Then he planted his hands against the stones on both sides of her and leaned in for a kiss. Slow, intense, and of single purpose...to make clear how much he wanted her. The kiss grew until she panted breathlessly against him, until her thighs clenched to quell the throbbing heat at her core that threatened to consume her.

She clung helplessly to him as his mouth swept along her jaw to her ear. Every touch of his lips to her body only increased the longing she felt for him. He nibbled teasingly at her earlobe before drawing it between his lips and sucking, before the tip of his tongue circled the outer curl of her ear—

His tongue swirled inside her ear, and she gasped.

"Beautiful Belle," he murmured, plunging his tongue inside once more and rewarding her with a shivering, aching shudder. "Finally mine."

She dug her fingers into the hard muscles of his shoulders to keep from falling away, even with the solid rock beneath her. The world whirled around her, and her only anchor was Quinn. And oh, what an anchor! Even now his hard muscles rippled beneath her fingertips, his body solid and broad. Nervousness flooded through her at the thought of what that very large, solid, and broad body was going do with hers tonight.

"Quinn." Her voice emerged as a tremulous whisper. "I don't know...what to do."

"Don't worry," he murmured teasingly against her throat as his lips kissed lower. "I do."

"Quinton!" She smacked her palm against his shoulder to get his attention, then repeated softly with a bit of embarrassment, "I don't know what to do."

He lifted his mouth from her neck and cupped her face delicately in his hands. In the shadows, his face was solemn. "Nervous, Belle?"

She nodded. At her silent acknowledgment, he tenderly touched his lips to hers.

"If it helps," he admitted, "I'm nervous, too."

That did help...but not much. Compared to those experienced ladies in London, he must think her a boring, backward dolt.

He brushed his thumb slowly back and forth across her bottom lip in a caress that was more soothing than seductive, yet still left her craving more. "I'll teach you, all right?"

She nodded jerkily, feeling like a wanton for wanting

exactly that—for Quinn to instruct her in all the arts of intimacy, so she could bring him the same pleasures he brought to her.

"It's simple," he assured her. "There's only one rule."

Rules? Dear God, there were *rules* to this? A new panic sprung up inside her, and she felt like an utter cake as she asked, "Which is?"

"You can do anything you want. If it feels good to you, do it. And if it feels good to me..." He grinned. "Do it twice."

She laughed, and the nervousness ebbed from her, replaced by a happy anticipation that tickled at her toes. Only Quinn could make her laugh at such an important moment in her life. And her heart sang because of him.

His grin faded as he stroked his knuckles across her cheek. "You'll be ruined."

That no longer mattered. She'd come to her decision. Tonight would be the first and only time she would ever give herself to a man.

Leaning forward, her mouth captured his as she tried to convey all of that to him. She poured every ounce of her aching heart and soul into that kiss, singular in its importance and in the overwhelming love she felt for him.

Tender and sweet, with the tantalizing promise of more, his lips caressed hers in equal measure of both demanding and coaxing for her to deepen the kiss. So she did exactly that, slipping her tongue tentatively between his lips to explore the spicy depths of his mouth and stroke her tongue along his, the same way he'd done to her.

He groaned. His arms clasped around her as he thrust his tongue between her lips in a rapid series of plunges and retreats that left her breathless and aching.

Oh, how much his kisses had changed from six years ago!

There was none of the fumbling of before; now there were only smooth, masculine movements that savored at the same time that they intensified with growing arousal. While the eagerness was still there, now pulsing electrically through both of them, it had been tempered by time into a tantalizingly seductive control.

And a very wicked part of her wanted to make his control snap.

He'd urged her to do whatever felt good, so…"I think this would feel good," she whispered as her hands slid down his chest to unbutton his waistcoat.

"It does," he assured her between gentle nips of his teeth at her throat.

She laughed. "I meant for me!"

And it did. The brocade was soft and smooth beneath her fingertips as she pushed it open and down over his shoulders, letting it fall to the ground. She trembled at the boldness of what she was doing. A secret thrill pulsed through her and landed deliciously between her thighs. Still, she wanted more.

"This, too," she whispered, then did the same with his cravat, untying the long cloth of white silk and dropping it away.

She hesitated then, not knowing what to do next.

Sensing her uncertainty, he slid his hands up her back, where his clever fingers made quick work of unfastening her dress. The loose bodice sagged low over her breasts, and with a gasp, she crossed her arms over her chest, catching it before it fell away completely. She wasn't wearing anything beneath the silk gown except for stockings, the tightly fitted bodice making both shift and stays unnecessary. A hot blush flushed her face as she realized what he must think of her, that she must be a wanton to dare to dress so boldly.

But when his hands slipped beneath the silk and caressed warmly over her bare back, all embarrassment fled, and she gained a new appreciation for her dressmaker.

"Does that feel good?" he whispered, brushing his mouth back and forth across her bare shoulder.

"Yes," she admitted. Oh, a great deal!

She slowly relaxed and released her clamping hold over the bodice. And that—oh, *that* was the exact right thing to do, because his hands at her back slipped around to her front, somehow nudging the bodice down while simultaneously stroking in featherlight touches across the bare skin beneath. When his hands captured her breasts, she shrugged her shoulders and the bodice slipped down her arms and fell away, baring her from the waist up.

She closed her eyes, not in embarrassment but because the cool air on her hot skin felt so heavenly. So did the way his work-roughened palms gently kneaded her bare breasts, how her nipples puckered impossibly tighter beneath his flicking thumbs. She moaned deeply at the throbbing he flamed inside her. Her breasts grew heavy against his hands, and the ache at her nipples pulled straight through her to the moist heat gathering between her legs.

"Dear God, Annabelle," he rasped out. "You are so beautiful."

His lips closed around her right nipple. She gasped at the exquisite sensation of his mouth suckling at her, at the bold way he tongued her. He released her nipple and drew back just far enough to blow a stream of cold air against her moist skin.

"Quinton!" She jumped at the sharp sensation, then

moaned in sheer pleasure as his hot mouth once again closed over her, heating away the cold until she melted against him like butter. "You are...wicked," she panted out, digging her fingers into his thick hair.

She laughed when he looked up at her and grinned impishly before moving his mouth to her other breast to start the sweet torture anew. "Very much so," he mumbled against her bare skin.

A thrill shivered through at the delicious hope that he'd show her exactly how wicked he could be. Because if what he did to her was wicked, then it was also so very, very good.

"I think," she whispered as she licked her lips and bit back a soft moan as he worried her nipple between his teeth, as if deciding whether to devour her slowly or gulp her down all at once, "that I know what else might feel good."

Her fingers slipped down to his sides, pulled the lawn shirt free from his trousers, and let it hang loose around his hips. Then she slipped her hand under his shirt to touch the warm skin beneath.

"It does feel good," she confirmed as her fingers fluttered across the ridges of his abdomen to his hard chest. Everywhere she touched, his muscles rippled beneath her fingertips. Like magic.

Her hesitant explorations grew bolder, her hands stroking higher and higher across his chest until her fingers traced over his hard male nipples. He flinched beneath the flick of her fingertips.

With a happy laugh, Belle pushed him back far enough to lift the shirt up over his head and toss it away.

"It's only fair," she challenged. After all, her own breasts were exposed both to the cool night and to his hot stare.

His muscular chest was bare to her now. She leaned

forward to take one of his nipples between her lips and suck shamelessly, the same way he'd done to her. He inhaled sharply when she nipped lightly at him, then she soothed away the pleasure-pain with feathery kisses until he groaned.

"I know what else might feel good," she whispered against his chest, then licked her way up to his throat as her hands moved lower, following the trail of golden hair down his stomach to his waistband.

"Annabelle," he whispered hoarsely, her name uttered in both warning and desire as her trembling hand cupped his bulging manhood through his trousers.

She laughed again, this time in wonder at the hardness of him against her fingers, the heavy weight of him resting against her palm. Then, somehow, he seemed to grow impossibly harder and larger as she caressed him.

Closing his eyes, he hung his head as his shoulders slumped, reminding her of a giant cat welcoming her petting strokes. From the blissful expression on his face, she almost expected him to purr. But this man was a tiger, and he starkly reminded her of that as he shifted his hips to press himself harder into her hand.

Without stopping her caresses, she kissed him, outlining his lips with the tip of her tongue. "Do you like that?"

With a low growl, he reached between them, flicked open his fall, and shoved her hand down inside his trousers.

She froze. His bare length rested against her palm, and his hand encircled her wrist to keep her from pulling away. Her heart pounded furiously in her ears. Had she gone too far? Had she done something that—

"Do it twice," he panted out.

Her heart somersaulted. He *liked* what she was doing to

him! And if it felt half as good to him to be touched like this as it had to her, then she knew he wanted it. Desperately.

Her hand folded around him, cupping him the same way she had through the trousers, but this time, no barrier prevented her from stroking the soft skin covering the steely hardness beneath. Her strokes became increasingly bolder, more confident as appreciative groans and growls escaped from the back of his throat, until she drew him free of the constricting material and he sprang straight against her palm.

She stilled. So large and thick, so long and hard—her stomach knotted. Suddenly their play had turned serious.

"Annabelle."

Her gaze lifted to his, and she lost her breath.

His eyes stared hungrily down at her and made her shiver beneath their dark heat. This was what it was like to be with Quinton all the time, she realized, not just in his arms but every moment—a fierce oncoming storm, filled with an intensity that left her breathless.

Slowly, he slipped a hand down between them and covered her fingers with his own, then guided her in a slow, smooth stroke along his length to show her how to give him the pleasure he craved. He was patiently instructing her, just as he'd promised, and she blinked at the unexpected tears forming on her lashes.

With his free hand, he reached up to cup her face and reassuringly touched his lips to hers in a kiss so light that it was barely a kiss at all.

"Do you know what happens between men and women?" His breath had grown ragged, yet he still guided her fingers in her slow strokes.

She gave a jerky nod. "Like how you…caressed me in the pond, except…"

"Except with this," he finished, squeezing her fingers gently as they encircled his thick girth. "This part of me slides inside you."

Belle knew she should have been embarrassed by that, but she wasn't. She didn't even blush. This was Quinn, and she would never be self-conscious with him. His patience with her, his willingness to put her at ease— Surely, there was some kind of caring behind that. There *had* to be. Because she certainly cared for him.

"I know," she breathed, so softly that the sound was nearly lost against the silence of the night surrounding them. "I've read about it."

He grinned at her. "Of course you did."

"But the books were wrong." They had to be. To do *that* when he was so big— "I don't think it's possible."

"Trust me," he murmured. "It's very possible."

"But you're huge!"

He laughed, a rich and throaty sound that filled her with warmth, as his arms went around her and hugged her to him. When he kissed her again, this time sucking softly at her bottom lip as he retreated, she suspected she'd said the best thing in the world to him…but she had no idea why that should please him so, when she'd only pointed out why they'd have to stop.

"It will hurt the first time," he explained, tenderly stroking his fingertips over her cheek. "I can't prevent that."

She drew a deep breath and nodded, knowing that he would never intentionally hurt her.

"But I can prevent getting you with child."

As he reached to retrieve something from his jacket

breast pocket, she felt a stab of panic sweep through her. Getting with child? She hadn't considered—but Quinn had, and she realized again how much she could trust him to protect her.

"It's not as nice, I'll admit." He gently nudged her fingers away from him. In the shadows, she couldn't see what he was doing, but when he brought her hand back to him, she felt a soft sheath covering his length, tied close to his body with a tiny ribbon. "But it's necessary. All right?"

Another jerky nod, although she wasn't certain exactly what she was agreeing to. But if Quinn thought it was needed... She sighed and trailed her fingers teasingly over his length just as she'd done earlier, careful not to knock the sheath from its place.

"Good," he growled and swooped his head down to plunder her mouth, this kiss hot and openmouthed, hungry and full of wanton invitation. "Very good." Her hand tightened around him, and he groaned. "And oh so wicked."

"I'm not wicked," she protested against his mouth.

"You are. A wicked angel." With a smile against her lips, he rested his hands on her knees. "You're a walking contradiction, Annabelle."

His hands slid slowly upward, pulling her skirt carefully up along her thighs. With each little kiss he leaned in to take, he gently rocked her back and forth, freeing the material from beneath her until her dress lay bunched around her waist.

"An alluring, luscious contradiction..." He tenderly kissed her brow, and she closed her eyes with a soft sigh. "All independence and strength on the outside, so soft and sweet beneath."

He gently parted her legs and stepped between her thighs.

He stood so close now that the heat of his bare chest warmed her breasts, and the sprinkling of golden hair tickled at her nipples. Excitement and nervousness warred within her. Goose bumps sprouted across her skin with a shiver as his hands caressed up her inner thighs, stroking over the bare flesh above her stockings, higher and higher—

When he touched her folds, she jumped.

"Shh," he whispered at her temple. "Relax, Belle."

"I—I am r-relaxed."

He chuckled, the deep sound rumbling into her. As one hand moved up to possessively cup her breast, he lightly stroked his fingers against her folds with the other. "You are so beautiful, yet you don't realize how much," he whispered. His words heated through her nearly as much as his fingers as he continued to stroke against her, and she bit her lip against the whimper of need that rose from her throat. "And you have no idea how very special this is for me, to be with you."

She wasn't naïve enough to believe him. "You've been with dozens of women. I'm not special."

"Look at me, Belle," he ordered, and she opened her eyes. His gaze met hers in the dark shadows. "You *are* special to me...this bluestocking who wears men's clothes and cheats at chess."

When she opened her mouth to bite out an angry retort, he slipped his finger inside her tight warmth, and the rejoinder melted into a low moan of pleasure as he slid in and out of her slippery core. Oh, what a wicked, wicked man!

She trembled helplessly as the undeniable ache inside her grew. So intense and wonderful that it stole her breath away, forcing her to bury her face against his neck and breathe in soft pants.

"I have been drawn to you since the first time we kissed," he murmured, continuing his tantalizing strokes inside her. "And contrary to what you may believe about me..."

A moaning gasp tore from her as his fingers gave a swirling, deep plunge inside her and his thumb flicked across the little bead buried at the top of her folds. She knew what came next because of what he'd done to her in the pond, how the pleasure would pulse through her in wonderful, breathtaking waves. She held her breath in sweet anticipation—

Instead, he withdrew from her. A whimper of utter desolation crossed her lips at the sudden loss of him.

"I've never taken a woman's virginity before," he finished quietly.

As her arousal-fogged brain tried to process that soft admission, she felt him reach between them, to position himself at her center and nestle his sheathed tip against her ready folds. His large hands encircled her waist.

"You, Annabelle," he murmured as he pressed his hips toward hers and the first inch of his manhood sank inside her, "are *very* special."

She trembled nervously as he slowly slid farther inside her, his hands on her hips drawing her against him even as he shifted forward to sink deeper between her thighs. Her body stretched to accommodate his thick girth as if she were made to fit him.

Inch by slow inch, careful not to hurt her, he gently slid himself deeper until his arms encircled her and her breasts pressed flat against his hard chest. He whispered her name, and the last traces of nervousness and embarrassment vanished from her, leaving only the certainty that this moment was right. Because of Quinn.

"Beautiful Belle," he whispered hoarsely, his shoulders tense beneath her fingertips and his body shaking with restraint as he held himself still inside her, not yet stroking her the way her body craved. The way she *needed* him to move inside her.

She writhed against him. "Quinn, please."

With a deep groan, he stepped forward as he pulled her hips toward him, thrusting through her resistance and plunging himself inside her tight warmth to the hilt.

She cried out at the sharp pinch. But within seconds the pain was gone, leaving only the wonderfully strange sensation of her body stretched wide around his, welcoming his strength and the precious security of having him close to her, until they were one.

"Are you all right?" he whispered against her temple, his voice hoarse with concern and arousal.

She nodded, unable to speak around the acute disappointment that swept through her that *this* was what making love was all about. Not exactly uncomfortable, yet not the wonderful pleasures he'd given her before.

But when he finally moved against her, each shift of his hips came as a delectable stroke inside her.

She moaned softly. Oh, the sensation was wonderful! Simply heavenly. She'd anticipated the same soft, fluttering strokes he'd given her with his fingers, but this was so much better, so much *more*. Each smooth retreat from her warmth came as a wicked tickle, each returning plunge an electric shiver.

Happiness swelled inside her. *This* was what her body had craved from the first time his lips had touched hers, this amazing physical joining that brought both breathtaking pleasure and trembling vulnerability. Even six years ago when he'd first kissed her, when she didn't know anything about the intimacies men and women shared, a secret part of her had longed for exactly this. With him.

She arched herself into his hard body, achingly whispering his name. Closer... she wanted him even closer.

"Wrap your legs around me, Annabelle," he instructed, not ceasing in his smooth rocking. Each little stroke inside her now came with a swirl of his hips that sent tingles shooting out to the ends of her fingers and toes. She did as he asked and raised her legs, locking her ankles together at the small of his back.

But immediately, she realized she couldn't move, not sitting perched at the edge of the wall. A frustrated whimper rose from her. Knowing what she needed, he lowered her onto her back and followed down on top of her, until his body covered hers.

In this new position, with the heavy weight of him pressed deliciously down on her pelvis and her thighs held open wide around the cradle of his hips, his movements changed. No longer giving the rocking strokes of before, he now thrust hard and deep inside her, each plunge shooting an intense shiver through her.

Squeezed between his warm body above her and the cold rock beneath, she gave over to the pulsating ache he flamed at her core, to the quivering tightening of her intimate lips around his thick manhood. Unable to remain still, she arched herself into his thrust.

He sucked in a mouthful of air through clamped teeth. "Damnation, woman," he muttered in an appreciative warning, his voice husky. "Keep doing that, and—"

"And what?" This time when she arched against him, longer and harder than before, an animal-like growl tore from him.

"This." He ducked his head and captured her breast in his mouth. Even as he continued to stroke between her thighs, he took her nipple deep inside his mouth and sucked hard in time to his relentless thrusts.

She gasped as flames licked at the backs of her knees. Every stroke of his body into hers only tightened her insides, like a coil ready to spring.

Now...she had to move *now*. Unlocking her ankles and lowering her legs, she planted the soles of her slippers firmly against the rock beneath her and pushed. Her hips rose up against his, audaciously lifting to meet each hard thrust. The movement brought him deliciously deeper inside her, yet that only temporarily eased the tension mounting within her. When it returned, it arrived with the intensity of a tidal wave, and she wrapped her body around his and held on for dear life.

She cried out his name as the tension broke inside her. Quinn smothered her mouth with his, to drink in her cry as a liquid heat pulsed out through her fingers and toes, engulfing her in its warmth. Her body quivered uncontrollably around his, and at that moment, she wanted nothing more than for him to become part of her forever.

Seconds later, the muscles in his back tensed beneath her fingertips, and she heard a low groan swell up from him as his own release came. He shuddered violently as his thighs strained against hers, then his body went limp. He rested his forehead on her bare shoulder and fought to regain his stolen breath.

Neither of them moved, and she was glad for it, because she wanted to stay right there in the protective strength of his arms, with the pulse of his heart beating so hard that it echoed within her. She was certain her own heart beat just as hard. How could it not? What he'd done with her was simply astonishing in its actions and utterly blissful in its wanton pleasures, and she'd never felt happier in her life.

At that moment, still wrapped tightly within his embrace, she was free.

Then he slowly shifted away from her, reluctantly sliding himself from her warmth, and she had no choice but to let him slip from her arms. He removed the clever little sheath, then buttoned up his trousers and reached down for the discarded cravat at his feet.

He leaned over her as she still lay draped across the stones, utterly satiated and relaxed, and placed a soft kiss to her lips. "Hold still. You've bled a little," he explained with a touch of embarrassment, gently stroking the silk between her legs to clean her. "We can't risk staining your dress."

But the soft caress of the smooth, cool silk brushing against her sensitized folds sent a new shiver of pulsing arousal through her. A sighing moan escaped her.

He grinned against her lips and murmured, "Insatiable."

She laughed, certain she was. But only for him.

When he finished and moved away to dress, she sat up and winced at the sharp pain. She would have bruises on her bottom and on the backs of her legs from the stone wall, but she simply didn't care. Tonight had been wonderful, and she would never regret it. Resisting the urge to seduce him into doing all those deliciously wicked things all over again—for now, anyway—she pulled up her bodice and carefully wiggled down her skirt.

He returned to her, his waistcoat hanging open and his neck rakishly bare. Her breath caught in her throat. *Goodness.* Even half-dressed and rumpled, he'd never been more breathtaking.

"Bluebell," he murmured as he smiled at her through the shadows, such a self-satisfied grin that she couldn't help but smile back. She didn't want to think about what lay ahead for them. At that moment, with her body still warm and pulsing with pleasure from his, she refused to think about anything past tonight.

He gathered her into his arms and held her close for a precious moment more, just long enough for her to rest her cheek against his shoulder and breathe deep the familiar scent of him, now deliciously tinged with the musky aroma of sex. Then he gently helped her to the ground, fastened up her dress, and finished straightening her skirts and bodice, making certain no trace of what they'd done was visible.

His careful attention made her heart ache. He cared about her, she was certain of it. This tender act proved it. Perhaps he would never love her, but at least she knew she mattered to him, if only in this small way.

When she moved to step away, he encircled her in his arms and pulled her back against him.

"You're not going anywhere," he insisted gently, his cheek nuzzling the side of her neck. "I want to hold you a bit longer."

She closed her eyes and nodded, sighing deeply, so happy and at peace within the circle of his arms.

"Are you all right?" he murmured.

She smiled. "I'm wonderful."

"Yes." His lips smiled against her ear. "You certainly are."

An easy, happy laugh fell from her lips. Only Quinn could make her laugh at a moment like this!

He placed a kiss against her shoulder and murmured, "I didn't expect for that to happen, you know. Not here, not like that."

"You didn't?" She stiffened, her body flashing with sudden apprehension. Had she made a horrible mistake?

"Oh, I wanted you all right," he drawled wolfishly. "From the moment I arrived here. That first evening when I found you swimming in the pond, I wanted to jump in after you and have my way with you."

She laughed.

"Repeatedly," he growled.

More laughter poured from her. She couldn't remember the last time she'd laughed so much. She squeezed her arms over his as he held her. Nothing else in the world existed at that moment except for Quinn and the cocooning shadows of the ruins, except for the strong beat of his heart against her back.

"But you should have had roses and wine, satin sheets, and a down bed," he added with regret. "It should have been something special that you'll never forget."

She drew a deep breath and admitted, "Six years."

In puzzled surprise, he lifted his mouth from her shoulder. "That's a bit exact for forgetting, don't you think?"

"No, goose!" She laughed. "You kissed me for the first time six years ago, and I haven't forgotten it." Not the rakish way he'd looked in his formal evening clothes, not the scent of the roses or the way the music wafted faintly through the dark gardens, not the way he'd kissed her so breathlessly...not the way he'd created that same intense longing inside her that he'd finally satisfied tonight. "So if I can remember one little kiss for six years, then how could I ever forget tonight?"

"Belle," he whispered, tenderness lacing his hoarse voice.

He turned her in his arms and cupped her face against his

palm as he lowered his head to kiss her. The moment was bittersweet, so much so that she ached with it.

He broke the kiss, and she wrapped her arms around his neck to keep him close, not wanting this moment to end so soon. Although she knew they only had tonight, she would have gladly remained right there in his arms forever.

Then he stiffened, not so much that anyone else would have noticed. But Belle did. She now noticed everything about him, so attuned had she become to this man. He asked quietly, "You'll make the announcement tonight, then?"

Confusion mingled with the satiated pleasure fogging her mind. She blinked. "Pardon?"

"When we return to the party." He inhaled a deep breath of resolve. "You'll announce that we're engaged. That I'm the man you're going to marry."

The realization of what he was saying—and why—spilled over her like icy water, instantly chilling the blossoming warmth inside her. Slowly, she loosened her arms around his neck and lowered herself back until she could look up into his face, which had grown suddenly grim.

Far too grim for a man who had just made love to the woman he wanted to marry.

The happiness inside her vanished, the loss of it pricking like petals ripped from a flower. She pressed in a trembling whisper, "But you refused before."

"I also promised to protect you, and now it's the only way to save Glenarvon." He glanced away guiltily. "I also just ruined you."

She leaned back against the rock for support as swift desolation sliced into her. "You made love to me," she corrected softly.

With each beat of her heart that jarred through her, her

soul yearned to hear him say the words...*I love you, Annabelle. I want to marry you because I love you and want to be with you, and no other reason.* But as each heartbeat ticked off the silent seconds, she knew he wasn't going to say any of that.

Instead, he replied quietly, "A gentleman marries a lady when he takes her innocence."

Her hands gripped the rock, this time to keep from falling to the cold ground. The pain that bore into her with each tortured breath she took filled her with a wretched anguish, so brutal that she could barely breathe. How did she not shatter from the pain of it, right there among the ruins?

When she'd chased after him into the darkness, she hadn't expected him to offer marriage, hadn't expected more than just this moment together. But this—oh, this was so much *worse*! Because he didn't want to marry her because he loved her.

He wanted to marry her only because she was an obligation.

"No...you're going to America," she reminded him softly. Marrying Quinton only to put an ocean between them—once she'd wanted exactly that, but now she couldn't have borne it. "You promised your father."

"I promised my father that I would make a good life for myself, that I would make him proud. I can do that right here. With you." His eyes turned solemn. "I need you, Belle, I know that now. And you need me."

How much pride it must have cost him to admit that! But need wasn't love.

Summoning all the strength she possessed, she forced herself to remain on her feet despite the legs beneath her that had gone numb and weak. Somehow she found the determination to keep breathing as she forced out, "That offer no longer stands."

He frowned, searching her face. "Pardon?"

"That marriage proposal I made to you—I'm taking it back." She choked down a sob, thankful that the shadows hid her face and glistening eyes. She'd never felt more alone or more helpless in her life, yet she was doing the right thing for her heart. The pain she felt now at rejecting him would be nothing compared to a lifetime of marriage without his love. "I won't marry you."

"Yes, you will." His eyes flared brightly with frustration. "Marrying is good for both of us, Belle. And it solves your problem."

It solved nothing. Because now she wanted everything—Quinn's heart, his laughter, his grins, a home and family they'd make together...his love.

If she couldn't have that, then she'd rather have nothing at all. Living with the specter of what she might have had if he loved her would be unbearable.

"I've made my decision." All of her shook with the effort of holding back her tears. Her frustration and humiliation. Her anguish. "I won't marry you, Quinton."

"Annabelle!" Her name echoed through the darkness as Lady Ainsley called for her from the house, shattering the cocoon of quiet shadows around them. "Annabelle, it's time!"

A dark desolation blackened her insides. *Time.* It had finally run out for her.

She tried to pull her hand away, but he wouldn't let go.

"We haven't settled this," he bit out.

Her heart tore. Still no admission of love...She blinked rapidly as the hot tears stung her eyes. "Yes, we have."

She tugged again, and this time, her fingers slipped free.

Leaving him behind in the ruins, she ran down the path and across the lawn, through the dark night toward the house, where Lady Ainsley stood on the terrace waiting for her.

When she saw Belle hurrying toward her, she held out her hands. "It's midnight! You have to make your announcement." Taking both of Belle's hands in hers, she looked past her to search the dark night. She stiffened, a troubled frown creasing her brow. "Where's Quinton? Isn't he with you?"

Belle shook her head, unable to stop a silent tear from sliding down her cheek.

Lady Ainsley's face fell. "But I'd thought when you both left the party—I thought for certain he would..." She lowered her voice to whisper the hope Belle knew she'd been keeping secret since she invited Quinton to Glenarvon. Perhaps for six years before that. "Ask you to marry him."

An excruciating pain pierced her. "I'm not marrying Quinton," she rasped out, her lips so numb that she had no idea how they were able form the words.

Deep sadness distorted the viscountess's wrinkled features. "No?"

"Quinton and I would never have suited." She forced a smile through her tears, even in the midst of her own anguish wanting only to comfort the woman who had been a second mother to her. "We want different things in a marriage."

He wanted to ease his guilt, while she wanted love...or they would prefer never to marry at all. After tonight, they would both get that last wish, at least.

"I'm all right, my lady." When that didn't seem to cheer Lady Ainsley, Belle placed a kiss to her cheek and squeezed her hands to cover the lie. "Truly."

"What will you do about Glenarvon?" Lady Ainsley asked, an expression of grief and regret so raw on her face that Belle felt her heart tear anew, this time for the viscountess.

"What I should have done all along," she answered in a trembling voice.

"My lady?" Ferguson appeared in the doorway. As Master of Ceremonies, it was his duty to keep the party on schedule. "Midnight has arrived."

Lady Ainsley wiped her hand at her eyes. "Of course."

Both women linked arms and walked slowly inside the house, where the crowd of guests were waiting expectantly for the announcement. Including Sir Harold, who snatched two glasses of champagne from the tray of a passing footman and started across the room toward Belle, beaming a smile. He was oblivious to the pain inside her as Ferguson called for the musicians to stop playing.

With the attention of the room on her, Belle inhaled a deep breath. She'd made her decision, and it was for the best. But where there should have been relief that the agony of the past few weeks was finally over, there was only unbearable grief.

"I asked you all to be here tonight because—" She fisted her hands at her sides, so tight that her fingernails dug into her palms. She welcomed that physical pain because it countered the emotional torment inside her. "Because I wanted to announce that I would be... marrying next week, in time for my birthday. I wanted to share with you the name of the man I'd chosen to be my husband." She forced down her misery. "And master of Castle Glenarvon."

Soft murmurs and whispers rose throughout the room. Sir Harold proudly stuck out his chest as he arrived at her side.

But Belle stepped away, unable to endure being next to him when she announced her decision. She pressed a clenched fist to her chest, as if she could physically push back against the fierce tattoo of her broken heart.

"And so I've decided..." The room spun around her, the heat suffocating and the stench of candle smoke dizzying. More whispers, this time louder and more anxious. Her heart pounded so hard that the rush of blood in her ears was deafening. How could the foolish thing keep beating like this, when it had already shattered into a thousand pieces of glass? "I've decided..."

"She's decided on a husband," a deep voice announced loudly from across the crowded ballroom.

Quinton. He strode confidently into the room with the determination of a man resigned to his fate. Bare-necked, with mussed hair falling rakishly over his forehead, he embodied every bit of the scoundrel his reputation avowed him to be. Belle couldn't stop the shuddering desolation that descended upon her as she stared at him.

"She's marrying me," he stated with such resolve that everyone in the room fell into stunned silence.

Then bewildered whispers arose, followed by scattered applause and puzzled congratulations. And a happy cry from Lady Ainsley so loud that it echoed through the house.

In the momentary confusion, guests craned their necks to stare at Quinton and at Belle—and at Sir Harold, whose face turned scarlet. Spinning on his heel, he stalked from the house. When he reached the stone terrace, he threw the champagne glasses into the wall, shattering both in a hail of shimmering crystal and bubbles.

Quinton's blue eyes trained on her, blazing for battle as he stalked across the crowded room toward her.

She jerked her arm away when Quinton reached to take it. As she backed away from him, she shook her head.

"I've made my decision." Taking a deep breath, she announced as firmly and loudly as all her strength allowed, "I'm not marrying anyone."

CHAPTER ELEVEN

I wish you would tell me what this is all about," Belle said quietly to Lady Ainsley as she nervously paced the drawing room. Around them, the house grew quiet as the guests took their leave and the last of the carriages rolled away from the front entrance, the party having ended early on the heels of her surprise announcement. "I'd very much like to retire for the evening." To her room, where she could undress, crawl beneath the covers, and weep herself inconsolably into sleep. To put this evening behind her and find a way to go forward, without both the home and the man she loved.

"As soon as Quinton arrives," Lady Ainsley assured her, but her normally unflappable voice held an uneasy edge to it. Although, after the spectacle she and Quinton had just made of themselves in the ballroom, Belle acknowledged that perhaps the viscountess had a right to be anxious.

And to request that Belle and Quinton join her in the drawing room.

But that didn't explain why Mr. Bartleby was here, or why he seemed just as uneasy as Lady Ainsley. Certainly, he'd witnessed her announcement, and as the family solicitor, he would be carrying out the conveyance of the estate to the Church. But the reason why didn't concern him.

As for Quinton... Dear heavens, he was the *very* last person she wanted to face!

He had been right all along about marriage and Glenarvon. This place was her home, and she'd always think of it that way. But she wasn't willing to purchase it at the price of a lifetime's imprisonment of marriage to a man who did not love her.

Ferguson opened the door, and Quinton strode into the room, looking just as unsettled as she felt. Right down to the wrinkles in his jacket and the haphazardly tied replacement cravat he'd donned after leaving the ballroom. For once, he was unable to muster the charming grin that he always had for her and Lady Ainsley, giving them both a sober nod instead.

"Aunt Agatha." His gaze darkened as it landed on Belle. "Miss Greene." Then he saw the solicitor as the man rose to his feet, and he stiffened in surprise. "Bartleby? What the devil are you doing here?"

"That's what I've been attempting to discover," Belle mumbled as she walked toward them. "Neither of them would tell me until you arrived."

She trembled at Quinn's presence. Why did the rascal have to look so handsome, even all mussed and aggravated? And *why* did he have to keep looking at her like that, as if he wanted to grab her to him and kiss her senseless?

"Please sit." Lady Ainsley nodded toward a chair, but she remained standing and nervously wringing her hands. "You will probably want something to drink." Then she mumbled, "God knows I do."

Belle looked at her with alarm. To see the viscountess this upset—a warning pricked at the backs of her knees that this summons was about far more than tonight's party.

The viscountess gestured toward the front of the room. "There's a bottle of Bowmore inside the card table."

"Thank you." Quinn retrieved the bottle and a glass, pausing to refill Bartleby's glass before sitting. But his every muscle remained tense, his spine straight. His hard gaze flicked to Belle, and finding no answers in her, he looked back to his aunt. "You wished to speak to me?"

"To both of you," Lady Ainsley corrected.

Oh no. Belle sank onto the settee across the tea table from Quinton as her stomach roiled. Did Lady Ainsley know what happened between them tonight?

The viscountess drew in a deep breath, once more wringing her hands. "It seems that matters concerning Glenarvon—and Annabelle's future—have now changed."

Oh no no no no. She pressed her hand against her belly to keep from casting up her accounts and darted her eyes toward Quinn, whose face remained remarkably inscrutable. That Lady Ainsley had figured out what they'd done— She bit back a mortified groan.

"Changed how?" Quinn demanded quietly.

His aunt hesitated, then swung her gaze to Belle, who caught her breath. The last time she'd seen the viscountess so out of sorts was when Lord Ainsley died. Seeing it again now deeply worried her. "Annabelle, are you quite certain that you do not want to marry?"

"Absolutely certain," she whispered as Quinn stared at her, saying nothing. Thank goodness that the rascal remained silent for once. She didn't think she could have borne a second argument with him about that in front of his aunt.

"That is a disappointment." Lady Ainsley's face fell as she admitted quietly, "I had great hopes that you two would marry."

Belle's heart stopped. So did Quinn's arm as he raised the glass of whisky to his mouth.

He drawled, "Why would you think that?"

The dowager shook her head. "Because I've seen the way you two have looked at each other since you were eighteen. Even then there were embers burning between you." Belle turned away from the viscountess's gaze, but was unable to stop the telltale blush from rising in her cheeks. Lady Ainsley pressed Quinton, "Why do you think I invited you here to Glenarvon?"

"Because you needed my help to separate the viable gentlemen from the fortune hunters," he bit out as he continued raising the glass to his lips. He clearly hated the idea of that as much now as he had when she'd first proposed it three weeks ago. "To find Belle a suitable husband."

She wearily breathed out a defeated sigh. "A husband in *you*, my dear boy."

He choked on the whisky. Coughing, he wiped the back of his hand across his mouth and stared at her, speechless.

So did Belle.

Lord Ainsley smiled faintly, clearly regretting that her scheme hadn't worked. "I have learned over the years that the quickest way to make a man want something is by telling him that he cannot have it. So I told you that I wanted you to find another man for her, hoping you'd realize that you wanted to marry her yourself." She looked hopefully at Quinton. "You did offer tonight, and I'm certain that—"

"I do not wish to marry," Belle interrupted as firmly as possible, the conversation growing unbearable. Perhaps if she said it enough times, she'd begin to believe it herself.

"Not to anyone?" the dowager pressed.

"No, my lady." She pulled in a deep breath, refusing to meet Quinton's stare in case he could see right through that lie. "I wish to remain in your company for as long as you'll allow me."

"Then it seems we have no choice." Lady Ainsley exchanged a questioning glance with Bartleby, who nodded and pulled at his neck cloth as if it were choking him. She took another deep breath. "Your announcement this evening changed everything."

Confusion struck her. How could that have changed anything? She didn't have a fiancé and was set to lose Glenarvon anyway. Her announcement simply made that loss final.

A frown creased Quinton's brow. "How so?"

"When Lord Ainsley set up his will," the viscountess continued, "he attached the marriage stipulation because he wanted to protect you, Annabelle."

"From my father," she whispered.

Lady Ainsley hesitated, paling slightly. "From Marcus Greene, yes."

Bartleby straightened in his chair, leaning forward on the edge of the seat. "Although Lord Ainsley was your guardian, if Marcus Green ever returned into your life, he would have had every legal right to assume control of your property. The only way to protect you was for the estate to become yours and your husband's."

"Yes, I know." Why were they telling her this? It made not one whit of difference now.

"But Ainsley and I always thought you'd marry, that you'd make a love match," she said a bit wistfully. "The stipulation wouldn't have mattered then."

"It doesn't matter now." Belle's chest tightened with a sharp mix of guilt and loss. And deep grief. "Glenarvon won't be mine after all, so my father cannot get his hands on it anyway."

"He cannot ever now, my dear," Lady Ainsley said somberly, "Marcus Greene is dead."

Dead. Numbness flashed through her like an electric jolt. Her heart skipped, one painful, jarring beat. That was all. The moment passed, and she was left exactly as she was before. It wasn't grief that struck her, but the lack of it.

Her father was dead. And she couldn't find enough affection for him inside her to muster a single tear.

"Annabelle?" Quinn asked softly, his deep voice filled with concern.

She turned to look at him, and the worry he wore for her pierced her. *That* made her eyes heat with tears, far more than the news of her father's death.

"I'm fine," she whispered, folding her hands in her lap. She had no idea what to do with her hands... She looked up at Lady Ainsley, who was still wringing hers, and a deeper wariness gripped her. "How do you know, for certain?"

"Lord Quinton tasked me with finding your father," Bartleby interjected.

She swung her gaze to Quinton. "You did? Why?"

"Because I didn't want any more problems for you," he explained gently. "I know the hell that man put you and your mother through, and I wanted to make certain he remained on the far side of England, where he couldn't harm you."

Her throat tightened. Drat him! Why did he have to be so

thoughtful and kind? He made it impossible not to love him when he did things like this.

"I hired a runner who traced him down in Liverpool," Bartleby added. "He'd gone there after he was released from prison and worked as a porter on the docks, until he was convicted of theft and sent back to gaol. He died there eighteen months ago. The parish records confirm it." His face fell. "I am sorry, my dear."

"Thank you," she murmured, struck by how everyone's grief for her was stronger than her own grief for her father. A man who had been in her life only long enough for her to despise him.

"When Mr. Bartleby learned of his death, he told me." Anticipating Quinn's question about that, Lady Ainsley explained, "Bartleby has been our family attorney for years, and he knows that if there is any issue regarding Annabelle's security, he is to contact me immediately."

"I appreciate that you told me." Belle shook her head. "But his death changes nothing. He cannot get Glenarvon now, but neither can I."

Lady Ainsley and Mr. Bartleby exchanged another look, another silent communication. Then the viscountess said quietly, "But you can."

"No," she said as firmly as possible, not daring to meet Quinn's dark gaze. Dear heavens, *why* wouldn't they leave her alone about this? "I am *not* marrying."

Bartleby replied carefully, "There is another part of the will that might now come into consideration and make your inheritance of Glenarvon possible without having to take a husband."

Her breath caught in her throat as a bubble of hope swelled inside her. Tonight, when she'd made her decision not to marry, to follow after Quinton into the shadows, she was certain she'd lost her home. She'd accepted it then, and coming to that decision had emboldened her, because she'd had nothing left to lose.

But now, she had a second chance. Her heart raced painfully, and she barely registered that Quinn had tensed and sat forward in his chair. She asked softly, "How?"

"As you know," the solicitor continued, "Lord Ainsley bequeathed all unentailed properties to his daughters to be split evenly among them."

"Yes, his daughters from his first marriage."

Bartleby glanced at Lady Ainsley, who hesitated, then nodded her permission for him to continue. He cleared his throat and explained, "Your inheritance of Glenarvon would have equaled their shares. Lord Ainsley made certain of it." He paused and nervously pushed his spectacles into place on his nose. "He wanted all of his daughters to be taken care of."

She nodded, noting from the corner of her eye that Quinn had pushed himself from his chair and moved to stand behind her at the settee. "Lord Ainsley was a good man. Of course, he—"

"Including you."

She caught her breath, stunned. Quinn's hand went gently to her shoulder as the soft words registered inside her. No, that couldn't be. What he was implying... *impossible*.

But when she looked up at Quinn and saw his sober face, she knew—

"My father was Marcus Greene," she breathed, so softly that her own ears couldn't hear it. Her heart leapt agonizingly, each thumping beat coming so hard that she thought it might burst free from her chest. Numbly, she reached up to cover Quinn's hand with her own, seeking an anchor in him to keep from falling away. "My father wasn't...my father?"

Lady Ainsley sat beside her on the settee and took Belle's hands securely in hers. The look of sadness and grief on the viscountess's face ripped through her, stealing her breath away and instantly forming hot tears at her lashes. When she felt the blood drain from her face and all of her began to shudder, Lady Ainsley placed her hand against Belle's cheek. "Charles North, Lord Ainsley, was your real father, Annabelle."

Sudden grief tore through her so fiercely that even in her stunned shock the pain was blinding. The world tilted beneath her. Only Quinn's hand on her shoulder gave her anything solid to cling to, his strong fingers tightening to let her know he was there.

"We never meant to hurt you by keeping this from you," Lady Ainsley whispered softly, her hand soothingly stroking Belle's cheek and hair while the other held tight to her hand. "But it cannot be kept any longer. You need to know now."

Squeezing her eyes shut, she gave a jerking nod.

She felt Quinn's hand slide away. *No! Stay with me!* But she couldn't speak through the terrible anguish shredding her from the inside out. Then she heard Lady Ainsley's voice through the painful fog suffocating her—

"...lost his first wife, Ainsley was devastated. He could barely leave his bed and wouldn't eat. Your mother was his housekeeper at the London house, and she helped him through his grief. They became very close." The viscountess's voice quavered, and Belle was only dimly aware through her own pain of how difficult this must be for her. "Ainsley loved your mother, very much, but he was a viscount with young children to care for and could never marry a housekeeper."

Another jerking nod, and her eyes squeezed tighter.

"Then one day, she left. No warning, no explanation... Ainsley looked for her, but she was gone. Yet he never gave up, and nearly a decade later, he found her. That was when he learned he had a daughter in you." She took Belle's face between her trembling hands. "Your mother had left because she'd discovered that she was with child, and she married Marcus Greene so that you would not be illegitimate. When Ainsley found you and your mother, you were eight. You thought Marcus Greene was your father, and your mother didn't want you to know the truth."

Belle gave a soft sob, unable to hold back a tear as it slipped down her cheek.

"Don't blame her, darling." Soft hands soothed at her temples and cheeks, gently brushing away the stray tears. "She wanted only to protect you, to keep you safe. But she allowed Ainsley to meet you, remember?"

"My birthday," she breathed out past trembling lips.

"He gave you a new coat and shoes, and a pretty doll, just like the ones he gave his other daughters when they were little." She paused, her own voice trembling with emotion. "It broke his heart to leave you behind."

Belle was certain it did. But *dear God*! Hearing the truth now stirred so much pain inside her that it hurt to take each breath.

"When Marcus Greene was arrested, Ainsley made certain that you and your mother had a safe place to live, food, clothes—everything you needed." The viscountess drew a deep breath. "Then your mother fell ill."

"And I came here," she whispered. She opened her eyes, and Lady Ainsley's concerned face blurred beneath her tears.

"He promised your mother on her deathbed that he would

treat you as well as his other daughters, that he would always care for you." Her eyes glistened. "He was at her side when she passed. The last words your mother heard were of how much he loved her."

Unable to choke down the flow of tears any longer, Belle collapsed into Lady Ainsley's arms. The viscountess held her tenderly and cooed soothingly to her as she rocked her in her arms.

Belle had no idea how long she lay there in Lady Ainsley's lap while she cried, but long enough that when she finally sat up and wiped away her last tears, Quinn had moved away to stand in front of the window, staring blankly outside at the night, his back toward them and his hand rubbing at his nape.

"Why?" Belle whispered, her hands tightly clutching the viscountess's. "Why didn't you tell me before now?"

"Life was hard enough for you as it was, having lost your mother to fever and the man you thought was your father to prison. Ainsley knew what happened to illegitimate children born to members of society when their father's true identity was made known, and he didn't want you to be hurt any more than you already were. He thought it was for the best to keep it secret and to give you the best life we could despite that." She squeezed Belle's hands. "We both did."

All those years...she'd never once suspected that Lord Ainsley was anything more to her than the kind and generous man who had taken her in as a favor to her mother. But he'd loved her, Belle had *always* known that. As much as any father could have.

"We treated you exactly as we did his other daughters, and he made certain you had everything you should, right down to a good education and a London debut." Lady

Ainsley smiled sadly. "He was always so proud of you, most of all whenever he found you in the library, lost in a book. You were his little bluestocking, and he constantly bragged about how smart you were, what new language you'd learned, what play or novel you'd forced poor Ferguson to act out with you in the gardens. He couldn't have loved you more if you were his legitimate daughter."

Belle nodded and lowered her face as she wiped at her eyes. And she'd loved him. The grief filling her heart now was not for Lord Ainsley but for herself, for never having the chance to know him as a father.

"He wanted to protect you, and so we agreed never to tell you. What good would it have brought?" She sadly shook her head. "But now, with circumstances as they are…"

When her voice trailed off, Bartleby interjected gently, "You can now receive Glenarvon as your share of the inheritance that he left to all his daughters."

Quinn glanced over his shoulder, his eyes narrowing angrily on Bartleby. "Tell her the rest," he ordered.

The two men stared at each other, and the silent communication that passed between them brought an icy frost over the room. A tension Belle couldn't fathom.

"Tell her what she has to do to claim it. That she can only gain her inheritance that way if she lets herself be recognized as Ainsley's illegitimate daughter." Quinn bit out distastefully, "His bastard."

"Quinton, please," Lady Ainsley chastised.

The harshness in his voice and face could have cut glass. But when he looked at Belle, his expression softened. "You'll never be accepted into society. They'll never let you forget who you are and where you came from. They'll cut you directly to your face—worse, they'll do everything they can to embarrass you, spread vicious and untrue stories about you, ruin what's left of your reputation."

She held his gaze for a long moment, each passing second marked by her pounding heartbeat. And by the increasing anguish in her heart, that he could care this much about her to once more attempt to protect her by warning her...but not love her.

She smiled faintly, a soft curl to her lips as she lifted her chin. "Let them. I haven't needed them in the past twenty-five years, and I won't need them going forward."

"You know what it means to be ostracized by society, how hard it can be," he pressed. "Are you certain you want this?"

"What do I care what society thinks of me?" She squeezed Lady Ainsley's hand. "I will have Glenarvon and my tenants, the workmen, the villagers...all the people I love, and all the people who love me." She saw the concern that darkened his face, but she also saw the flicker of admiration deep in his sapphire eyes. "I now get to tell the world that Lord Ainsley was my father, and I will make him so very proud of me. The way a daughter should."

His eyes never left hers as he murmured, "That's my Bluebell."

A warmth blossomed in her chest, even as her heart tore as she thought about her new future. One she wouldn't be able to share with him.

"If that is your decision," Bartleby interjected, "then first thing in the morning, I'll file to have the courts reopen the will. The magistrates will certainly want to question all of us, but I am confident that they'll grant you Glenarvon, especially after I show them the letters I have in my office, in which Lord Ainsley and your mother acknowledged your true paternity." He smiled at her. "Congratulations, Miss Greene. You are the new owner of Castle Glenarvon."

"Thank you," she whispered. Belle glanced at Quinn. She wanted to share the bittersweet joy of this moment with him, but he'd turned away, once again staring thoughtfully out the window.

Bartleby smiled proudly at Quinn. His chest puffed out beneath his waistcoat. "You asked me to find a legal loophole, Lord Quinton. It seems that's exactly what we've done!"

But Quinn only grunted to acknowledge the solicitor's comment, his eyes and attention still focused out the window, where he could surely see nothing but the inky blackness of the dark countryside.

Lady Ainsley rose to her feet, gently pulling Belle up with her. "I think we should go to your room now." She placed a motherly hand against Belle's cheek and smiled reassuringly at her. "You've had a long evening. I'm certain you could use some peace and rest. And I know that while I can never replace your mother"—she paused, her eyes glistening—"I hope you still hold affection for me, the kind a daughter would."

Unable to speak for fear of crying, Belle tightly hugged Lady Ainsley. Then the viscountess linked her arm around Belle's waist and led her from the room.

Belle looked back in time to see Quinn turn away from the window and slap Bartleby on the back.

"Bartleby, if you don't mind lingering a bit. I have a proposition for you..." Quinn's deep voice drifted away as Belle passed into the hall with the dowager.

CHAPTER TWELVE

$\mathscr{B}$elle sat on the window seat in her bedroom, her forehead resting against the cool glass, and stared into the dark night, unable to see anything beyond the pane. Although, in truth, she wasn't really looking. Her thoughts were too preoccupied, churning and spinning until she didn't know what to think. Or feel.

The solitude of her room hadn't given her the peace she'd sought, especially as Lady Ainsley had come by twice to check on her and then sent her maid to bring up a cup of warm milk to help her sleep. *Sleep?* A bubble of laughter spilled from her lips. How ludicrous that notion was! She'd never be able to sleep tonight. Not knowing that Lord Ainsley was her real father and that Glenarvon was now hers and could never be taken away.

And certainly not with thoughts of Quinn revolving through her mind, so foolishly replaying every moment that he'd spent making love to her.

No. Not making love.

She squeezed her eyes shut at the searing pain that gripped her when she thought of that special melding of bodies and souls. She might have made love to *him*, but what he felt for her wasn't anything near love.

To have him finally propose to her, only to have to reject him—oh, it had been torture! But she knew the hell that a marriage without love could be, and she would never put herself into that position. No matter Quinn's honorable intentions, or how much she longed to be his wife.

A knock sounded softly at the door, and she rolled her tear-blurred eyes. *What now?* Why wouldn't everyone just leave her alone so she could be miserable in peace?

But the knock came again. Dreading that it was another visit from Lady Ainsley, or more warm milk she didn't have the stomach to drink, she opened her door.

And gasped. "Quinton."

He leaned on his shoulder against the doorjamb and smiled down at her. For a moment she couldn't believe he wasn't a figment from her imagination, but she knew he had to be real. Because only the real Quinton could stir such confusion and yearning inside her, a riot of it leaving her not knowing whether to throw herself into his arms or throttle him. And for a moment not caring which as long as her hands were on him.

"Invite me inside," he murmured softly. His deep voice twined down her spine and blossomed goose bumps on her bare arms.

Taking a deep breath, she held her ground and prayed he couldn't see how he made her tremble. "That wouldn't be proper."

He trailed a searing look down her front that told her

exactly how little he cared for proper. That look cascaded memories through her of every breath-stealing kiss he'd ever given her, every delicious touch, and she shivered beneath his audacity.

As if he knew what confused desires he flamed inside her, he quirked the corner of his mouth higher with amusement. "Can't a man visit his fiancée?"

"I'm not your fiancée." She forced a playful tone, despite the hollow ache in her chest. "Haven't you heard? I'm an heiress now. You don't have to marry me to save Glenarvon."

Breathing deeply to steady herself, she longed to touch him, to brush her fingers through his mussed hair that even now had a golden lock lying rakishly over his forehead. But she wasn't naïve enough to think that it would stop with such an innocent touch and tucked her traitorous hands behind her back.

His eyes captured hers as he murmured, "What if I want to marry you anyway?"

Her breath caught painfully, her throat and nose stinging with emotion. She whispered breathlessly, "You don't."

"But I do. Let me in, and I'll prove it." He purred those words so wolfishly that a flush of heat rose in her cheeks, and his eyes sparkled at the reaction he drew from her. "Besides, I want to give you your birthday gift."

A bittersweet knot tightened in her chest that he cared enough about her to bring her a gift, to come to her bedchamber tonight...yet not enough to love her. "Someone might see you here."

He lifted a brow in challenge. "Then invite me inside so they don't."

Biting her lip, she hesitated. She should turn him away,

make him leave—and with that, to possibly lose her last chance ever to be alone with him, to be held safe and secure in his arms.

"Please, Belle." He told her honestly, "I'd very much like to come in and talk."

"Talk?" she asked dubiously.

"Perhaps more." His half grin blossomed into a wicked smile. "But we'll never know if you don't let me in."

A voice inside her head screamed in warning, but even that wasn't enough to tamp down the ache of desire she felt for him. Unable to deny herself the happiness of being with him, she stepped back to let him slip inside her room. She silently closed the door behind him, then paused to draw a deep breath before she turned the lock.

Quinn set the satchel he carried down on her reading chair and faced her. His sultry gaze swept languidly over her, from unruly locks to bare toes and back again, and everywhere he looked, heat prickled beneath her skin. The now familiar ache began to rise inside her, and her breath turned shallow and jerky. Her body knew now what he was capable of doing to hers, and she longed for those wonderful sensations again. Just as she knew that only Quinton would ever be able to make her feel such pleasure, such freedom and joy.

"You shouldn't be here," she protested weakly, unable to keep the aching tremor from her voice.

"You're beautiful." His eyes gleamed in the firelight.

Trying to ignore that, she sucked in a deep breath to steady herself. "We shouldn't be alone like this."

"*Very* beautiful."

Exasperated, she sagged her shoulders at his attempt to charm away her frustrations. "Quinton—"

He stepped slowly to her, then took her chin and tipped her face up to tenderly kiss her lips.

Belle closed her eyes, overcome by the nearness of him, his masculinity filling her senses.

She shifted closer. The heat of his hard body against her soft one made her tingle everywhere they touched, and his lips kissed hers so thoroughly that already she craved more. That secret space between her legs throbbed for him, with a need only he could satisfy. Why Quinton Carlisle, of all men, created this desperate longing inside her, she simply couldn't fathom. But he did just that.

He didn't love her, but he did desire her. And tonight, their only night together, that would have to be enough.

His mouth left hers to dance light kisses along her jaw to her ear, then down to the bare stretch of flesh where her neck curved into her shoulder. He ran his hand over the scooped neck of her night rail, stealing a caress of his fingers across the top swells of her breasts.

"You truly are beautiful tonight, Annabelle," he murmured.

That was a lie if ever she heard one. Her cheeks flushed at being caught wearing this old nightgown, which covered her in a formless tent of white cotton from wrists to ankles. "I am not, not in this frumpy old thing." And certainly not with a red nose and eyes from crying.

"I think," he murmured as his fingers untied the bow at her neckline and let the gown fall open around her shoulders, "that you look delectable."

With a soft laugh at his flattery, she snaked her arms around his neck. "I'm not delectable." Her fingers played flirtatiously in his hair at his nape, and excited anticipation grew inside her. Feeling feminine and light, with a nod toward silliness, she teased, "Puddings are delectable, not women." Feigning insult, she arched a scolding brow. "Am I a cake, then?"

"Of the most delicious kind," he murmured. He placed a delicate but possessive kiss in the valley between her breasts, and she shivered at the promise behind it.

"Of strawberries and cream?" She arched against him, inviting his mouth on her body. A wanton part of her wanted to tease him to the brink of losing control, to make him crave her intimacy as much as she did his. "All pink and luscious, sweet to the taste…"

He groaned at the image her words conveyed as his hands roamed freely over her body now, stroking the unseen curves beneath the billowing cotton. "You're killing me, Belle."

She laughed wickedly. "And so much buttery icing," she panted out as his hands squeezed her bottom through the cotton, "just waiting to be licked—"

His mouth captured hers, stopping her in mid-temptation and turning the teasing description on her lips into a low moan. She met the hungry passion of his kiss with her own, fisting his silky hair in her hands as the ache pulsed relentlessly between her legs.

"I want to taste every tempting inch of you, Belle," he murmured against her mouth, not pausing in his kisses. "I want to devour you."

He grabbed the sleeves of her night rail and yanked, expertly pulling the cotton down over her body in a single tug and letting it fall to the floor around her bare feet.

Belle gasped. She was naked! Completely and utterly bare as she stood in front of him. Her cheeks blushed scarlet.

He stepped back to gaze at her, and she felt the heat of his stare as it seared over each of her breasts, then down her belly to the curls between her legs. His face darkened with raw desire. Suddenly, there was no more charm or teasing in him. He wore a look that told her he would keep his promise—to devour her.

And God help her, she wanted just that.

She huskily murmured her consent, "Yes, Quinton."

He scooped her into his arms and carried her across the room, then placed her on the bed. When he pulled away to quickly shuck off his shirt and trousers, Belle stared shamelessly. This was the first time she'd seen him without the cover of clothing, and the sight of him was a sweet intoxication. Her eyes swept over the hard muscles of his chest and the ridges of his abdomen, following the faint dusting of golden hair down his chest, over his belly, and brazenly lower to his manhood, which was already hard and thick with his need for her.

She lost her breath.

He was simply magnificent, all golden in the firelight, with long, sinewy muscles in his arms and legs, and blue eyes staring at her so intensely that she shivered. At the warmth of his fingers touching her ankle and trailing along her bare leg to the curve of her hip, a helpless whimper of desire escaped her. What a wanton woman she was to lie here like this, draped naked over the bed while she let him run his hands over her, touching and exploring her body as he desired.

But if this was being wanton, then she welcomed it. Because she would never be embarrassed at the pleasures Quinn brought her.

He knelt beside the bed and placed his hands on her thighs. "Annabelle...please..."

Knowing what he wanted, she spread her legs to welcome

this new intimacy between them. She wasn't ashamed of opening herself to him, not when she heard him murmur how beautiful she was, and not even when she felt the heat of his strong lips as he placed a tender, delicate kiss right *there*. This was Quinn, and she loved him—hadn't she always?

Soft and gentle, his lips caressed against her in slow kisses that didn't flame the ache inside her so much as soothe and relax, and with a contented sigh, she reached her hand down to stroke her fingers through his hair. How could one man be both so passionate that he'd torn cries of desire from her earlier and yet now so gentle that he sent a calming warmth radiating through her?

But each delicate kiss grew stronger, his mouth more insistent against her. When he licked deep—

"Quinton!" she gasped, squirming beneath his mouth.

"Shh." He stroked his hands along her inner thighs to still her, as if petting a kitten. Each breathy word pulsed hot against her wet folds. "You are so delicious, Belle...Let me have this taste of you."

She took a deep breath, then exhaled in a long sigh. Closing her eyes, she gave over to the decadent sensation of his mouth against her, to the wonderfully wicked licks of his tongue delving deep into her, to the soft sounds of his lips enjoying her most secret place. The fluttering ache inside her began to blossom again, throbbing so shamelessly right there against his mouth that she was certain he could feel the pulsation of her need against his lips and taste her readiness for him on his tongue.

"Quinn." His name was a plaintive whimper as all of her began to quiver.

"I know, darling." He placed one last, lingering kiss at the hot heart of her, then slowly slid up her body, his mouth leaving a wet trail of kisses all the way up to her throat.

With his large body now covering hers, he reached a hand between her thighs and gently parted her with his fingers. As if understanding the inexplicable new need inside her, one that was far more than just a physical ache for release, he slowly slid his manhood inside her, pushing gently forward until his hips were seated against hers.

"Slowly this time," he murmured against her temple as his body began to stroke tenderly inside hers. "I want to savor you."

His hard chest rubbed against her breasts as he slid up and down over her with each gentle plunge and tantalizing retreat. None of the urgent thrusts of before, none of that desperate need to possess her—this was tenderness and affection. Never had she felt this feminine and powerful before in her life, this *transcendent*. And it was all because of Quinn.

If any doubts remained inside her that she loved him, this moment vanquished them all.

Murmuring her name, he continued his rocking caresses inside her. She clung to him as he swirled his hips slowly against her before retreating, rubbing tantalizingly against her sex and pulsing a soft ache deep within her. Every stroke inside her branded her as his, and she tossed back her head with joy as her body welcomed the intensity of him, filling her completely. She arched herself beneath him and rocked against his hips to bring him as deep as possible inside her. She would have let him crawl beneath her skin, if he could have, and inundate her soul with his essence.

Her hands clutched at his shoulders as the first flames shot through her, and the throbbing ache inside her fanned out to the ends of her fingers and toes. For one desperate moment, she fought against her release, knowing tonight would be the last time she would ever be with him and wanting to make it last as long as she could. But restraint was impossible, and she broke.

Her release came not as a wave of hot pleasure but a gentle, warm lapping at her toes that crept up her body until it engulfed her. He brought her to climax this time not with a cry of passion but a blissful sigh of love.

"Annabelle," he whispered as he rested his forehead against her bare shoulder and released himself inside her.

At that new sensation, her body shivered with a second, even more intense pleasure. He hadn't used that clever little sheath this time to separate them, and he had been right—making love was far nicer this way, with no barriers at all between them.

Only then did she realize that she was whispering his name over and over. But she couldn't stop herself. She knew she would never again feel as perfect and complete as she did when Quinn was holding her in his arms.

* * *

Quinton leaned over to place a kiss in the middle of Belle's bare back as she lounged on her belly across her bed, all sex-rumpled and relaxed. His lips curled against her warm skin, and he couldn't resist the urge to chuckle, so happy was he to have Annabelle with him like this.

He hadn't meant to take her like that, certainly not without using the last of the condoms he still had in his possession. But the surprising little bluestocking had aroused him to the point where all that mattered was being inside her. It was a risk he shouldn't have taken, but he simply couldn't help himself. Especially since he fully intended to marry her.

There was no doubt inside him about that now. He belonged right here with Annabelle. If any hesitations had still been lingering inside him, this second intimacy dashed them all. He'd been right about her from the beginning—a man didn't give himself to her and then walk away.

She turned her head to gaze up at him, with her cheek resting on her folded arms and her caramel hair tumbling around her shoulders. A contented smile played at her lips.

His chest tightened as he stared down at her. Sweet Lucifer, he could certainly get used to nights like this. And once they were married, there would be no reason not to.

He traced a fingertip over her mouth, drawing her smile. When she closed her lips around his finger and sucked suggestively, the sensation pulsed all the way down to the tip of his cock. He groaned softly.

"Keep doing that," he warned as he pulled his hand away, "and I'll have you on your back again."

Her eyes sparkled mischievously. "Is that supposed to be a warning or an enticement?"

"Wanton," he scolded. Yet he grinned at her, unable to resist her infectious happiness tonight. She had every right to be happy. Glenarvon was now secure, and she knew that the viscount had loved her as a true daughter.

The only issue left unresolved was marriage.

She didn't need to marry at all now, but he fully intended to marry *her*. The new conditions of her inheritance made not one whit of difference to him. They belonged together; tonight proved that, and she needed him, now more than ever. Being recognized as Ainsley's illegitimate daughter wouldn't be easy. Neither would running the estate. He could help her with both, while she helped him become the man he wanted to be. Successful, hardworking, devoted to his family and the village…the kind of man who would make his father proud.

But he had to convince her of that. And if it took repeatedly making love to her to do it, then he was most definitely willing to sacrifice himself to the flames.

"You know," she commented in a throaty voice as she sat up to bring herself into his arms, unwittingly giving him a perfect view of her full breasts and the sweet curls between her thighs, "if I had known that being naked with you would be so much fun, I think I might have stripped you bare right there beneath St James's roses six years ago."

He laughed and nuzzled his face against her shoulder, not wanting to dampen her amusement by telling her that many couples had done just that beneath that same bower, if rumors could be trusted. Of course, that gossip was also entwined with apocryphal stories about leather and bayonets, so he wasn't certain what to believe. Except that if she had tried, he certainly would have let her.

With a soft growl, he leaned over and kissed her, teasing fresh arousal inside her until he felt her shiver. He smiled against her lips. The fire he so loved to flame inside her now belonged solely to him, and he planned on never letting it go.

He cupped her face in his hands. Her eyes were closed, her lips red and wet from his kisses, and never had she looked more alluring. She tilted her face toward him in invitation to be kissed again, and it took all his strength to keep himself from doing just that. And more.

"Would you like your birthday present now?" he asked, his fingertips stroking her cheek. If he didn't distract both of them, and quickly, he'd be hard and between her thighs again before she could whisper his name. While the thought was deliciously tempting, he also knew how sore she would be in the morning. The last thing he wanted to do was hurt her, in any way.

Her eyes fluttered open, and she looked up at him, puzzled. "My...what?"

He laughed and kissed the tip of her nose. "Did you think that bedding you was your gift?"

"Of course not." Then she confided in a breathy whisper, staring at him seductively through lowered lashes, "But it *was* the best present I've ever been given."

Hiding his pleased grin, he lowered his mouth to place an openmouthed kiss against her shoulder. Her comment stirred more pride inside him than he deserved. Still, he liked it. Immensely.

Before he got caught up in her again, he slipped away and crossed the room to his satchel. He pulled out a blue velvet pouch tied with a gold-tasseled cord. He handed her the bag, then reclined across the bed beside her on his elbow.

"Go on." He leaned over to kiss her bare thigh as she stared down at the weighty velvet sack in her hand. "Open it."

Belle slid him a suspicious glance as she carefully untied the gold cord, opened the cinched pouch—

She gasped. Her eyes grew wide as she slowly withdrew the four-foot-long rope of white Persian pearls, long enough to loop around her neck and down her front thrice. His great-grandmother's pearls.

His mother gave them to him when he said good-bye to her a month ago at Chestnut Hill, wanting him to have this heirloom to remind him of who he was and the importance of family, even when he was half a world away. He'd sent all his other belongings ahead to Liverpool in a wagonload of trunks, but these he'd kept with him. At the time, he'd done it only to keep them from being stolen. But now he knew. As if Fate had been guiding him.

They belonged with Belle.

"Oh, Quinton," she breathed, awestruck. "This is...this is..."

He grinned at her. Even when stunned, she was beautiful. "Do you like them?"

Struck speechless, she only nodded as she draped the rope of pearls across her palm and down her forearm, luminescent white lying luxuriously against her pale skin. Her bright eyes glistened as she stared at them, her lashes wet with tears.

His chest pinched. Good Lord, he hadn't expected her to *cry*.

"Mother always said that a lady should be given pearls," he explained softly.

She arched a dubious brow but couldn't drag her gaze away from the strand as she let it spill through her fingers and across her palms. She whispered hoarsely, "To the lady who refuses to marry you?"

"Mother wasn't specific," he replied, deadpan, despite the sharp pang in his gut.

She might have refused before, but he planned on changing that. Starting now. He sat up and kissed her, so delicately and tenderly that he drew a soft sigh from her lips.

"You deserve them, Annabelle," he whispered between gentle nips to her bottom lip. "And many, many more gifts just like them to come."

Her shoulders sagging, she shook her head and shifted back, breaking the kiss. A sad expression darkened her face. "They're too much," she whispered. "I cannot accept them."

"Of course you can." He sat up and took the rope from her hands to loop it over her neck, then again to double it down her front. He wanted there to be no mistake that the pearls now belonged to her. And she belonged with him. "And you will."

"No, Quinton." She blinked hard with a determined shake of her head and choked out, "Truly, I cannot accept them—I won't. You need the money for America."

"Then you *can* accept them, because I didn't buy them," he explained quietly. They were beautiful around her neck, seeming to glow as they rested against her bare skin. "They're a family heirloom."

Remorse darkened her face. "Then even more reason to—"

"And they're staying right in the Carlisle family." She caught her breath at that firm declaration of his intention to marry her, staring at him with wide eyes glistening with tears. Dear God, he hoped those were tears of happiness. "They're yours for now, Annabelle," he pressed on quietly with full resolve. "But someday, you'll pass them along to our son to give to the woman he marries."

Our son. He wasn't prepared for the electric jolt that pierced him when he uttered the words, but he meant every one. Theirs would be a proper marriage.

"You're going to America," she breathed out, not moving except for the trembling of her lips.

"I'm staying right here," he told her, and meant it. Dear God, how could he even contemplate leaving her now? "My future is right here in the borderlands. With you."

Tonight had opened his eyes. He could make his success

here, where proving himself would be difficult and complicated, and become a better man for it. The borderlands certainly weren't the soil-rich lands that he had wanted as the foundation for his future, yet the offer he'd made tonight to Bartleby for Kinnybroch would put him well on the way. And make for equal partners in his marriage with Annabelle. The new combined estate would be *theirs*, a grand property to oversee together, where they would launch their lives and raise their family. Where he could prove himself away from Trent's shadow and make his father proud of him, just as he'd wanted. And where he was needed.

"I don't want you to give up your dream for America," she protested breathlessly. "I know how important that is to you, and I would never ask that of you."

"You didn't. I came to that decision on my own," he assured her. "With a little help from Robert. You need me, Annabelle." He leaned over her and lowered her down onto her back on the mattress with a deep and hungry kiss. "Haven't you realized that yet?"

"Quinton." His name was a heartbreaking ache for mercy, but he had no intention of giving her quarter. Not until she stood next to him in a church and pledged her life to him.

"I'm staying with you." He sucked gently at her bottom lip, then groaned at how sweet she tasted, that delicious flavor of the northern wilds, of heather and mountains and sky... "And I want you to have these pearls, something as special and precious as you are. Besides," he murmured, placing a kiss on the side of her neck where the two strands crossed, "they're beautiful on you."

Exquisite, in fact. The first loop of pearls draped down across her bare breasts, flirting tantalizingly at her dusky nipples, while the second fell down farther to graze her belly. Warm arousal stirred inside him at the erotic sight.

"You will keep them," he insisted as his lips went to her throat to suck at the pearls resting on her delicate skin. "And you will wear them on the day we're married. Understand?"

She shook her head. "I can't—"

"Annabelle." Her name was a warning that he would brook no argument about this. Because his next course of action would have been to tie her up with them to make her see reason . . . although, he considered as he rubbed the smooth pearls back and forth across her nipples and watched shamelessly as they hardened beneath the soft friction, tying her up might not be such a bad idea after all.

"I can't accept them, Quinton," she rasped out chokingly. "And I won't marry you."

"You will," he argued softly. Marriage was the right future for both of them, making both their dreams come true. *More*—she needed him, and he certainly needed her.

"No, I won't."

"Why not?" he cajoled softly as his mouth followed the rope down to her breasts, to lave at her nipples with his tongue. Whatever her reason, he would prove it wrong—

"Because I love you," she whispered, and the anguished sound sliced through him like a saber.

* * *

Belle held her breath as Quinn froze, his mouth stilling against her, and waited for him to reply. Her heart pounded brutally as it ticked off each silent second, and each passing moment only made her more miserable than she'd ever been before in her life. Because she knew the harsh truth.

For all his pretty words and charming smiles, for all his insistence that she marry him, he did not love her.

When she could bear his silence no longer, she slid out from beneath him and off the bed. Thankfully, he let her go, but the heat of his puzzled stare fixed on her as she snatched up her discarded night rail and pulled it over her head. Her shaking fingers tangled the ribbon at her neckline into a knotted mess.

She squeezed her eyes shut against the stunned expression on his handsome face and pressed her hand against her chest, where her foolish heart continued to pound away. Didn't the silly thing know it was broken? The irony burned inside her. Three weeks ago she was desperate to marry him; now she couldn't bear the thought of being the wife he didn't love.

Pulling in a deep breath, she forced down the hollow pain smoldering inside her chest. "Do you know why I followed you into the darkness tonight during the party? Because I'd already made my decision to not marry. Tonight was to be the one and only time I would ever make love to a man," she said softly. The raw sincerity came easier than she'd imagined, but it didn't stop her heart from bleeding. "And I wanted it to be with you."

He stared at her, stunned at her confession. "Belle, I—"

"It was wonderful, Quinton. *You* were wonderful. But I never expected you to marry me because of it. Not then, not now." She squeezed her eyes shut, unable to bear seeing his shocked expression. "In the end, you were right about me. I couldn't bring myself to marry someone who didn't love me." Shaking her head, she forced a smile, but it only deepened her sorrow. She choked out—"And I still can't."

Years of marriage to him, living with him and loving him,

even bearing his children— *Dear God.* A different kind of hell than the one her mother suffered in her marriage, but still agony. To dedicate her life and heart to a man who did not love her in return, to be so close to his love that she could feel it and taste it, but never have it...how would she ever survive?

He rolled off the bed and stalked toward her. "We need each other, Annabelle. As estate partners, as friends, as lovers...I want all of that with you. You're beautiful and intelligent, and you make me feel alive. How could I *not* want you for my wife?"

A soft sob tore through her. Damn him for saying such wonderful things! And damn him for putting his arms around her, for drawing her close against him...Oh, he wasn't helping, not at all! Because for all his sweet words and tender touches, there was no admission of love. And she knew in her heart that there never would be.

"Quinton—" Her throat tightened as he caressed his lips across her shoulder, her eyes closing tightly against the unbearable tenderness of his kiss.

"I care about you, Annabelle. And I want to make you happy." He kissed her gently and murmured against her lips, "We need each other, and that's enough. What more could love do but cause problems?"

"Allow for a true partnership, for one," she whispered. Something her parents never had.

"We would have that." He took a deep breath and confessed, "I spoke to Bartleby about it tonight. I'm taking the money I saved for America and purchasing more land for us. For *us*, Belle. Property we'll own and manage together."

What should have made her heart soar only made it tear more deeply. "And inside the house where we live?" she murmured, unable to find her voice beneath her sorrow. No matter how much the hopefulness of his words warmed her chest, owning property together would only be part of their lives. "Would we be partners there, too? When we disagree—and we *will* disagree, Quinton, it's our nature—without love to get us through the bad times…" She shook her head and whispered, "Our marriage becomes nothing but a prison."

"No, it won't." The determination inside him was strong, but it didn't bring her comfort. "We were friends first before we ever considered anything more, and we'll stay friends after we marry."

"I saw what my parents had for a marriage." She blinked rapidly as his handsome face blurred unrecognizably beneath her hot tears. "They didn't have love, which meant they didn't have respect for each other. But they had resentment, bitterness, anger…so much anger!"

"I'm not Marcus Greene," he countered fiercely. "I would *never* lay a hand on you or treat you the way he treated your mother."

"I know that," she whispered achingly. "But I also know that the damage you could do to me could be so much worse, just because I love you. You wouldn't have to do anything except not return my love, and the pain would be unbearable." She shook her head, the anguish already burning inside her so hotly that she shuddered. "I couldn't bear that kind of marriage with you."

"You think love would make it better?" His arms tightened around her, as if he were afraid she'd leave him right then. "Love can make things *worse*, Annabelle. Look at my parents—when my father died, my mother was devastated. Her entire life was ripped out from under her. It took her weeks to crawl out of bed, and every breath she took filled her with such grief, such desolation, that it nearly killed her, too."

"Quinton," she whispered, struck by the raw emotion in him. His jaw tightened as the grief of the memories mixed with his frustration, until it seeped inside her, as palpable as falling rain.

"And your real parents, Belle…what did love do for them?" He shook his head. "In my experience, love causes nothing but destruction and heartache. Why would you want that?"

Slowly, she stepped back, just out of his grasp, should he attempt once more to reach for her. Because she wasn't certain she had the strength to push him away if he did.

"You're wrong, Quinton," she said softly. "Without love there's nothing." She ached with a sorrow for him so intense that she couldn't stop trembling, with so much grief that each breath burned in her chest. The breathless whisper fell from her lips. "Those hours of grief and pain can never add up to all the years of happiness and love."

"Annabelle." Her name was a plea as he closed the distance between them and pulled her into his arms. Squeezing his eyes shut, he rested his forehead against hers.

A sob choked from her, and despite herself, her arms went around his shoulders, to press herself close. One final time. "Can't you…" she breathed out, so softly that she could barely hear her own voice over her pounding heartbeat, "can't you find a way to…" She couldn't stop the hot tears from spilling down her cheeks. "Do you think… someday…"

"I don't know," he murmured, so softly that it was barely a sound at all.

But she heard it, and it ripped all the way down to her soul. Every breath emerged as a blinding pain, and every pounding beat of her heart was agony.

"I care about you, Annabelle, and I want to spend the rest of my life protecting you and laughing with you, holding you close every night." All of him shook as he dragged in a jerking breath. "Needing and caring, friendship and respect...we have all that," he rasped out, each word a tickling warmth against her lips. "Let that be enough."

But it would never be enough. Not without his love.

Her heart began to crack, like a thousand fingers splintering through glass. She felt each one slice through her, a thousand tiny cuts, each one more painful than the last.

He tipped up her face, to make her look at him, but she closed her eyes, unable to bear it. "Marry me, Annabelle," he urged her one last time.

"No," she breathed, and her heart shattered completely.

CHAPTER THIRTEEN

Quinton sat in one of the leather reading chairs in the library and stared at the walls of books surrounding him. Through the tall windows, the morning sun inched higher over the mountains in the distance, lighting the large room that Belle loved so much.

Books...books...everywhere he looked. And not one answer to be found in any of them.

Blowing out a hard breath, he leaned forward in the chair, knees on elbows. The confusion that had clawed at his insides since he left Belle's room last night pulsed inside him as fiercely as ever.

Good Lord. The Bluebell *loved* him.

She was mistaken, that was all. Confused. God knew *he'd* been plagued with enough confusion of his own since the moment she'd shattered in his arms. No—since long before that. Since the moment he first kissed her six years ago.

She drew him the way no other woman ever had. Nor

most likely ever would again. One of her smiles sent his heart racing, and her needling criticisms only made him want her even more. And would he ever be able to enter a library again without thinking of her and all the things about men and women she'd learned by reading? The alluring, delectable way she looked, whether in silk gowns or men's work clothes, had him half-hard right now just thinking about how that caramel hair of hers fell around her shoulders, how those honey-amber eyes melted into him. *Never* had he wanted a woman as much as he did Annabelle.

Yet his attraction wasn't only lust. Which was the most bewildering of all.

He'd found himself enjoying her company and looking forward to spending time with her, even if only to argue over the newspaper at breakfast or to battle over a chess game. Her laughter was like music, and whenever she looked at him, her eyes shining, a warmth filled his chest. Happy. Energized. He cared about her and liked spending time with her, he would admit to that. He'd been happier here in the borderlands with her in the last few weeks than he'd been in the last several years.

But she wanted love. Would he ever be ready for that?

So he'd come here, to the one place she loved most in all the world, in a desperate attempt to understand her. He stared at the room around him as if it were a puzzle to be solved. But he couldn't find the answer.

"What on earth are you doing in here?" his aunt asked, dumbfounded, as she stopped short in the doorway.

Quinn glanced up quickly, only to be struck by a pang of disappointment that Belle wasn't with her. "Why shouldn't I be here?"

"Because it's the library," she explained as she came forward into the room.

He rolled his eyes as he grumbled beneath his breath, "I studied at Oxford, you know." Why wouldn't anyone believe that?

She added quietly, "It's also Annabelle's favorite room." She paused. "Were you hoping to find her here?"

Exactly that. In more ways than his aunt realized. But admitting that would make him sound exactly like the kind of lovesick pup he wasn't.

He shoved himself out of the chair and stalked across the room to the shelf that held the Bibles and reached behind them for the Bowmore. He held up the bottle in silent offer.

"Awfully early for a drink," she commented. When Quinn arched a brow at that, she added, "Well, someone had to say it, for propriety's sake." She pointed at the row of hymnals on the next shelf. "We keep the glasses there. Don't be stingy on my pour."

"Of course." He splashed the golden liquid into two glasses and carried one to her.

"If you're waiting for Annabelle, I'm afraid you've missed her." She accepted her glass. "Angus Burns sent a message to the house, just after dawn. There was a problem in the fields last night."

He paused with the glass halfway to his lips, his gut twisting with dread. There hadn't been any trouble in the past fortnight. He'd hoped the barn fire had been the last of it. "What kind of problem?"

"One of the gates was accidentally left open, most likely by a departing party guest, and the sheep wandered out of their pasture. They've strayed all over Kinnybroch, and the men have set to rounding them up."

Suspicion prickled at the back of his neck. That was no accident. "Where's Belle?"

"She's gone out with Mr. Burns and the others. That's why I was surprised to find you here." She studied him over the rim of her glass. "I was certain you'd be out in the fields with her."

He carefully kept his face inscrutable as he pretended to take interest in the whisky swirling in his glass. "Why would I do that?"

"Because in the month that you've been here, you've come to care about this place as much as she does. And to care about Belle as much as she cares about you." Her old eyes softened on him. "You two belong together. I've known that since you were children." She slowly shook her head. "Six years ago, though, you very nearly ruined everything. She hated you for such a long time after that."

And deservedly so. He was only now beginning to realize—and accept—all the wrongs done to her that night.

Dear God, the stupid, silly things he'd done in his past! Had he really been so immature and naïve to think that he could keep slipping through life by solving all his problems with fisticuffs? Or that he could avoid all responsibilities of the heart and emotional attachments with only a grin? A fine mess all that had gotten him into. Fate had twisted everything into a knot until the one woman he should never have cared anything about was now the only woman he wanted to marry.

But not love.

He wouldn't put himself into a position to be wounded the same way his mother had, and something deep in his heart whispered that loving Belle would do exactly that.

She sighed. "I had hoped that this time around would be different."

"It is." Frowning into his glass, he quietly admitted, "Annabelle loves me."

His aunt froze, except for her eyes, which widened like saucers. "She...said that?"

"Yes," he whispered. He would have puffed out his chest in arrogant pride if Belle hadn't made it sound like a prison sentence.

Or expected him to love her back.

"Yet she refused to marry you?" she breathed out, still staring wide-eyed. If he'd sprouted a second head, his aunt couldn't have been more surprised.

"She did." He tossed back the rest of the whisky.

Her face fell, and she blinked, utterly bewildered. "Why on earth did she do that?"

He stared at the empty glass. "She doesn't want a loveless marriage."

"But it wouldn't be loveless. If you both—" She narrowed her eyes knowingly on him. "You did tell her that you love her, too, did you not?"

"No." That familiar pang of uncertainty returned to his chest in full force.

She gaped at him. "For heaven's sake, why not?"

"I won't start my marriage with a lie."

"My dear boy, you won't start your marriage at all at this rate." Her eyes swept over him, as if desperate to notice something important that she'd missed before. "You don't love Annabelle?"

The quiet question was a punch to his gut. "Annabelle is wonderful."

Amazing. Beautiful. Free-spirited and kindhearted. The

only woman who had him longing to hear her laugh and see one of her smiles, who had him rereading *Don Quixote*, for God's sake. Who had him looking forward to a long lifetime of morning swims in the pond, afternoons working on the estate, and quiet evenings spent together in front of the fire. Who had him wondering what she would be like as a mother, if their daughters would have the same caramel-colored hair and warm honey eyes, if their sons would be wild handfuls like him or quiet scholars like her. Their family and future. Right here in the place she loved, the place he was coming to appreciate just as much.

And yet... "But I don't want to love her."

Aunt Agatha grimly shook her head. "From what I've seen of love, you don't get a choice in the matter."

He clenched his teeth, his frustration rising. "And *I've* seen enough of love to know that I want no part of it."

"You've seen nothing," she shot back, suddenly angry, her eyes blazing. "To be so foolish as to reject someone's love."

He forced out through gritted teeth, "It isn't love that's the problem."

"Then what is?" she demanded.

"When love ends!" He raked his shaking fingers through his hair, the frustration nearly unbearable. "It *always* ends. And the more you love someone, the worse it is when it does."

Her lips parted at his outburst, and she involuntarily stepped away, as if knocked back by the force of a physical blow. With wide eyes, she stared silently at him, as if trying to see down into his soul.

Then her expression softened, as if she'd found what she'd searched for in him. The look of understanding she sent him pierced him even more painfully than her angry accusation of only moments before.

"Yes, it does," she agreed softly, lowering her face. "Which makes the love before it ends even more precious."

Her eyes glistened as she reached for the locket she wore around her neck. With a flick of the tiny clasp, she opened it.

"I understand your reluctance to love," she said quietly as she gazed down at the locket, her features softening with a mixture of love and grief. "It isn't always happy and wonderful."

She showed him the locket and the miniature inside of his uncle. Understanding struck him then of why she always wore it, to keep her late husband close to her heart. But wasn't this exactly what Quinn wanted to avoid, the sorrow of losing someone he loved? Whatever lesson she was hoping to impart about the blessings of love, she'd failed, because her locket only exemplified the pain that struck when love ended.

"When my Ainsley died, I thought my own life was over," she whispered. "I couldn't imagine living on without him. For a time, I didn't want to. I wanted to join him."

She touched a trembling finger to the portrait, and Quinn tightened his jaw at the gesture. He didn't need a lesson in the grief that came of love. He'd witnessed it firsthand with his parents.

"It hurt so terribly, not having him with me. Not only an emotional pain but a physical ache, as well. It was torture to breathe, to keep feeling my heart beating, to simply crawl out of bed and face the dawn...to suffer the hours of dark night alone in an empty bed."

"But you kept living and made it through," he drawled,

unable to keep the cynicism from his voice. He didn't need platitudes. "Is that your point?"

"Not at all."

Surprising him with that, she snapped the locket shut, but she closed her hand around it. To protect it in her grasp.

"*My point* is that even with the grief and all the agony and desolation I suffered, I would not trade away the love we shared. I would never deny myself a single day with my Ainsley nor sacrifice a single minute that I spent in his presence, just to protect my heart from being pained. Not one smile, not one laugh." She squeezed her eyes closed, as if she didn't trust herself not to cry. "What I wouldn't give to have just one more argument with him! To have him infuriate me to no end just once more. To have back those silly days when we were so angry at each other that we didn't speak." She choked on the words, and her voice softened to a hoarse whisper. "To hear him say just one more time that he loves me."

The same words he couldn't bring himself to say to Belle.

Quinn's heart thudded, each beat a jarring jolt in his hollow chest. "Even knowing how much pain his death caused you..." He sucked in a deep breath as his gut twisted into hard knots. "You'd still want that?"

When she opened her eyes and looked at him, they shined with unshed tears. "I'd give everything I possess for that. And I'm certain your mother feels the same." She gave him a faint, bittersweet smile and looked down at the locket in her hand. "All the days and weeks of anguish and grief can never triumph over a lifetime of love. Or even one moment of it."

Belle had said nearly the same thing last night. At the time, he'd thought she was simply being melodramatic, too optimistic for her own good. A bluestocking who believed in the happy endings found in her books. But now..."And if it doesn't? If there's not enough love, or—" he rasped out, his voice suddenly thick and hoarse. "Or if the grief is unbearable?"

"Then you rely on the love you had to give you the strength to continue. Because that kind of love will always live on in your heart." She tenderly rested her hand against his cheek. *"That's* the kind of love you share with Belle, isn't it?"

A long, ragged breath tore from him. He shook his head as he put voice to his deepest fears. "I can't take that kind of risk." Too much was at stake, too much to lose—too much pain and grief to survive. "Especially with Belle."

"If you love her, then it won't—"

"Not her," he bit out. "Her love for *me*. If she ever loves me as much as my mother loved my father, the grief and pain she suffered when he died—if something happens to me—"

He choked off, unable to continue as he looked away, his eyes burning. He shook his head as a wave of guilt crashed through him just imagining Belle in that kind of relentless suffering.

He sucked in a deep, jerking breath. "To know that I've caused her that same kind of grief, that same pain, simply because she loved me—" A shudder sped through him, and the anguished truth ripped from him. "I would never do that to her. I would *never* hurt her like that."

Her old eyes softened. "It's too late, I'm afraid. She's already given her heart to you." Her heartache for him was audible in her soft, slow whisper. "You've always wanted to protect her. You two got into that mess six years ago because you wanted to defend her, even then. But you cannot protect her from loving you, just as you cannot stop the tide from rising or the sun from setting." She paused. "Or from loving her yourself."

With the affection of a mother, she brushed at the lock of hair falling across his brow.

"Love isn't at all what you think it is. But Belle can show you the goodness of it, because she loves you." She smiled at him. "And you *do* love her, I know it. I suspect that so does Belle." She rose up on tiptoe to place a kiss to his forehead. "So go tell her you love her. If you let the words come, the heart will follow."

His heart pounded, the damned thing not knowing whether to be terrified at opening itself up to love or elated at the possibility of loving Belle forever. Dear God, if he made the wrong decision— "It isn't that simple."

"Yes." Her tear-filled eyes sparkled knowingly. "It is *exactly* that simple."

* * *

Belle walked down the dew dampened lane toward the far pasture with her hands shoved deep into her coat pockets and her eyes fixed to the ground but not seeing anything. She'd dressed in her work clothes and left the house as soon as she'd spoken to Angus Burns, not because this morning's trouble was anything too serious but because she couldn't bear to linger within the same walls with Quinton a moment longer.

Around her, the early morning was quiet and still. The birds weren't fully awake beneath the layer of clouds that the rising sun had yet to burn away, and the soft scrape of her boots against the gravel was muted by the fog that clung to the pasturelands like a veil. She wore the collar of her coat turned up against her neck, but it proved poor protection against the damp cold that seeped into her bones and seemed to chill her all the way down to her soul. Summer was over.

And so was any hope of being loved by Quinn.

She'd wanted the biting cold of the damp air and the physical exercise to chase last night from her mind, if not from her body's memory, of how joyous it felt to make love to him. But the quiet morning served only to churn the emotions inside her even more, the images and sensations of being in his arms repeatedly pummeling her senses until hot tears blurred the ground in front of her.

She hunched her shoulders and blinked hard. *No.* She wouldn't cry again. That was all she'd done since he'd left her room last night, until she thought she didn't have any tears left. But she scowled at herself when she swiped a hand over her eyes and felt the warm wetness on her fingertips.

How dare that scoundrel come sweeping back into her life! Until he came along, she'd been perfectly fine. She'd grown used to being alone with her books and her swims in the pond, with managing the estate all by herself, and with the villagers and Lady Ainsley to care for. She would have lived out her life here, contented and satisfied with her lot. But then Quinton came along and ruined everything by making her fall in love with him, and by not loving her back.

She pressed her hand against her chest, where the man's waistcoat she wore covered her pounding heart—as if the foolish thing didn't know that it was supposed to be dead. Because surely it had shattered, this time beyond all repair. Oh, *dear heavens*, how much it hurt! She'd thought that the pain from six years ago could never be topped. But that girlish infatuation and humiliation had been nothing compared to this loss.

And she had no idea how to survive it.

"Miss Greene," a voice called out from just beyond the edge of the mist. "Good morning!"

She glanced up, blinking rapidly to clear her eyes enough to make out Sir Harold sitting on top of his curricle that he'd stopped in the lane. The perfectly matched pair of bays pawed at the ground, impatient to continue their morning drive.

"Sir Harold." She forced a smile. "What a surprise to see you up this early."

He returned her smile, but it shivered through her, striking her as equally cold as the misty air around them. "Couldn't be helped, I'm afraid. I seem to have a problem on my hands."

This morning's trouble with the sheep, of course.

Belle sucked in a deep breath to brace herself for the lecture she was certain to receive about the necessity of having better fences and gates, about how women had no place running an estate. The same set-down she'd received from him for the past year whenever trouble struck Glenarvon.

"I'm terribly sorry about the sheep," she said, offering her apologies to keep the peace between them. Now that Glenarvon would be completely hers, they would have to deal with each other for a long time to come. And she wasn't entirely certain that the wound she'd given to his pride last night had yet healed. "But it should all be cleared up soon. I've got Angus Burns and my men rounding up the flock right now."

"I know." His smile widened, but somehow remained just as stiff as before. Just as icy. "They're down in my south pasture. Should be occupied there for several hours, I think." He looked past her into the morning mist. "No guard dog this morning to escort you?"

"Lord Quinton is at the house." She smiled tightly, even though his question tore at her heart. "I thought I'd come out early to help the men."

"Can I offer you a ride to Kinnybroch, then?" He set the brake and tied off the ribbons, then stood to help her up onto the rig. When she hesitated, he added, "Might as well save your energy for rounding up sheep instead of walking all the way there."

But she needed to walk, and to walk until she'd exorcised away the anguish still clawing inside her and the unbearable loss of a future that could never be hers. She forced her smile not to waver. "I don't want to bother you."

"It's no bother." He reached out his hand. "I insist."

A prickly unease tingled at the backs of her knees. Something wasn't right about him this morning. Something was… off. She couldn't quite name what exactly, but it made her apprehensive to go with him.

Yet when she looked at him, his gloved hand outstretched, a stabbing guilt told her that she couldn't refuse.

She was being silly! He'd driven her around the countryside dozens of times in the past, and often like this, just the two of them without a chaperone. This would be no different. What would never be allowed in London among the so-called quality was commonplace here in the country. After all, how much could she beg off for propriety's sake when she was wearing men's clothing, ready to join the field hands in herding sheep?

"I hold no grudge against you for what happened at your party," he assured her, misreading her hesitation, "although I'd hoped to be the one you chose to marry."

"I am sorry for that," she said softly. And she was. Although she'd never cared for him, Sir Harold was a gentleman, and he didn't deserve to be embarrassed.

"Then make it up to me by letting me drive you." Another smile, just as strangely stilted as before. But now she understood the tension behind it. "We're still neighbors and friends, are we not?"

Her shoulders eased down. "Yes. Of course."

She slipped her hand into his, and he helped her up onto the curricle. She sat next to him on the bench. With a flick of his long whip, he sent the team forward.

When they reached the bend in the lane where it joined the main road, Sir Harold sent the team the wrong way—not toward the fields to the south but toward the north.

Turning in her seat, she glanced over her shoulder, to try to glimpse the men in the fields. But she could see nothing around the raised canopy behind them. Her heart began to pound as the same unease she'd felt when she first saw him bubbled up inside her.

"It seems we've gone astray," she told him, forcing a lightheartedness into her voice that belied her rising uneasiness. "We'll never find the sheep by heading in this direction."

He kept his gaze straight ahead, but this time, he made no attempt to smile. "We're not going to find the sheep."

The short hairs on the back of her neck prickled in warning. "Where are we going then?"

"To Scotland." He flipped the ribbons, and the horses jumped into a fast trot. A dark determination hardened his features. "Where we'll be married, just as we should have been all along."

Alarm flooded through her, and her hand gripped at the

seat rail so tightly that her fingertips turned white. "I don't find your teasing amusing, Sir Harold." She forced out in panic, the jarring beat of her heart coming so hard that she winced, "Please stop and let me down this instant!"

"I'm not teasing." He glanced sideways at her, with an expression of such raw hatred that she flinched. "And we're not stopping until we reach Scotland and the blacksmith."

Dear God, he was serious! Fear shot through her, and a bitter metallic taste formed on her tongue as her breath came in fast, frightened gasps that matched the terrified racing of her heart. Then she knew...

He was kidnapping her.

Her gaze darted to the hard and rocky ground speeding past, her mind spinning as fast as the curricle's wheels. If she jumped, she could clear the wheels and run for help—

"You'll break your neck," he warned, reading her mind.

She pressed herself against the edge of the seat to put as much distance between them as possible. "Why?" she breathed out, panic burning inside her chest. "*Why* are you doing this?"

"Because you left me no choice," he bit out. "Everything would have been fine if you'd simply married me, as you should have done all along." His eyes narrowed on her, darkening until they were almost black. "But you've always been stubborn. Even with all the trouble I've caused for you at Glenarvon, you still refused my help when I offered."

Terror flashed through her. "It was you," she breathed out. "You were the one who destroyed the floodgate, let out the sheep..."

Worse. He'd set the fire in the hay barn that could have injured the workmen and that had nearly killed Quinn. She'd mocked Quinn's intuition that Sir Harold had been involved. Oh God, she'd been so wrong about him!

"You forced me. Even then, you were too obstinate to realize that you needed to take me as your husband. You should have been honored to have a gentleman like me give you a second glance, let alone offer marriage." A sneer pulled at his lips. "*You*, the worthless daughter of a convict and a maid, who should have been washing pots in my scullery. Who should have been begging me to marry you instead of forcing me to make overtures to you and that insipid Lady Ainsley."

Confusion swirled with her panic. "If you hate me so much...why are you doing this?"

He snapped the whip over the horses' backs to keep up their fast pace even as the wheels bumped and jumped over the rocks and dips in the old road. "Because of your announcement at the party that you wouldn't marry."

"No, you don't understand! I don't need to marry now." She tugged at his arm, pleading desperately, "Please stop, and we'll forget this ever happened. A misunderstanding is all, you wanting to help me—"

"Stupid gel!" His hand shot up and grabbed her by the neck. He yanked her toward him, his eyes flaring as he glared down at her with his fingers clenched around her throat. "I don't give a damn about you. This is about saving Kinny-broch. The only way I can get my hands on enough money to pay the mortgage is to marry you and sell Glenarvon."

"No," she choked out, her body flashed numb with terror, even as she clawed at his arm to loosen his hold. "You'll never have it!"

His eyes gleamed, and he tightened his fingers on her neck. "Once we marry, it becomes mine."

"I'll never marry you!" she ground out.

"You'll have no choice. There's a blacksmith just across the border who'll do anything I ask, if I pay him enough. Including marrying you by force over the anvil and swearing you went willingly. And his wife will witness it."

"Then I'll—I'll have it annulled!"

"You can't. Not without your husband's permission." An icy smile spread across his face. "And I'll *never* give it, unless you give me Glenarvon."

A sickening helplessness overcame her, and she whispered in horror, "You're mad."

"Worse." A muscle ticked in his tightened jaw. "I'm a gentleman in debt."

With a hard shove, he released her throat and pushed her away, then flipped the ribbons and set the horses into a faster pace.

Annabelle cowered to the side of the seat and stared at him with revulsion and fear, her hands grasping the rail to hang on as the curricle bounced beneath her. In desperation, she looked down at the road again, now speeding by beneath the deadly wheels.

She took a deep breath to resolve herself and inched closer to the side of the carriage to jump—

"Annabelle!"

The deep voice boomed across the countryside, only seconds before the sound of racing hooves reached her.

"Quinton!" With relief pouring through her, she tried to rise up from the seat and wave for help over the large canopy. "Help me! Help—"

Sir Harold let fly a sharp curse and grabbed her by her hair. He yanked her down onto the seat.

Annabelle cried out in pain as she fought to keep hold on

the seat, now bouncing wildly beneath her as he cracked the whip and the team jumped into a run. She could do nothing more than hang on for her life and trust in Quinton.

* * *

Quinn lowered himself over the back of his horse and urged the large gelding into a run after the curricle. His heart pounded as hard as the hooves thundering beneath him as his horse ate up the distance between him and the carriage.

When he pulled even with the carriage wheels, he saw Belle clinging in terror to the seat. Beside her, Bletchley ignored her cries to stop and whipped the team into a dangerous frenzy.

Something inside him snapped. A fury and fear unlike any he'd ever experienced before flared through him, and he focused every ounce of his being on saving Belle.

"Let her go!" he shouted at Bletchley.

In answer, the man gritted his teeth and yanked on the ribbons to send the curricle careening at Quinn, the tall wheel spinning dangerously toward his horse.

With a curse, Quinton reined in. The well-trained gelding darted out of the way just seconds before the wheel cut across their path.

Quinton dug his heels against his mount's side, and the horse surged forward again. This time, before Bletchley could swerve toward him, he reached out to snatch the ribbons from Bletchley's hands.

"Damn you!" Bletchley struck back with the whip, cracking it at Quinn's horse, who jumped to the side just far enough to put Quinn in reach of the whip.

Bletchley smiled wickedly and snapped it again. The

metal tip struck Quinn's cheek and sliced through his skin, drawing blood from a painful gash. Belle screamed.

Growling and furious, and increasingly terrified for Belle, he ignored the sting of the whip as he rode in close. When Bletchley let fly another snap of the whip, Quinn grabbed at it, catching it and ripping it from Bletchley's hands.

But Bletchley still had control of the ribbons and the team, and he pulled sharply, turning again toward Quinn's horse. The gelding darted away from the spinning wheel, safely out of danger, but *damnation*! The weaving carriage kept him too far away to stop it.

"Annabelle!" he shouted, needing her help.

She looked up, and for one heartbeat, they locked gazes. In that instant he saw the terror leave her, replaced by a fierce determination.

Carefully keeping hold of the seat, she moved closer to Bletchley, whose attention was still set on running Quinn down beneath his wheels. With a cry, she drew her right hand into a fist and swung with all her might. The glancing blow caught the tip of Bletchley's chin and flung his head back. Not enough to make him stop the team but enough to distract him while Quinn charged again toward the lead horse.

From the corner of his eye as he moved up even with the team, Quinn could see Annabelle slapping at Bletchley, kicking and clawing at every part of him she could reach.

His chest warmed with pride. The Bluebell was no shirking violet. Bletchley had made a terrible mistake by attempting to abscond with her. *Thank God* that he'd gone after her, that he'd ridden into view at the far end of the lane just in time to see her climb into the carriage and ride off, that he'd gotten close enough when the curricle had turned to the north to see Bletchley grab her by the throat.

When he caught them, he'd murder the bastard for that.

Quinn leaned far to the right, dangerously hanging off his saddle by only a single stirrup, and reached toward the lead horse's head. He glanced back at the spinning wheel just behind him, the ground rushing past beneath them. If his horse stumbled and he fell, if his stirrup snapped—he was as good as dead.

Belle cried out, and white-hot anger and fear for her drove him on. He lunged for the rein near the bit, grabbed it, and held tight as he slowed the team.

Behind him, the wheel smacked a large rock jutting up from the road. The curricle jumped, both wheels coming off the ground. When it landed, it careened out of control to the right. The rein yanked from Quinn's hand.

His horse darted away as the carriage tipped. The axel broke with a splintering crack, and the wheel snapped. He watched helplessly as the carriage bounced into the air before slamming into the hard-packed road. Annabelle flew from the seat and hit the ground with a dull, sickening thud that stopped his heart with a soul-shattering jolt. The team ran on, dragging the wrecked carriage behind it with Bletchley clinging to the dashboard. When it hit another hard bump, he was flung to the road, where he lay moaning, too hurt to scramble to his feet.

Quinn yanked his horse to a stop and jumped from its back. Terror pulsed through him at the sight of Belle lying still in the dirt. *Dear God, no!* He ran to her side and dropped to his knees, scooping her into his shaking arms.

"Annabelle!" He clutched her to him, all of him trembling and shuddering. Fear clasped an icy fist around his heart as he cupped her face in his hand. "Open your eyes, darling," he ordered breathlessly. "Please, dear God…Open your eyes. Annabelle…"

Her name was a pleading rasp on his lips. But she didn't open her eyes to look at him.

"Don't leave me," he whispered against her temple, his own eyes now squeezed shut against the pulsing pain. "Not now, now that I finally have you…Annabelle, please!"

Pained heat stung at his eyes, and he held his breath, desperately listening for any sound of her breathing, of her heart beating—*anything* to signal that she was still there with him. But she lay so terribly still in his arms, her body limp and lifeless against his as he cradled her against his chest.

Wetness burned at his lashes. Each beat of his heart was agony.

"I love you, Annabelle," he rasped out and kissed her.

A soft inhalation tickled against his lips. Then her eyes opened and she stared at him, dazed and unfocused.

With a shudder, she gasped and gulped in a deep swallow of air as she tried to catch back the breath that the fall had ripped from her. Her hands clutched at his shoulders as she struggled to breathe, and her eyes never left his as she forced out hoarsely, "Quinn…"

He crushed her to him and buried his face in her hair, which had come loose and now fell in disheveled curls around her shoulders. Her clothes were dirty and ripped. An ugly scrape bloodied the side of her face and both of her palms where she'd tried to arrest her fall, and her right ankle lay at an unnatural angle. Each breath she took was labored and rough, filled with pain.

But she was alive.

Thank God.

Then she winced as she lifted a hand to touch his cheek and the streak of blood from the whip wound. Her brow furrowed with worry as she breathed out, "You're... hurt..."

Relief poured through him, like a liquid heat that filled him to overflowing, and he gave a soft laugh. Only Annabelle could be worried about a scratch on him when she had nearly been killed herself.

"I'm fine," he assured her, gently rocking her in his arms. "I have you. And I am *never* letting you go."

"You said you loved me," she whispered. "Did you... did you truly mean it?"

"Yes." *Sweet heavens, yes.* He cupped her cheek against his palm. "I thought I couldn't love you, that I could keep from being wounded if I kept myself from you. And my heart." Closing his eyes, he touched his lips to her forehead. "But when I saw that bastard hurt you. And then when you fell..." He silently shook his head, unwilling to put into words the terror he'd felt at nearly losing her.

"It's all right," she assured him, so softly his ears barely registered the sound. But his heart heard every word. "I understand."

"I was a damned fool. But now I'm not willing to miss a single moment with you, Annabelle." He slid his hand down her arm until he clasped her hand, lacing his fingers through hers. "Can you forgive me?"

Not moving her eyes from his, she slowly raised his hand to her bosom and guided his fingers beneath the gaping front of the torn waistcoat and shirt. He felt the rope of pearls she wore beneath her clothes, just as his aunt wore her locket. In order to keep him close to her heart. "Always," she whispered.

"Then marry me, Belle," he urged, his voice trembling

and all of him shaking. "Not because we made love or because I need you to let me care for you and protect you—although I do, more than I realized. But because I love you, and because I hope that you still love me." He traced his fingers over the pearls and the warm skin beneath, feeling her heart beating strong beneath his fingertips. "I want every moment with you that I can have, for as long as this life gives us."

"Then it must be love." A tear slipped down her dusty cheek as she lightly teased, "You keep asking even though I keep refusing."

He crooked a half grin. "I'm not the kind of man who lets a woman's absolute refusal stop me from marrying her."

A small bubble of laughter escaped her, then she winced at the pain. Guilt washed through him. "Belle, I'm so sorry that you—"

"Yes, Quinton," she whispered.

His heart stuttered. "Yes?"

Her fingers tightened around his, as if she never wanted to let him go. A smile of joy lit her face. "I will let you marry me now."

Grinning at her stubborn pride, shining in her even now, he felt his love for her warm inside him until it permeated every ounce of his being and soul. Aunt Agatha was right. There was no choice in love. *Thank God.*

He lowered his head to kiss her.

EPILOGUE

Four Very Busy Weeks Later

$\mathcal{Q}$uinn stood on the other side of the door connecting his room to Belle's and took a deep breath to calm himself. God's mercy, he was nervous. *Nervous!* Although why he was, he had no idea.

They'd been intimate before, for heaven's sake. What did he have to be nervous about? Nothing...except that this would be their first joining as husband and wife. Except that tonight would be the first of all their nights together for the rest of their lives.

He wiped his sweaty palms on his dressing robe. Nervous, indeed.

Belle was making him wait, extending the very long and tiring day they'd already had. They'd taken their wedding vows before friends and family that morning in the Braeburn parish church. Robert, Sebastian, and his sister, Josephine, stood up with them, while his mother and Aunt Agatha cried from the front pew, with his sister-in-law, Miranda, dutifully patting the backs of their hands. Then came breakfast at Glenarvon beneath special tents he'd had erected among the ruins of the old castle. Everyone from the village came to congratulate them...and to welcome him permanently to Braeburn.

All the loose ends were tying up perfectly. Bletchley had been sent out of the borderlands and out of their lives forever. When the bank foreclosed on Kinnybroch, Quinn purchased it with the money he'd saved for America. Now, he and Annabelle would start their lives as equal partners, their combined lands forming the second-largest estate in Cumbria. The land would be *theirs* now, not hers or his. And although it was too early to receive a reply to the letter Quinn had written to Asa Jeffers and his wife, he knew they would be just fine as well. Their sons-in-law would care for them as they deserved, perhaps even deciding to keep the land in the family and farm it themselves. He suspected that any ill will they felt toward him for not claiming the land would dissolve when they received word of the birth of his and Annabelle's first child. One he hoped would be their godchild.

And then, there was Belle herself. The little bluestocking had refused to let him into her bedroom during the past month, even after her sprained ankle and other wounds from the accident had all healed. She'd insisted that they wait to make love until after their wedding.

Four weeks. Four *very long* weeks without touching her luscious curves, without holding her sultry body against his, without kissing her sensuous lips and licking his tongue over every delectable inch—

He groaned and knocked impatiently on the door. "Belle?"

"Just a moment longer," she called out. "I need to fix the ribbon along my thigh..."

His gut wrenched with ravenous yearning. *Sweet Lucifer*, just the sound of her voice describing what she was wearing was enough to turn him hard. For the past month, she'd seductively teased him with snippets of what she planned on wearing tonight, a lace and silk confection from her trousseau. The same silk and lace he planned on slowly peeling from her body, one tempting inch at a time, then following along with his lips—

Another groan. Good Lord, he would die if she didn't open the door and let him inside!

"I'm ready," she announced. *Finally.* "Come in, my love."

He threw open the door and charged into her room—

Then pulled up short. She wasn't there.

He glanced around. What kind of cruel joke was she playing? The room was ready for them. The fire glowed warm, and two glasses sat next to the bottle of scotch on the bedside table. The coverlet had been turned down, the candles extinguished, and the drapes drawn so they could linger in bed as long as they wished in the morning without being bothered by the dawn. And he was certainly ready for her.

But there was no Belle.

He frowned. "Annabelle?"

"Bluebell, you mean," she corrected teasingly as she stepped out of her dressing room.

Quinn saw her and grinned.

Instead of wearing the gossamer negligee he'd expected, she sashayed slowly toward him wearing her rope of pearls, a pair of very blue stockings tied with bows around her thighs...and nothing else.

"Do you still want me?" she taunted as she lifted her leg to rest her foot on the chair beside him, giving him a tantalizing view of her smooth thighs and a teasing glimpse of that special place which lay between. "Even though I'm an unrepentant bluestocking?"

"I wouldn't want you any other way." With a growl, he lifted her into his arms and carried her across the room. "I love you."

She sighed happily. "I know."

Then he placed her on the bed and followed down after her.

The only thing standing between Lord Robert Carlisle and the business empire of his dreams is one woman: Mariah Winslow, known about town as "the Hellion." Robert will do anything to win—even help Mariah's father find her a suitable husband and force her into respectability. But as the desire flares between them, will he dare sacrifice his dreams to get in bed with the enemy?

A preview of

As the Devil Dares

follows.

CHAPTER ONE

London
January 1823

I suppose you prefer White's," Henry Winslow drawled.

With a knowing smile tugging at the corners of his mouth, Robert Carlisle let his gaze drift from the smoke curling off the end of his cigar to the man sitting in the leather chair across from him in the smoking room at Brooks's. Before them, a crackling fire warmed away the chill of the winter afternoon whose gray sky once more threatened to snow.

"I prefer being here at Brooks's. I'd rather be in a club with the real leaders of England." In truth, Robert preferred Boodle's, where the gambling required more skill, the stakes were higher, and the women allowed in through the rear entrance were more interesting. But he raised his glass of whiskey to salute Winslow anyway. "Businessmen and merchants, traders, importers—the men who truly make England run."

"Hear, hear!" Winslow lifted his own glass and gasped softly as he took a large swallow.

Robert popped the cigar between his teeth before Winslow could see the self-pleased smile at his lips. *Pompous arse.* But he would gladly flatter the man's choice of club, where he'd been invited for a lunch of roasted pheasant and conversation about business afterward, because he needed Henry Winslow.

Rather, he needed Winslow Shipping and Trade.

Given the fierce pounding of his heart at the reason why Winslow wanted to meet with him, he drawled as nonchalantly as possible, "I've heard that you're considering expanding into real estate."

"Ha! Where did you hear that?" Winslow flicked the ash from his cigar onto the floor.

"I have good contacts." The best, in fact. Winslow knew that, too, or the man wouldn't have reached out to him in the first place.

Robert eased back in the chair and kicked his Hessians onto the fireplace fender. A model of a confident businessman, when he was actually nervous as hell.

He'd been waiting two years for this chance to finally prove himself worthy of the Carlisle name. Two years of taking calculated risks to build his wealth and connections, purchasing unproven shares of ships from India and the Far East just so he would have a presence among the men who drove the auctions, buying and selling warehouses full of goods so he could make a name for himself among the traders...all of it coming to this moment.

He'd be damned if he let it slip away.

He pinned Winslow with a level stare. "I've also heard that you're looking for a partner."

"I am." Winslow's eyes gleamed, appreciating Robert's bluntness. "I'm looking for new blood to energize my company. Someone with the drive and ambition to make a name for himself. And someone who has contacts in Parliament and at court." He pushed himself from his chair and stepped forward to the fire, to take the liberty of grasping the brass poker and stirring up the flames. "I have an extraordinary company, and I need extraordinary men to help run it."

Robert smiled tightly. *Extraordinary*, all right.

Henry Winslow might have been an arrogant braggart, but he was also one of the most cunning, most successful business minds in England. As sole proprietor of Winslow Shipping and Trade, he was one of the few import merchants who had managed to emerge from the wars wealthier than before. All due to determination, a willingness to risk capital, and good old-fashioned luck. A titan of fortune and power who was now looking to diversify his holdings into warehouses, real estate, and storefronts, Winslow had never taken on a partner before. But Robert had thoroughly studied the business and knew that he would be the perfect man for it.

And that this partnership would be the answer to his prayers.

"I'm considering offering a limited share, you understand." Winslow puffed out his chest, a gesture more propriety than proud. "A small stake. Perhaps five or ten percent."

Robert's eyes narrowed. Much smaller than he'd hoped. But it would do. For now. "You've never taken on a partner before. Why now?"

Winslow stared into the fire. "Changes need to be made.

A man who doesn't recognize when it's time to adjust his ways might as well retire."

He jabbed the poker at the logs, sending up a shower of sparks and drawing the irritated attention of the manager as the man passed through the room.

"But the timing of it—*daughters*," Winslow spat out distastefully, as if the word were a curse. "When what a businessman needs is a son to carry on what he's created. It's about legacy, Carlisle." He heaved a hard breath and shook his head. "How does a man guarantee himself a legacy when all he has are daughters?"

Robert didn't answer. His own father hadn't been bothered with such worries. Instead, Richard Carlisle had concerned himself with character, hard work, and devotion to his family. And Robert would do everything in his power to make certain that legacy continued. He *would* become the kind of man his father could take pride in raising, at all costs.

"Two troublesome daughters," Winslow grumbled as he replaced the poker, then slapped his hands together to remove the soot from his fingers. "That's what fate gave me."

"Perhaps one of them will marry a gentleman you can bring into your business." For his own selfish sake, Robert prayed both Winslow daughters were toothless, bald spinsters well into their third decade and beyond the possibility of marrying ambitious upstarts who might snag this opportunity from him.

Winslow laughed. "You don't know my daughters, do you?"

Robert shook his head. His usual concern for female companionship fell more toward experienced women who knew how to please a man than to spinster daughters of trade merchants.

"My daughters' reputations precede them, I'm afraid." Winslow folded his hands behind his back and stared grimly down into the flames, his round belly jutting out. "Their mother died when they were young, only ten and eight. I suppose I should have remarried, found them a stepmother who could have raised them into proper young ladies. But there was barely enough time to find an appropriate governess, let alone a wife."

"Are they both out for the season?" Robert couldn't care less, wanting to focus on the partnership instead, but polite conversation was expected. And it was essential that he get to know the man better so no surprises would arise later.

"Yes." The single word was spoken with grim chagrin. "But it's their seventh and fifth seasons, and I'm afraid it might be too late for them."

"Never too late." Especially for shipping heiresses. How the two didn't have fortune hunters pounding down the man's front door, Robert couldn't fathom.

"Hmm. Didn't both of your brothers wed last year?" Winslow inquired, knowing as well as every gentleman in Mayfair that the Carlisle brothers had been picked off one by one. Robert was the last man standing from a threesome that had once been considered the bane of marriage-minded mamas everywhere.

"They did," he confirmed. Then he placed a hand over his heart. "May God rest their bachelor souls."

Oh, they both seemed happy enough. Sebastian, especially, appeared more relaxed and carefree than Robert could remember his older brother being in years, which was all due to his wife, Miranda. The perfect duchess she certainly wasn't, although even Robert had to admit that she proved completely perfect for Sebastian by being nothing he wanted in a wife yet everything he needed. His brother had gone happily over to the ranks of the domesticated, doting on her like a smitten pup. Of course, the attention he heaped on her was made all the worse by her being six months along with child.

Quinton was little better. Annabelle had his younger brother up to his neck in tenant leases, farm improvements, livestock, and crops, yet Quinn had never been more focused on his future. From what Robert could tell, he was perfectly happy to be shackled to a woman who was more than his match in wits and charm.

But *marriage*...Good God. Would Robert ever be ready for that?

"Are you planning to follow suit, Carlisle?" Winslow accepted his drink from the attendant and tossed the man a coin.

Popping the cigar between his teeth, Robert shook his head. "No reason to rush into captivity."

His mother, however, had other ideas. Elizabeth Carlisle was simply beside herself with three of her four children happily married, two grandchildren already here, and one more on the way—which meant she was determined to bring the same wedded bliss to Robert. Even if it killed him.

He dearly loved his mother. And while he would do anything to make her happy, he drew the line at marriage. Just as he would never rush into a business deal, he certainly wouldn't rush into wedlock. Especially since he'd come to believe that matrimony was simply another business arrangement, negotiated and bound by contract. Yet one a man could never escape when it went bad.

Robert exchanged his empty glass for the full one held out by the attendant and explained, "I had the great fortune to be born a second son."

Winslow guffawed, so loudly that he drew an irritated

glance from Lord Daubney as he sat in the corner reading the *Times*.

"A second son with a happily married older brother—*very* happily married, you understand," he clarified. That innuendo brought another fit of laughter from Winslow. "I am a man in no danger of becoming an heir, so in no hurry to find a wife."

But he *was* a man in desperate need of a partnership. Not only for the potential wealth and respect it would bring among London's business elite, but also to prove himself to his family. To his mother and siblings…and to the memory of his late father.

Which was part of the reason why he'd not disclosed his plans for the partnership with them. His family was already uneasy about his choice of business for his life's path, rather than the usual posts available to second sons. But he couldn't stomach the law or medicine, and he lacked the discipline necessary for the military and the moral fortitude for the Church, with no desire to either end men's lives or save their souls.

Of course, the other part of why he hadn't told them was that they still blamed him for their father's death. He knew they did. Because he still blamed himself.

Pushing down the sickening guilt that rose inside him, even two years later, he leaned forward, elbows on knees and keen to nail down the terms of the partnership. "So the offer you're considering—"

A clatter went up outside in the street. Angry shouts and laughs joined the loud rattle of running hooves approaching wildly down the cobblestones.

"What on earth?" Winslow frowned and stepped toward the tall window overlooking the street.

Robert shoved himself out of his chair to join him, tossing the butt of his cigar into the fire. Lord Daubney dropped his newspaper as he gave up all hope of attempting to read it and hurried over to the window, joining the group of men gathered there to stare down at the spectacle below on the street.

Daubney peered over Winslow's shoulder and uttered in disbelief. "A phaeton—driven by a woman?"

"On St James's Street!" The club manager was appalled.

"That's no woman." Another gentleman clarified with a grin. "That's the Hellion."

Standing several inches above the others, Robert looked past them as the rig raced by.

Oh, that was definitely the Hellion, all right, the notorious woman who delighted in outraging the staid old guard of the *ton*. No other woman but her would dare such a thing.

Had she been at a ball, the dark beauty would have had gentlemen fighting among themselves like dogs to gain the favor of her attentions. But here, men shouted obscenities and jeered at her from the street that housed London's most exclusive gentlemen's clubs and where a respectable woman would *never* have dared to venture a slippered foot, let alone race a phaeton.

Robert couldn't help but smile in admiration, despite knowing the gossip such an outrageous act would rain down upon her head.

"And that is why my daughter is in her seventh season," Winslow muttered beneath his breath as the rest of the men dispersed back to their seats, the excitement over.

"Pardon?"

"*That*, Carlisle," he explained, his back straightening

under the weight of humiliation as he turned away from the window, "is my daughter."

"The *Hellion*?" Robert exclaimed before he could stop himself, flabbergasted. His mind ran wild searching for the woman's name, if he'd ever known it at all. Then it hit him...Mariah Winslow.

Winslow Shipping and Trade.

Christ.

Winslow's mouth pressed tight, not seemingly offended by the epithet that the gossips and dandies of Mayfair had branded on her but more by his daughter herself. "And beside her sat her sister, Evelyn, who is just as determined to mire herself in scandal."

This certainly explained all those seasons without proposals, and judging by this latest antic of theirs, none would be forthcoming this year, either. If the Carlisle brothers were the scourge of Mayfair, these two were its female equivalent. Two young ladies who somehow managed to thumb their noses at the quality yet creatively skirt the dangers of ruining their reputations completely.

"Mariah needs a husband to rein her in," Winslow muttered, "to keep her occupied with housekeeping and babies."

Robert sympathized with the man, but he couldn't help a touch of admiration for his daughters. They certainly weren't part of the boring, pastel-wearing lambs following the suffocating rules of the marriage market like sheep going to slaughter. They should consider themselves lucky to have escaped the chains of domesticity that society shackled onto its young ladies, who were expected to do nothing more in life than host parties, birth heirs, and then retire quietly into the countryside with their embroidery and watercolors.

"But I've no female relatives in society to give her proper

introductions," Winslow lamented, "so no chance of gaining proper suitors for her."

Robert raised his glass to his lips and murmured dryly, "That's a damned shame." It was hard to sympathize with the man when his daughters had practically glowed with freedom and excitement as they'd raced past.

Winslow faced Robert, his gaze hard. "But you do."

Robert choked on his whiskey. Coughing to clear his throat, he rasped out, "*What?*"

"I need a partner with connections in the *ton* and the audacity to use them," he said frankly, laying all his cards on the table. "Call on your acquaintances and relatives to guide Mariah through this season, and if she's engaged by the end of it, I'll have my proof of your capabilities and will guarantee you a partnership."

Robert gaped at the man. He was mad.

And utterly serious.

"A partnership," he sputtered out, echoing the man's words to make certain he understood him, "in exchange for marrying off your daughter?"

Winslow nodded curtly. "A twenty percent stake is yours if an offer for her is made from a respectable gentleman by the last day of Parliament." When Robert only stared at him, shocked, he drawled, "Seven months to secure a suitable match for her doesn't strike me as unreasonable for a man of your connections. *If* you truly possess them as you claim."

His eyes narrowed. "Be assured that I do."

"Then come by the house tomorrow at eleven, and you'll have your chance to prove it."

The offer was preposterous. A test wasn't out of line to prove his abilities, but *this*? Good Lord.

And yet...how difficult could it be? His daughter might be the Hellion, but she was also a shipping heiress with the beauty of an Incomparable. And he had his mother to help him, a dowager duchess longing for something interesting to do this season rather than attend the same boring society events. A few balls and garden teas, a few new gowns, and even Mariah Winslow would be offered for by March. April at the latest.

And his future would finally be set.

"Agreed," Robert said, extending his hand for the man to shake. "I won't let you down."

Winslow dubiously arched a brow.

But Robert was confident, both in himself and in his mother's matchmaking abilities. After all, if Sebastian and Quinton could be sent packing into matrimonial bliss within three months of each other, how hard could it be to marry off the Hellion by the end of the season?

ABOUT THE AUTHOR

Anna Harrington fell in love with historical romances—and all those dashing Regency heroes—while living in London, where she studied literature and theater. She loves to travel, fly airplanes, and hike, and when she isn't busy writing her next novel, she loves fussing over her roses in her garden.

You can learn more at:
 www.annaharringtonbooks.com
 Twitter at @AHarrington2875
 http://facebook.com/annaharrington.regencywriter

Sign up for Anna's newsletter to get more information on new releases, deleted scenes, and insider information!
 ow.ly/iqdu300gByj

If you love Anna Harrington, don't miss Grace Burrowes's *Too Scot to Handle*, available now!

From award-winning author Grace Burrowes comes the next installment in the *New York Times* bestselling Windham Brides series! As a newly titled gentleman, Colin MacHugh has no wish to entertain all the ladies suddenly clamoring for his attention. But when the intriguing Miss Anwen Windham asks for his help to save a London orphanage, he has no idea how much she'll change his life forever.

Fall in Love with Forever Romance

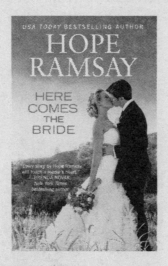

HERE COMES THE BRIDE
By Hope Ramsay

The newest novel in the Chapel of Love series from *USA Today* bestselling author Hope Ramsay will appeal to readers who love Jill Shalvis, Robyn Carr, and Brenda Novak.

Laurie Wilson is devastated when she is left at the altar. How long will it take her to realize that Best Man Andrew Lydon is actually the better man for her?

Fall in Love with Forever Romance

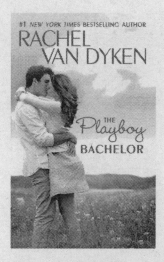

THE PLAYBOY BACHELOR
By Rachel Van Dyken

**New from #1 *New York Times* bestselling author
Rachel Van Dyken!**

Bentley Wellington's just been coerced by his grandfather to spend the next thirty days charming and romancing a reclusive red-haired beauty who hates him. The woman he abandoned when she needed him the most. Bentley knows just as much about romance as he knows about love—*nothing*—but the more time he spends with Margot, the more he realizes that "just friends" will never be enough. Now all he has to do is convince her to trust him with her heart...Fans of Jill Shalvis, Rachel Gibson, and Jennifer Probst will love this charmingly witty and heartfelt story.

Fall in Love with Forever Romance

WHEN THE SCOUNDREL SINS
By Anna Harrington

When Quinton Carlisle, eager for adventure, receives a mysterious letter from Scotland, he eagerly rides north—only to find the beautiful—and ruined—Annabelle Greene waiting for his marriage proposal. Fans of Elizabeth Hoyt, Grace Burrowes, and Madeline Hunter will love the next in the Capturing the Carlisles series from Anna Harrington.

Fall in Love with Forever Romance

HARD JUSTICE
By April Hunt

Ex-SEAL commander Vince Franklin has been on some of the most dangerous missions in the world. But pretending to be the fiancé of fellow Alpha operative Charlotte Sparks on their latest assignment is his toughest challenge yet. When their fake romance generates some all-too-real heat, Vince learns that Charlie is more than just arm candy. She's the real deal—and she's ready for some serious action. Don't miss the next book in April Hunt's Alpha Security series, perfect for fans of Julie Ann Walker and Rebecca Zanetti!